Dedicated:
To my wife, Kristin, who encouraged me in all things.
To my son, Harrison, who decided that I didn't need to sleep anyways and should write.
To my family, who always told me I could write a book if I sat down and tried.
To my friend Nick, who has too much patience with my insanity.

Special Thanks to:
Tamara Blain
Steven LoBue
Peter Morena
Justin Johanson

OTHERLIFE
DREAMS
~The Selfless Hero trilogy~

By William D. Arand

Chapter 1 - Soup Bowl -

Runner stared at the login screen for Otherlife Dreams as the text rotated slowly. His fingers drummed against his thigh idly. He considered the virtual window as if it were a beast hunkered down before him. Beyond the screen, there was nothing but inky darkness that expanded unendingly in every direction.

With a flick of his hand he accessed the window for perhaps the fiftieth time. It transitioned from the logo to the login screen. It only held two pieces of information, but it told him more than enough.

Username: NorRun001
Password: ***********

WARNING: This game is intended for an adult audience. N-18

Without any actual proof he knew his user name was correct. That little name was a mutilated IT version of Runner Norwood. Unfortunately, he couldn't begin to guess at the password. Being that it was already entered gave him the clue that he'd clearly logged in at some point previously. A game of this nature shouldn't be on a military vessel; it could only have been installed with permission. On top of that, he had apparently allowed the program to save his password. Yet he had no memory of logging in or even approving saving his password. He had no memory of anything. At all. In fact, to him his mind felt a lot like the place in which he found himself. Devoid of everything other than a few pieces of information, and a general feeling of who he was.

Frowning, he executed the replay message command line once more. It had been waiting for him when he appeared here in this virtual lobby. The duration slider reverted to the starting position. The play button cycled for a moment and the file began playing once more.

Static cut over everything after the music was paused. With a crackle, the distorted message started. The loud buzzing that garbled much of the audio and filled gaps between what little he could make out taunted him. "…and no time -bzzzz- damaged the bridge -bzzzz- bleeding -bzzzz- atmosphere. You won't -bzzzz- everyone's brain waves into -bzzzz- database since the main server died -bzzzz- didn't lose -bzzzz- not rea -bzzzz- hap - bzzzz- no chance.

"I -bzzzz- diced up the crew's memories into level brackets -bzzzz- they won't know anything about themselves -bzzzz- level up. Here's -bzzzz- if you die, it'll delete your character -

bzzzz- No biggie, right? Big deal actually -bzzzz- your avatar is deleted, and a new one is created based on its default settings -bzzzz- you go brain dea -bzzzz- become an NPC. Like an empty PC -bzzzz- Ha, an MTC rather than an NPC.

"Sorry -bzzzz- dark here in -bzzzz- died a while ago - bzzzz- pretty sure we're -bzzzz-" A distant explosion could be heard on the recording. It was followed by a muffled klaxon. "Fuck, long story short, don't die! Level up and get your memories -bzzzz-"

With that, the message ended and the music resumed.

"Options. Audio. Set music levels to ten percent."

The verbal control picked up his command, and suddenly the music was nearly muted. It was pretty enough, but he could only listen to it looping endlessly for so long before he began to question his sanity.

He needed to think things through, order his mind, and come to a decision about what to do.

"The message is for me. There is no doubt of that. Who sent it, I don't know since the video was missing and the audio is…well…bad at best. He mentioned not knowing who you are, and that's certainly true for me. I can't even tell if talking to myself is normal for me. Damn. How long have I been sitting here contemplating all this? Minutes? Hours? Days?"

Sighing, Runner hung his head and stared at the darkness below him. "I know there are others with me. It's only a vague recollection, but quite a few are with me. I think. Hundreds. Thousands. Hundreds of thousands, it feels like. Did they all get the message? Am I the only one who got it?"

Runner lifted his head and pulled down the developer console with a glance upward. He contemplated it, mentally thrashing at his mind to drum up any memory he had about the ship's console, before typing in a number of requests.

/Status
User: NorRun001 logged in

/Time
09/01/43 10:13am Sovereign Earth time

/Current active Users
499,928

/Permissions
Admin
Systems Administrator-All systems access
Restrictions in place due to emergency conditions

/System Status
L O **A** D **I** N G
System is unresponsive
Abort, Retry, Quit?

/Abort

Request Aborted

/Current active Admin
1

/Active Process Status
L O **A** D **I** N G
Milwin.exe
TGDB.exe
Life Support-Emergency
Power Plant-Emergency

Runner minimized the console with a frustrated grunt, and then he stared into the login window once more. They were on a military ship, and military ships served contracts based in years. Judging from the plotted course in the navigation system, the journey had been expected to take three years. From the time indicator it had only been around a year since departure, which would put them somewhere in between the two planets. "Sit in limbo until help arrives, if ever, or play a video game where it's permanent hardcore mode. What a shitty game. I bet the damn things learn by death with cheap-ass tricks."

With a sudden burst of courage, he stabbed his finger into the login button. Before him the window went dark and was no more, taking with it what little light there had been in the void.

Snapping back into focus, the bleak world of darkness was replaced by an open field with a Human avatar at its center. Posed in a casual sort of way, the naked man looked around but made no reaction to Runner's sudden appearance. Leaning forward, Runner found he was staring at a computer-generated version of himself. Standing five foot nine, he looked like a typical nobody to himself. He couldn't recall being referred to as attractive much in the past, but with a brain like Swiss cheese, that didn't amount to much certainty.

Fair skinned and sporting a decent complexion Runner could only assume he was somewhere in the middle, he supposed. Going in close, he concentrated on his eyes, just to assure himself of their color. Bright blue. Eyes that popped out with their vibrancy, and a shock of dark black hair finished his look. Staring at himself naked was a surprise though.

"Well, at least I know everyone will look like themselves, if nothing else," he said dejectedly. He tapped the flashing indicator in the corner. It had been blinking steadily, begging for attention. Listed simply as "Create," it could only be the character creation screen.

With a click, the window maximized and presented him with a character sheet. Expecting to find a table that showed him stats, such as strength, dexterity, and intelligence, he was surprised when he received none of that.

He tilted his head as he leaned in closer to get a good look at the jumbled mess of characters and grayed out arrows. Most of the information displayed was actually glitched and resembled punctuation and symbols rather than English. On top of everything else, only one selector responded to any interaction.

Sighing disappointedly, he took the singular option available to him. He pushed the one arrow that was selectable. Eventually even that failed and there was nothing else he could do but push the "Complete" button near the bottom of the page.

"Let's hope it's at least a decent attribute. Not like I had a choice if it wasn't."

The circle spun clockwise as it processed the command. "If it even loads," he mumbled. "Sure is taking its sweet time. I mean, really now, what centu-"

Amid a loud chorus of chimes, Runner found himself in a field, staring at a copse of trees. "-ry. Nice trees, good foliage. What a lovely place to load into… that is clearly not the starting area. Good times," he muttered.

Glancing around at his surroundings, Runner couldn't help but blow out a breath in complete frustration. Whatever was wrong with his ability to create a character was causing problems within the game. Because it was already done, it wasn't as if he could restart the game client and see if that would fix it either.

"I can't even bitch about it to a game admin because apparently I'm the only one."

Grumbling to himself, Runner started to work over his heads-up display, and went about rearranging it to his liking while giving verbal commands to modify his game settings.

No self-respecting gamer would ever leave the default options on, or use the default HUD, he thought to himself.

"Options, game options, nameplates on, health bars as numbers and percentages, enemy health bars on, enemy health bars as numbers and percentages, casting bars on, decline all friend requests, decline all trade requests, decline all duel requests, anonymous mode on, auto attack upon selecting enemy off, miscellaneous sound at fifty percent, ambient sound at seventy percent, distance indicators on, d-"

Runner was rocketed forward, his knees striking the dirt before he tumbled forward in an impromptu roll. Tucking into himself tightly, Runner tried to reorient himself as he came to a stop. He quickly rolled to his feet and turned to face his would be killer.

A quick analysis provided him with fur, fangs, and a sizable skull. It was the best view he could manage given the circumstances. Taking a few desperate steps backwards, he managed to gain some distance. Runner had gained his footing, but didn't stop backpedaling from the very large wolf chasing him.

"Fuck me, fuck me, fuck me. Fuck you, dog! I'll put you down like Old Yeller and use your skull as a-FUCK!" In seeming disagreement with him, Yeller bit deep into Runner's forearm.

His health bar was already in the final ten percent, in the red zone, and he was only a hair's breadth from being a corpse. Yeller was clearly a higher level than he, when he himself couldn't be anything other than level one. Dying minutes after having entered wasn't exactly a great start. A terrible end to his glorious career as a hero. As soon as the wolf released his arm, he punched it in the throat and activated whatever ability was loaded up first in his quick slot loadout. He turned without waiting to find out what it did and sprinted for the trees.

Knowing that he couldn't run faster than his character's preset speed didn't stop him from feeling as if he were moving at a dead sprint. Heart thumping in his chest, he didn't so much climb, as fly up the first tree he came to. Runner hadn't stopped to consider what would happen if he couldn't get up the tree fast enough. Or if he could climb it at all.

Looking down, he found Yeller staring up at him unerringly with lifeless eyes. Resting his forehead on a branch in front of him, Runner took slow breaths to calm himself. With his health not regenerating, he could only assume he was still in combat. That and the fact that Yeller wasn't leaving. He let his eyes close and rested a few moments before lifting his head and taking stock of his situation.

Alternating from a dark red color to a bright red, his health bar showed he had eight hit points left. Mana and stamina were both at one hundred, well and full, but those weren't as life and death important as his hit points. Literally.

Calling up his inventory window, he grunted at the sheer number of items. He pulled up his character sheet and worked through the information that was available to him. Tapping each item and description one by one for a pop-up tip, he went through the definitions to figure out what he had to work with.

Nothing out of the ordinary jumped out at him from the attributes. They were all pretty standard traits to be expected of any role playing game. Strength, dexterity, agility, constitution, intelligence, wisdom, and finally charisma. As he went through each to check the value, he grew more depressed until he reached the bottom. He felt his stomach clench, then drop, his head swimming at the number that stared back at him. Charisma. It just had to be a non-combat attribute. All his points, giving him the ability to actually survive a fight and to become dangerous, had been wasted on charisma.

"Charisma, sixty-four. Every single attribute is at one but charisma. What am I supposed to do about you with charisma, Yeller?" he asked the wolf staring up at him. "I don't think asking you out for dinner and a holomovie will work. Don't get me wrong, you're a handsome animal, but I just don't swing that way."

Laying his chin in his palm, he closed the character window and started sorting through his inventory. There were a number of tools, weapons, armor, clothing, general items, and a truly healthy amount of food. It made no sense how much was stuffed into his inventory.

It was far more than a starting character should have. Bulging to the very limit of what he could hold in the starter backpack. From a skinning knife, to a smith's hammer, to a frying pan. It was as if he had equipment for every class possible in there.

Wrenching open his skill window, he could only stare. Every skill was already listed and set to level one, from One-Handed swords and alcohol tolerance to fishing. Runner could distantly remember that Otherlife Dreams, in their marketing campaigns, boasted hundreds of pre-built skills and that, given enough server allocation, the game could generate more based on the players. The problem here was that they would need to be unlocked and that many of those skills were classified as "hidden" until unlocked. Which meant no one would really know if it was a valid skill until investing time into it. Scrolling through the list, he was able to actually see hidden skills since they literally had an "H" in front of the name.

"Need to sort these," Runner muttered.

After he closing his skill window, he re-opened his character window. There, under his name and level, was his class. While he had not been able to select one, he had assumed he could play whatever was given to him and make it work. Instead, it seemed he had no class. In fact, the space where it should have been was just blank. It appeared as though he had a very glitched-out character, and he truly didn't know why. Or if he could fix it.

Runner tagged Yeller with the selector. The basic information for the animal popped up in a small box.

Runner confirmed its level as thirteen, full health, and full stamina. Level one versus level thirteen didn't really sound like a main venue prizefight to him. Not one he would bet on at least.

Placing his palms together in the "call console" gesture, he reached up and expanded the window when the indicator presented itself.

/Status
Game Master: NorRun001 logged in

/Active Process Status
Permission Denied

/Permissions
Please enter Password: **********
Invalid Password

/Permissions
Please enter Password: **********
Invalid Password

/Permissions
Please enter Password: **********
Invalid Password

/Permissions
Please enter Password: **********
Invalid Password

User Locked
Please contact System Administrator

/System Status
Permission Denied

He stabbed his index finger into the X in the top right. Rubbing his eyes, he was faced with the horrible realization that he could probably end this entire problem if he could just remember his password. If the message was true, the only way he would get those memories back was by leveling up.

He opened his eyes and found another console in place of the one he had just closed. The last response from the system in this new console differed from the one he had just entered. It was the ship's system console he had interacted with back in the lobby. He brought up the main console and set them up side by side. He closed both again after confirming the other one was the console for the game itself.

It should have been obvious they were two separate consoles, as the new one had listed him as a Game Master rather than a User. A finger flick was all it took to pull open the action logs from his social pane. He went to the start, and low and behold, everything made a lot more sense.

> *Unable to log into GMHub.*
> *Unable to log into GMHub.*
> *Unable to log into GMHub.*
> *Unable to log into GMHub.*
> *Unable to log into GMHub.*
> *Loading into coordinates 0, 0, 0.*
> **You gain Spawn Invulnerability**
> **Plains Wolf uses Tackle on you**
> **Plains Wolf damages you for 149 points of damage**
> **You are invulnerable**
> **Spawn Invulnerability has ended**
> **Plains Wolf bites you for 92 points of damage**
> **You punch a Plains Wolf for 1 point of damage**
> **You use Distract on Plains Wolf**
> **Plains Wolf is distracted**

Once he had read through the log, he realized he should be dead already. Having checked against the help manual, he knew everyone had one hundred hit points regardless of class or race. Everything came down to how much you could mitigate. It didn't matter if it was through armor, resistances, or skills.

Runner definitely wouldn't do much of that with only one point of constitution, starter armor, and level one skills. If it had been a few seconds later, his spawn invulnerability wouldn't have soaked up that damage, and he would already be a corpse.

Throwing up a thank you to the Random Number God, he sorted out his starter gear into what he could use immediately and what he couldn't. A simple sword and simple shield went into his equipment slots, followed by pulling on a sturdy leather tunic, leggings, arm guards, gloves, a belt, and boots. Everything else stayed in the backpack until he could do a proper audit later. He would sell the duplicates and maybe make a few coins on the deal. Provided he got out of this mess.

Now suitably attired for a night out with his dear friend Yeller, all that was left was figuring out how to end this without becoming a meal. Initializing the ability section of his HUD, he was unsurprised to find it was not what he would have expected. Every page in his ability book was filled with level one abilities.

Given that he also had every skill available, it would seem he was given the starting loadout that every level one character began with. All of them. Every class. Going over his quick slots, he found *Distract* to be the first skill there. *Cure* was in the second position. When he highlighted *Cure*, the display box came up and confirmed what he expected. It was the level one healing ability for the Healer starting class. *Distract* was a level one Rogue ability.

With a mental flick of his attention, he targeted himself and cast *Cure*. Turning his attention to the social pane, he gauged the results.

You cast Cure on yourself
You gain thirty hit points

Fifteen mana points fell out of his full mana bar as his health bar refilled. Nodding to himself, he paused and considered the situation anew. He definitely wanted his health back, but it might be a waste to spend all his mana just to find out it didn't regenerate while in combat. After a few seconds, the bar started to refill. It came back at about two points per second, which wasn't great, but it surely wasn't terrible either. Casting the skill twice more, he brought himself up to ninety-eight hit points. Going back to his ability book, he read over what was available to him while his mana refilled.

A few minutes passed before he felt like he had sorted the book into three usable categories: combat, non-combat, and crap. Only a few things, primarily less powered or duplicates of other abilities that a different class already had, ended up in crap.

Opening the non-combat section, he tapped the entry at the top, Strengthen, and then cast it on himself.

You cast Strengthen on yourself
You feel stronger

Twenty points of mana for fifteen strength for fifteen minutes was far from prohibitive. Activating four more buffs, he was out of mana but now had increased armor, agility, dexterity, and constitution. At a guess, he was probably just barely a true level one now. Maybe a level two since he was able to wear heavier starting gear than others.

As for combat abilities, he was torn between *Regeneration* or *Fireblast*. Targeting the wolf below him with a swift glance, he cast *Fireblast*. The wolf burst into flames and let out a surprised yelp before whimpering and running in a circle around the tree, settling down in very nearly the same spot it had just vacated. The small amount of damage done was instantly healed as the AI realized Runner was in a place that couldn't be reached. There would be no cheesing the system with being in an inaccessible area.

With a dismissive gesture, he closed his ability book, contemplating the wolf at the bottom of the tree. In the middle of his contemplation the world became gray, like a historical drama attempting to simulate black and white movies. Everything stopped. There was no sound. Try as he might, Runner wasn't able to activate a single window or move. Panic set in and his mind raced. Then even his ability to think wound down, like a toy's energy cell running out of power. Only surface thoughts floated by, and even those were far distant things, almost like clouds in a distant sky.

In this limbo, Runner simply was. As the world was, and as the wolf was.

The world exploded into color and sound as it roared back to life. The sun above seemed to proclaim victory as if it had banished the gray alone. The wind picked up, and the tree in which Runner sat swayed gently.

A scratching sound below drew his eyes to the wolf. Scrabbling at the base of the tree, the wolf eyed him anew as it clawed at the bark, trying to reach up to get at his perch. No longer patiently waiting as if cycling its AI commands, it was actively trying to get to him. The eyes of the wolf were what made him nervous now. Before, they had a creepy doll like quality, hazy and unfocused. Otherlife was one of the newest MMOs out there, the bleeding edge of technology. It combined sleep, time dilation, and entertainment. Even it had limits though. Eyes that were alive and full of hunger, that wanted nothing more to tear his throat out, gazed up at him hungrily.

Runner opened the console, desperately hoping for an answer. Unfortunately, there was nothing visible in the console for Otherlife Dreams, which seemed correct, as he wasn't able to log into his admin account completely. Moving to the ship's system console, he tapped the up arrow a few times to retrieve all previous commands, and he found what he was looking for.

User § ⌐îτ has logged in.
User § ⌐îτ has paused the server.
User § ⌐îτ has started patch σ\q.'Ç.
Patch σ\q.'Ç completed.

Resource allocation program has been automatically activated.
User § ⌐îτ has logged out.
User § ⌐îτ has logged in.
Allocation program has finished. Resource allocation has found an additional
4,179,821,031% available assets.
User § ⌐îτ has attempted to cancel the program.
Permissions request from User § ⌐îτ received. Logged to inbox.
Permissions request from User § ⌐îτ received. Logged to inbox.
Permissions request from User § ⌐îτ received. Logged to inbox.
Permissions request from User § ⌐îτ received. Logged to inbox.
Permissions request from User § ⌐îτ received. Logged to inbox.
Permissions request from User § ⌐îτ received. Logged to inbox.
Permissions request from User § ⌐îτ received. Logged to inbox.
Response from User NorRun001 timed out, proceeding with Allocation program.
User § ⌐îτ is now away
Allocation complete, server reloading with new resources.
Server reload complete, server unpausing.

There was a fuzzy memory oozing by in his empty head that told him one of the biggest draws of Otherlife Dreams was that it would take whatever resources was given to it. It would then use those resources to develop emergent game features, quests, and AI behavior. Four billion percent additional resources would make the game pretty damn advanced. Deep in his heart, Runner quailed. Two hundred percent would have been unprecedented: a gigantic leap in technology. This was simply incomprehensible. He had to consider just who this *§⌐îτ* was and where such massive resources had come from. Had their target planet jumped ahead in the technology race? Were they now in enemy hands? Had an engineer on Earth accidentally hooked them up to a mainframe and misunderstood what Otherlife Dreams was?

"I'm not alone," he murmured to the wolf. "Beyond you that is, Yeller."

With a casual wave of his hand, he flagged all seven requests from the unknown user, declined them, and deleted them.

"IT doesn't just grant privileges all willy-nilly. We ask them why they need it…then deny them anyways," he said, his face twisting into a shit-eating grin. Nodding to himself, he typed up a response, then sent it over to user *§⌐îτ* and hoped a response would be swift in return. With any luck they were an engineer from the government outside and could help. Help somehow. He really wasn't even sure what was going on. This of course was all well and good, but didn't solve his immediate problem: Yeller.

Even with the buffs and gear, he was quite a bit under the ability to fight the damn mutt one-on-one.

Murmuring nonsense to no one in particular, he eased his way through the skill list, character sheet, and his abilities one more time. Once more he came to the conclusion that there really wasn't much more he could do to even the odds. Even with an additional level or two, this confrontation would probably be lost through sheer level difference. With a growl of irritation, he threw a *Fireblast* at Yeller. He felt a little better watching it smolder and run around below, but it didn't accomplish anything.

The missing hit points quickly filled back up after a few seconds when the system confirmed Runner was unreachable. Drawing his sword with his right hand, he briefly considered hurling it at the animal. No, he'd probably break the damned thing.

He reared back screaming, ready to throw another *Fireblast*, but almost fell out of the tree as his foot slipped. Wrapping himself around a large tree limb, he hung on for dear life and tried not to stab himself with his own sword. Gripping the trunk, he watched as the *Fireblast* played over the sword. When his foot had slipped, his mind had wavered, and the spell had been launched without a target. Apparently he had come very close to scorching himself…or the tree, but by sheer luck it had struck the sword instead.

"Wouldn't that be just ironic. Burn yourself to death, with your own fire, and the tree you're in. Fan-fucking-tastic, really."

After a few seconds the fire died. The sword seemed unharmed despite its fiery ordeal. It had burned longer than he expected-metals weren't the most flammable of substances. The main effect had disappeared almost instantly when it hit Yeller, though the damage over time effect had continued.

Releasing his death grip on the trunk, he settled himself on a branch, using it for a bench. He lightly set the sword tip against a limb that was a little lower than his seat. He contemplated the blade as he rotated the hilt slowly.

With a deliberate slowness, he reached down with his left hand and cast *Fireblast* with a fingertip against the simple steel. Once more it burned for a few seconds before going out. He would swear that it lasted a moment longer. He cast it three more times, watching as the fire lingered longer each time.

Tuning out the incessant scratching and low growls of Yeller, Runner concentrated on this newfound mystery.

Runner let his mana bar refill and then cast *Fireblast* into the blade five times more, draining his mana bar. He was sure of it now. The blade remained lit longer each time. It was on the third cycle when he received a pop-up notification.

You have developed the ability Enchant.
Simple Steel Sword gains Fireblast.
Cong-

Runner minimized the window before it could finish the message.

Thrilled, but concerned at the same time, Runner was overjoyed that something happened. It didn't feel quite right that creating a unique skill should be this easy or quick. Unwilling to get lost in it, or to spurn this glorious gift, he wrote it off for later.

"Alright then, let's do this shit!" he shouted. Closing the minimized notification screen, he steadied himself and found the right ability in the list. Runner quickly cast *Vitality* on every piece of equipment he had, other than his sword and shield, and confirmed that all of these enchantments were stacking. They were on a timer. They were actively adding their bonuses one on top of the other.

He checked his character screen just to be sure.

Name:		Runner	
Level:	1	Class:	
Race:	Human	Experience:	0%
Alignment:	Good	Reputation:	0
Fame:	100	Bounty:	0

Attributes-			
Strength:	1	Constitution:	1 (106)
Dexterity:	1	Intelligence:	1
Agility:	1	Wisdom:	1
Stamina:	1	Charisma:	64

He now had a glorious constitution of one hundred and six. He gave his shield the *Stoneskin* attribute just for some extra mitigation. Pushing himself to a standing position in the tree, he found that he had nothing else he could do.

Well, I could stay in the tree until my food runs out, but that just seems cowardly.

"Ok, Yeller, I believe I was just commenting that I was going to use your skull as a soup bowl. Going to cook you, turn you into soup, and eat you out of your own damn skull. Love me some soup. Yeller soup in a Yeller soup bowl."

Taking a firm grip on his sword, he leapt, aiming the point at the damned wolf even as he fell. If he could time it just right, he could score a *Flank* attack and do double damage. The blade struck the wolf's spine, nearly being wrenched from his grip as he landed awkwardly. Runner took a few steps away from the beast as the *Flank* attack completed.

Settling himself into an attack position, he tried to activate the basic *Slash* ability as Yeller spun to face him. The ability fired just in time to land before Yeller's attack. As the ability finished, Runner did his best to raise his shield while activating *Block*, fully expecting a counterattack.

Just as the shield seemed to be in the right place, it impacted his arm and shoulder. A worried upward glance to his health bar was all Runner could spare before he looked back to Yeller. With a feral grin spreading across his face, Runner addressed the wolf. "Oh puppy, puppy. Baaaaad dog. Bad."

Yeller's health was down to ninety percent, and his own health had grudgingly shed a few points. Stinking of burnt fur and still smoldering, the Plains Wolf was suffering the aftereffects of the fire-enchanted blade. Runner watched the angry creature even as he went through the normal auto attack process to keep chipping away at its health. Trying to throw in a dodge while pulling his shield in line, Runner did his best to mitigate every attack. Overconfidence was the straightest path to becoming lunch. Preemptively casting *Regeneration* had definitely helped to keep his health in the upper green portion of the bar, but he was by no means safe.

Whenever *Block* was off cooldown he instantly used it to take care of the next attack and then immediately weaved his sword in for a *Slash*. Over time he was able to drag down Yeller's health, bit by bit. Occasionally he was forced to top himself off with a *Regeneration* cast, and it took most of his concentration, but he didn't feel as helpless as he had earlier.

Runner finished the fight with a thrust aimed at Yeller's chest. When the strike landed, Yeller whimpered and keeled over dead. Runner ended the fight with thirty percent of his health left and only a little bit of mana. Every spell cast had been used to keep pushing his health up as high as possible. From the first attack to the finishing blow, the ordeal had taken around five minutes. Runner would swear it had been hours; and that it had been a battle between titans.

Runner slammed his sword home into its sheath with a grunt. He tapped open the loot window and sorted through the pickups. Shattered teeth, a ruined wolf pelt, and meat were all he was able to salvage. After taking everything, he closed the window and looked to the corpse. He briefly considered hacking away the head to make a proper soup bowl, but found himself growing queasy at the thought. All in all, this was still just a game. A game with only one goal: level up, get his memories back, get the password, and get everyone out.

"Maybe next time, Yeller," he suggested. Turning from the corpse, Runner once more surveyed the landscape and patted his tree. "Nice tree, good foliage. I dub thee Bastion. I'll come back and cut you down so I can take you with me. Plenty of wolves to go around. Much soup to make."

With that said, Runner walked out into the field, enjoying the feeling of the warm sun on his face.

Chapter 2 - Blackjack -

Runner sat up, his groggy mind struggling to a state of wakefulness. Blinking away his dreams, he held up a hand to block the morning light from his eyes. Grumbling, he clambered to his feet and half walked, half stumbled, towards the bathroom to start the day. His bare feet on the grass rattled him back to reality, and disappointment stretched his face as he looked down. "Oh."

Wiggling his toes in the grass, Runner contemplated them. Yesterday was coming back to him like the coming of the dawn, slow, sharp, and almost too bright. After fighting several more wolves, he had accidentally happened onto a road. Just beyond the road there was a small clearing that promised seclusion and safety. With night coming on quickly, he had scrambled through the ability list on the hunt for something he swore he had seen earlier. When he found it, he had smiled to himself in victory. Also at the prospect of sleeping warm, safe, and sound. He'd tapped the *Campsite* and *Campfire* abilities and read their information. One provided a twelve-hour safe haven from the monsters of the world. It would warn him if any uninvited players attempted to enter as well. The other would give him access to a fire pit that gave off warmth, morale, mental security, and a means to cook. Otherlife boasted actual temperature levels to reflect world location, time of day, and actual specific areas. A warm fire sounded sublime at the time, as darkness was always a fear.

An icon of an empty stomach dully flashed in his status tray. Next to it in the tray was a blue thermometer.

Hungry and chilled.

It wasn't important to him at first, until he confirmed he was losing fifteen percent of his stats due to hunger. An additional five percent was lost for the cold weather.

He'd found *Forage* in his quest for the *Campsite* ability. On activating it, it surprisingly came back with a positive result. A root covered in dirt was the prize, randomly pulled out of the ground.

He supposed it was edible. Maybe. He really didn't like the feeling of a virtual empty stomach, resenting the fact that such a large portion of his stats were missing. In the end, he ate it. It tasted exactly like one would expect. Wet dirt.

Activating *Forage,* he grunted inarticulately. Reaching down into the grass, he came up with a large twitching beetle. Dangling between thumb and forefinger, it made a soft clicking noise, its legs clawing at the air.

With a face full of displeasure, he considered the bug. Conflict warred in him as he debated the question.

To eat, or not to eat.

Slowly moving the insect to his mouth, he settled on the fact that he wasn't willing to deal with the stat loss. Tilting his head, he got the beetle in a position where he felt he could dispatch it rapidly, and swallow it, without tasting it. Hopefully.

It was a scant inch from his mouth when he heard the clatter of metal striking metal. A series of crashes came from up the road, freezing him in place. Hesitating, Runner put his mind through the possible scenarios that this could possibly be. The beetle hung in front of his open mouth, its imminent doom on a brief hold. The staccato of clashing metal continued for a brief time; then an abrupt wail sounded and all noise faded to silence.

Shocked from his contemplation by the sound of a voice, he stuffed the beetle in his mouth. Chewing it to bits while deactivating the Campsite, he hurriedly got his boots on from his inventory. Swallowing the remains of the beetle, he slipped deeper into the growth beside the road and made his way towards the commotion. Activating the *Stealth* function, he crept onwards until he found the source of the disturbance. Moving up to the roadbed from the scrub brush, he was able to spot a handful of men spread out across the road. There was also a woman, a horse, and by all appearances, a corpse.

The one closest to him was simply labeled "Thief." He was level eleven and gave Runner no cause for concern. The wolves he'd been fighting were higher level.

The Thief was actively rooting through a cluster of packs that were resting on the ground. Two of the other men were going through the belongings of the corpse on the ground, who was facedown in a pool of what could only be his own blood. Those two jackals were titled "Bandit," and both were flagged as being level thirteen. Rounding out the trio in the road itself was the aptly named "Thug," who was level fourteen. He stood looming over the woman and was apparently going through her pockets while helping himself to a handful of her figure at the same time.

Runner eased away from the entire ordeal. After creating some distance between himself and the situation, Runner felt safe enough to begin casting. Regardless of his choice of acting on this little drama or not he'd be a fool to not be prepared one way, or the other.

Runner had no delusions that this would be anything but a swift, ugly fight. Preparing with a mindset for caution, he decided he could only afford to enchant two pieces of his gear:

his sword and shield. He loaded *Fireblast* and *Stoneskin* respectively. Either he would kill them quickly and brutally or they'd gang up on him and wear him down, drown him in their numbers.

Creeping back to the roadbed, he found only their locations had changed in the thirty seconds he had been away. Both of the bandits and the thug were now circled around the woman, who was pressed to the ground by Thug's boot.

Runner scowled. The situation set off a small explosion in the pit of his stomach. Going through the mental gymnastics of the situation, he desperately wished for more time. Mentally calling up the information for *Analyze*, he confirmed it would provide him with basic information. Hit points, mana, level, name, faction, and level. A quick check with *Analyze* found that all of them were NPCs. Even the corpse, which had been left to rot where it fell.

"Odd" was perhaps the best way to describe the situation. NPCs fighting and killing one another for nothing more than what could only be described as a mugging. If he didn't know better, he'd swear the men with the woman over there were behaving a lot like they were planning on sexually assaulting her. Considering this was a game, he didn't believe for an instant this was a normal situation. This left the only plausible blame to be left at the feet of the patch. Seemingly, it made some serious changes, and the AI was now running headlong in any direction it chose.

Admittedly the game held an adults-only rating, but this was just too much. Now the question was, risk everything for an NPC or wait for a better opportunity to earn easy experience? There was only one of him after all and four of them, including Quickfingers McGee. At least Quickfingers was still doing his impression of a raccoon in a trash can and was far enough from the others to be dealt with separately.

It was the sound of the woman's quiet sobbing, when it finally reached his position, that demanded his action. Enraged at a level that defied his comprehension, he was filled with a murderous rage. NPC or not, the sobbing, whimpering, and low cries of the woman as they toyed with her drove him to action.

Lurching forward with *Stealth* active, he fixed Quickfingers with his glare first. Hands shaking with fury, Runner barely kept himself from lashing out instantly. A detached thought skimmed by that maybe Quickfingers could be sidelined entirely.

Utilizing the *Sleep* ability on the lone Thief, Runner passed by him without engaging him. Continuing towards the trio, he crossed the Thief from his list of concerns. Behind him, Quickfingers toppled over and went motionless. He would be out for at least five minutes, which meant there were now only three to deal with.

Targeting one of his foes, he closed in on the closest bandit. Runner used *Distract* in the opposite direction of his approach, and all three men turned their heads in tandem. Getting within arm's reach of the group, he firmed up his plan.

Letting go of his shield's front handle, Runner reached out, the shield hanging limply from the forearm strap. Fingers closing around the hilt of one of his foes, he jerked the weapon back in an attempt to rip it from the sword belt. Milliseconds after, he activated *Slash* into Bandit One's back. Bandit One bent around the blade, the full weight of a critical *Slash* that did six times the damage taking his life. It'd counted as a *Backstab* on top of the critical.

Bandit Two stumbled sideways towards Runner, the force put on the sword belt staggering him. Runner hadn't managed to clear the blade from the scabbard, but he'd definitely earned a few seconds of time to act.

Leaping forward over the corpse of Bandit One, Runner drove his blade into the Thug's midsection with the intent to skewer him. Unfortunately, it wasn't able to break through his defense completely, but it did count as a *Flank* attack. Thug took a step backwards as Runner raised his left hand. *Fireblast* burst from his palm and slammed into Thug's face. There had been no distance between them, and no warning, ensuring Thug without the means to dodge the magical attack.

Runner turned himself around to face Bandit Two, who was in mid attack. Surprised by the attack, Runner twisted himself sideways in a desperate attempt to dodge.

Failing miserably in his attempt, Runner felt the sword slice right through his Basic Leather Armor and into his hip. Carving through the Basic leather armor Runner felt it bite flesh as it went. The fact that he felt pain at all was surprising, but it was a bearable. He could take it. What choice did he have?

Runner quickly cast *Regenerate* on himself, then launched a return stroke aimed at the opponent's sword. With a screech, the Bandit's sword was forced to the side, giving Runner a moment to cast *Fireblast* into the man's face. The man screamed as he spun away, his hands going to his smoldering face.

According to the info tab, *Fireblast* had two effects outside of its direct damage. The first was the obvious one, the opponent catching fire and suffering a damage over time burning effect. The second was a direct attack on their morale, which had no visible representation.

Scuttling backwards, Runner reevaluated the situation. Glancing at his health he found it to be below half, near the forty percent marker. His mana was depressingly at twenty percent. Receiving that attack from the Bandit had nearly ended him. In retrospect, berserker charging a group of four was a bad idea.

Focusing on the Thug, it took but a second to confirm his health. He only had fifteen percent of his life left. Not only that, but *Fireblast*, coupled with the destruction he'd meted out to his friends, had caused the Thug's morale to visibly drop. It was something you had to rely on visual cues for, but Runner was certain of it. The Thug was wavering.

Wisps of smoke trailed up from the top of his head, and the skin of his face had a light pink color. Animals were programmed to fight nearly to the death, unless the odds were overwhelming or they believed death was imminent. Humanoids on the other hand had a tendency to run if their hit points fell fast enough, regardless of the situation.

Time to try a bit of psychological warfare then maybe? All aboard the crazy train.

Speaking in a sing-song voice, Runner tilted his head and opened his eyes wide. "Scott thinks your face is interesting. Linda disagrees. She says I should cook it in a pan. I can't trust her because she's hungry. Personally, I wonder if it'll fit me after I carve it from your skull? I need a new mask for Sunday, you see. You won't need your face anymore, right?" With a giggle and a crooked smile, Runner began to move closer, letting his sword casually slip into its sheath. He produced a skinning knife, holding it up as if to display it, his face twisting in a grin from ear to ear.

Thug spun on his heel and ran, his fear overwhelming him. Sprinting after him, Runner cast *Fireblast* into his back and then drove the skinning knife into the man's side. Ripping the knife free, the Thug collapsed in a heap. Runner pivoted around once more, searching for the last enemy.

Facedown in the roadway was Bandit Two, smoking like a spent match. Putting the little dagger into his inventory, Runner hooked his shield onto his back. It was mildly uncomfortable, but there was no other option other than unequipping it.

Runner cleared the Thug of his inventory quickly and moved on. Walking back to the woman, he winced. She had eyed him just as fearfully as she had her attackers. Nodding to her, he looted both of the Bandits of their worldly goods. Sighing, he selected the corpse of the man to be certain of his fate. On a scale of alive to dead, the unmoving man was unarguably rapidly cooling meat.

Scratching at the back of his head, Runner squatted down in front of the woman who was aptly named Peasant. Feeling a touch of embarrassment, he cleared his throat first before speaking.

"Hey there, name's Runner. I promise I'm not actually crazy. I was trying to get him to run. Figured if he was running, he couldn't fight back. This may sound tawdry, but can I help you?"

Blinking slowly, the woman considered him. After a brief consideration she seemingly decided that he wasn't to be feared. Eventually she nodded her head a fraction, yet said nothing. Taking this for reluctant acceptance, Runner stood back up and walked over to Quickfingers.

Pulling out one of his many starting cloth undershirts, he ripped it into strips, the number coming out to an even ten. With quick movements, he pulled the Thief's hands behind his back and bound them along with his feet. He made sure to stuff a gag in the Thief's mouth. Based on the actions prior to this point, he couldn't trust that he would wish to be civil.

The ability to tie up NPCs and gag them felt a touch ludicrous. Better yet, he destroyed a piece of clothing without working through the crafting menu. Confusion worked through his mind as he thought on it.

Many of his actions up to this point felt wrong in retrospect. Many of the rules a normal player would adhere to almost appeared to be malfunctioning for him. Much like the fact that NPCs were attacking each other, possibly raping each other, he added this one to the list of concerns. Eventually he'd need to figure out what was going on. Shaking the thoughts free, he refocused his mind on the current task.

Behind him, he could hear the Peasant shuffling about. It was clear to even his untrained eye, she had yet to fully come back to herself from the shock of the situation. That or she was truly a low-grade AI.

Humming to himself, he reached down and hefted the Thief up, promptly dumping him over the nearby horse's rump. He cheerfully smacked the Thief on the ass. Jerking his bonds, the Thief woke up from the single point of damage. After taking a second to confirm the Thief wouldn't be going anywhere, Runner then went back to the woman.

"So," Runner supplied uselessly. "Uhm, quest? Quest activate? Help? Quest help?" Targeting the Peasant, he tried using the interaction command.

Runner waited quietly, hoping for a reaction, anything.

It would be great if she was a quest giver, or I got a reward for saving her, or seriously just anything. At least maybe directions to a town? Damn, I didn't get a quest acceptance notification, did I? I wonder-

"No. I appreciate your help. It's sad you couldn't save my friend. He was helping me back to town."

"Ah! That, yes." Runner hurriedly made an offer. "Uhm, perhaps I could help you back to town in his place?"

"Yes. It would be good. I can't offer much in return."

The way she spoke was offbeat, close but not quite right.

A Quest has been generated
"Escort the Woman home"
Experience Reward: 5% of current level
Reputation: 1
Money: 5 Silver
Do you Accept?
Yes/No

WARNING! Experience Reward is adjusted based on current level at turn in

Eager to accept the quest, Runner opened his mouth, then stopped. Since the quest hadn't been available until he questioned, perhaps he could make alterations? He'd already broken many aspects of the game that would appear immutable. Why not one more?

"I accept, though I ask nothing in return, except for perhaps directions. That and any other information you or your townsfolk can provide," Runner countered, with a short bow and a smile. While experience would certainly be useful, he'd rather generate some goodwill and assistance. If it cost him experience or coins, so be it. Levels could be gained at any time, and coins came and went like the weather, but a good reputation could not.

Quest Modified
"Escort the Woman home"
Experience Reward: 5% of current level
Reputation: 5
Money: Forfeited
Alignment Shift-Good
Quest Accepted

WARNING! Experience Reward is adjusted based on current level at turn in

The woman slowly nodded her head. A few minutes later, they were traveling on the road. Runner had a vague notion they were traveling west, assuming he could judge it off the location of the sun and its movement; he confirmed with a quick use of *Sense Heading*. After suffering in silence with the NPC for half an hour, Runner started activating his abilities to try to improve their efficiency. Every ability and skill had its own leveling system. Runner was determined to utilize every chance to strengthen himself, even if it happened to be a non-combat skill.

Through foraging he got three beetles, two bunches of wild strawberries, and a pod of water he couldn't begin to explain. He found he could cycle between a number of his skills and return to the start as they all refreshed. *Forage*, *Sense Heading*, *Stealth*, *Analyze*, *Distract*, and *Enchant* on his boots. It was in this manner Runner passed the day:` quiet contemplation and ability usage as a counterpoint to his silent traveling companion.

As evening settled in, Runner established a *Campsite* and *Campfire*. Hauling the Thief down from the horse, he dropped him unceremoniously next to the fire. He'd done his best to ignore the Thief entirely and pay not a bit of attention to him. The Peasant had already fallen fast asleep. She'd taken her dinner from something in her pack and passed out.

Runner chewed down another beetle for supper. While he wasn't exactly unhappy with his new all natural diet, he missed civilized food.

Bored, Runner flipped the Thief over to look him over. Or rather, her. Runner was staring into the face of a female Thief.

Surprised by this, Runner found himself wanting to catalog her. Looking at her closely, he'd put her age in the mid-twenties. A dirt-stained face held a pair of dark blue eyes. Eyes that stared up at him with cold resentment.

Growling at him, she tilted her head to one side as the wind pulled her bedraggled black hair over her eyes. Between the splotches of dirt, she looked like she had a fair complexion and skin tone. Even as road stained as she was, it was clear to even a casual observer she was quite fetching with alluring features set in a triangular face with clean lines.

Breaking eye contact with her, Runner looked her over once without lingering. She was put together in a clearly athletic way, but held a womanly shape. She was moderately endowed in the chest for such a lithe figure. She'd never compare to some of the sculpted insanity that science or video games could provide, but she certainly had an appeal.

Angrily yelling through the gag the Thief got his attention. Runner belatedly realized his eyes might have hugged her curves for a bit too long after all.

"Oh shut up. You'll wake the idiot. I have no intention to carry out the crime your cohorts were clearly planning on committing on her. Besides, is that even possible? You're a damn NPC for crying out loud!" Runner explained. "I mean, I know they have certain NPCs flagged for that, but I didn't think they'd be out wandering the woods. Or did that patch change far more than I give it credit for?"

Runner let his mind wander, thinking deeply on the subject, his vision becoming unfocused. Blinking rapidly after a little time had passed, he came back to himself. "Sorry, I can zone out pretty fast," he apologized. "So, I'm going to remove that gag now, you're going to tell me your name, and we'll proceed from there."

Waiting for a response, he stared at her.

"Mmmph."

Assuming she'd behave by the response, he reached over and unwrapped the cloth from around her mouth, pulling the gag loose. Sporting a grimace, he set the drool-soaked wad of cloth to the side. Looking to the thief, Runner watched as she attempted to work some moisture into her dry mouth. Runner could only guess she was thirsty. Deliberately but firmly, he eased her head up with his left hand and caught her eyes with his own.

"You can help me, and open your mouth as I pour, or you can get a bath," Runner explained. He scooped up one of the foraged pods of water with his right hand. Wasting no time, he popped the lid of it off and moved to pour the contents into her mouth.

She stared at him hatefully but complied, her mouth open. Watching carefully, he waited till it filled halfway and stopped. Closing her mouth, she swished it around and then spit it into the grass. She must have been thirsty considering she swallowed the next two mouthfuls, rather than spit them out. Runner watched the water fade out of existence as its last charge was used. He fixed his attention on her again, the back of her head cradled in his left hand.

This all makes very little sense. An NPC shouldn't be experiencing fear of being assaulted, or have a need to clean out their mouth. Very advanced game it may be, but still a game. Nothing makes sense right now. Just how much did the patch change? Can I no longer rely on the few memories I have of video games in general?

He wondered just how much might be different as he stared through the Thief's face, seeing her not at all. So deep was his reflection, that it was as if the sound and area around him no longer existed.

He came back to himself suddenly, his mind jolted back to reality when the Thief shifted her weight around. The Thief was breathing heavier yet had not attempted to move from his grasp. With an abrupt smile, he tilted his head to the side, his hand tightening in her hair. "Feeling chatty yet, Thief?"

He waited for her to respond to his question, but she looked to be at a loss. Visibly mastering herself, she gradually controlled her expression until she'd built a mask of neutrality. Hesitating, she licked her lips before finally speaking in a clear, crisp voice.

"Yes, I'll speak with you. I'm not sure what you want, though. I swear, if you do anything to me, I'll kill you in your sleep."

"How about we start with your name, rather than threats? I hope it isn't Thief," Runner said. Smiling, he quirked a brow at her.

The thin mask she had put up broke apart as her face contorted with anger. Jerking at his hand holding her hair, she tried to lash at him with her forehead with little success.

"No, my name isn't 'Thief,' you bastard, so stop calling me that. I have a name, it's Hannah. Hannah Anelie."

"Holy shit…you have a surname? That's different for an NPC."

"Yes, I have a surname, damn it. Why wouldn't I? Wouldn't it be more strange if I didn't have one? What the fuck is an NPC?"

"Right, Hannah Anelie it is."

Her expression changed to mild irritation at the sound of her name. Staring at him, her eyes unsteady, it was obvious she didn't know what to do or how to respond to his statement.

"Why were you with those lovely men, Hannah? They clearly meant the Peasant harm, as simple as she seems to be, and had already murdered her friend."

"I wasn't with those pig fuckers. I was robbing everyone there. I'm a Thief, not a murderer. I may have killed people before, but never someone that would be missed. Not worth the attention."

"I think I get it," he acknowledged. He moved his head back and forth a little as if he were juggling a thought. "Essentially, you were just capitalizing on them being distracted. You didn't consider helping out?"

"What would you have me do? They were stronger than me. Outnumbered me. I'm just a Thief from the city, I'm not some Ranger like you, traipsing around through the woods and fucking deer by moonlight. Pulling food out of the ground, all magical like, with nary a care."

Deer fucking aside, she had a point. It also made him realize he hadn't looked at her outside of a cursory inspection. Fortunately, he had spent the day trying to level *Analyze*. He'd even managed to work it to beginner level three. Rectifying that, he targeted her and used the ability.

Scrolling down with a thought, he parsed the information and it matched what she had already told him. Hannah Anelie, Thief, level eleven, basic gear, no weapons since he had disarmed her already. She had a series of status ailments, but he wasn't able to see what each one individually signified.

Pulling up the game console with a directed mental command, he shook his head to concentrate and focused in on it while selecting Hannah.

/Target
Target Acquired: Thief0084

/Status
Flag Status:
Flag1Active=2
Flag2Active=1
Flag3Active=0
Flag4Active=0
Flag5Active=1

Condition:
Starving
Afraid
Bound
Wounded
Confused

He closed the console window and looked into Hannah's face once more. He was pleasantly surprised with how much information he was able to acquire and what he could infer from it. His mood had vastly improved.

An immediate problem he had to handle was the Starving condition. While it would take an actual human being a considerable amount of time to starve to death, the game had simplified it. As the time without food increased, constitution would decrease until it reached zero. At which point you would die and respawn in the cemetery. This didn't apply to NPCs of course as they wouldn't respawn, they would simply cease to be, replaced by another NPC.

Doesn't apply to me either, actually.

He sucked in a startled breath as he checked her constitution. Five percent of her total constitution was all she had left. With that much gone, it was a wonder she hadn't expired to any encounter she had. Could have been a wild rabbit and it would have ended poorly for her. He'd have to feed her if he wanted to keep her alive.

It was unlikely she would make it through the night otherwise, and Runner didn't want to lose her as a resource. The plan was to keep her alive long enough to turn her over to the town and no more. That, and he was hoping she maybe had a bounty on her.

He clicked his tongue and opened his inventory, dragging out one of the bunches of wild strawberries. It was the most substantial thing he had foraged as of yet, and had five uses. He'd been looking forward to eating them, but it seemed fate had other plans for him. Alone, it might just get her back up to just hungry status.

"While I admit to believing what you've said, you're still a Thief with a potty mouth. I have no intention of untying you. If I do decide to untie you, it certainly won't be in the woods at night," he declared. With mercy forcing his hand, he regretfully continued. "I'm willing to sit you upright and feed you, rather than have you starve to death overnight. I promise to be gentle, if you can promise to not bite me, or anything stupid like that. Otherwise, we go back to you starving. You start your career as a worm buffet while I go along my merry way. Well?"

Rather than reply, Hannah nodded once and watched him with hooded eyes.

With anger burning his mind but mercy guiding his heart, he levered her upright into a sitting position and fed her. In the end it took both sets of strawberries.

They arrived at a small town early the next morning. Runner drew everyone up short when the buildings came into view, far in the distance. Inspecting it, he found it was a simple thing, houses and shops built close together. Meandering streets, which had been placed as the population grew, ran throughout like twisting paths. It seemed like any other village that one might see in a fantasy setting.

"Would that be our destination?" he inquired of his quiet companion. She had said precious little this entire trip. When he tried to converse with her, even about the simplest of subjects, her responses never varied from single word responses, or silence.

"Yes."

"Mm, you don't say. I do hope the reason you've been so quiet is you're contemplating a speech for the town about our little adventure. Or maybe all the delightful things you'll tell me when we arrive, like the town's history. Maybe even give me a tour, introduce me to the mayor or your family."

"No."

"Ahhh, fantastic. Lead on, fair farm maiden, she of the reticent articulation, master of the spoken word!"

Said fair farm maiden only nodded her head in response and set off with her horse walking alongside her.

Runner started walking again with an unsatisfied groan, Hannah falling in beside him. They had left the gag off today, though her wrists were still bound. Runner had tied a lead into the bindings and then looped that into his belt. It wasn't the brightest idea, but he figured he could handle an unarmed Thief even if she decided to yank on the cord.

"Hah, real winner with the ladies there, shit head. Really wooed her right out of her skirt," Hanna chirped from his side. She had recovered quite a bit overnight. Once he had finished feeding her, he'd used *Cure* to get her health back up to full. She still had the bound status, but that was unavoidable, since he had to keep her tied.

"Yes. It does seem that way. Either way, I don't imagine I'll get much from her other than meeting other people I can speak with. Hopefully they're a bit more verbose. We shall see." He shrugged, the conversation leaving him. Runner was left with the impression that he was missing something. After a moment's thought, and looking up at his mini-map, he realized what it was. There had been no notification he had left one zone and entered another.

Making a nonplussed noise, Runner was disheartened to see that he had minimized the notification window. It was separate from the social pane and held notifications that held a higher value than skill leveling or experience gains.

In his carelessness he had triggered the default setting for the notifications to remain minimized until the window was restored to its proper place. That also meant he had not received any notifications, which would include discovering new areas. Thinking back, he realized he had actually turned it off the day before yesterday in his titanic battle of the ages with Yeller.

Letting out a frustrated breath, he brought the notification window back to the front.

Congratulations! Server first: Discover an ability
You've earned 100 fame
Congratulations! Server first: Defeated an enemy five levels higher
You've earned 50 fame
You've earned the title Unyielding
Congratulations! Server first: Defeated an enemy ten levels higher
You've earned 100 fame
You've earned the title Indomitable
Congratulations! Server first: Level 5
You've earned 500 fame
Congratulations! Server first: Have over 500 fame
You've earned 100 fame
Congratulations! Server first: Level 10

You've earned 500 fame
Congratulations! Server first: Level 15
You've earned 500 fame
Congratulations! Server first: Level 20
You've earned 500 fame
Congratulations! Server first: Have 10 unspent attribute points
You've earned 100 fame
Congratulations! Server first: Have 20 unspent attribute points
You've earned 100 fame
Congratu-

Runner stopped in his tracks. Reading through the messages one by one, he could only shake his head in disbelief. He didn't care to read through all fifty-four notifications and what each one meant, so he started mashing the Accept key as fast as possible.

It turned out he had earned a number of server firsts, achievements, titles, and created abilities.

There were five abilities he had created: *Enchant Weapon, Enchant Armor, Intimidate, Persuade, and Seduce.* Of those Seduce was disconcerting. Maybe he had been pushing the Peasant a bit harder than he realized, and Hannah wasn't just teasing him.

Everything else boiled down to the fact he had earned over five thousand points of fame, and twenty levels worth of experience. Now he had twenty pending level ups to spend. That would put him at level twenty-one exactly.

Chapter 3 - Memories -

08:17 pm Sovereign Earth time
09/03/43

Drumming his fingers along the windowsill, Runner stared out into the slate colored afternoon sky. Clouds hung heavy from horizon to horizon, drenching any and all foolish enough to be outside. Rain suited him just fine right now to be perfectly honest. Mentally laboring over how to proceed with his level ups, he found himself at a loss.

No matter which way he went with his attribute points, he'd be lacking in every other way. While his enchanting would certainly help shore up some deficiencies, it would in no way balance him enough to be as strong as any other class. He would never fully measure up against anyone else in their chosen forte.

Once accepting that fact, Runner came to the conclusion that he was now faced with two choices. Dedicate himself to one class and be second best to every other person out there. The other option was to dedicate himself to every class, and spread himself wide. Wide and very thin.

On top of everything else, he had made the mistake of querying how many people were in graveyards. It had been an errant thought, that if people died, they'd reappear in the graveyard, right? If it was true that death brought true death, the graveyard would be populated.

Finding the command to find everyone in a graveyard only took the barest of searches in the help section. Before he took the time to consider the consequences of the query, he had already gotten his answer. He had not been prepared for the number, though it provided confirmation of his worst fears.

"In a situation where I need to level up the fastest, is it better to have a bigger toolbox or just one really good tool?" Runner mused aloud. Stifling a yawn, he rested his forehead on the cool glass of the window. Runner only had one goal. Level up fast, hard, and get everyone left out of this trap. Game or not, it was actually killing people. By the thousands. Three thousand fifty-seven to be exact.

"I have no idea what you're raving about now, but if it's about a job that needs doing…I try to keep my toolbox as small as possible. Fit it with the best tools I can. Anything that serves a second purpose is perfect, and if I can find one that can do three things, it's even better," Hannah supplied from the table. Rope creaked as she noisily shifted around in the chair, causing Runner to glance back at her.

Bound from the waist down to a chair, she appeared content. Leaning back after she finished her meal, she waited. The bowl burst into blue motes of light and faded to nothing. As the little lights disappeared, she rested her arms lightly on the table.

"That seriously doesn't bother you? The way things just, poof, turn themselves into an electric fart and disappear?" Runner asked. He turned himself around completely to face her.

She'd cleaned herself up since they'd arrived. Leather armor had been replaced with simple peasant garb.

Runner had purchased it on the cheap from the innkeeper downstairs. Pricing had been only a few copper coins, on top of which he paid for two days' lodging. A tub of water to bathe in was the last purchase to round out their stay; all told, it only cost two silver coins.

Copper, silver, gold, and platinum coins were the measure of wealth in Otherlife. Coinage was on a ten base system. One platinum coin was worth ten gold, which was worth one hundred silver.

That group of thieves had a number of silver coins between them that went to Runner's war chest. Selling off all the duplicates in his inventory, then selling the raiders' gear to boot, he'd made a tidy sum. He already had three gold to his name and a fistful of silvers. He couldn't think of a way to confirm his financial standing, but he'd bet on being ahead of the curve.

"Not in the least, I had no use for it. There was nothing left, either. This is how the universe works. What's so hard to understand? The fact it bothers you makes you even more strange. You using magic to rewarm the water, now that's a topic. Or when you used magic in that fight with the bandits. Care to explain, or are you still pretending that didn't happen? I'm not blind you know. I may not be the most intelligent, or even the best spoken, but I'm not stupid," Hannah said with a Cheshire's grin.

Runner shook his head with a grunt and refused to comment. Casting *Fireblast* into the water hadn't immediately worked, but after a few tries it eventually took hold. He'd decided to try because of the fact that so many of his previous experiments had been successful.

"Let's just say I know a bit of magic and leave it at that. Back to what you were saying earlier though. It definitely has merit, though now I wonder if it's even possible? I'd have to find an attribute that fit every class. I'll probably need to find two actually, as I doubt dexterity would cross into the realm of casters. Best place to look will be in the second promotion tier for end results," Runner said.

Calling a system window into existence, Runner opened the in game help file. After a moment he found the section dealing with the classes. It had tables, charts, and diagrams of the information he needed. Studying that section he, focused on the second tier of promotions.

Doing a cross comparison against each and every one would take time. It would be worth every second of the time spent if he found attributes that transcended base classes. Hannah was absolutely right; this called for a multi tool of the finest caliber. He could build himself into a jack of all trades, one that was proficient in each area. Rather than the bargain bin, everything must go, on sale version.

Time passed in this way. Rain smashed itself to bits on the window pane while Runner continued ever deeper into his analysis. Meanwhile, Hannah kept her hands on the table as instructed. Runner noticed that over time her posture became more rigid, her fingertips lightly tapping the wood of the table.

She jumped when Runner suddenly sat up straight and laughed.

"Ah ha! Dexterity, intelligence, and a dash of agility. It's not perfect, but it'll definitely hit a second promotion for every base class. Thank you, Hanners, that was a wonderful thought. Now, let's see," Runner muttered, his voice fading out. He tilted his head down and peered into the character window.

Name:		Runner	
Level:	1	Class:	
Race:	Human	Experience:	100%
Alignment:	Good	Reputation:	5
Fame:	5,150	Bounty:	0

Attributes-			
Strength:	1	Constitution:	1(106)
Dexterity:	1	Intelligence:	1
Agility:	1	Wisdom:	1
Stamina:	1	Charisma:	64

Every stat stared back at him. Taunting him with their disgustingly low value.

"You realize you're insane, right? You told that idiotic peasant you weren't, but I'm starting to wonder if you truly are. You're not even listening anymore, are you? Jackass," she muttered. That said, she put her head down on her forearms in resignation.

"I'm not insane, thank you. I will admit to being eccentric, but an NPC would never understand. You don't even realize this is all a game. To you, it's completely natural.

Dexterity, dexterity, dexterity, intelligence, intelligence, agility," Runner continued. "And so, we who had become error, are now Win."

With a nod of his head, he tapped the Accept button with his thumb for emphasis. Losing complete control of himself, he leaned forward as the world swayed crazily. Collapsing to the ground, he bounced once and came to rest on the wooden floorboards. Mobility and thought were lost in the turmoil that enveloped his mind.

It wasn't pain exactly, though extremely uncomfortable. His head felt two sizes too small. The large number of memories twenty levels provided felt like too much to take in at once. Like a light switch being hit, his brain shut down, and he was unable to control himself. Blitzing through the material as efficiently as it could, his mind sorted and processed everything. It couldn't keep up. A human mind wasn't built for this.

Memories settled into places that felt natural to him. Only now was he aware of how much had been missing. Distant memories of childhood: sunlight filtering through windows at his parents' house back on Earth, watching bits of dust flutter through beams of light to disappear as they passed into the shade. Enrolling in and subsequently being expelled from college. Joining the Corps and being promoted to a Senior Systems Admin after a brief stint Earth side. There were gaps here and there, but he could guess at his own history from the things he could remember.

One memory stood apart from the rest by virtue of being the most recent. Boarding a capital ship bound for an outer colony that was in revolt. The travel would take years, but it would count towards his deployment, and he'd even be considered for hazard pay. For a non-combatant, it was a dream job.

He stared at the ceiling as he gathered his thoughts, trying in vain to put some order to his life. His life according to the memories he now possessed.

Then his view was filled with Hannah, her black hair framing her face like a darkened halo against the muted light. Cold sapphire eyes appraised him as if he were an insect. Runner could only track her with his eyes, unable to turn his head. As suddenly as her face appeared, she pulled away again.

Realization settled over him like a wet blanket. Shifting his weight around was the extent of his control. There would be no cry of alarm, or defense of his self.

It was no use. His brain felt like it'd been rewired by an apprentice electrician. Nothing was connected to where it should to be. He'd need time to let his brain rewire everything. Time was something he didn't have.

Metal rattled quietly, coming from the direction of the door. He guessed that Hannah was checking the lock, confirming it was engaged probably. The clatter was replaced by fabric whispering across the floorboards. Hannah popped into view, peering down at him once more.

Runner figured this to be the end. When he'd explained the situation to the mayor, he'd been informed that thieves were hung. There was no jail, no willingness to put the community at risk when the thieves were eventually released. Runner had declined their invitation, stating that he'd escort her to a city for actual justice.

The mayor emphasized the point forcefully when he mentioned Hannah was partially of the Sunless race. Runner hadn't been sure how the mayor had made that distinction; he hadn't been aware of it himself. Did NPCs distinguish the Sunless race by black hair? Blue eyes maybe? His own hair was black, though, and his eyes blue. Did he not qualify since he was a player? Chalking it up to a distinction of players versus NPC, he let the thought drop.

Exhaling slowly, Runner did his best to control his emotions. He waited, gaining a little peace in the acceptance of his expected end. It wouldn't do to face her with fear. To go out with a whimper, so to speak. Truth be told, the worst part of this was not even being able to see her hands.

"Try not to struggle, it'll just make this harder," she said, leaning in towards him. Runner closed his eyes in response, accepting and waiting. He listened to his own heart for several beats, no strike came.

His head was lifted from the floor, then gently placed on what felt like wadded up fabric.

Combed from his eyes with a delicate touch, his hair was brushed aside. It was done while avoiding touching him, as if he was made of poison, and contact would burn the fingertips.

"There. Is that better? I can't do much for you," she admitted quietly. "Your pack is full, and looks like a rat's nest. Like someone upended a gods damned cellar into it. Very fitting for you, but not very useful."

Runner's eyes snapped open, and he fastened them to Hannah. She was bent over him with her hands resting on her knees as she looked into his face.

I'm not dead? How the hell did she get into my pack? She shouldn't be able to, she's an NPC, and I'm not dead?

"I'm assuming whatever you were doing backfired. Or something," Hannah said, her head tilting to the side as she watched him.

"Uhm. Can you blink?"

He blinked.

"OK. How about we go with once for yes, and twice for no?" she asked him.

Yes.

"And to make sure you're not blinking to blink, please blink twice."

No.

"Great. Did you manage to cast *Paralyze* on yourself or anything like that?"

No.

"Did you activate a curse or something?"

No.

"OK. Not paralysis, not a curse, maybe it's similar?"

Yes.

"Was it a spell?"

No.

"Are you insane?

No. No. No.

"What exactly are you? Who are you? You talk to yourself, you do things that contradict the laws of the world. You use spells, *Stealth*, and clearly can handle a weapon. You killed others, but want to punish me for my crimes. When they wanted to do exactly as I thought you wanted them to, you refused. You treat me like any other Human, though I'm not. You purchase meals for me that cost you as much as what you buy for yourself. You talk like an educated twat, but you don't talk down to me."

Yes.

"Yes what?"

No.

"I guess you can't really answer any of that since it's not a yes, no answer."

Yes. No.

"You're a real fucking shit, you know that?"

Yes.

"Sleep, idiot. I'll keep watch till this, whatever this is, wears off. It will wear off, right?"

Yes.

He closed his eyes.

Unexpectedly, and like a bad made for web drama, Runner had fallen asleep. Coming back to wakefulness, he did his best to feign sleep. From his new memories he knew the technology that powered Otherlife was very cutting edge. One could have said it was nearly an adaptive AI in its base state. Clearly that massive resource boost had taken the game and elevated it to a whole new level. NPCs acted like people for the most part. They accepted the rules of the game as if they were normal.

The game's original operating shell was supposed to sync with the user, nesting itself in the user's mind, utilizing it as the hardware for visualization. That would leave the entire server to be able to process everything else. That still wouldn't be in keeping with the amount of resources it was increased by though.

Clearly, the difference between NPC and PC isn't normal anymore either. Something has gone horribly wrong here. Hannah was actually digging through my inventory. My inventory! That shouldn't be possible on any level.

Opening his eyes, he found he couldn't distinguish the time of day, as the darkened room offered no clues. Each room came with a few endless burning candles that did a fair job of lighting the room with a gentle light, but did nothing to dispel the shadows in the corners. He was covered by a blanket now, his head resting on what felt like an actual pillow.

Hannah sat a few feet from him, not paying attention to him. She'd taken control over his pack and emptied its contents. Everything was sorted and laid out on the floorboards. She must have worked quietly during his convalescence since she hadn't disturbed him. Evidently, Hannah was the type of person who wanted things to be in a certain order, or done in a particular way. Even if it didn't concern her.

Left hand propping her chin, her right hand hovered over a mound of crafting supplies. With a smirk, he guessed she was troubled by the fact that some crafting classes shared resources, though they had different tools.

Stretching his shoulders, he tried to flex his back and gauge his control over himself. Runner felt gratified by the immediate response to the demands he gave his body. Runner felt normal. Letting his head roll to the side to watch Hannah, he ended up making eye contact with her instead.

With a room that was silent except for breathing, he'd managed to alert her to his waking by shifting under the blanket.

"Do I greet you with good morning, good afternoon, or good evening?" Runner asked.

Hannah tilted her head and regarded him for a moment before responding.

"Good early morning. You slept through the afternoon and well beyond the night," Hannah explained. "Color me curious as to your plans considering the brand of justice by these inbred, farm tending, racist fuck wits. They'd have you dancing at the end of a rope for being a non-human, even those who aren't thieves. Humans are such gracious bastards."

And there it was. Her tone was light, despite the vulgarity, but had an edge of lethality to it. Runner had been wondering about her lack of, well, killing him. She hadn't escaped during the night and had even taken the time to care for him. Now she wanted to know his plans.

There was more going on here than he could reason out in the time he had to answer her. Her every action singled her out as a very unique NPC, beyond having five flags even. There was no telling what plans she had prepared for him while he blissfully slept the night away.

Now the choice was here and his alone to make. Runner couldn't deny that this world drastically veered away from his expectations the longer he spent here. Turning her over for the town's version of justice would be the end of her. Perhaps explaining everything to her would placate her, or maybe not. Truth or lies.

He was positive she was more than willing to try to kill him, given the chance, if his answer displeased her. After all, what did she have to lose?

"My intention yesterday was to turn you over to the city, not the town. For actual justice that is. Let them mete out your punishment."

"And now?"

"Now I'm unsure. Perhaps you could help me fill in a few gaps about the local culture? As you mentioned yesterday, I'm not exactly from around here," Runner conceded.

"That's true enough. Well, the simplest answer is that out here in the frontiers, it takes a different type of person to survive. So it's full of those dipshits you've already met. Life is cheap. Those who can't pull their weight, or aren't part of the community, are unnecessary. You heard them. Thieves are hung. What city in the world hangs thieves? Being half Sunless and half Human puts me pretty low on the worth scale to start for this bunch of east of nowhere bumblefucks. Now add being a thief, an outsider, and involved in a murder with one of their own," she said quietly. Fresh memories of humanity in hand, Runner felt it had the ugly ring of truth to it.

"I see. OK, that makes sense. Especially if I use that as a point of reference as to why you didn't try to slit my throat and escape. They would have been more than eager to grab you. Would it be safe to believe that the closest oasis of civilization is more than a month away?"

"About a month, a week shy of that perhaps, depends on how fast you can walk and what route you take. Most just take the trade road."

Coming to a decision, Runner cleared his throat and barreled ahead.

"I propose the following. I employ you directly. Specifically, to help me get to civilization. More to the point, off this little island. My goal is to reach the larger island east of here," Runner said. He'd briefly consulted the in game map the previous day to determine he was currently on an island. One that had been meant to bridge the gap between the starting island and the main continent.

"We can consider the theft thing as if it never happened. I'll provide funds, food, and whatever else travel expenses we incur. There is one further thing to note. I'll need your assistance in becoming stronger as we travel. If we encounter a dungeon, a cave, a band of what-the-hell-ever-nasties may be there, it's likely I'll stop and smell the roses. And kill things. Then loot their corpses while smelling said roses. But hey, who doesn't love money, right? Or roses."

Runner then did his best to present a winning smile at her. Thinking in the moment, he tried to use whatever he could, mentally grasping at whatever social skills he had. Leaning heavily on his character's ridiculous charisma, he could only hope.

You use Persuade on Thief
Thief is not Persuaded
You use Seduce on Thief
Thief is Seduced

Cursing himself in his mind, he managed to stop a groan from escaping.

Seriously? Seduce? Now? The fuck is wrong with you, Runner? The hell is going on with this game?

During the conversation Hannah had decided on how to sort the crafting materials, separating them into two equal piles. Runner could only imagine her AI algorithm was processing everything at light speed while in accordance to whatever personality she had drawn up at creation.

He'd have to be careful of how far he pushed the system. At least until he could determine its ability.

Even with all its new resources, there was only so much it could handle. How rapidly it could adapt to changing circumstances and the needs of its players was a finite thing.

Whatever *Seduce* did, it thankfully wasn't what he originally feared. Contemplation and hesitation were plainly written across her face from his point of view.

At least she's considering it and didn't turn me down flat.

She'd made no secret of the fact that she believed he was disturbed on some level. He couldn't really argue that he wasn't from her impressions of him. His offer would give her a very real way out, a way to remain clothed, fed, and taken care of.

No stipulations attached. Other than being a tour guide and providing assistance in combat.

She continued to noticeably work her way through the question. Giving her time, Runner stood and began stretching himself out. Stretching did nothing for him, but it was comforting at least to his mental health. Mental fatigue could always be relieved in repeating habits, or routines, that brought on normality. Normality and routine calmed the mind for him.

"I accept. My fee is four copper a day, not including food."

"Fantastic. Please take twelve copper from my purse over there. Four for today, four for yesterday, four for the last day. Consider it a security deposit," he said gratefully. She'd asked for a pittance, and he wasn't about to argue with her. Four copper was truly nothing to him, but she only knew the world based on her storyline.

"As for your meal, help yourself to whatever fare I have in my pack. I'm getting pretty good at finding things."

Runner decided to put action to his thoughts of routines and go through a rotation of his abilities. One by one, he activated them. For safety's sake, he only fired off those that would be safe to do indoors. *Forage* went off without a hitch even indoors. Producing yet another beetle. Without pausing to consider it, he popped it in his mouth and devoured it.

"Ugh. Do you have any idea what a lovely fucking surprise it was to find beetles in your pack? Why the hell are they still alive? You don't actually expect me to eat those as my 'meals' do you?" she berated him. Beetles weren't on her menu it seemed.

"Not always? Sometimes I find wild vegetables and fruits. You remember those strawberries, right? Good example, that. No?"

"No."

"Fine, fine. I'll buy travel rations and you can eat those. Missing out though. After the first one, the beetles actually go down easily and have an interesting taste. As to why they're alive, I'm afraid they'll go stale if you kill them. They might not have that same crunch."

Runner shrugged and then started stuffing everything into his pack, uncaring to the piles they were put into. Squawking noisily at him, Hannah slapped at his hands in an attempt to stop him from ruining her neat and orderly arrangements.

"Arrange your own pack, Hanners, mine's just fine as it was. Thank you regardless."

Hannah said nothing more, sulkily giving him the silent treatment. Having stolen her inventory back from his pack during the night, she made herself ready. He honestly didn't want to know where she got a pack from since she didn't start with one, so he didn't bother asking.

Minutes later, they stood outside the inn, contemplating what to do next. The rain of the previous day had muddied the roads and paths, but the sun was warming everything as it moved further from the horizon.

Runner had no luck previously in his attempts to get a quest from anyone he came across. He'd come to the conclusion that it was either reputation or faction that was preventing him from receiving anything from them. For most games, players would have spent many levels getting here, building normal relations with the kingdom and its people.

"Right then. Despite being higher level than the area, I can't get a single quest from anyone. I honestly was hoping there might be some stupid SovEx fetch quest. 'Oh, dear Hero, please deliver this worthless letter to my Aunt in Bendover, just east of here. Let me mark it on your map for you, because I'm secretly able to read your map perfectly and know exactly where we are despite never having seen one before.' Kind of thing, ya know?" Runner said, turning his head to look at Hannah.

"I understood maybe a third of what you said just now. This is just a frontier town. Only reason people come this far out is for trapping, hunting, or exploring old ruins."

"I'd like to do all three of those things, preferably at the same time, and in the same direction as the nearest city. Which according to my map-" Runner said, opening his in game map with a flick of his fingers. After a moment he closed it again. "-is to the east, by northeast. Any thoughts? Normally villagers are supposed to give you a clue, some gossip, or an indirect quest without meaning to, but everyone around here just stares at me till I walk away. Maybe it's my breath? Do I have beetle breath? Maybe part of a shell on my teeth? Bad beetle death breath?"

Runner sighed and put his hands on his hips and contemplated the hamlet around him.

After a moment of thoughtful silence, Hannah offered him a solution.

"You could try asking if there's a large monster den or an old ruin nearby. Might not be on the way. No, you don't have beetle breath, but it'd be a blessing if you'd rinse your mouth out after eating one. I swear if I find a leg between your teeth, I will leave you the fuck behind."

"Hm. Solid deduction skills there, Watson. You there, Villager number twelve," Runner accosted a man nearby, resting his hand on his shoulder. He was named exactly as he called him,

Villager. "Would there perhaps be a monster den or ruin nearby? Teeming with wildlife, the possibility of loot, or delicious treasure?"

"There'd be nothing like that around here, sir. Though if you follow the road east for a day, you'll find a path leading into the North Woods. Take that for a day north and you're sure to find an Orc village that's made itself a home out of a fort. They're not real friendly to outsiders, but they've left us alone and trade with us on occasion," replied the Villager.

> **A Quest has been generated**
> **"Cleaning House"**
> **Experience Reward: 230% of level**
> **Reputation: 5**
> **Do you Accept?**
> **Yes/No**

> **WARNING! Experience Reward is adjusted based on current level at turn in**
> **WARNING! This quest is rated above your current level**
> **WARNING! This quest is rated as a group quest**

"Oh? Fantastic! That's just what we needed. East, to the North Woods, where we travel north. Hopefully we'll get some gear. I'm tired of running around in these newbie leathers. Don't get me wrong, Hanners, it definitely flatters your figure and works your curves, but it doesn't do anything for me at all."

Accepting the quest as he finished speaking, Runner set off down the path to the east.

Glancing to the side as she fell in beside him, he nearly laughed at a furiously blushing Hannah. It'd be two days till they arrived, but Runner was excited. Progress. He was making progress. Calling up the system console, he confirmed there were no new messages from the mystery user.

Chapter 4 - Train Incoming -

It took two days to reach their destination. They followed the directions and reached the area exactly as described.

Hannah turned out to be an acceptable traveling companion to share the road with. They conversed occasionally, but overall they were still getting used to being in close proximity to each other. It wouldn't be described as companionable, but neither was it awkward.

Runner kept himself occupied by cycling his abilities to build them up. In between cycles he attempted to piece together what he could from the ship's systems to determine the status of the ship.

He was by no means an engineer, but even with the limited experience he'd gained before being expelled, it was obvious the ship was a wreck. All external sensors were offline, the power grid was a mess of blown out conduits, and the junctions between decks had multiple bulkhead failures. The hull looked as if it'd been peppered with micrometeoroids. The hull had more holes than actual metal on some of the decks. From the overwhelming amount of hull penetrating, it was clear the ship would be exposed to the vacuum of space. The damage was extensive.

Only life support and the general systems were online and functioning. Maintenance nanite droids could keep those systems running indefinitely. They were running emergency conditions, which of course meant no work would be done to repair anything that wasn't essential to life support. An extensive hull repair would need to be conducted so they could flood the ship with atmosphere. There would be no way to disengage the emergency override until that occurred.

During his survey of the ship, he detected an outside network patched in to the ship's main computer. He hadn't been able to access anything on it or even determine the extent of their integration. Perhaps the only thing he could monitor was the extreme amount of bandwidth flowing from the network into the ship's core computer, and straight into the system the game server was running on.

Mystery user $\S\ulcorner\mathring{r}$ must have been riding this line in to have gained access in the way they did. It also explained why this person had no privileges or authorized access.

Runner broke from his reverie to look down the road. He could just barely see the crest of a tower sticking up from the horizon of treetops. Around them on all sides was a lightly wooded area that would be ideal for a concealed approach. Which meant the little fort had been abandoned a long time and now valued its secrecy rather than its ability to withstand foes.

"What exactly did you want to do here? It sounds like any other Orc village I've heard of before. I don't think they'll be able to direct you to ruins any better either."

"My dear Hanners, they're the target. I'm going to kill every single one of them, loot them, and move on. We'll start at the fringes and work our way inwards, one corpse at a time. With any luck we can do it with single target pulls and avoid pulling groups of them."

"Wait, wait, wait. That's just straight-up murder. You realize that right? You sick psycho fucker. They're just a village of Orcs. They haven't done anything to anyone."

"You'd think that, but they're not just NPCs, but sheep NPCs. Put there for the explicit purpose of gaining experience from killing them. Not to mention, they'll attack us if we show up regardless of our intentions. It's too conveniently set up to be a dungeon, rather than anything else."

Nodding to himself, he walked off the path and into the surrounding countryside. Using his mini-map, he navigated his two man party to the side of the Orc town's entrance. Checking his coordinates regularly, he gave the entire town a wide berth. Buildings and crumbled walls passed by as he continued his circle of the town. According to the map he was nearly on the opposite side when he reached an open patch of ground, devoid of trees and cleared of debris.

Figuring this as likely a starting point as anywhere else, Runner halted and went down to a kneeling position.

They were just outside of a small clearing that looked like it had been cleared and kept clean. A training area perhaps. It provided a clear line of sight to a cluster of buildings and anything that would be coming their way. Casting a wary eye over the area, he found nothing out of the ordinary.

Runner glanced over his shoulder to confirm Hannah's position before addressing her.

"Hold here a moment. I wanna take a peek. I'm pretty certain I'm right about this place, but I can't spare the loss of reputation for killing them if I'm wrong. Keep an eye on things. There could very well be patrols coming through here. Rather unlikely though."

Hannah's head bobbed in acknowledgment. It seemed she was taking his advice seriously. Her face had the appearance of concern as she moved away from the tree line. Her head swung to the left and right while she considered her options as to the best place to hide. Leaving it to her as she entered the shadows, Runner turned back to the buildings.

He set about the process of enchanting his gear up for whatever might lie ahead. The duration and mana costs had been improved through the two days of training. Leveling the *Enchant* skill up had well and truly paid off.

Although being able to offset his extreme lack of stats originally, it was quickly becoming apparent the bonuses were not scaling with his level. Benefits that once put him above or on par with enemies were now only barely capable of keeping him on an even playing field most of the time. He would need to find other solutions for his problems. And soon.

Runner did a quick character check to confirm his stats.

Name:		Runner	
Level:	21	Class:	
Race:	Human	Experience:	13%
Alignment:	Good	Reputation:	5
Fame:	5,150	Bounty:	0

Attributes-			
Strength:	1 (31)	Constitution:	1 (31)
Dexterity:	10 (25)	Intelligence:	10
Agility:	3 (18)	Wisdom:	1
Stamina:	1 (16)	Charisma:	64

It wasn't perfect but a generalized set of stats would get him through the next set of encounters.

Completing the work, Runner activated *Stealth* and looked over the map one more time. Most of the town was laid out in a basic fashion that centered around the fort. In truth, beyond the fort, there was nothing out of the ordinary or remarkable about the place.

"Fucking unnatural bastard," Hannah said aloud. She probably hadn't meant for him to hear it, having expected him to immediately step away after going into *Stealth*.

Smiling ruefully, Runner could only shake his head. Striding towards the closest buildings, he set off. In light of her unrelenting belief that he wasn't normal, it was readily apparent that NPCs were well aware of the rules of the game. To them, he probably was as impossible as fish flying.

Approaching the back of what he could only guess was a stable, he checked his surroundings. Nothing was in the immediate area. Feeling his mind starting to wander a little, he advanced.

I wonder who this place belonged to before. It seems rather developed, maybe it was a frontier fort first? From reading the wiki, Orcs regard everything other than Orc-kind as food. Horses included. And Humans.

An Orc's eating habits and their general disposition had been the foundation to Runner's certainty this was a dungeon. Passing the threshold, he was prompted with the entry message. He absently closed it without a second thought.

Whatever it's called is irrelevant, because it's about to become a body farm. Plant me some Orcs, bring in the red harvest, and collect my bounty.

Runner eased himself around the corner and walked towards the entryway. His actions were slow and cautious. He wanted to observe and scout first. Reckless aggression had its place, but it was not here.

Advancing on the entry door carefully, he checked for guards, yet found none. Peeking in through the doorway, he scanned the interior.

Stalls lined both sides of the stable. Early morning light filtered in from above through rotten boards. Each stall had been converted into a cage, and more than three-fourths of those were full of people. Starting here, he could begin to depopulate the fort. It was defensible, out of the way, and lightly guarded.

Must be the pantry. Except instead canned goods we've got livestock waiting for slaughter.

Two red names floated clearly in the middle of the room. Both were named Orc Guard, their levels both set to eighteen. Every other name in the room was green and ranged from Merchant to Priest.

Rationally working through what the scene meant, it made sense. Villager twelve had said they left them alone and would trade on occasion. Clearly the Orcs were picking up travelers, merchants, and adventurers, but nothing local. Better to not anger or panic the local wildlife after all. Especially when there was this much easy game walking the roads nearby.

They definitely weren't his goal, but he figured he could earn some easy experience for freeing them. So long as it wasn't a "Free ten slaves" quest. That would just make that eleventh one weird. *Sorry, quota's all full, can't free you. Enjoy being a late night snack.*

Waiting for a bit, he saw no change in their patrols or habits; they were simple NPCs placed to protect an easy experience grab. They'd walk close enough to the middle to confirm all prisoners accounted for, and return to their original post. Their origin of the patrol was close to the entryway but not in it, thankfully. Confident there would be no change after he departed, he made his way back to Hannah.

Upon reaching the place he'd left her, he was unsuccessful in trying to find her. Realizing how stupid this was, he knew why he couldn't find her.

Frustrated, he dropped his *Stealth* and looked around. Almost immediately, she appeared off to his side, stepping out from behind a tree trunk.

"Yeah, no, that's not going to work. If you're not in my party, I can't see you. Trouble is, you're an NPC, so you can't join my party," Runner explained. Hannah tilted her head to one side.

"I'm getting used to you just spouting absolute bullshit, but it doesn't mean I actually understand you any better. I feel like I'm getting tired of you saying NPC, too. You've called me that several times, and it's starting to sound degrading."

"Right. OK. To simplify, I couldn't see you while you were stealthed, and vice versa. That won't work if we go into that open dungeon back there," Runner said, throwing a thumb over his shoulder to indicate the Orcs. "Which means I have to talk aloud, which will break my *Stealth*, and you'd have to be in range to hear it. Which leaves it to me to solo them, which I honestly doubt as possible considering I'm still in nub gear. I could hold your hand, but that'd only work up to a point. I can't even guarantee that it'd not break *Stealth* either. Don't get me wrong, I'm sure holding your hand is an enjoyable experience, I just don't think it'd work here."

Frowning, Runner stared up into the sky, thinking quietly. "Damnable music. I appreciate the artistry, but not right now. In need of some silence."

With a harrumph, Runner mentally silenced the music with the mute option. The last musical notes faded to nothing, and silence reigned supreme. No solutions had come to him working within the rule set of a player. Runner tried considering the problem from a strictly systematic point of view instead.

NPCs aren't allowed to be a part of the party. They can be followers but that's different. Is it too different? What if I used the targeting function through the server console, identified the base ID for the NPC, and pushed the Party invite through the server to that specific ID? A GM without rights would still be allowed to access all the game's console and basic system commands, like getting the database ID for a spawned NPC. So long as it didn't require a password that is. That and I've been breaking the rules for everything else so far with impunity, so why not try? Soooooooo...

Runner threw out a mental request for the game console, and the window appeared. Inputting "Select Nearest NPC" into the console, he posted the command.

Hannah was immediately selected, and her nameplate went from green to yellow. It was no different than how a normal player would do it, though it was done utilizing the server itself.

So far, so good.

"One step down," Runner muttered. Runner shrugged and entered the invite command through the game console to push an invite to the selected target. Appearing in front of him was a request to confirm that he'd like to invite Thief0084 to his party. Memorizing the position of the yes button, he approved the request. His eyes flickered to Hannah to gauge her response.

There was no change in her behavior. Her eyes scanned the woods, watching for patrols. It was apparent she did not get the request.

His face turning into a frown, Runner decided to change his approach. The system had responded to his desires and actions so far. Truth be told, it was creepy in the way that it seemingly responded to his wishes.

"Come over here please, Hanners. Stand directly in front of me, facing away."

"Uhh. Stupid question since I'm asking you, but you're not going to do anything strange, are you?"

"Nothing out of the ordinary, I promise."

"Ordinary for you maybe," said Hannah, sighing.

Standing as directed, she looked up over her shoulder at him.

"And now? What then?"

"Hold out your right hand. No, not there. Up a little more. No, errr, to the left. A little to the right. For crying out-OK, look, here," he huffed. His hand snaked out and grabbed hers, guiding it into the position he wanted. At the exact place a window would have appeared if she were a player. "Now concentrate everything you can, every single thought towards the idea that, 'Yes, join the party.' Once you feel like you've concentrated enough to crush a stone with the power of your mind, move your hand forward two inches. No more, no less."

"Right, this isn't out of the ordinary at all. Who was I kidding? More insanity from the Lord of Idiocy."

As she stood in front of him, working on the request he gave her, Runner called up the invite command through the server once more. Keying up the command to invite her, he sent it off. Accepting the confirmation immediately, he waited for her.

Visibly frustrated, Hannah complied. Facing forward she fell silent, ostensibly doing as he'd instructed.

Waiting as patiently as he could, Runner merely held her hand and looked at the crown of her head. Watching the light play across her black hair, his mind began to spin random thoughts off.

One such thought landed in right smack dab in the middle of his vast curiosity. *Do NPCs have a scent?*

Leaning forward on that impulse, he smelled her hair quietly. Surprisingly enough, she did indeed have a scent. She smelled of the road, woods, sweat, dirt, and leather, and under all that there was just a hint of something else.

Runner was broken from his woolgathering when her hand shot forward, punching the button neither of them could see.

In that moment, the world spun crazily. Vertigo assailed him as he felt his equilibrium stretched to the limit. Trying to blank his mind, Runner attempted to steady himself, his left hand clutching the fabric of Hannah's clothes.

It was as if his mind was pulled open, turned upside down, and shaken violently. Conscious thought stretched out until he could barely hold a thought together. He became nothing more than a shrieking fear flying through the void. Then it ended as quickly as it had come.

"The fuck is wrong with you? Let go of me, damn it," Hannah declared angrily. Spinning around, she broke his grip on her clothes and shoved at him.

"Please tell me that whatever the fuck it was that you wanted to do, worked. Because I swear if that was some strange need of yours to get close…" Hannah said dangerously.

Blinking a few times, he focused on her face. While the vertigo was gone, he was left with a vague feeling of deja vu.

Looking to the game console, he read over the log. Nothing suspicious lurked in the log, and everything there was benign. There was no massive update patch, the world hadn't gone gray, and the only person who felt it was him.

Focus, Runner, focus. Check your medical log later. It's probably stress.

Closing his system windows, he shook off the vestiges of the strange feeling. Pulling open the party window, he was elated to see it'd worked. Turning his face to Hannah, he gave her a bright smile.

"It worked, though I must say I'm surprised it says your name rather than Thief in the Party window. Whatever. OK, tell me if you can see me when I *Stealth*."

Without waiting for her to respond, he activated *Stealth* and moved to the left. Sure enough, her eyes tracked him even as he moved, though she seemed at a loss for words.

"Oh? Seems you don't even need to respond if you just watch me like that. Fantastic. Outside of a really awesome game of Marco Polo, I think not being able to see each other would not have worked out very well," Runner said happily.

"Kind of? You, you're there, yes. I can see you. Which I shouldn't be able to do, but I can. Bu-but it's like I can see…well, that I can see through you. Like you're made out of fog, or a ghost. A misty version of you."

"Mist? Oh. I'm transparent almost? Kinda see through? Yeah, that makes sense, I guess. Though, not sure what you expected to see, do you just notice people as they come out of *Stealth*? As if they were standing there the whole time? Like they walked up to you but didn't? That seems even more weird."

Runner worked his way through the new party options as he spoke. Casually he turned the group loot options on and changed the item rolls to uncommon or higher.

"It sounds strange when you put it like that, but yes. In fact, everything is a little strange right now. Really fucking strange actually. My head feels heavy," Hannah complained, her lips pressed into a thin line.

Pushing his *Analyze* ability into an active state, he confirmed quickly that there were no status ailments troubling her. Then he cast *Cleanse* on her anyways on the off chance it was a hidden status effect. Runner cocked his head to the side with a smile as the soft azure light faded from around her.

"Better? Head a bit more clear, hopefully? I didn't see any status ailments, but that doesn't mean there weren't any, only that I couldn't see any."

"A little? Maybe? Thank you. I'm fine," she replied quietly. It was clear she was still in distress, but Runner wouldn't press. "I'm fine" usually translated to "I don't want to talk about it" when it came to women. Not being anything to her afforded him the luxury to take it at face value.

"Alright then, the battle plan, ready for it?" Runner asked, looking directly at Hannah. When she nodded her head to signal she was indeed ready, he continued. "There's only two of them, at opposite ends of the stables. They're fairly alert, so we'll need to be swift. I'll attack the first one after I hit him with a *Distract*. It's extremely unlikely I'll drop him in one, but I figure you should be able to drop him with your own *Backstab* attack. Now that I think about it-"

Runner stopped and came in close to Hannah and dropped *Stealth*. Resting his hands on the pommels of her short swords, he called up his *Enchant* functions. She leaned back from him, but didn't move further back as he began casting.

"Kay, that'll help. Gear next. Hold still. Stop squirming," Runner admonished her, his hands pressed to her shoulders as he cast *Strengthen* on her leather guards and chest piece. Hannah continued to fidget as he worked his way down her equipment.

Kneeling at her feet, Runner rested his hands on her ankles. He started to go through the motions to cast *Strengthen* but stopped. In the last moment he decided it'd be a good idea to enchant them with *Regeneration* instead. No sense in putting all this work into her if she couldn't get back into a fight. With a light pat on the toes of her boots, he stood up and brushed himself off.

"Anyways, come on, slaves to free, Orcs to kill, blood to spill, loot to take, stuff to do. Skulls for the skull throne, blood for the blood god. Onwards and all that."

Stealth flashing into an active state, he made his way back to the stable and the Orcs who were waiting for him. He could feel his heart speeding up and the cogs of his mind spin up to a high revolution as the distance shrank. Closing in on the sentry, he wondered at those feelings. This was no game, it was life and death. Beyond the joking, teasing, and irreverence, this was a deadly sojourn.

His gear was woefully below his level, and his stats were just barely adequate. It would come down to an appropriate application of tactics.

Runner skulked along the side of the building. He slowed down as he approached the entryway. Slowly, carefully, he took a quick peek inside to confirm locations. Standing at the outside of his patrol route, the Orc was still. There'd be no time for confirmation or extensive setup, just enough time to cast *Distract* and stab before it turned to walk back.

Slipping into the stable, Runner threw out his hand and activated *Distract*. There was a noise followed by a glint of light at the base of one of the stalls. It pulled at the Orc's attention, and it turned to inspect the area.

No sooner than it took for the Orc to be absorbed in his scrutiny of the bait, Runner was on the move. Stabbing deep into the beast's spine, he felt the blade twist in his hand. Pulling the sword free, the Global refresh timer began.

Facing him, the Orc raised its lip in a snarl, his weapon coming up to strike out at Runner. Then it promptly fell forward, straight into Runner, who was roughly knocked to the side. The Orc crumpled to the floor and laid there unmoving.

Letting his eyes travel up to where the corpse had been standing, he found only Hannah. She stood at ease, blade held loosely in her hand, positioned perfectly to have delivered her *Backstab*. There was no discernible change in her countenance at having killed the Orc.

"Good work, Hanners. We have to move to the other side and catch the other guard before he turns."

Runner immediately stealthed as he finished talking. Ghosting along, he crossed the stable as quickly as he could. Glancing to the side as he went by, it was clear the prisoners were in dire straits and many seemed unkempt. Most of them had noticed what had happened though acted as normal as possible so as not to alert the other guard. A few began praying, while others watched quietly.

Refocusing himself on the task at hand Runner, targeted the Orc at the end of the stable. To his surprise, Hannah was outdistancing him and was now a good bit closer than he was.

She had a natural ability he wouldn't be able to compete with regardless of what he did. Nothing could change that fact; at best he'd be the quintessential jack of all trades.

Whipping her hand, out Hannah used *Distract* and moved past the Orc as it turned to the side. Runner came within range as she rammed her blades home. Dancing backwards, she pulled the short swords clear of the Orc's lower back.

Runner couldn't deny she had a certain feline grace to her. Banishing the thought, he thrust out at the guard. The green-skinned monster collapsed while a tinkling noise indicated the attack inflicted critical damage.

Sheathing his weapon, he indicated the corpse. "Loot it quickly, I'll get the other one. You're looking for a key."

Hannah's brows came down and her head tilted to the side. Realizing she didn't truly understand, he elaborated.

"Focus on the body, in your head picture the words 'Loot All,' and put your hand forward over the corpse. Should move everything to your pack that can be taken."

Ending the conversation, Runner made his way back to the first Orc in a light jog. Halfway there he thought of a second problem and groaned.

Hannah might not even be able to loot. He'd completely forgotten that NPCs couldn't actually loot, not really at least. NPCs had an inventory of sorts, but only what was visually on them, or what one would expect them to have. Maybe a few coins or a random piece of junk to be sold.

Sliding to a halt, he looted the body and spun towards the cages in the same motion. Flipping through his inventory windows, he paged to the quest items. Sitting there was an old key. Grinning, he went to the furthest cage at the end.

"No key on this fucker, but everything did appear in my pack. Much like everything else about you, this makes no gods damn sense. At all. Answers soon or I start killing your beetles while you sleep."

"What? No, seriously, they won't taste right if you kill them," Runner whined. Pushing the key into the mechanisms slot, he gave it a quick twist. Swinging open as it came unlocked, the door creaked on rusty hinges. Moving on to the next cage, he proceeded to insert the key.

"Oi, listen up everyone. I'm freeing you all, consider yourselves saved, go do what you need to do. The End," he said loudly. Unlocking the cage, he gave the door a small pull, opening it partway to confirm it was open.

"Stop!" a masculine voice demanded. It came from the next cage over. Runner stopped with the key in the lock of the third cage. He glanced over to identify the speaker.

"Eh? Why? You're not the eleventh slave if I keep going in this order, are you? I'll unlock all of the cages regardless of the number of prisoners. Scout's honor," Runner promised.

"They're murderers! Evil! That Barbarian clubbed a man and threw him to those beasts. The other is a Sunless. Even your little halfbreed pet over there is better than that," the voice said. Moving to the front of the cage was a man who was gesturing towards Hannah. Blonde haired and blue eyed, he cut the appearance of Prince Charming. Built like an athlete and a touch under six foot.

There were subtleties that spoke of dark things lurking in his eyes. The fool gave off the impression of a bully. His eyes were those of a person who viewed others as inferior, backed by the absolute belief that they were correct in treating other human beings as beneath them.

"She's not a pet, and I'd appreciate you not address her as such or you can stay in your cage. As to them being murderers…"

Taking a step back he studied the occupants of the cage he stood in front of. There were only two occupants. In the back a woman was leaning against the bars, her hands clasped tightly on the cold iron. She was clinging to them as if her body was unable to stay upright. A simple robe proclaimed her as a caster, since that was typically all they could wear.

When she looked up at him, Runner raised his eyebrows in curiosity; she was the definition of different. Alien and exotic were words that could be applied accurately.

Her eyes were clear, piercing, intelligent. The color of her eyes had the look of warm honey. They were perhaps a touch larger than normal as well. Black hair hung limply behind her, partially unbound, and shaggy in a matted braid. Her face was heart shaped, open, and her skin tone a very fair white. Her age wasn't something he felt comfortable guessing at, but he'd feel comfortable with "mature" instead. Features that ran on the fine side, bordering on delicate. Her height was at best a smidgen over five foot. An hourglass shape almost overwhelmed her small figure. Without a doubt she was beautiful. Then she offered a tired smile. It was a truly amazing smile. She did not have the teeth of an herbivore at all, but a full set of sharp pointed teeth. More akin to a predator who subsided on a meat only diet.

"Charming," Runner said, offering a wide and open smile back at her.

"Let me out, now. I'll only give you one black eye for ignoring me this long," stated a towering woman at the grate door. Guessing her age was a bit easier since she was much closer to a Human in appearance. Tentatively, he'd put her at barely past twenty. As she was hunched over to glare down at him, it made her height a little harder to guess. Using his own height for reference, she'd top out at a few inches over six foot. That kind of height was primarily the domain of the Barbarians. One could only describe her as muscular. Her smooth skin was clear in complexion and lightly tanned from days spent outdoors. There were curves to support a womanly figure but one could never mistake her as anything other than an athlete in her prime, lean and fit. Long, elegant, yet callused fingers flexed around the bars of the cage as she pressed her forehead to a crossbar. Looking into that snarling face, he immediately was struck by the fact even the smallest smile would change her appearance. Eyes as black as coal and without a hint of warmth bored into his own. Those dark eyes were dynamically offset by red hair tied back in a loose ponytail.

"Yes, I did it. Tried to rape her. I broke his arms. Gave him to them when they came. Do it again. Do it to you, if you keep looking at me."

"Be still my quivering heart. Such a sweet talker. I'm Runner, that's Hannah, excited to meet you. No danger here then. Except to my sanity, though that's debatable," Runner said. Rotating the key, he popped the lock and swung the door open. Standing to the side, he let the two prisoners out.

"Hey, you promised one black eye only. Pay me later, things to do. Blood for the blood god, skulls for the skull throne. And you," Runner said abruptly, looking to the Sunless woman. Rather than spending the time to *Analyze* her, figure out what was wrong, and then solve it, he'd just go straight to what he'd end up doing anyways.

After tapping his inventory screen open he pulled out two servings of salted pork and handed them over to the worn looking caster as she shuffled out of the cage. "Eat this before you collapse. Based on those pretty teeth of yours, I'd wager you line up more closely with a carnivore than us silly omnivores. Betting your hosts didn't provide you with the right nutritional needs and you're technically starving even though you're full. I'd offer you some beetles but I'm saving those for me. Sorry. Actually, could you hold still for a second?"

He cast *Cleanse* on both the Sunless and Barbarian. Then he followed it up with a *Regeneration* spell, in case one of the ailments had been hindering their maximum health.

You use Persuade on Sorceress
Sorceress is Persuaded
You use Seduce on Sorceress
Sorceress is Seduced

Seriously? Can this not happen? They're clearly not normal NPCs, so I was hoping for maybe a reward. This is just ridiculous. I feel like I'm triggering flags for a dating game. Was this game made for lonely men sitting in bed at night? This is just getting obscene.

Runner turned with a grunt and made his way to the next cage. Belatedly he realized it was the last cage with actual living inhabitants. All of the other pens were filled with bundles of clothes, packs, grain, anything that an Orc wouldn't actually want from those they captured. In his mad dash to and fro he hadn't even noticed they weren't people.

Runner quickly unlatched the lock on the last cell. The last group of ten or so filed out. Most of them made themselves scarce as fast as possible, much like everyone did from the earlier cells. Only four of the prisoners remained: the nasty blond haired man, an older companion, the Barbarian, and the Sunless.

Runner turned his back to Mr. Personality and congratulated Hannah instead.

"Nice work on that last one by the way, Hanners."

Hannah sheepishly nodded her head and partly turned from his scrutiny.

Smiling, he slapped her on the shoulder and then turned to address the foursome again.

"Clearly I'm not a tour guide, so I would think it best you make yourselves scarce. Shoo, be gone, off with you. Things to do, remember? Skulls and blood? No? If you head south along the road, then west there's a town. How about you bugger off in that direction?"

"You're just like them. You consort with filth and allow it to run free. If I had my blade I'd-"

Mr. Personality put his hands to his throat as he started sputtering and gagging. Runner's punch to his larynx had been swift and accurate.

"Please take him away from here before I just kill him. Yes?" Runner addressed the older man. His title labeled him as a Priest, but it didn't stop Runner from considering murdering both of them. The old Priest nodded hurriedly.

"Good man, off with you."

Runner spun the two men around and shoved them towards the exit.

No sooner had Runner cleared one obstacle than another had to present itself. As Runner turned back to the three women, he made eye contact with the Barbarian. In that moment he felt she had just now decided to give him that black eye she promised, but only after robbing him.

"Runt," the woman said, stepping up to him. Runner felt his skin prickle at being addressed as such. His patience, which was low to begin with, gave out. Her level was nineteen but she had no equipment. She wasn't a threat to him in any way. Time to end this swiftly. "Hand over your pack, you can tell people Katarina pr-iiiiaaeee!"

Growling, Runner reached up and hooked his fingers into her hair, catching her in mid-sentence, and yanked her head down. He smashed his forehead into hers and kept it there. He stared into her eyes from no more than an inch away, his nose pressing into hers. Before she could do anything more than meet his gaze, he did his best to pierce her bravado with his own. His intent was to intimidate her so there wouldn't even be a challenge, only acceptance.

"Listen here, Kitten. I don't care. Seriously, I don't. Just stay out of my way and everything will be fine. Not in the mood right now to beat you into the floor just so you can give me some idiotic quest to go back to your home town. I don't care if it's to help you or your people, whatever. I've got green skins to kill and not a lot of time before something goes wrong. Something always goes wrong. So, consider me tempted, I mean you're certainly pretty enough, when your face isn't screwed up in a scowl, but right now is a terrible time for this."

Sighing, he released her hair and patted her cheek with a bit of force before pushing her shoulder, forcing her to stand up and away from him. With a little more time, it might be interesting to investigate a population that was full of large able-bodied women. There'd be men too, but he'd put up with worse. After all he was on a ship full of the worst kind of people from all corners of the Sovereignty. NPC or not, it never hurt to admire the scenery.

You use Persuade on Fighter
Fighter is not Persuaded
You use Intimidate on Fighter
Fighter is Intimidated
You use Seduce on Fighter
Fighter is Seduced

Great good Sovereign Seven. Could this just please stop? I just practically assaulted her and that's persuasion and seduction? This really was made for a bunch of loners with cold empty beds.

Hannah was eying him quietly, her brows drawn down as he turned back to her. They needed to get moving soon if they wanted to clear the fort before nightfall.

Much like he'd cast a prophecy, it was in this moment that everything went wrong. Everyone turned to the far door as a shout was heard, one of courage, bravery, and vigor. Such a thing could only be some type of Battle shout coming from outside of the stable. This was quickly replaced with the sound of a group of Orcs yelling in return from a considerable distance further. Mr. Personality came sprinting in through the open door and bolted past them. He came in wide of their position and exited out the other door.

Staring at the back door, everyone stood dumbstruck as the door closed and the clank of a bar falling in place was heard. Mr. Personality was gone.

"Fuck me, we just got trained. That pack of greenies are going to path right through here as they follow his trail."

Chapter 5 - Sword and Board -

"Right. You," Runner said, pointing to the Sorceress. She'd just finished off the second piece of pork like a hungry wolf before everything went to hell.

"Thana, Thana Damalis," she responded to the question.

"Thana? Like Thanatos? As in death? Cute. Lady Death then, got any spells that are a wall type? Preferably Earth or Ice? We've only got a little bit before those Orcs arrive, and we need that entryway sealed."

Runner gestured over his shoulder to accentuate his point.

"I'm unsure. I'll inspect the area and ascertain what I can do," she reported. Her voice was serene and measured, bordering on musical.

Nodding, Runner cast her from his mind and locked eyes with Hannah.

"Get on that door and see what you can do. he locked it on his way out. Keep in mind it might not be worth the trouble. If you can block it firmly from our side, it'll keep them from flanking us as much as it'll keep us from getting out."

"Got it. On my way," Hannah acknowledged.

Hannah moved off to carry out his orders. Crackling Ice came into being, pulling his attention to the entryway. It was a solid cloudy wall that stretched the width of the entry.

Runner really couldn't gauge the thickness from here, but he could only assume it'd buy them a few minutes. The Ice groaned ominously under its own weight. Eying the wall as it creaked, he mentally willed it to remain solid. He needed this, needed this badly. Finally it settled itself and became quiet. Thana made her way back to him with a pleased look.

"Good work, Lady Death, remind me to never underestimate you in a critical situation. Next, next, next. Kitten, Lady, come stand in front of me please."

Thana complied immediately, though Katarina stared at him. Before it could become a standoff, she did as instructed, breaking eye contact with him. Thanking whatever AI decided it would be good for her to obey, he moved to stand behind Katarina.

Placing his hands on Katarina's hips, he opened up the console with a thought. A single breath later he had completed and approved the party invite to Katarina.

"OK. Hold up your hand," Runner commanded. Once she held up her hand, he wrapped his around it and held it. "Now, in your mind, focus on the words, 'Yes, join the party.' When you feel like your will could crumble mountains under the sheer force of it, move your hand forward two inches. No more, no less. OK?"

"Mmm."

Taking her non-verbal response for acquiescence, he waited patiently. Within a heartbeat of his instruction, Katarina's hand shot forward. Runner received the party acceptance notification, elation filling him. Nodding to himself he released her hand while patting her hip.

"Good show, that was quick. Some impressive mental fortitude. OK, my Lady, your turn."

Moving to stand behind Thana, who had been watching him the whole time, he smiled at her.

"Eyes forward, little miss. OK. Same thing. Hand up please," Runner insisted, resting his hands on her hips.

Thana hesitated and then raised her right hand. Runner placed his hand over hers and leaned forward, then down, then forward again. Her diminutive height made it harder to judge the right placement for her fingers. Finally he felt fairly sure he had her hand in the right spot.

"Same instructions for you. 'Yes, join the party.' Two inches, no more, no less."

Silence dominated the area as Thana stood there, her hand held in the air. Trying to remain patient was a difficult thing for Runner, as his mind tended to run into strange thoughts when he wasn't keeping it busy.

Thana's cool hand hung motionless in the air, his own hand keeping it steady. Swinging his head over to look at Katarina, he paused midway. Without even straining his eyes Runner could see a vein at the side of Thana's neck pounding away.

Frowning, he stared at her neck, wondering why the game had decided to add such a minor detail. It was more than likely that it would be overlooked by ninety-nine percent of the player base. Watching it beat rapidly, anyone could see she had an elevated heart rate. Why would an NPC even display such a characteristic in such a way? Let alone have a heart rate to begin with now that he put a thought to it.

Letting go of her hip with his left hand, he brushed a fingertip over the pulsing skin and then pressed his finger into it. Feeling it throb under his fingertip, he was more than a little surprised. In that touch he was able to confirm her heart rate was indeed racing and that she had a heartbeat. *Such a strange thing for an NPC. She's little more than the most basic layer of coding for a game this size, yet this was put in.*

Without warning Thana's hand shot forward. Before he could even confirm the party invitation was accepted, she was walking away from him. Glancing to Katarina, who was just watching him, he shrugged, then checked the party window. Sure enough,

Katarina Saden and Thana Damalis had joined the party. *More surnames, such a strange thing. I'll need to check their status later. I bet they'll have flags as well.*

Taking a moment to confirm their levels, Runner was pleasantly surprised. Katarina was sitting at level nineteen and Thana at twenty-two. In this situation that was an immeasurable blessing.

Thana had turned and was now glowering at him from under her dark brows, her hands clenched into fists at her sides. Ignoring her, Runner continued on with the plan.

"Now that you're in the party, that'll make it easier to target you later. OK, nex-" Runner started, and then stopped as he heard crunching noises from up near the ice block. "Ah, our party guests have arrived. We aren't ready to receive them yet. No refreshments, the band isn't here, and the waiters haven't even prepared the glasses. We must freshen up a bit first," Runner lamented sadly. He quickly made his way over to the cages and their tightly packed contents and opened the closest one. Rummaging a bit through the pile of clothes, he began sorting out various pieces he could use.

"I don't think they'd store weapons of any sort in the place where they're holding prisoners. Unless the writers of the game treated this like a horrible fanfic or really dodgy writing. That leaves what I've got on me, as far as weapons go at least. Let's see then."

He threw open his inventory window and he flipped through it rapidly. He had kept one type of each weapon but had sold all the extra armor. A regret to be sure, but how could have known he'd be supplying others with gear. Pulling out a shield from his inventory and then his own long sword from his character panel, he set them on the ground. These two items were followed by a small oak wand and a focusing crystal sphere.

Sparing the time to bolster their strength, he placed *Fireblast* on both the wand and sphere. His limited repertoire of spells was narrow in scope and primarily stuck to enhancing the most basic of things. It'd just have to do. After all, there was nothing else.

"Okie dokie, take these. They're pretty much garbage equipment but should be a decent focus until we can outfit you better," Runner apologized, handing over the focusing sphere and the wand to Thana. He turned to Katarina, picking up the long sword and shield. With a brush of a finger, he enchanted the shield with *Stoneskin* and walked over to her.

"Kitten, this is my sword and shield. Take them," Runner requested. Passing the items to her, he looked between the two of them. "This next bit is for both of you. Focus on the items, put the word 'Equip' and nothing else in your mind. Eventually they'll pop, shift, or just appear in your hand. They'll fit better than you even thought they could. That sword might even get a bit bigger in its reach, Kitten. Next."

Leaving them to the task of equipping the weaponry, he went back to the cage and started going through the other crates and barrels, sorting them into his existing piles. Grumbling to himself, he dismissed nearly everything that he came across. Perhaps a minute passed before he found a set of workable clothes with a bare amount of armor and a set of Light Leather. He walked back to his new party members while organizing his haul into three sections.

"Lady, take these. Same thing, just hold in your hand with 'Equip' in your head."

Handing over the stack of lightly armored clothes, he turned to Katarina.

"There's a slight problem, Kitten. No armor in there that actually would be useful in a stand-up fight. I'm going to give you mine. Don't worry about the size, it'll adjust on its own and fit you just fine. Oh, my sword has a fire enchantment. If things catch fire, don't be startled. Kay? Kay."

Katarina nodded to him and watched him wordlessly. Her lack of a response after having been so confrontational was disconcerting. For the moment he was grateful that he didn't have to solve it immediately. Running his hands over himself, he updated all the spells to be a mix between constitution and strength, noticing halfway through that the timers had increased to an hour.

Must have leveled that up again. Neat. Hopefully it doesn't cost as much to cast either.

Equipping the set of light armor, he went through the *Enchant* process again. Having leveled up, the cost of each cast was indeed less, which he was thankful for.

With fewer casts and a longer timer they could be ready faster. Ice could only take so much abuse before completely falling apart. Even one made through magic and conjured up as a solid block.

Runner held out his sturdy Heavy Leather to Katarina. Taking a moment to sheathe her sword she then clipped the shield into the harness clip on her back. She took the proffered armor from him. Patting her shoulder, Runner indicated the armor.

"Just like last time, 'Equip.'"

Diving through his inventory, Runner pulled out a short sword and a dagger. Giving both a quick *Fireblast* enchant, he equipped them. Looking to Katarina, he watched as her peasant clothes disappeared and the snug leather armor replaced them.

Feeling run-down and with a touch of vertigo, Runner closed his eyes. Allowing himself a deep breath and a quiet moment, he

fought against the dizziness. It was a feeling he'd long ago
associated with looking over steep heights. He let the air out
of his lungs and took another deep cleansing breath.

Cracking open an eye, he retrieved his canteen. Unscrewing
the cap quickly he then exhaled once more and took a drink. Cool
water filled his mouth and charged down his throat, chasing the
nausea away. Finally it felt like his head wasn't going to go
spinning off.

Opening his eyes fully, he gave Katarina a once-over, and
he couldn't help but be impressed.

"Lord knows I love a woman who looks dressed and ready to
kill," Runner said, giving Katarina a broad smile.

"Do you have anything bigger? A great sword? An axe?" she
asked him, sounding unsure.

"I do, but Kitten, I need you to tone down that bloodlust.
I don't need a crazed Barbarian to wildly swing themselves
through the fray. That wouldn't serve my goals, my needs. I need
you as you are right now. I need you as my sword and shield. I
need you to use your head, put yourself where you're needed, and
keep them busy. I need you to use that Barbarian gift in
accordance with your intelligence. You can do that, and do it
well. Lady Death and I can start lowering their numbers as you
work. Please."

Marginally she nodded her head and said nothing more. Her
long fingers wrapped around the hilt of the sword. She redrew
the blade swiftly from its sheath. She held it at her side,
hefting it, clearly feeling the weight of it. After a long
moment, she clearly gathered herself and met his gaze, nodding
her head fully this time.

*Well, she didn't smile, but she's not going to run away or
just get herself killed. Fine, moving on.*

Turning, he caught Thana staring at him again. Locking her
eyes with his own, he addressed her once more.

"Kitten will be the front line and I'll be working to keep
them off her by bouncing their aggro list around a little. I'll
also be trying to chip at their health or eliminate one if I
can," Runner explained. "I need you to let us attack them a few
times to generate enough aggro so that they'll ignore you and
not just run straight for you. Err, aggro as in who they hate
the most. The more damage you do, the more healing you cast, the
faster you end up at the top of their priority list."

Runner waited, watching her eyes, to see if she understood.
With a practically imperceptible acknowledgment, she signaled
for him to continue.

"Then, and only then, cast at that target. For every two
attacks she lands after that, you can cast again. Orcs have

thick hides, so go for something that is piercing. That or will lower their ability to fight. Understood?"

"I understand. I also recognize you're correct. Your plan is sound though it has a large flaw. I fear that we will be overrun. Katarina can only take so much punishment, even with your ensorcelled equipment," Thana said, concern tinging her voice.

"A fair point. It will not be an issue. I will be acting as healer as well. This isn't exactly ideal, but we'll make do with what we have. The damage shouldn't overwhelm my ability to heal," Runner assured her. At the mention of him being able to use restoration spells, her eyebrows jumped upwards.

Ice shattered and sprayed bits of itself in every direction. A gap large enough for Orcs was coming to shape- they'd start piling through it any minute. Their time had expired.

"Kitten, get in that breach! If we can bottleneck them in that break, this'll be easier," Runner shouted. Moving even as he spoke he sprinted for the opening. The distance wasn't great but he was still sure most would get through before he got there.

Katarina started out ahead of him by a few paces, but left him behind as if he was standing still. Red hair trailing behind her like a streamer, she pulled further ahead of him. Roaring from deep within, Katarina advanced on them. She cleared the distance with blazing speed and charged them like the angry fist of a goddess of war.

Shield held high like a ram, she bashed them into each other and wedged them into the opening. Two had seen her coming and had gotten out of the way before she could get to them. Engaging those at the front of the rift, she wasn't able to respond to those who had escaped and now circled around her.

Runner would arrive at her side too late to prevent them from scoring easy *Flank* attacks. Their aggro list would only have her on it as no one else had acted. He needed to do something now, in this instant, or she'd pay for his inaction.

He used the *Regeneration* on Katarina to bring her health up, and both Huck on the left and Puck on the right turned to face him. Ignoring Katarina, they focused on the new target, Runner the healer.

Weapons clanged as blows were exchanged in the melee at the breach. Katarina's shouts of pain and anger resounded over the Orcs' bellows in return. Sliding up to the two Orcs facing him, he attacked Puck's cleaver. Sword rebounding from the ugly little blade, Runner targeted Huck and activated *Slash*.

He only managed a basic hit on Huck and a partial disarm on Puck. His timers were refreshing as both Orcs attacked. Turning to the side, he was unable to dodge the cleaver and barely parried Huck's club. The ugly crunch of the cleaver hitting his flesh filled his ears. It came away bloody from his arm.

Runner was immediately affected by the Bleeding status ailment. It would continue for the next five seconds for an extra five damage on top of the damage from the strike.

Pain was still a surprise to him, and a grimace painted his face. Perhaps relying on the pod so deeply had raised the immersion level. Though it was a serious wound that would debilitate a person in real life, it did little more than cause pain here. It was still just a game after all.

Casting *Fireblast* in the face of Huck, he tried to disarm Puck once again. Fire played over Huck's face and the Burning effect took hold with a *whoosh*.

Puck's cleaver went spinning from his hand and clattered noisily into a wall. Turning to Huck, Runner launched his *Slash* attack as it came off from cooldown. His attack cleared the Orc, and from out of nowhere a large spear of ice impaled the Orc through his chest. Falling backwards under the weight of the attack, Huck hit the ground and died.

Runner checked on Katarina and found she was losing ground. Her health ticked away under the continuous pounding she was receiving and was already at half. In that glance he saw she was suffering under several different status ailments as well. Puck was still in the process of retrieving his cleaver. Taking the opportunity, Runner cast *Cleanse* on Katarina and immediately snapped off *Cure* twice in rapid succession. Mana pool now seriously depleted, he turned his attention back to Puck, who was rapidly approaching him.

Runner activated a quick slot item he'd prepared earlier. Slamming down a mana restoration potion, he tossed the bottle aside once he'd emptied it. Using the potion had reset his global cooldown though. It would give Puck another attack before Runner could respond in kind.

A partial deflection was the best he managed, and it was only a glancing blow, but once more he was afflicted with Bleeding. Scrutinizing his health bar, he saw he had forty or so points left. His supply of mana was definitely limited, but it was coming back under the strength of the potion. He would need to be sparing with it and keep its use restricted to keeping Katarina in the fight. He'd need to work harder at improving his restoration magic if they got out of this, that and his mana pool.

Returning the attack with one of his own, Runner was able to score a hit off Puck's thigh. Aligning himself once more with his foe, he cast *Regeneration* on Katarina when the first casting wore off. Puck's return stroke landed solidly and took another deep bite from his dwindling hit point pool. With such little armor and low stats, he just couldn't take hits. Another attack and that'd be game over for him.

Resolving himself to casting another *Fireblast* rather than risk his life, he raised his hand. Ice exploded from the Orc's neck, a spear of ice ripping through the green skin. The magical attack nearly decapitated the poor creature with its sheer power.

Mentally crossing both Orcs from his list, he pivoted to face Katarina who was inexorably being forced from the bottleneck. Three Orcs bulled their way in, Katarina felling the fourth as they moved to encircle her.

Not missing this golden opportunity, Runner sunk his short sword into the back of the closest one. Critical tinkling noises filled his ears with its beautiful siren song, a confirmation of a powerful blow. With the critical attack and the *Flank* attack bonus, the Orc was no more and deflated like a popped balloon.

Casting *Cure* on Katarina followed by *Regeneration* drained his mana pool. He stalked around to the rear of the Orc on Katarina's left.

Katarina had her shield out to it, keeping it distracted, while she kept the second Orc busy with her sword. As he neared his target, an Ice spear took its life, entering one side of it's chest and exiting the other.

Runner turned to face the last Orc and found it was in mid swing to end his life. There was nothing he could do, there were no actions he could take that would be able to halt, deflect, or dodge that blade. Apparently his last cast of *Regeneration* on Katarina put him at the top of his aggro list. Thus fixating on him and ignoring Katarina. He hadn't heeded his own advice and charged in foolishly with no health.

Then Katarina was there, putting herself in front of him and taking the blow on his behalf. Standing behind her, he watched her shoulder flex and then the Orc drop to the ground at her feet.

Runner closed his eyes and rested his forehead on the back of Katarina. He had truly believed that he was going to die.

"You blessedly quick-witted and gorgeous woman. That would have been the end of me if that connected. Definitely going to share my beetles with you."

Runner took deep quivering breaths, his short sword and dagger forgotten on the ground, having fallen from nerveless fingers. He rested his hands on her sides now for stability, not trusting himself to stand on his own.

Katarina made no reply nor did she move. Barbarians were warlike people who thrived in battle but paid for their bloodlust in the aftermath. Unable to confirm it but fairly sure of it, he believed she was probably trying to quell the burning desire for combat. It was as much a positive racial passive as it was a detriment.

Patting her on the hip, he lifted his head and looked to Thana. She was standing a fair distance back, ready for whatever came next.

"Solid spell work my, Lady Death. Those spears were definitely on another level. You really pulled out a few clutch hits there. OK, clean up time I guess. I don't think we'll ever fight a group that big again thankfully. That was like two patrols, maybe even three," Runner mused aloud.

Runner walked over to Thana and surveyed the other end of the building. Hannah was there, looking back at him, guarding their flank as he'd requested. Signaling to her to remain where she was, he also provided a thumbs-up for her. Hannah apparently had been a little tense as even from this distance it was clear she relaxed at the signal, then threw a thumbs-up back at him.

It's a pity party chat only works the same distance as normal chat. Annoying to not be able to communicate with her from here. Damn game designers and their realism, woooo.

Rounding on Katarina, he walked over to her after scanning the area around them.

Katarina stood watching the exit still, shield and sword clutched in her hands. Eyes focused, her stance loose but ready, she seemed the embodiment of a Fighter waiting for the next battle.

"You alright, Kitten?" Runner asked her quietly. "I won't hold you and Thana to anything, if that's what you're thinking. You're free to go after we split the loot from the dead. We'll not have another fight like that until we actively begin pulling to this location."

Katarina said nothing at first, though she did glance at him and then away. She shifted her weight slowly from foot to foot, her thumb tracing the line of the sword's hilt. As there was no rush Runner, left her to think.

Keeping himself busy, he went to loot and drag the dead to an empty cell. Ugly but necessary work. Though it felt like a good amount of time went by, it only took perhaps five minutes to clear the field and loot the dead.

While Runner finished his grisly Task, Thana rooted around in the cages that held the stolen belongings of travelers while Runner had finished his grisly task.

Standing before Katarina, he reached out to touch her shoulder with his fingertips, trying to get her attention. Hesitating a moment longer, she finally spoke.

"I would remain. I…would be your sword and shield. Though I am unsure of these beetles."

Runner didn't reply immediately. In fact, he seriously considered rejecting her. Realization came to him though when he considered how much damage she soaked up. How she held against everything with the barest of support, that she had put herself before him without a thought to her own well-being. Grinning at her, he chuckled.

"I accept. The pay is four copper a day, you get eight upfront. Four for today, and four for your last day. My goal is become as strong as possible, as quickly as possible. I expect a lot of bloodshed and a lot of problems. Do you accept these terms?"

"I do."

"Fantastic, glad to have you aboard, Kitten. As to the beetles, trust me, they're great. Have a real good crunch to them, like biting into a firm apple. Let's go see if Lady Death will be joining us as well."

Shifting gears from Katarina, Runner walked over to Thana while signaling for Hannah to come over. Thana was still in the process of sorting through the myriad of items that had been haphazardly packed by the Orcs.

"Thana, I'll not hold you up any longer. You're welcome to depart as you wish. You are also welcome to one-fourth of the spoils that can be found if you choose to leave."

"I'll be taking the equal of the offer you gave Katarina, thank you. You weren't as quiet as you think, and I have exceptional hearing to begin with," Thana said confidently, not even pausing from her task.

"Right. Good. The company of an intelligent, young, and beautiful woman such as yourself is not something one should ever turn down. Ah, good timing, Hanners. Lady Death and Kitten will be joining us. I must confess that this one's earned the right to my beetles. Don't be jealous," he said, gesturing his thumb at Katarina.

Hannah looked from Runner to Katarina and said nothing. They fixed their gaze on one another before both looked to him at the same time.

"She's fucking welcome to them then. I can't get over the clicking noises they make, remember?" Hannah explained exasperatedly as a shudder played over her.

"Hey, hey, they're delicious. Watch, watch. Kitten, close your eyes and open your mouth. Just start chewing and don't think about it."

Runner was already moving things around in his inventory window and pulled a squirming, clicking beetle out. Surprisingly, Katarina did exactly as he asked. Not waiting or letting her change her mind, he pushed the beetle into her mouth.

Thana and Hannah were both watching with interest as Katarina chewed it up and swallowed. Tilting her head to the side, Katarina opened her coal dark eyes and looked at Runner before smiling. Runner had been right. A smile was the best thing for Katarina. It opened her entire face in an entirely different way and made those dark eyes smolder.

"Very crunchy. Tastes odd at first. Probably grow on you, get used to them," Katarina critiqued.

Laughing triumphantly, Runner pulled another beetle and set it into Katarina's hand.

"Ha? See? I was right. They're delicious after the first one. More for us, ain't that right, Kitten? Forgive me, I'm sidetracked. Next we clear the area of every single Orc. Peasant, woman, warrior, whatever it is, it's gotta be put in the ground. I doubt very much we'll run into anything that large in number from here on out either. Hanners, any thoughts on how to keep that back door from opening up?" Runner inquired.

"None of them came over during your little party over here. There's a bracket to hold a beam in place to brace the door. I found the beam when I got over there. I dropped the fucker in place, wanted to be sure. I figure it's enough to give us a warning to expect a problem if nothing else. Shit else we can do about it though."

"Close enough. Hanners, you're on pulling duty. Do it like we talked about on the way over. Shouldn't be too bad. Kitten, I need you to stand at the front. Once Hanners gets past you, close it up and hold them there. Lady Death, I would ask that you stand back with me and cast from there. With your *Ice spear*, my *Fireblast*, and Kitten holding them in place, we should be well off. Scratch that, extremely well off. If Hanners gets the chance to put work in with her blades, we'll drop them quickly," Runner summarized. "I'll keep you healthy, Kitten, so have no fear of that."

"I indeed have no fear of that. I will do as you've instructed. Second one was a lot better," acknowledged Katarina, the beetle now absent from her hand.

"Good, a repeat of last time with fewer Orcs. I have absolute faith in all of you."

Squaring his shoulders, Runner grinned wolfishly and flexed his hands and shook them out.

"Shall we begin?" Runner asked, looking to his companions.

Chapter 6 - King of Cliches -

Runner ran his eyes over the map spread out over the table. It was only a map in the vaguest sense of the word. Runner had pulled out a roll of parchment from his inventory, put it down, and started drawing in everything that was visible. Hannah filled in gaps here and there where she could. Each building became a rough box, and the fort began to take shape on the paper.

They'd turned the stable into their operating base since it was already clear and reasonably defensible. A frown creeped up on him while he shaded in one of the squares marking a building. Hannah tapped a different square on the map and Runner moved a small rock to the building that she indicated.

"Marked," he confirmed. Standing, Runner blew out a breath and stretched his back. Hannah slipped out of the stable to go get the next set of Orcs.

"You came amazingly prepared. I did not consider you would have put so much planning behind it. Let alone any thought at all. You don't seem the type."

Runner made a displeased face and turned to Thana. Pinning her with a glare, he drew his brow came down. He could feel frustration seeping out of him and tried his best to battle it down.

"Why? Because I choose to be who I am? Because I care little for social niceties? Because I refuse to play the games others do? That same kind of thinking would have me leaving you in the cage. A set of societal norms that would condemn you for you and Hanners for your race. To be used and disposed of based on whatever flight of fancy tickled me."

Thana said nothing and looked away from his furious glare. Runner sighed and tried to smooth out his emotions as he scanned the room. Eventually his gaze fell on Katarina.

In the short time he'd spent with her he'd quickly discovered she wouldn't mince words. She'd tell him exactly what she thought and expected, regardless of anyone else's views. It was certainly refreshing considering he'd only had the swarthy mouthed Hannah for company for days.

Katarina stood at the entrance, sword in hand and on guard. Silent, stoic, waiting. What he would have considered originally a boisterous personality turned out to be shockingly the opposite. Now she seemed the immaculate warrior maiden, stern and unrelenting, the shield that protects and the sword that delivers swift retribution. He'd judged her incorrectly and unfairly.

Thana, on the other hand, had already been pushing his buttons with questions and mildly irritating statements. Half of what she said forced him into a reconsideration of his opinion and the other half outright annoyed him into debating with her.

It's frustrating because I know what she says isn't wrong, just a different way of looking at things.

"That would be your doing you realize," Thana said, as if in response to his eyes falling upon Katarina.

"You forced her into a role she had never considered. One she hadn't even truly realized existed. She merely was content to do as she willed. With a handful of words and a compelling appeal, you've broken the sharp edges off her and slapped a purpose into her. I wouldn't have thought it possible if I hadn't seen it, but there it is."

"I did nothing of the sort. All I did was intimidate her, put a sword in her hand, and demand things of her."

Thana's gentle laughter drew his focus from Katarina. Smiling widely at him, Thana shook her head at him.

"Yes. The woman you intimidated, yet you didn't deny interest in. Who you threatened to break completely if she didn't bend to your will, then you gave her your own sword and stood before her defenseless. A woman who had always done as her free spirit wanted, you denied it, and demanded she use herself for you," Thana explained patiently. Moving to stand in front, of him she looked into his eyes defiantly. Daring him to deny any of her statements.

"You shattered her self-assurance in her physical strength and then replaced it with confidence in her judgment and intellect. You gave her your trust without demanding hers. It's honestly terribly cliche, but that's the problem with cliches, they tend to originate in reality."

"Cliche, she says. I'll have you know I planned no such thing. I merely did what was required of me."

"So you say. I'll believe it to a point, but would you now cast her aside if it were required of you? Perhaps for a more convenient tool, a better warrior? Would you dismiss Hannah? Me?" she asked, her voice softening near the end.

Runner was angry and frustrated with the Sunless woman. Again. They'd been systematically clearing the village of Orcs, eliminating any and all, for the entirety of the day now. Corpses were stacked in the cells, looted completely of everything worth a coin. Minutes into this systematic cleansing, the Sunless Sorceress had started with her questions. Like a fencer, they started with light probing things. Easily answered and thrown away. By the second hour she'd brought him into philosophical debate.

It wasn't until the fourth hour that he realized she was enjoying the exchanges, which only served to get deeper under his skin. Spanning any number of subjects, it seemed Thana lived to debate, question, and prod him. Katarina was no help in this situation as she was devoted to her duty and wouldn't leave the door. Though he doubted she would have added much to the conversation. She wasn't unintelligent, she merely didn't wish to concern herself with subjects of no interest to her.

Clenching his fist, he considered ejecting Thana from the party. It'd be that simple, he told himself. Removed from the party, she'd have no reason to stay and would leave. Perhaps he'd kick her in order to prove he could do what was required of him. Required of him to save everyone.

Deciding to do just that, he started to form the command to see the kick party member command. Then he hesitated as he thought about how much he did actually need her. Hand trembling in barely checked frustration, he let it fall to his side.

"I can't afford to do anything else. I have to do everything I can to level up. You wouldn't understand, none of you would. You're just NPCs. You're not even real, just random bits of code strung together, powered by electricity and a guiding AI. Don't you get it? You're not real. You're characters in a story. Not even major characters."

Runner struggled with himself. The weight of the problem wracked him with guilt at night. Nightmares waited for him built on the fear of how high the graveyard count would reach each morning. Five thousand souls was the tally now. Five thousand.

Seeking rest each night, his mind wanted only to circle around the idea that everyone was trapped. Every single person was stuck in this game, with no way out, unless he could manage to log into the system and begin to make changes necessary to protect everyone. Game Master controls could bring everyone to one spot, then they could plan. Organize everyone and put people on the path to getting out of this situation, or at the least, safety. They were all waiting on him.

"I will admit, I only understand some of what you've said, but I can tell you now, I am a woman. A Sunless Sorceress to be exact. I think. I feel. I have memories. I…I feel some of them are strange, they don't seem to match up…and…and things are missing. Everything from the moment you appeared is different. A subtle difference in flavor you could say. Yet here I stand, discussing a "am I me" philosophical debate with you," Thana said, flashing that predatory smile at him.

Chuckling, he shook his head and grinned in return. "I think you enjoy frustrating me. Your questions grow more provocative every minute, more wolfish. More hungry than that clever smile of yours. You seem to enjoy pulling me into arguments just to argue with me. Soon you'll have me debating the finer points of cheese making."

"Of course," she agreed. "You're clearly intelligent and have a fine mind for debate. You're also without any doubt suffering. Inside you there is a piece that isn't healthy, whole, complete. I can't fix it if I can't find it. Besides, you like my smile. You always smile back."

Sighing, he started to respond, fighting the smile that threatened to break free, but he was interrupted by Katarina.

"Incoming."

"Ah, to be continued, Lady Death."

With a deep mocking bow, he gestured for her to proceed him.

Thana inclined her head slightly and moved to her assigned position. Runner came to stand beside her and they stood shoulder to shoulder. Placed here, they were angled in such a way that they could see the door and target enemies easily. They'd left the ice as it was since it would operate as a bottleneck if need be. Thick as a fog, silence hung over them all as they waited for Hannah.

Hannah came sprinting in through the gap in the ice. "Two Warriors!" Hannah gasped out.

Two Orcs pounded into the stable a dozen paces behind her. Katarina stepped out and swung her shield at the second one as it neared her. A sound like a frying pan hitting the floor filled the air. The Orc's face was crushed behind the weight of the Shield bash. Landing flat on its back, the Orc was stunned and lay there motionless. Mercilessly, Katarina moved in to skewer it with her sword.

Locking his eyes to the first Orc, Runner held up his left hand and threw a *Fireblast* at it. Screaming in pain and fury, it focused on Runner and continued its charge. It didn't charge far since an Ice spear tore through its face. Its feet shot out from under it with the force of the impact. Propelled backwards, the Orc crashed into the wall of cells and fell dead. Thana must have scored a Critical to kill it on the first shot. That or it was weaker than what they'd experienced up to this point.

Flicking his eyes back to Katarina, he saw her standing over the corpse of the other Orc. Smoke billowed from the wound, a silent testament to the showmanship of a *Fireblast* enchantment.

Katarina gave the body a heavy kick to confirm its level of deadness. Satisfied, Katarina next grabbed it by a boot and dragged it to a nearby cell. Unceremoniously and without a care, it was left next to a pile of corpses. The corpses would fade over time, but they didn't feel like tripping over dead bodies until then.

Runner walked over to the corpse Thana had made and hauled it into the same cell. As he pushed it up against the other corpse, an arm flopped out. Nudging it back inside, he looted the creature of its worldly possessions.

"That pull came in a bit faster, Hanners, and weaker to boot. Did we miss a patrol?" Runner inquired, going over to the map where Hannah was standing.

"No, they came in on the path out of the thrice damned woods. For whatever fucking reason I don't know. Maybe they had a group out there hunting? I'll keep an eye out for them. Not much we can do about the goat fuckers. They just decided to show up," Hannah groused.

"Got it. Come're for a moment. I think your enchantments will run out before you find the next group. Call me a paranoid fool and I'll be forced to agree."

Runner waited for her to face him so he could begin. She ignored him until she finished with her inspection of the map. Facing him, she held up her hands with a raised eyebrow.

"I think you just like putting your shitty paws on me," Hannah teased, smirking at him.

"Can't deny that, though this is hardly the time or place. Not to mention you feel, gasp, a lot like Leather Armor. Realistically though, I think pushing your armor and constitution up would be ideal. No real need for you to do more damage right now, it would increase your survival rate too, in case the unexpected happens."

Rolling his fingers over her gear a piece at a time, he bolstered her constitution and armor as he'd said. Now that he'd admitted his fear aloud, he knew it was the truth. He wasn't willing to risk her life. Not surviving a fight for the sake of an easier kill wasn't a trade-off he was willing to make.

Finishing up, Runner patted her on the shoulder. "Alright, you're good. Go on. Skulls don't just collect themselves ya know. You can't expect me to make a Skull stool do you? Need a throne."

Rolling her eyes, Hannah trotted out the door without a word. Katarina had been nearby and took Hannah's place after she'd gone.

"With her being more sturdy, I should be shifted towards damage," Katarina asserted.

Grinning smugly behind Katarina, Thana looked like she wanted nothing more than to laugh. Runner had no real argument to refuse Katarina with, and it wasn't a terrible idea either. It wasn't as if they were pressed by time. Resetting the enchantments would give him a break from Thana as an added benefit. It'd only be for a few minutes, but it wouldn't cost him anything.

"Fair enough. Let's see…" Runner muttered and laid his hands on Katarina's shoulders. Concentrating for a moment, he set on recycling the empowerments. Giving her constitution and strength in equal amounts, he worked his hands over her equipment the same way he had Hannah's. Finishing with her boots, he looked up to find Katarina watching him quietly.

"All set, Kitten. Wouldn't want you to scar up that pretty skin of yours."

Not acknowledging that statement, Katarina walked back to her post at the entry.

"You're spoiling her. She's like, awkwardly enough, a kitten. Taking any and all attention you're willing to give her since you're treating her as an equal, rather than an inferior or a superior," Thana chided, laughing at him.

"Oh shut up. Don't be jealous. I'd be happy to do the same for you if you like."

"You could, but I'm not wearing armor, remember? Thin clothes that stink of dirt and better suited to working a field. You'd get a lot more than a handful of stiff leather if you tried."

Challenging tone matching her wolfish grin, Thana took a step and put herself in the same spot Katarina had been standing in. She held her hands up and turned her wrists outward as if inviting him and surrendering simultaneously. Runner found the idea tempting but controlled himself. His body made him painfully aware of the fact that Thana was beautiful despite being an NPC.

"Foul temptress. You realize how weird that is? An NPC shouldn't be like that. Why am I even considering this? This is insane. I'm insane. I need a drink. A lot of drinks. And a beetle."

He'd turned his head to start rifling through his inventory when her cool fingers caught his chin and forced him to look into her upturned face. Though the view was impressive considering the height differential between them, her eyes held a dangerous glint that demanded his attention.

"Again, and for the last time, I am a woman. A Sunless woman but a woman. You will not address me as that ever again. The NPC part, not the temptress part. I am certainly finding the role of temptress to be amusing. I don't know what an NPC is, but you say it in an insulting way. Runner Norwood, you are a man in dire need of manners and a person who will argue with you, rather than do as you ask. I will take this position, and I expect you to fully cooperate."

Runner could only nod his head at this and let his inventory screen close. Seeing his agreement, she released his chin, smiling at him once again.

"I'm not normally so forward, but it seems the other roles are already filled in your building harem. Besides, it's a lot more fun to not hide my actions in politics or diplomacy. Just to do as I would. As Katarina has always done, up to now at least. You yourself said it, no? I believe it was along the lines of not caring for societal niceties?"

"I suppose that answers one question I had about you," Runner started. Thana tilted her head, inviting him to continue. "You give off the impression you're from nobility, Lady Death. Your manners, etiquette, vocabulary, and honestly your very looks, all scream fine breeding and a grand education," he finished.

Blushing from hairline to neck, Thana didn't break eye contact with him. Brown eyes flashing alarmingly, she gave no response. While she might try her hand at playing the seductress, pester him, spar with him, be forward, and dare him, it was transparent that she had only recently left court life. She was quiet, well spoken, kind, and a polite young lady at heart.

"Forgive me, I did not intend to make you upset or offend you. I'm impressed with you. I cannot for the life of me fathom why Mr. Personality would declare such a creature as yourself as filth," Runner confessed apologetically.

Coughing delicately into one hand, Thana gestured at the map with the other. "Once you've depopulated the area, or zone as you called it, then what is your plan? While I am in your employ, I would know my future."

Permitting the change of subject with unspoken thanks, Runner looked to the map again.

"Elementary, really. I need to level up as fast as possible. This is just a quick means to an end that will provide a good experience reward. That and loot. Really need an upgrade to our equipment and funds to that end as well. This'll be a wealth of both I hope."

"So you've said. And beyond that? Why work so hard? You've not spoken to that goal."

"I don't think you actually want to know. Perhaps another time. Let's just say that I have nearly half a million people waiting on me. I'm hard-pressed for time. Very-hard pressed," Runner answered. Taking a moment, he squeezed his thumb and forefinger to the bridge of his nose, sighing, closing his eyes. "I'm not even sure if they're alive to be honest. It's very possible they're all already no longer among the living. Maybe they all existed a long time ago. Maybe I'm the last. Maybe I'm alone."

Thana said nothing at first but placed her small hand against his upper arm. Runner felt her hand rubbing up and down in a soothing manner. Such a plain gesture of comfort, yet it offered so much to him. Underneath it all he'd felt like he was struggling to uphold this burden.

"You're not alone, of that I am certain. Even if your worst fears were true in the way you stated them. Hannah may not be what a person would normally trust as a companion, given her heritage and job, but I truly believe she'd lay her life down for you first. It goes without saying that Katarina would probably cut off her legs if you asked her to."

"And you, Lady Death? You suspiciously left yourself out of that," Runner said. Opening his eyes, he angled his head to watch her, waiting for her response.

"I did, didn't I," Thana tauntingly confirmed. Looking pleased with herself, Thana let loose that smile of hers once more.

Chuckling to himself, he couldn't help but return the smile. Leaving it at that, Runner returned to his quiet study of the map and his abilities, making plans for both the worst case and best case scenarios here and abroad.

As time is wont to do, it moved on without a care for anyone else. Late afternoon came and went. Early evening found the group hunched over the map, each confirming the same thing. Only the fort remained unshaded, all other buildings, patrols, houses, and sheds had been cleared of all enemies and loot. All guards, soldiers, and menial labor had also been cleared from the fort. Only the town leader, the dungeon boss, remained, residing on the central floor of the fort. Hannah had scouted the room but made no attempt to try and pull him from the keep. Unlikely, to say the least, was the chance he'd leave his little throne room.

"I suppose it's time to just go in there and end this," Runner said. "We've cleared everything, there's nothing left but him. What do you think, Lady?"

"I trust in Hannah's reconnaissance. I've no doubt there's nothing left for us to do. Time to end this sordid affair."

"Thanks for the confidence. Still the same damned problem though. Bastard will sit on his throne and shit himself to death rather than leave. Katarina, what do you think?" Hannah asked.

"We go in, I keep him busy, you kill him," Katarina outlined.

Catching himself before he could start laughing, Runner coughed roughly. Clearing his throat, he tapped the fort. "I suppose that's it then, let's go finish up. Kitten, take these and put the thought of 'Quick Slot 1' in your head while holding it. If you suddenly find yourself cursed, bleeding out, on fire, afraid, or honestly anything out of normal, think 'Use Quick

Slot 1,'" Runner explained. In his hands he held out several small vials.

Katarina scooped them out of his hand with her own, her long fingers enveloping them as if they were children's toys. He briefly considered how lifelike NPCs could be. They were so real at times that Runner found himself having to rethink them with each interaction. Before his brain ran from him, he pivoted on his heel, collected the map, and exited the stable.

Fingers of sunlight slanted in from the west, the sun hanging beyond the tree line. Soon it would set and plunge the land into night. Taking a full day to complete, the town was now a desolate place, the sound of the wind was the dominant sound. Distantly a shutter tapping against the wall could be heard; a melancholic harmony to the tomb-like stillness. It was unnerving in its own way, like a corpse freshly picked clean.

Setting a steady pace, Runner angled himself for the fort. Katarina paired off with him directly on his right, matching his stride. Hannah was a shade to his left and back a step, occupying the same space as his shadow. And while he couldn't see her, Runner knew Thana was directly behind him and within arm's reach.

Their boots drummed against the flagstones as they entered the keep. Perhaps it was a trick of the acoustics, but to Runner it sounded like a single pair of boots as they invaded the courtyard.

Upon reaching the throne room, Runner paused and cast an eye around the area. Quickly he confirmed it was all that Hannah had stated it to be. Front and center was a terrible imitation of a throne that sat in a large audience room. What might have once been art or tapestries were moldy hangings on bare stone walls. Near the rear of the open room was a curtain that probably led to a private room.

Atop the cheap throne sat an ugly old Orc who glowered at them as they entered his immediate domain. Red eyes glared from below bushy white brows. His green skin was mottled and webbed with wrinkles. Robed in a light fabric the color of wine and with a rod clenched in his hands, he had the very image of an old magician.

So…very uncreative. Need to remember this moment when I write my review.

Finding nothing out of the ordinary, Runner sighed heavily and looked to Katarina.

"Kitten, I'm betting he's a caster. Close with him, get his attention, hurt him, keep him busy. Keep your *Shield bash* ready until he starts to cast, then interrupt him with it. It'll be obvious when he starts channeling. I'll get your health back up should he actually get a hit in on you," he said, patting

Katarina's arm. Swiveling to his left, he addressed Hannah next. "Get around behind him, start working his spine with your kind ministrations."

Turning on his heel, he found Thana close behind him, her honey-colored eyes boring into him with a smirk just waiting to be unveiled. Blinking, Runner had to force his mind into action once more. "Lady Death, if you would be so kind as to cover the magical aspect of the battle. Once Kitten has his undivided attention that is. I'll be with Hannah but holding myself in reserve to make sure we can handle whatever he throws at us."

"Prudent and rational. Consider it done, Master Runner," Thana answered. She evidently was unwilling to tease him as mercilessly when the others were present.

"Kitten, if you would?" Runner asked.

Katarina's deep roar filled the room and echoed from every wall. She launched herself at the Orc lord, her wordless cry carrying her forward. Sword trailing low, her shield held before her, her long red ponytail flying out behind her like a pennant that declared war.

"Glorious," Runner whispered, watching her.

Hannah went *Stealth* next to him, shaking him from his reverie. Activating his own a second after Hannah, he moved in to engage. Hannah reached the target a moment after Katarina did and set into the elderly Orc immediately. Runner circled to the right before delivering a thrust of his blade into the wrinkled Orc's spine, *Backstab* activating on the contact. Ice slammed into the chest of Wrinkles, shattering and spraying ice chips everywhere.

Raising his arm to the sky, the Orc lord was only able to utter a single syllable before Katarina's shield clipped him in the head. Stumbling under the weight of the blow, the Orc instead threw a fire spell into Katarina's chest. In return, Runner cast a *Regeneration* spell on her to make sure her health would remain near topped off. *Regeneration* cost far less than *Cure*.

Another *Ice spear* cracked into Wrinkles as Hannah pierced his side with a thrust of her sword. Throwing his arms apart, Wrinkles shouted, and Katarina, Hannah, and Runner were flung back a few feet from the explosion of energy. Before Katarina could reengage him, Wrinkles had managed to complete a spell. Four Earth Elementals clawed their way from the ground, forcing the stones apart as they sprung from the earth. Comprised of stone and dirt, they had a vague humanoid shape. Overall, one could call them dirt men and be completely accurate.

With a shout Katarina peeled three of them onto herself in addition to Wrinkles. Hannah tagged the fourth, and Runner turned to assist her with it. Battering at the dirt monster with his sword, he was rewarded with a critical hit. Following his attack up with a *Fireblast* to its back, he immediately danced backwards expecting a counterattack.

As the Elemental began to move, Hannah attacked, blades cracking off stone and sending the remains flying as it's health ran out. The combat strength of Runner's team was orders of magnitude greater than it should be from the number of enchants he'd placed upon them.

Surveying the battlefield, Runner confirmed Katarina was at the center, holding Wrinkles and two Elementals in place. Near the entryway he caught sight of Thana backing up from another Elemental. Pointing to center stage, he motioned Hannah over. Deciding that Thana was the more immediate need, he veered in her direction.

Passing by close to Katarina, he cast *Cure* as he closed in on Thana, her situation now becoming desperate.

Unfortunately, the creature had knocked Thana to the ground violently and struck her several times before he was able to cross the throne room to her. Apparently it had used some type of ability to root her in place and she was unable to flee.

Fireblast exploded from his open hand and caught the Elemental squarely in his rocky back. Chasing his magical attack, he struck out with his sword.

It was enough to get its attention and it jerked towards him, swinging a stone fist. Dodging to the side, he hammered his blade through its midsection, the enchantment on the sword activating and dislodging a *Fireblast* into its internals. For good measure, Runner removed his blade from it and swung around with a *Slash* attack, the sword cutting the top part of its humanoid head off.

It collapsed heavily at an angle from him, dirt sprayed out in a cone, and the Elemental was no more. Glancing to the party window, he saw Thana's health bar was flashing red, Katarina's was yellow, and Hannah's was green. Triaging the situation, he cast *Regeneration* on Thana while offering her a hand up. Thana took his hand and levered herself upright. Snapping open a mana restoration potion from his Quick Slots, he pressed it to his lips and downed it swiftly. Dropping the vial to the ground, he targeted Katarina.

Casting *Cure* on her caused one of the Elementals to fixate on him. Katarina apparently noticed and slammed her shield into it, bringing its attention back to herself.

Thana threw an Ice spear that tore through it like wet paper and ended its magical life. Hannah smoothly dispatched the last in the next heartbeat, clearing the dance floor of the extras.

Wrinkles stood alone again in the middle. Katarina kept him occupied and involved. Under the focused barrage of the party as they reformed around him, Lord Wrinkles floundered, and died to Katarina's blade.

Quest Complete
Experience gained: 230% of level
Level up!
You've reached level 22
Level up!
You've reached level 23
Level up!
You've reached level 24

Bellowing, Katarina held up her sword in triumph and then stamped her foot down viciously on the head of Wrinkles. Runner could only shake his head with a small smile. Tapping the decline message for his level up, he took a breath and let it out slowly. He'd take care of it later.

Sheathing his blade, he confirmed Thana's health was slowly refilling, now that they were out of combat. Attempting to get Thana's attention, he touched her arm gently, and she focused on him with those large eyes. Noting the trembling in her hands and shoulders, he could only wonder at how bad the shock was to her. Being pinned in place without the ability to move and having a dirt monster beat you to death didn't rank high on the "To Do" list.

"Care to talk about it?" he quietly asked her.

Thana gave no response immediately to his question, but then shook her head slowly. Her hair fell across her face like a curtain, hiding her from his view.

"Later then?" he suggested.

Her hair shook as her head bobbed once in acceptance.

He'd have to settle for circling back with her later, after she calmed down. Perhaps the close brush with death would have her rethink her position in the group. Coming to grips with the assurance of a violent death would tend to do that to a reasonable individual.

Rejoining Katarina at the center, he laid one hand on her shoulder and looted Wrinkles with the other.

"That was some great work there, Kitten. Solid work. I couldn't have asked for more. I'm well pleased with you," Runner gushed. He craned his neck to peer up at her. Her dark eyes were riveted to his own, glistening black with a fiery center fueled from the heart of battle.

Katarina had sheathed her blade. She slammed a hand down onto his shoulder and smiled widely at him. Her hand pressed down firmly on him and she gave him a light shake. Katarina opened her mouth to speak but was interrupted.

"Runner, you better get your ass over here. There's a woman back here behind the drapes. She's alive but pretty fucked up. If you can call that alive? Fuck me…" called out Hannah from across the room.

Katarina jolted at the sudden shout from Hannah. Runner frowned and patted Katarina once more. "We'll talk. I promise, Kitten. Let me see what's going on though?"

Runner trotted over to the drapes without waiting for a response. Hannah was crouched down near the curtain he'd assumed was a partition. At her feet was a shapeless lump of clothes lying in a pool of dark red blood. Activating the *Analyze* ability on the NPC who was named "Merchant," he found that her health was slowly draining. Status ailments flashed crazily in reds and yellows, warning of some pretty severe problems.

There was no way to get any information beyond that it was a Human female, level four. *Cleanse* would only do so much for this poor wretch. Figuring time was of the essence, he produced a costly vial of Remedy.

Reaching down and gently lifting up the woman's head in his right hand, he lifted the vial. Rolling her neck towards him, he inspected the face that was presented to him. Swollen with bruises, cuts crisscrossing her face, lips cracked and puffy, she had been very badly mistreated. Bright green eyes, aware yet dull with pain and sorrow, tried to focus in on him. He attempted his best smile for her as her gaze finally settled.

"Hey there, I'm Runner. It's okay now, I've got you. We took care of every one of them. I'll have you fixed up shortly, try to relax. I'll take care of you. You're a bit of a mess, but that doesn't make you any less human or in need of kindness," Runner said softly. Placing the vial to her bloody lips, he started to upended the vial.

> **You use Persuade on Merchant**
> **Merchant is Persuaded**
> **You use Seduce on Merchant**
> **Merchant is Seduced**

Holding back a sigh, he could only smile as the glass tube emptied and a pair of green eyes watched him.

I am suddenly the lord and master of terrible cliches. All bow before my royal self.

Chapter 7 - Problem Solving -

Empty, the vial was carelessly dropped to the ground. Checking her status with *Analyze*, he found the vast majority of debuffs were gone. A few he wouldn't be able to dismiss without her allowance remained. Hungry, Thirsty, and Fear, to name a few.

Using his free hand, he lightly brushed golden strands of her hair from her eyes. Green eyes tracked him like a hunting dog, unswerving, unwavering. Her health still flashed in the danger area but was now steadily refilling.

"You OK? Can you talk at all?" Runner inquired.

Studying her reactions, it was safe to say she was in shock. That or she was a really low-grade AI that wasn't meant to be conversed with.

Whatever had actually been done to her definitely fell on the violent side. She was fully clothed, so that dismissed any type of sexual assault. Large rents in the fabric of her clothing, the blood that covered the clothes liberally, and the volume of status problems she had it made it was clear she underwent a very brutal attack.

Chimes sounded in his ear in a preprogrammed alert. A flashing icon presented itself in the console tray. Before he could respond to it, the light flickered off again. The indicator had been programmed to go off when §┌ír was no longer Away. They'd only been around for a few seconds-he'd just have to wait for next time.

Runner moved his attention back to the young woman. Nothing physically with her had changed, but the dim haze that had clung to her eyes was receding.

"You a bit more coherent now? Care to try some food? Water? Maybe sit up on your own?"

Her eyelids drooped before she blinked twice and then haltingly nodded. Doing his best to encourage her, he smiled and retrieved a melon he'd managed to forage up earlier. Holding it out with his free hand, he kept himself still. Without letting her gaze drop, she took the melon from his fingers and started nibbling at the food. Once she finished the first piece Runner handed her a second, and glancing up, he established eye contact with Hannah. Tilting his head subtly, he indicated Thana, who was standing by herself at the other end of the hall.

Hannah flashed a look to Thana and back to him. She held her hand out to indicate her understanding and acceptance. She ambled off towards Thana.

Promising himself to thank Hannah later, he couldn't help but feel blessed in having met her. With a quick scan of the room he confirmed that all was still as it should be. Katarina moved around the area, patrolling it as if there might be a counterattack, focused on her task of defending the team. Feeling more at ease he let himself return to the young lady.

The merchant had not taken her eyes from him, and Runner had the impression she was unsure of what to do. A quick inspection confirmed that her status was free of negative effects. Letting go of her shoulder, he took her hands in his own and then stood up, pulling her along for the ride.

"Upsa daisy, little lady," Runner said. Fearing that she might collapse, he kept a tight hold of her hands. He waited for a few moments to see if she'd strike up a conversation, but in the end couldn't wait any longer.

"Safe and sound, whole and healthy. My comrades and I have cleared the entire fort, nothing alive in the entire place except for us."

Flinching at his words, she tugged at her hand that was still locked in his own. Unwilling to let her go just yet in case she bolted or worse, he gripped her hand. As his fingers pressed more firmly to hers, he realized they didn't fit quite right. Letting his view drop down, he finally understood her reaction to him holding onto her hands. Two fingers were missing from her right hand, and his own hand was engulfing the nubs.

Brushing his thumb over one of the stumps of the missing fingers he rotated his hand over to get a better look. Pale puckered scars and long white tracks extended the length of her wrist. They continued all the way into the cuff of her tunic at her bicep.

"Interesting. Clearly unrelated to what happened here. Long healed from the looks of it. This, something like this wouldn't happen normally. One can only assume it's part of your backstory," Runner said thoughtlessly. Meeting her eyes with his own he grinned. "Surprise, you're unique. Got a name that I can put to those pretty green eyes?"

"N-n-n-n…Nadine. Nadine Giselle. Traveling m-m-m-mer-merchant," stuttered the woman in a warm timbre that was on the higher pitch side of the scale, but trapped behind a stutter. On closer inspection, Runner was able to make out large amounts of scar tissue across her throat that reached up to her cheek. It ended abruptly under the eye socket, probably having struck the bone there. Most of her left ear was simply gone, missing. Putting it all together, it would seem she had been savagely mauled by a beast in her youth.

Well, character creation.

"A true pleasure to meet you, Nadine. I'm Runner, Runner Norwood. Those are my companions over yonder. Were you to arrange them by height, that is Katarina Saden, Hannah Anelie, and Thana Damalis. Fighter, Rogue, Sorceress, respectively. We were in the area simply to dispatch the Orc tribe here and collect all their belongings. You happened to be a pleasant bonus for us. You'll need to excuse me, but I'm afraid I have things to attend to. Please," Runner insisted, pulling her over to the throne and forcing her to sit in it, "have a seat, make yourself comfortable. You're welcome to accompany us when we leave here. We planned to head onwards to the next village to sell our ill-gotten gains."

Releasing her hand from its forced captivity, he patted it gently with his fingertips. Nodding to her once more, he went over to where the rest had gathered around the corpse of Wrinkles.

"Not wanting to add more troubles to your shoulders there, but we've got more fucking bad news. Or maybe good? Don't know. It's fucking weird regardless," Hannah greeted him as he approached.

"I see. What's the current issue? Or issues if more than one," he asked.

Sighing, Thana put her fingers to her brow as she took the explanation over. "The first problem is we couldn't loot him. Now we have a second problem that is precluding the first one from being solved. Ahem." Thana cleared her throat and her eyes fixed on nothing a few inches in front of her chest. "You have leveled up, would you like to assign attributes now?"

Like slamming into a brick wall, his train of thought came to a screeching halt. Runner could only look from Thana, to Katarina, and finally to Hannah. Each watched him, looking for his reaction as they all apparently could see the same system notification. Cupping his chin in his hand, he lowered his head and thought hurriedly.

Technically speaking, this was all completely impossible. NPCs didn't level up, they remained as they were. Plans had been drawn up for the eventuality of the day he'd have to leave them behind. It'd be due to the level differential and he'd be forced to find new companions. NPCs were tools, made to be utilized and set aside, without regard to their longevity. There were outliers to this of course, household NPCs one would keep in their homestead for altogether different reasons.

Yet here I am, surprised once again. When I thought I'd seen how deep the rabbit hole goes, I find I'm nowhere near the bottom. The system had changed itself, again. Now it's pushing NPCs deeper and deeper into a PC role. More and more human.

Clapping his hands together, he made his decision. "So be it. You've discovered the secret to this world. This is a much larger and very long conversation, but for now I need you to memorize the following. Character, Inventory, Quest, Party, Skills, and Map. As an example, say Character inside your head, in a very similar way to what we did earlier. Another floating box will appear. You'll see yourself, numbers, and information. This is how the world views you. Should you have a question, place your finger over the area and think, 'Help.' You'll receive yet another floating box with more information. To close them, simply hit the little X in the top right. This isn't permanent and can be recalled or dismissed whenever you wish. Whatever you do, do not accept the level up invitation. Decline it for now. We'll pull it back up later in your Character window. Your homework is to read over all the information in your Character, Skills, and Inventory as we make our way to the next town. We'll get a room when we get there and discuss what to do next. Please save your questions for then, I promise I'll answer them all as best as I can. Now, for Lord Wrinkles of the Rotting Meat Clan."

Runner put out his hand and called up the Loot window. Sure enough, there were a few uncommon items, a rare, and a unique on the corpse. Since Runner had disabled party rights, the others were unable to loot the body.

Two gold pieces immediately went into his pouch, bringing his total wealth up to a staggering five gold pieces. He'd have to convert all the copper and silver they'd collect into higher denominations, then sell all their loot, but he expected his little fortune to grow.

There was a heater shield that added additional block and armor, a piece of parchment that he'd need to read over later, a silver ring that increased *Stealth* ability, a second ring made of platinum that provided a bonus to all items sold, and a short sword appropriate for the level range with a small bonus to damage. Putting them to one side of his inventory, he pulled up the rare item. It was another ring, one made of white gold that provided the wearer additional strength. Finally the unique item's turn came and he inspected it eagerly. Once again it was a ring, palladium metal formed into a simple band. Analyzing it, he found that it added points to intelligence but also provided a large amount of hit points.

A frown creased his brow as he considered the four rings.

This is too much. Too convenient. Unless my lack of a class is breaking even the loot system, then something else is going on here. I mean, awesome haul, but really?

Deciding to thank whatever god or goddess of loot proclaimed him the winner of the loot lottery, he moved on. With a plan for all of the items, he stowed them separately from the rest of the loot they'd taken and looked to his companions.

"Time to vacate. We've done our business, though I'm afraid we'll need to leave the Skulls for later. They're quite heavy, and we're loaded down with weapons and armor. I'm not aware of the local area outside of a very generalized idea. I know I need to get to the island to the east, but not the fastest way to port. Or which port will offer the fastest crossing. Now comes a time of choice-which road will get us to a coastal town the fastest?"

Silence was the answer to his question. None of his companions were local to the area, or had even visited it until whatever brought them here. Realizing his error, Runner relegated himself to the idea that he'd simply have to travel the road and hope for a town.

"N-n-north east by north. It's a central t-t-trading town. I frequen-n-n-nt them often when I pass through. For a com-m-m-mission I'll sell your wares. I'll get a better price tha-n-n-n you will," Nadine interjected confidently. She'd walked up during the conversation unnoticed.

"Aren't you the trooper. Say five percent commission, but you guide us all the way to a port town," Runner offered.

"T-t-ten percent. Trooper? No, com-m-m-mon sense. Can't stop no m-m-matter what happens. You have t-t-t-to dem-m-m-mand your due. Final offer," Nadine countered. A grin blossomed on her face. Runner couldn't help but laugh while adjusting his perception of her entirely. Attitudes like that moved mountains. Not everyone would be able to overcome their lot in life and bounce back this capably.

Standing no taller and no shorter than himself, one could consider her pretty if they could move past the scars and disfigurement. She held herself upright and confidently, her figure fairly average and presenting nothing out of the ordinary. With tanned skin from days walking the roads, she wouldn't stand out in a crowd. Straight blonde hair and green eyes felt out of step when paired to the background cruelly written for her.

"Done, on the condition that you allow me to be present when you make your sales. It isn't that I don't trust you, it's that I don't trust those you'll do business with."

Runner held out his hand to her, his eyes daring her to deny him the informally formal way of sealing agreements.

Hesitantly she held out a trembling hand. Before she had time to change her mind, Runner reached out and took it in his own. Firmly squeezing it, he smiled at her.

"How would you feel about accompanying a traveling band of bloodthirsty mercenaries? Pay starts at four copper a day, food, room and board will be paid for you. You receive eight up front, four for today, four for your last day. You'll earn two percent commission beyond this first sale for all future sales. Though I do value your courage and tenacity, no beetles for you. They might be up for negotiation down the road, but for now you'll have to look on with envy as Kitten and I enjoy them."

Possibly sensing that he couldn't or wouldn't offer her more, she delayed only a fraction of a second before nodding her head. "I accept. Uhm, bee-t-t-t-tles? Who's Kitten? Katari-n-n-na? N-n-not very clever of you."

Laughing, he could only agree. It really wasn't that clever at all. Runner could only shrug and reached out to pat her hand with his left even as he clenched it in his right, preventing her from pulling away.

"No, I'm not very clever at all."

They'd been traveling the road for a few hours in the dark of the night. Nadine assured everyone that they'd reach the next town just before daybreak. Traveling by night didn't sound the most pleasant of experiences but reaching town rather than camping did.

Katarina walked point position, Runner took the middle with Nadine and Thana, and Hannah pulled rear guard duty. They made idle chitchat but nothing in depth or groundbreaking. In truth the entire group was still feeling each other out.

Fingers brushing over his chin, Runner figured this to be an opportune time to try and work a few of the hiccups out of the party. He looked back to Hannah and threw a thumb towards the road ahead. She nodded her head in confirmation to his unspoken signal. Then he tipped his head to Thana and Nadine and jogged to catch up with Katarina.

"Come along, Kitten, let's do a recon up ahead a bit. Stretch those long legs of yours," Runner called back over his shoulder as he passed her.

You didn't need to be a psychic to know Katarina would take him up on the unspoken challenge. Runner knew there was no contest in this, she simply had better synergy between her stats, passive abilities, and traits than he did. It didn't make it any less thrilling to compete with her though. Losing didn't remove the enjoyment of a contest.

Katarina came parallel with him swifter than he anticipated. She didn't overtake him but ran alongside him companionably. Catching her eyes with his own, he grinned at her, receiving her smile in return, and they jogged along in silence.

In time, Runner let his pace deteriorate, eventually coming to a complete stop. He felt like they'd gone too far already but there was an appeal to running in the dark. A slight quickening of the blood as shadows danced along at the edges of his vision.

He glanced back down the way they came. The rest of the group was now too far back to be seen in the dark. Runner turned back to Katarina and faced her directly.

"Can't say I'm surprised that you caught me so easily," Runner complimented her. Pulling a beetle free from his inventory, he looked askance at her to see if she'd like one. Still smiling, she inclined her head towards him in acceptance. Katarina clearly enjoyed competition as much as she did battle.

Handing her two beetles, he began chewing on the first one for himself. Looking around at the roadway and the surroundings, he was struck by the fact that the world truly was gorgeous. Nothing like this had existed on Sovereign Earth in a long time.

"I admit as much fun as that was, it wasn't my only goal. I wanted to talk to you about the battle the other day."

Grunting, Katarina waited, chewing quietly.

"You did wonderfully. Such a performance made me wonder how I could function without you leading the way. You're a sight to behold, Katarina," Runner confided. Still admiring the scenery, he let his eyes gravitate to Katarina as he finished with her name. She'd frozen up as he spoke and now stared at him, waiting for him to continue. "I'm afraid I have to ask more of you though. Thana almost died because she made a mistake. She attacked an Elemental you didn't have control over yet. It ended up separating from the group and attacking her alone. Damn near killed her."

Katarina nodded at his words.

"I need you to search your abilities. You'll need to be looking for any skill that has the word 'taunt' in its description or name. Anything that'll let you hit multiple enemies would be good too. A cleave, an intimidating shout, anything. You did nothing wrong, so don't blame yourself. I guess I just have to ask more of you. I'm sorry for that."

"I will not fail you, Runner. I won't," Katarina declared. Runner blinked at the strength of her words. Her hand was clenched on the hilt of her sword as if she were swearing an oath.

"You never have, Kitten. I truly doubt you could fail me."

With that said, Runner let the subject drop and enjoyed her company as they stood there in the road making small talk. Eventually Runner could just barely see the outlines of the rest of his group trailing behind. Letting his feet start carrying him down the road again, he walked side by side with Katarina. Her eyes scanned the roadbed for anything suspicious while Runner did the same. Runner eventually felt like he could dismiss himself to move on to his next planned conversation.

"Alright, time for me to fall back. Think on what we talked about. I'm going to wait here for them. Oh, and Kitten? Thank you."

Runner watched her as she slowly, reluctantly, continued walking down the road. As she left, he could see her left hand sorting through unseen windows. Hopefully she was already looking through her abilities. Though it would detract from her role of being on point. Details, details.

Deciding to have a bit of fun, Runner stealthed himself and slipped sneakily from the roadbed to a small scrub brush nearby. Pickpocketing them and giving them each other's inventory sounded like a riot. Camouflaging himself, he lingered there, watching the rest of his group near.

"…appeared? Like just out of thi-n-n-n-n air?" Nadine questioned, her voice carrying just enough for him to hear her.

"Quite right. Started opening the cages without a thought or care. A Priest and one of his flock tried to convince him to leave myself and Katarina there. Contrary to that, it seemed only to infuriate him. Ultimately he freed everyone. And then the abhorrent man insulted him and called me filth. To which he disagreed by punching him in the throat and casting him out," Thana explained.

"I see. M-m-m-my initial im-mpression of him was right then. Is Han-n-n-nah his wife or…?"

Runner frowned as they passed his position. *My wife? Now that's a strange thought.*

"Not in the least. As far as I can tell, he's uninvolved with anyone. Hannah said he caught her robbing murderers, that's how they met. Hired her directly on as a companion after that. She swears he's never even made a hint of desiring her to warm his bed."

"That soun-n-n-nds right for Hannah, I guess. Maybe he's…"

Nadine's voice trailed off as they got further down the road.

Stepping out from his position, he unstealthed himself in the middle of the road. Eavesdropping wasn't what he'd in mind, yet he couldn't have revealed himself without admitting he'd heard their conversation.

Hannah was coming up the road towards him, still holding the rear guard. Falling in lockstep with her, he shared the road with her, his eyes roving, lost in his thoughts.

"Going to fucking say something or keep walking along like a stupid jackass?" Hannah snapped irritably. Now that he thought about it, she'd been annoyed with him since they'd invaded the stable. Guessing at what the cause was, he held up an apologetic hand, as if asking for mercy.

"Thank you, Hanners. I'd be lost without you and value you dearly. I ask your pardon for not consulting you before I added to our group. I realized they'd be beneficial but didn't consider your own personal thoughts on the matter."

Hannah said nothing at first but her head dipped down once. "Accepted. I'm sorry for being snippy with you. I don't do terribly well with rapid change. It feels like since I've met you, there's been nothing but change. I'm not good at that. I plan, I prepare, work the angles."

"That's why I need you all the more. I can plan when I need to and I can do it fairly well, to be sure. But I'm more of a consultant type of thinker. Bring me a problem and I'll figure out how to crack it. I guess what I'm saying is, I need you, Hanners. I need you and thank you."

"Sure. Don't mention it," Hannah responded, her voice quiet.

"Since you're being civil and I don't think I heard a swear word in there, Nadine asked Thana if we were married. Can you believe that? I didn't realize we had the old bickering couple act down," Runner shared with a chuckle.

Hannah failed to counter while tucking her chin closer to her chest. Her bangs fell forward to block parts of her face from view like a black curtain. Leaving it at that for a while, their conversation lapsed to talking about the siege of the Orc fort. Once more Runner could no longer postpone the next leg of this little train-stop tour.

"If you don't mind, Hanners, could you trade places with Thana? Send her back here to rear guard that is. Might do well to send Nadine up to relieve Kitten as well. Time for you two to get a break."

Hannah inclined her head and moved forward at a trot. Runner could only keep watch and contemplate what to tell Thana. In the light of hindsight, Thana erred and almost got herself killed. Pretty clean cut and dry, really. Now to tell her that without alienating her completely.

Up ahead the Sunless Sorceress in question awaited him. Her face was turned to him, watching his approach. Runner did his best to prevent his eyes from roaming over her as he neared. Real or virtual, she could certainly draw his attention without trying. Finding inspiration in the moment, Runner smiled and offered his arm to her.

After a flicker of surprise crossed her face, Thana returned the smile and linked her arm into his.

"Lady Death, I'm afraid I must make you aware of some details. Details that will be unpleasant, I'm afraid. I wish to let you know upfront that I respect you greatly and wish no harm either to your self or ego. If I critique you, it is only because I do so out of care for your well-being."

"As we're being formal, Master Runner, I'm well aware I acted rashly. And that I nearly paid with my life. After reading through the abilities, it would appear my Ice spear has the secondary effect of spraying damage out in a cone behind the target. Area of effect, I believe it was labeled. From what you told me of aggro, and based on your instructions, I can infer that because the ice struck the creature before Katarina had a chance to engage it, it attacked me. Is that accurate?"

"Yes. Yes it is. I'm glad to hear you putting the situation forth as such, Lady Death. Part of me was concerned that might have been more than you were willing to tolerate. Not everyone is cut out for a life of mercenary work. A refined, intelligent, and warmhearted young lady like yourself probably shouldn't be running around with us ruffians."

Thana started to snicker but that turned into full laughter a heartbeat later. "Oh, you couldn't be closer to the truth, and further, at the same time if you tried. That's not my story to tell though. As for me, you're right, I probably shouldn't be amongst you. Though it is my life and my choice to squander it as I see fit. Besides, I already feel you're working to make sure everyone is healthy, both mentally and physically. It's not as if I wasn't there when you went to talk to Katarina, then Hannah comes up to ask me to fall back, and there you are. I'm guessing one of them, or both, is now looking into ways to make sure they can react swiftly to a similar situation in the future."

"Ah, yes. This is true," Runner admitted, embarrassed. It really was rather obvious when put together as she said.

"You see? I have no cause for concern. I must simply own my mistakes and build off them. I'm sure you have a plan to speak with our dear merchant in due time. Oh, and don't mince words with her or even begin to pity her. It'll just infuriate the dear woman."

Runner nodded to her point but said nothing, nor released her arm. He scanned the terrain looking for threats, feeling the warmth of Thana's arm against his own. Virtual world it may be but it certainly was pulling out every stop to make it closer to life every time he checked.

There were vague memories in the back of his head, that the game attempted to be as close to life as possible. If given the resources for it, the programming could do wonders. He couldn't pin it down to a similar memory though he wanted to say it was designed as a therapeutic tool originally. It had programming built in to allow memories to be repressed and dealt with in a safe environment. It also strove for realism for those who were locked in their own bodies or suffering great mental torment. An environment people could identify with and heal in.

Thana rested her free hand on top of his arm and patted it lightly, reminding him that a response would be appreciated. Her hand rested there comfortably while Runner worked through his thoughts.

Finding that her answer was certainly acceptable, he could only take it for what it was.

"You're a wise counselor and a beautiful temptress, Lady Death. Be sure to steer me accordingly in the future. I need someone to tell me when I'm being an incompetent jackass."

"Such a full-time job on top of the one I have already. I should try to get my pay increased. That or better benefits."

Chapter 8 - Man Puppet -

Morning found Runner on the point position by himself. Occasionally he caught a glimpse of the town ahead as the road wound its way through gently rolling hills. From the distance he originally spotted it, it had been little more than a discernible change in the landscape.

An outer wall secured it to the coastline and provided it safety. Everything inside the wall had the appearance of a jumbled up mess of buildings that ran into each other the closer you got to the water line. Keeping an eye on the mini-map HUD, he continued to close on the outer wall.

It had taken longer than they had originally planned. They'd been cautious and moved off the road several times when spotting others traveling the road. You could charitably call it being overly suspicious instead of paranoid, but it resulted in the same end. Runner wasn't willing to risk anything at this juncture if he didn't have to.

He stopped at the border of the town when his combat icon flashed to a solid yellow from red. The swap in color indicated it was a punishable-player vs player zone. The guards would immediately attack anyone who attacked another player inside of this boundary if they witnessed it. That or they had an orange or red name tag, which indicated they were complicit in an attack on another player.

Inspecting the town walls and the guards, Runner passed the time in silence while taking mental notes. All the NPCs he could spot were named "Guard" and seemed to average sixteen in level. It was glaringly evident as they traveled that the zone difficulty was decreasing with each mile. This of course meant they were heading in the right direction.

They'd have to journey all the way to the starting town to start building his reputation. Killing level one wolves for a copper didn't sound enjoyable, but it would be necessary. It would also be where he could get his starter class.

Fighting both sides of an internal debate and losing, Runner called up the Graveyard query. *Seven thousand three and hundred fifty-two lives.*

Blue dots appeared on his map at the edge of the compass as his group neared his location. Orienting himself to face the road, Runner forced his attention off the graveyard. Finding his eyes drawn to the luxurious blue sky, Runner watched absolutely nothing.

"Runner? How the hell did you get all the way out here? Whoa, how'd you get level twenty-one so fast? I'm just barely thirteen and I thought I was the highest level. Did you find a great place to grind?" A young man rattled off questions, one coming right after another. Pulling his gaze down from the blue morning sky, Runner looked at the speaker.

Runner recognized him from a fuzzy memory deep in his head. Floating above the newcomer's head was the name Ramsey Bell. *Doesn't ring a bell. Hah, yeah…that was terrible.* Figuring he could use the memory problem to his advantage, he put on a frown and turned fully towards him.

"Sorry, Ramsey, I'm afraid I can't recall you. Were you in IT with me or…?" Runner asked the man. Receiving no response, Runner looked at the man closer. Ramsey was preoccupied with whatever was behind Runner.

Looking back over his shoulder, he found Thana and Katarina approaching him. Falling in behind Runner, they looked from him to Ramsey, then back. Ramsey's eyes lingered in all the wrong places and Runner felt a spark of anger come to life in his chest.

Snapping his eyes back to Runner, Ramsey did a fair impression of a fish. Mouth agape and wide-eyed, void and vacant of anything resembling intelligence.

"Uh. Oh! Yeah, huh. Uhm, Ramsey. Ramsey Bell," the man sputtered.

"Yeah, got that part," Runner agreed, indicating the man's name floating above his head. His annoyance at the man leaked into his voice.

"Uhm, geeze, yeah. Sorry, Lieutenant. Infantry, Private 1st class. You helped fix my HUD cross-link with my auto-armor. You uh…helped me get rid of something I'd downloaded that screwed up the OS," Ramsey quickly explained, saluting. With that bit of information it was clear Runner would gain nothing from this man. He was one of hundreds of thousands. Of the lowest rank and trusted with nothing of value outside of his equipment.

"Yeah, nope. No memory. Sorry. Anyways, nice to see you. Don't die, it's permanent," Runner said hurriedly, giving a brief salute in return. Glancing over his shoulder, Runner watched Hannah and Nadine fall in next to Katarina and Thana. He attempted to move past the infantryman, but Ramsey moved to block him and leaned in to whisper to Runner.

"Hey, uh, where'd you get all those followers? I heard there were a few you could have some fun with. Or could I borrow yours?" Ramsey asked hopefully.

"Don't. Just, stop right there. If you say anything more, I'll remember it and you'll regret it. I'm going to keep walking and you're going to walk in the other direction," snapped Runner. The heat in his voice surprised even him. Rage flitted in the back of his mind, lighting a fire in him he hadn't felt when he'd met Hannah.

His stomach felt like it boiled from the sheer heat of the anger that was thrumming through his veins. Perhaps being up for twenty-four hours was affecting him more than he realized. Teeth locked together, his hands cold and balled into fists, Runner wanted to escape. Needed to escape. Now.

Pushing the infantryman roughly aside, Runner passed the town guardsman. Stomach twisting itself into an uncomfortable knot, Runner kept up a swift pace, not pausing until he'd reached the plaza at the center of town. His hands went to his hips and he hung his head as he bit his lip. Closing his eyes, he focused on the sound of the nearby fountain. It helped to hide most of the sounds of the market, drowning them out to the level of a soft growl. It also provided him a blessed focus.

Without having to confirm it, he knew his party was fanned out behind him, waiting for him. Runner knew beyond a shadow of a doubt that the ladies were likely to draw attention if they weren't doing so already.

It went without saying that game designers tended to steer towards the visually pleasing with this kind of stuff, but through sheer luck, or perhaps bad luck, his little group for the most part exceeded the average. Thankfully they weren't at the front of the bell curve. That'd be unbearable.

This caliber of attention though could create some ugly situations. Most especially since the PVP restriction only really protected him, not his followers. If a player got it into their head to kill an NPC, all they had to do was get them alone and finish the deed. Their distinction as an NPC wouldn't turn the player's name orange. There'd be no consequences to those actions.

Runner would need to amend a few of his plans to put their safety to the forefront. Placing Hannah, Katarina, and Thana together in one group was his best bet. Taking Nadine with himself to complete the transactions would limit exposure all the way around.

Whipping his head up, he turned and addressed the small company. "Kitten, Lady Death, Hanners, please secure us room and board. Please track and record whatever you spend to acquire those and I'll reimburse you. Don't fuss over the price, just find somewhere for us and settle in. Nobody split up, don't go down alleys, no mysteries to solve, stay out of other people's business. If one of you needs something, go together, all of you. If it comes down to you or coin, give up the coin and get out of there. Coin is replaceable, you're not. Nadine, you're with me while we make our rounds. Questions?" Runner queried them. "No? Good, meet back here by noon. Use the 'Time' command in your head to see the current time."

Runner waved Nadine over as the others began discussing how to go about getting lodgings. Taking a few steps to the side, he came clean about his problem to Nadine.

"I'm afraid I must confess I have no knowledge of this place. You'll need to lead us to the best place to sell the loot. Oh, I had everyone transfer the loot to me before we set out on the road so we can start whenever you're ready."

"How could you n-n-not com-m-m-me through here? Everyone has to com-m-me through here. It'd take days to go aroun-n-n-nd. And what do you m-m-mean you had them transfer it to you? You couldn't-t carry all that," Nadine said suspiciously.

"I enchanted all of my equipment with strength."

"That doesn-n-n-n't make sense… Fine, for n-n-now. An-n-nd never bein-ng here?"

Runner looked around to check who might be listening before answering.

"Long story honestly. Short answer is, I'm not from this world. I appeared far southwest of here. Where I met Hanners actually. Honestly, I don't even remember the name of the village I came to first. Can we go now?"

Runner started walking instead of waiting for a reply, not really caring in which direction it was. His emotions were still running hot and he was uncomfortably tired. Standing around and explaining to someone that their world was fake didn't appeal to him right now.

Nadine caught up to him easily and then turned left at an intersection, redirecting their path. Runner made no comment but fell in behind her. Lost in his thoughts, he was trying to figure out what made him so angry at Private Bell. Lurking under the surface of his psyche was a tension, one that so far had been on a hair trigger. He could only guess it was something that happened close to him. Proximity aside, it also apparently centered on men showing undue interest in women.

It stands to reason that it's a loved one, sexually or romantically charged, and involving me? That leaves sexual assault, cheating, or sexual abuse. Ugh. None of those are exactly pleasant things to consider. I can't even remember family yet. Can't even remember if I'm married, seeing someone, or a bachelor. Why couldn't I get some useful memories? I've got memories of boot camp, traveling, school, training, but nothing even remotely concerning a personal life. Am I a hermit? Who am I?

Nadine had stopped in front of a building and Runner had to catch himself from running her over. Surveying the area around them, he set a hand on Nadine's shoulder and guided her to one side, into the entrance of an alley. Leaning in close to her ear, he spoke quietly.

"For this to work correctly I need to invite you into my party. It'll seem odd, but just follow my instructions. It'll take but a minute."

Nadine gestured angrily for him to hurry up, her head inclined in agreement.

Moving around behind her, Runner grabbed her right hand in his own and positioned it correctly. Once he'd activated the console command to invite Nadine, he spoke again.

"Take a breath, close your eyes, and think in your head 'Yes, join the party.' Focus on it exclusively compared to everything else. Once you're at that place, move your hand forward two inches. That's it."

Runner drew in a breath and waited, his fingers gripping her trembling hand. Nadine gave the impression of a strong woman with little social grace or experience. Personality wise she resembled Hannah with her distaste of society but didn't have the underlying hostility towards everything. Her general unease of people was especially present in concern to her disfiguration. Holding her hand didn't feel any different than holding any of the other party members', despite two of her fingers being missing.

Thoughts interrupted by her hand going forward, Runner caught the change on the party screen to the left of his HUD-her name suddenly appeared at the bottom. Closing the notification that Nadine had joined the party, Runner patted her shoulder with a smile.

"There we are, welcome to the party, Nadine. Now we can proceed in and we can get this over with."

"Th-th-thank you. Let's go get m-my m-m-money," Nadine demanded. With a glint in her eye, it was clear the merchant in her drove her forward. Nadine nearly dashed through the shop entrance and approached the counter.

"Even-n-n-ning, good sir. I have wares to sell and you'll be buying them. I expect you'll find m-m-me reason-n-n-able."

Runner caught the shopkeeper eying her ear, her throat, then finally her hand. Disgust showed plainly on the pudgy man as his eyes moved back to her face. Runner could almost feel the disdain the man had for her. Society would shun someone who stood out and an outsider doubly so. With smoldering anger still hiding in his heart, Runner could easily picture this response from everyone Nadine did business with. That they all dismissed her as an easy mark, a regrettable existence that had to be dealt with as quickly as possible.

Feeling annoyed, Runner targeted the middle-aged man and brought the flat of his hand down on the counter top with a

sharp crack. Deliberately activating *Intimidate* and *Persuade*, he
tilted his head to the side, growling at the man.

"Did you hear her? Were you listening? Or were you too busy
being an asshole? Tell you what, when she gives you a price,
you're going to agree and thank her. When we're done, you're
going to give her a bonus for being such a great person to deal
with, one unlike you've ever met. Else I'm going to tear your
tongue out and use it to paint you a fucking mural using your
own blood and stomach bile as paint. Got it?"

You use Persuade on Shopkeep
Shopkeep is Persuaded
You use Intimidate on Shopkeep
Shopkeep is Intimidated

Moving his head up and down rapidly, the man shrunk in on
himself.

"Good, now bless this waste of genetic material with your
presence, Nadine. I'll try to not redecorate his shelves in the
meantime. I was thinking they'd all look great out on the
street. Start a bonfire right there in the middle of the avenue,
invite the kids, have a grand ol' time while we contemplate if
his skull would make a better toilet or a trash can."

"That was certainly profitable. We've got more than enough
money to equip ourselves better and move along the agenda.
You're all dressed in little better than rags. Can't have that
now, can we?" Runner asked Nadine.

"You didn-n-n-n't have to th-threaten the man-n. I'm-m used
to it," Nadine grumbled.

"You shouldn't be used to it. He shouldn't have acted that
way. More so than you realize. Next time he'll think
differently. Look, I'm making the world a better place. I'm a
saint. Worship me for my benevolence and grace."

Honestly he'd enjoyed terrorizing the man. The shopkeep
being a valid target for his anger made it justified enough for
him to truly get a kick out of it.

"Whatever that m-m-m-an said at the gate really worked you
up. I on-n-nly caught part of it. What'd he say to you?"

The option of ignoring her and not responding tempted him.
They were sitting on a bench near the fountain while waiting for
the rest of the group. They still had an hour to go, and it was
clear she wasn't going to let the subject drop. Nadine's
personality, even this early in their working relationship,
plainly wouldn't allow her to relent once she decided she was
owed something. NPCs went about their business, and here and

there a PC navigated the streets. Runner didn't recognize anyone, and it seemed no one recognized him.

"He asked if he could borrow you girls. For the night that is. Or an hour? Whatever way you wish to phrase it. I'm not sure what Lady Death has told you, or what you've been able to deduce, but this. All of this," Runner explained, gesturing to everything around them. "It's all fake. This entire world is a story that is currently being told. That everyone and everything here isn't actually here. You feel pain, joy, anger, loss, but it isn't real. Here, let me ask you this. Think back to a time before you met me, now compare it to the moment we met. Do they feel different? Lady Death described it as a different 'flavor.'"

Nadine had gone utterly still and silent, gazing into nothing as she listened to him. He'd wager her mind raced with his words. That she was processing it as fast as possible. After a few seconds of introspection, she focused on him again.

"Yes, there's m-m-more to it than that, b-b-b-but yes. Th-there is a defin-n-nite difference before and after. You're saying, you're saying that I'm not m-me. I'm a character in-n a story?" Nadine whispered.

"Yes and no. How to explain. You're real and you're not. Time for a metaphor. Imagine a fishbowl that you cannot see in or out of. To the fish, that is the entirety of the world. Especially since they cannot see beyond the glass. Now imagine I walked up with a fish puppet on a stick. I put it in the fishbowl and pretend to be a fish. To you, I am a fish. To me, I am a man holding a fish puppet. I can pull the puppet out whenever I want and walk away. As the fish, you cannot."

Eyes downcast to the ground in front of them, Nadine's face was a picture of concentration and thought. Blinking away unshed tears, she rubbed at her eyes. Runner was only mildly surprised by this since he'd come to expect much more from the AI running the whole thing. Every day it seemed to grow, adapt, and change.

"S-s-sorry. It's h-h-hard to t-take in. I s-suffer-r-red so m-much for the am-m-musement of oth-thers? M-my l-life is a j-joke?"

"No, no, Nadine, no," Runner said, sighing. He wrapped an arm around her and drew her head into his shoulder, holding her there. "You might be a fish but you're still very real in your world. To be honest, I'm no longer a man holding a fish myself, but a fish puppet. I can't leave here any more than you can. Something went wrong, and all the puppets are now trapped here. No one did anything to you for their amusement. The AI created you as a unique NPC with your own traits, history, and beliefs based on its database of preset information."

"I-i-is AI g-god?"

"I suppose in a way that's true, but not really. The AI didn't create the puppets, the puppets created AI. Created the AI and then joined it. The man I was speaking with at the gate views NPCs, or fish in this metaphor, as things. Things to make his story more interesting or fun. I was upset because he wanted to use one of you as a sexual plaything. I can't really explain why it made me so mad, other than it really did."

Runner gently rubbed Nadine's shoulder as he finished his explanation.

What of my own views though? Are they just fish to me too? Are they real? Am I just giving her a false platitude to comfort her?

Runner patted her back awkwardly, unsure of himself now. He did what he could to assuage her as she continued to cry into his shoulder.

Am I fooling myself? I may not have the sum of my knowledge previous to this but I'm fairly certain I wouldn't be handling my followers as I have been if this were reality. Have I been viewing them no differently than Ramsey? Am I truly any better?

"Nadine, you have a favorite color. You prefer certain foods. You can debate whether it's lawful to steal from a thief or murder a murderer. I would classify all those things as having a mind of your own and the ability to dictate your future. To work towards your self-interests and better yourself. The fishbowl has been revealed to you, but that doesn't make it any less real. For all I know, I myself am a man puppet in a manbowl using a fish puppet to play in a fishbowl. Come on, it'll be alright."

Waiting for her to wind down, Runner could only wait as she cried. People would stop and stare occasionally, but for the most part people kept to their own business. In this situation he was finally thankful to the selfishness of humanity as a whole.

After his own inner dialog Runner found himself wondering if he could keep treating his companions as he had been. Reviewing his actions, he'd been quite forward with all of them. Much of what he did and said would have been considered extremely flirtatious and sexual harassment in a workplace.

"You're r-right. I'm m-m-me. I m-make my choices and th-they are m-m-mine. I can on-nly be what I am. Dem-m-mand my due."

Runner had to respect her strength of character. Not everyone would handle being told their life and the world they lived in was in truth a lie.

"Gotta respect that attitude of yours, Nadine. Want a beetle? They tend to cheer me up. They're so weird to eat that they tend to distract me. The taste really isn't bad, and after one they grow on you," Runner offered lamely.

"O-okay. Why n-not?" Nadine muttered. Sitting up she scrubbed her hands across her face, wiping tears away before holding out her crippled hand.

Surprised at her sudden acceptance, Runner pulled two beetles free from his inventory and handed them over to her. During the long journey here he'd managed to collect a veritable fortune in beetles. Nadine watched the clacking, twitching insects, then shoved one into her mouth. Ranging from apprehensive to mild surprise, she finished the morsel and then frowned at him.

"It really wasn-n-n't that bad," Nadine said, putting the second one into her mouth.

"Nope. They're pretty good after a while. I have no idea why. Kitten enjoys them too."

"What do I enjoy now?" said the woman in question.

"Beetles, my dear. Want one?" Runner said disarmingly. She'd been rather quiet on her approach, and he'd failed to notice her. Thana and Hannah flanked her on either side.

"Yes, yes I do."

Katarina held out her hand expectantly to Runner, who complied. Runner let his eyes find each of the trio and confirmed they appeared healthy and whole.

"I knew you'd be fucking early, Runner. And sure as shit here you are. See?" Hannah said exasperatedly, her head turning to Thana.

"I concede you were correct, Hannah. Runner, we were able to acquire accommodations at a reputable inn. I've notated all that we spent and have receipts for each item. Unfortunately they only had one room and two beds available. Apparently there's a large influx of people from the mainland. Supposedly there is the possibility of land being granted? I only overheard a bit of it," Thana advised him. Katarina said nothing, still enjoying her beetle as she inspected the immediate area.

Holding out a piece of parchment to Runner, Thana waited until he took it from her hand. Runner gave it a glance, found the sum at the bottom, and then dug out the amount listed. Placing the coins in Thana's hand, he crumpled the paper and executed the destroy item command.

"You didn't even read it, Master Runner. I'm not sure if I should be complimented or insulted that I wasted my time," Thana said archly, quirking a delicate eyebrow at him.

"Complimented, Lady. Please, lead on. I know it probably goes without saying but I'm exhausted. I'll bunk between the beds, you four can figure out who sleeps where otherwise."

Runner stood and brushed his hands over his backside as the group began moving off. Falling in behind them, Runner let his mind revisit the conversation he'd just had with Nadine.

Sprawled out between the beds on the floor, in a strange nest of blankets and pillows, Runner read over the classes and attribute descriptions. Hannah had managed to convince Katarina, Thana, and Nadine into a game of cards. Nadine was winning so far, with Hannah right behind her, Thana pulling up a third, and Katarina a distant fourth. Stakes were small, nothing more than two copper being the biggest bet, and many of the bets were personal favors instead of coinage. Katarina owed Thana a promised switch on night watch, and Nadine had suckered Hannah into taking her next cooking duty. Thana owed everyone at the table lessons in etiquette and manners after a series of particularly bad hands. It must have been something she offered to cover a bet since it didn't really match up with what any of the other girls would view as valuable. The likelihood of anyone claiming that prize didn't seem high either.

When they had asked him if he'd like to play, Runner had declined but thanked them, asking them to please invite him again next time, though, as he was interested.

Right now though, there was leveling to do, inventory to sort, and plans to be made.

"I call. I say you have n-n-nothing, Kat-t-t-arina," Nadine challenged.

"Fold. Fuck both of you," Hannah grumped.

"Now, now, don't be vulgar. You got greedy and got caught red-handed. Don't be bitter that you're losing now you don't have an extra card. Though I must agree, I fold. Odds aren't in my favor," Thana said, laying down her hand.

"YAH!" shouted Katarina triumphantly, laying down a flush. "Unless you can beat that, you owe me two beetles!"

Runner looked up at that, confusion taking precedence in his thoughts. He hadn't heard them betting beetles, but couldn't help but laugh at the situation.

"You're seriously betting beetles?" Runner queried.

"Yes, and Katarin-n-na is right. I owe her two," stated Nadine, sighing heavily as she threw her cards into the center of the table.

"Ah ha! Hear that, Runner? Pay me her beetles!" Katarina shouted, chortling boisterously.

Shaking his head Runner closed the ability window and pulled open his inventory as he stood up. Retrieving eight of them, he gave six to Katarina and two to Nadine.

"Here then. Extra currency I suppose. You're lucky. I foraged these in the hundreds on the road. It seemed like they were all I could find," he explained.

Katarina immediately ate one of the beetles and started pushing the rest of them into what he could only guess was her inventory. To him it was as if they disappeared.

Katarina had put in some true time and effort to not just learn but understand all the commands he gave her.

"Ugh, how are they not disgusting to eat? I mean, you're eating a bug. I will admit I have preference to eat things that were living, but I think I draw the line at bugs," uttered Thana.

"Not a-t-t-t-t all, they're crun-n-nchy. A little odd, yes. But they're good!, The first on-ne was odd, but after that th-they were easy," answered Nadine.

Katarina nodded her head in absentminded agreement while she fiddled with an unseen window.

Runner had given Nadine a few more on the way back to the inn after she pestered him about wanting another.

Thana didn't argue further, though she was unquestionably unconvinced. Pulling the cards back together into a deck, she began the next hand.

"Mm, well, don't forget to level up tonight. If you have questions about your abilities, the classes listed in the wiki, or anything else, hit me up first. I'd rather we made sure we get it right than have you regretting it later down the road," Runner said, moving back to his little nest. He sat himself down and started rechecking his choices, wanting to be absolutely sure of his selections.

Jolted awake from a nightmare, Runner looked around the room, confused and unsure. Blinking rapidly, he rubbed at his face with one hand as the world started to make sense.

Levering himself up with his other arm, he got into a sitting position. Checking the system clock, he saw it was deep in the night and the lights were all out. To the left, Katarina and Thana lay cuddled against one another in one bed, while to the right Hannah and Nadine slept back to back in the other. Placing his head to his fingers, he closed his eyes and let out a sigh.

"Dreams can't hurt you but they leave their marks. I don't know how much it'd help, but I'd listen," whispered a voice to his right. Tilting his head to peer in that direction, he found a pair of dark blue eyes staring at him from the bedsheets.

"Thank you, Hanners. I might take you up on that some time. For now I need to heed my own advice and level up. Would-would you keep an eye on me? In case, err, in case I end up paralyzed again? Oh, did anyone else experience anything like that?"

"Yes, I'll watch you. No, no reactions. We all talked to Thana before we made our choices, but nothing happened when we leveled up. That's what you called it, right? Thana spent a lot of time reading those shitty ability and attribute definitions. For everyone. They just made me mad honestly with their convoluted circle speak. She helped everyone, made sure we were doing the right things."

"Good. Good. Remind me to thank her. Right, no time like the present."

Runner grimaced and called up his leveling screen. His leveling and class goals remained the same as previously. From slaughtering the fort he'd gained three levels and now sat on three level ups, which on completion would put him at twenty-four.

Focusing on three abilities would give him the best result. Duelist, Scout, Blade, Doctor, and Elementalist all had a subclass at the second promotion that built their abilities off dexterity, intelligence, or agility. Much like last time, Runner opened the level up screen and placed the points accordingly. Bracing himself, he lay himself back into his blankets and pressed the Accept button and waited.

Memories filtered in and took their place, filling in holes in his mind, clearing questions but creating more with each one. Not being destroyed by the level up process this time, Runner was thankful.

He now knew his ship's administration password. He hoped it happened to be his account login password for the game too.

MayOrOfFailTOwn

Fighting back the excitement, he pulled up the game console to give it a try.

/Permissions
Please enter Password: **************
Invalid Password

Groaning, he let himself relax into his sleeping bag. He'd hoped, hoped it would be correct.

As he lay there recovering from the failure, one memory stood above the rest, demanding his attention.

"I'm fine, nothing wrong this time, thank the Sovereign. It's hard, every time I level up I get more memories back of my life before this world. Before being trapped here." Hannah didn't reply, but Runner could still feel her eyes on him.

He could finally answer at least one question that had been nagging at him though. Dinner several days before the mission started. A private dinner, in an apartment, alone with a woman. Feelings were attached to it, but they ran counter to his expectation to the setting. Love, joy, passion, anger, hurt, sick, distrust, jealousy, hate, and finally betrayal. He was seeing someone. Had been seeing someone.

Struggling against the missing blocks, Runner fought with his own mind. Ultimately he could call nothing else up. Not a name, an end, or even what happened after. He knew she was on the same task force he was on, though, even if it was nothing but a vague intuition. Knowing she was part of the mission helped-it meant she was here in the game with him. Even if he couldn't put a name to her yet, perhaps he'd run across her? It was probably too much to hope, but it was all he had at the moment. With any luck she could provide him with a better picture of himself, their relationship if they still had one, and what happened to the ship. Maybe she was in IT with him?

If she isn't in the graveyard.

"Thank you, Hanners. Goodnight."

Adjusting his sheets, Runner did his best to sleep.

Chapter 9 - Conscience -
06:18 am Sovereign Earth time
09/08/43

Pachelbel's Canon in D woke Runner from his sleep; his mind came to a slow state of wakefulness. Blinking, Runner let the alarm play on as he stood up.

Each bed still held its occupants, blissfully sleeping away. Thana had eventually moved to take up most of the bed and managed to corner Katarina. Hannah and Nadine remained back to back having not moved at all during the night.

Though it served no purpose any longer, Runner continued his morning routine as he always had. Moving to the table, he took a seat and eased out a pod of water from his inventory and pooled it in his hand. Scrubbing his face with the water, he repeated the action a few more times. Noticing with a smile that the debuff "Wet" appeared, he stretched his arms over his head.

As the memories of the previous night rolled in, the smile slipped from his face as he considered them. While he now had an answer to one question, many more had taken its place. Unfortunately, it wasn't something he could solve right now either.

Another mystery, another question, another answer. Another time.

Shaking off the morose feelings as the song ended, he silenced the alarm.

Tempus fugit, carpe diem, hop to. Run on, Runner.

Runner fingered the inventory screen open. Pulling free a beetle he ate it quickly and considered the loot from the previous day. With a furrowed brow he pulled the four rings, the shield, and the short sword out of the window.

Laying the shield facedown on the table, he placed the four rings into the concave center. He then laid the sword across it lengthwise before returning to his pack. Rummaging through his currency, he removed two months' worth of pay for each companion, assuming each month had thirty-one days at least.

He created four stacks on the table and leaned back into the chair eying, the glittering gold pieces. Even after portioning out such wealth, he had seven gold remaining in his purse. They really had increased their financial standing the other day by a considerable margin.

Making sure that each companion still slept, he opened up the ship's console screen and began cycling through the systems once more. They all reported the same as they had before. There were no changes.

After closing the ship's command screen, he powered up the Otherlife wiki through the in game browser, then stopped.

Sighing inwardly, he started to surf pages he'd already read. He was only delaying the inevitable.

Putting the worst ghost to rest first, he opened the social pane. Checking the graveyard, he held his breath. It'd increased slightly, but it hadn't passed eight thousand mark thankfully.

The second issue would need a delicate touch and would need everyone awake and alert. Nadine would of course eventually tell everyone what he'd told her about their fishbowl reality. He'd need to get ahead of it and talk to them first rather than have them hear it secondhand. On the off chance he'd need demonstration material for the talk, he logged into the IT portal and created them each a login into the ship's operating system and granted them access. Completing that task, he centered himself as best he could. Preparing in his mind what he'd need to say to them when they woke, he waited.

Sporting just a touch of luck, the ladies woke up within minutes of each other. That and Katarina woke up first. Upon doing so she let out one of the loudest yawns Runner had ever heard. To himself he admitted it fit perfectly with her character and only barely kept from laughing aloud at the audacity of it. Thana had sat bolt upright at the noise but clearly wasn't coherent. Hannah and Nadine had both startled in their bed and were now eying the Barbarian. Nadine launched her pillow from across the room to smack Katarina in the face. Shrugging it off, she dropped it in Thana's lap as she stood up from the bed.

They'd only been together perhaps a little over two days, but already it was feeling like a close-knit group. Nothing brings people closer than a unifying foe. Shared fears did wonders for making allies.

"Good morning, everyone. Before we break our fast I'd like to make sure I give you part of our bloody loot. After that I'd like to talk to you a bit more about what you experienced back at the fort and where to go from there. If you don't mind, would you please join me over here once you're all awake and functioning?" Runner asked of them.

One by one they joined him, each taking one of the open chairs. Katarina took her seat first, her eyes scanning an unseen window she was reading. Thana was present but visibly ready to return to the bed if allowed, her eyelids fluttering at times. Hannah and Nadine were both bright-eyed and bushy-tailed at the very mention of loot.

"First, I have one of these for each of you," Runner informed them. Katarina closed her window and Thana managed to finally shake off her lethargy.

After collecting the four rings, he handed them out accordingly. Stealth boosting silver was given to Hannah, platinum ring of the merchant to Nadine, white gold strength to Katarina, and finally the unique palladium ring of intelligence and hit points he gave to Thana. Each accepted their ring gratefully but none made a move to equip them. They all stared at their new jewelry and each other but none attempted to return them to him either.

Taking it as a general acceptance, Runner pulled the short sword clear of the shield and handed it over to Hannah. Once she'd taken the weapon from his hand, he lifted the heater shield and moved over to Katarina's chair.

"You'll have to forgive me, it's all I can offer for the moment. I would like to give you better or more, but at this time I'm woefully lacking. I'll do my best to provide for you all eventually. It'll take time though of course. We'll also need to look into a place that we can call home. A base of operations on the off chance that my goal takes longer than I wish. Sovereign knows an inn room and two beds just won't cut it for long. I imagine the harder part would be to find a city that would accept all of us. Fairly racially intolerant places we've visited so far."

As the group processed his words, he moved the stacks of coins to their respective owners.

"This is two months of pay up front. Obviously it's a lot of your time to pay for, but it's a reasonable assumption we'll be together for at least two months."

Exhaling loudly, Runner prepared himself for the hardest part of the conversation.

"As you all know, my overall goal is to level rapidly. What you don't know is the reason. This'll be hard to explain but I'll do my best. Imagine if you will, two thousand years from now, boats made out of metal that travel through the sky above. Between the very stars in the sky themselves."

It took a few hours' time and dozens of questions, but in the end the telling was complete. Runner had ended up using the shipboard wiki to help illustrate his points. Once they logged themselves in and started using the search function, the questions came fewer and further between. They now knew of their world, of his original world, and the difference between PC and NPC.

Katarina cared not at all since it changed nothing for her. She was still who she was and nothing would be able to change that. Thana took it gracefully, yet at an intellectual level. She'd asked the most questions though she seemed accepting of the dilemma. Nadine had been told of the more troubling aspects of her world the day before, yet her posture and tone dictated it still troubled her at some level. Hannah had no response one way or the other. This only made Runner all the more nervous for her in particular.

Runner suspected the young thief might be going through the same mental pathways Nadine had the day previous. A hard life lived on the streets in the city as a young woman. More than likely she had been given a far greater share of poor life experiences than she deserved.

"That brings us to here and now. I need to get everyone out, or as many as I can. Failing that, I need to create a situation where they at least stop becoming a vegetable on death. Perhaps sending them to the login screen. To that end I must get to a starting city to level my reputation, classes, and my first promotion. I technically don't have a class and once I hit level twenty-five, my progress will be halted. If I'm to succeed, I need you, all of you. Collectively you're all greater than the sum of your individual parts. As individuals you all excel at your individual roles, whereas I cannot measure up to you. Any of you. Now you know my goals, my plans, my quest. I've given you all that I know and wish. Will you join me?" Runner asked.

Katarina shrugged and handed over her old shield to Runner and picked up the heater shield with an overeager smile and equipped it. Large for Runner as it had been originally, it appeared gigantic to him when it sized itself for Katarina. There was no doubt in his mind she'd be able to wield it easily. Her face turned thoughtful as she stared at the large shield. Using both hands, she lifted the shield over her back and made a motion as if clipping the shield to her back. Instantly it appeared there and fit correctly.

Apparently satisfied with its placement, she equipped the ring and promptly stored her pay.

"In the end, knowing this changes not a thing. It certainly provides an interesting frame of reference to view the world in and it's an interesting philosophical discussion for later, but I am still me. And I choose to follow you. Thank you for the ring, it's quite lovely in truth," Thana stated.

Before Runner could respond to Thana, Nadine vied for his attention, addressing him directly.

"Run-n-n-ner, leave buying and selling to m-m-me. I'll t-take care of it for us all," Nadine enthused.

"I appreciate that, Nadine. Your ring can help build on that idea. It offers benefits suited for you alone. In fact, all of your rings are ideal for each of you."

Hannah had taken the money, equipped the sword, and wore the ring yet said nothing. Runner wasn't going to push her into a corner, so he'd assume she had agreed for the time being.

Runner reached over the table and picked up the discarded short sword. He handed it and Katarina's old shield over to Nadine, then leaned back into his chair.

"Equip 'em, use 'em, store 'em. We'll see about getting you a ranged weapon in the starting city when we get a chance to reset your class. I figure ranged would be best for you. A crossbow to be specific. A medium sized one with a cranequin, that's a hand crank on the side to re-cock the weapon, or a heavy one with a windlass on it, that's a two-handed crank. You put the nose of the thing in the ground and wind it at the butt," Runner said.

Seeing no one had anything further to say and everything had been distributed, he continued.

"I say we get food and head for the coast. Any objections?"

In the month it took them to travel to Bren, a little harbor town on the coast of Vex, little had occurred. Occasionally they'd had a skirmish with an over enthusiastic bear or wolf. Those little bouts of entertainment never lasted long since the animals' levels barely got above ten. One could have called it a hiking trip with friends. What had started as strong bonds in fear and death only grew stronger in peace and idle time between days of walking.

Water sloshed against the wooden supports beneath the pier's decking. It all sounded real to him, and there was a nagging familiar sensation in the back of his mind. Out on the water a mist clouded the horizon and obscured visibility. The ferry continued making its way towards them through the fog, though at a glacial pace. Leaning forward with his forearms resting on the handrail, he breathed in deeply.

One could taste the salt of the ocean on the brisk air. With each day he spent in the world it felt more real to him than he would like to give it credit for. There was no longer a separation in his mind between what was virtual and what was reality. Virtual reality felt like the real thing when it came to the sights and sounds of the world he now inhabited. Admittedly there were still a few disconnects, like eating but not needing to use the restroom. Or that every building lacked bathroom facilities.

Viewing the area around him, he checked to confirm that Thana sat in the shade nearby, reading a book she'd picked up from somewhere. Hannah was nowhere to be seen, but the distance readout in the party window showed she was within fifty meters of his position. Nadine and Katarina were listed at three hundred and seventy-four meters away. Based on that one could assume the merchant quarter sat at least three hundred and fifty meters away.

"I see your filthy pet but not the mutt. Did you get rid of her for the pure breed? At least the mutt was only half," a spiteful voice said.

Turning his head around, Runner was able to confirm his first impression of who that voice belonged to.

"Oh ho, Mr. Personality. I believe I owe you for that lovely gift you left with us while you ran like a whipped dog. Tell me, did you leave your balls behind along with your pride?" Runner happily replied, smiling at him.

"Watch your mouth, heathen. You consort with castoffs and whores, you might as well sell them to the church and m-"

You have developed the ability Throat Strike
You use Throat Strike on Warrior
Warrior is silenced

Gurgling, Mr. Personality struggled to move back from Runner. The punch had been swift and accurate, connecting with his throat with a meaty thwack. Grabbing the man by the shoulders, Runner leaned in close and tightened his grip, staring into the man's eyes.

"Insult me all day, that's fine, but say another word of my companions and I'll end you here and now. Damn the guards and their interference, I care the fuck not," he snarled at the man. Holding himself in check, Runner had images in his head of tearing the man's nose from his face with his teeth. Distantly Runner could see a guard patrol coming up the street towards him. With a final growl, Runner pushed the man away. Only then did he notice the Priest from the fort and another man standing beside him.

"Ah! Hello there. We really should stop meeting like this. I seemingly can't stop from just punching him in the throat. Though I do appreciate the fact that it's always right into your waiting arms, wouldn't want to dirty his noble bum," Runner admitted with a smirk to the Priest. Blood pounding with the heat of anger and the desire to throttle the man, Runner had to focus.

As Mr. Personality regained himself, Runner targeted the man and used *Analyze*. Named Bullard Griffin, the man was a level twenty-four Warrior. Unfortunately, that was the only information available. It was enough for now.

"Bullard, you've ruined my lovely morning. Do you not realize just how damn lovely this scene is? Perhaps you should leave before I end your sorry life."

"You could try, my cause is just, and I believe in my triumph and my gods. You consort with ill-bred filth that are looking for an excuse to sacrifice you as an offering. Give them to the church and you'll be forgiven! You can keep the half-breed, but turn over the Barbarian and the w-other," enthused Bullard.

"Ill-bred. Hah. I'd wager bronze to gold she's more educated and cultured than yourself. As for being forgiven, I've done nothing other than free those who were wrongly imprisoned. You would argue that I should have left them there based on your account. On what was said then and there. I am not one of your gods, nor theirs. Why must I stand in judgment of them? You would condemn them for doing their best to cling to life in a bad situation and survive. Condemn them for their very race alone. I ask no forgiveness from such an intolerant people. Go now. You bore me."

Waving his hand at the man, Runner looked to the ferry coming towards them. He didn't notice them depart, didn't even hear them if they had continued to speak once he'd turned his back. Nor did he even care.

Apprehensive, he could feel the pressure overwhelming him, bit by bit. Runner shook his head and closed his eyes, trying to find the peace he'd had minutes before. Frequent nightmares, being quick to wrath, slow to relax, unable to quiet his mind, and honestly feeling like he wasn't going to measure up, all pointed to the fact that Runner was cracking. Resting his head on his forearms, he tried to find a semblance of calm, a place to let his mind recover, to push out the fury.

Creaking wood and the gentle play of water under him provided a framework to reorder his mind. Screwing his eyes shut tightly, he attempted to empty his mind, his psyche straining at the edges as if he might come flying apart. Sunlight warmed the top of his head and the backs of his arms as he battled within himself.

Light scuffing from the soles of shoes alerted Runner to another person joining him at the railing. Every muscle in his body locked tight for a split second before he realized it could only be one person and relaxed. Location, personality, and a request he'd made to her previously told him who it was.

"Am I already lost? I've yet to begin and I'm already crumbling. It's been a month I admit, but I truly thought I was stronger than this. I must continue, though I'm terrified to do so. Yet who else? No one else can do this. That fact is only reinforced by the nine thousand dead. I have to unlock my memories. I have to free everyone. I can't do this."

The quiet whisperings of the wind and play of water answered him. Runner feared in his heart there would be no response coming, no forgiveness or consolation.

"My understanding of the situation is thus. You are missing large swathes of your memory. From what little I understand, it sounds as if a large portion of your life is blank. Perhaps not the broader strokes, but much of the underlying detail. Your life experiences. Beliefs you hold dear. Decisions you've made. Battles you've fought and ideals you've challenged. They're missing. The sum of what we are, our experience, is what we draw upon to make choices. It's what we use to defend ourselves from doubt. We compare them to things we've done previously and judge it based on what the outcome had been then," breathed Thana. She'd pitched her volume low enough that only he could pick it up.

"With all that being said, I would say you're doing as satisfactorily as could be expected for a man who has very few life lessons to draw on. For both taking action and defending those actions. Stay the course. Run on, Runner."

As she finished talking, she patted the back of his arm but didn't leave his side. Thana tended to radiate her proximity without much effort and he could feel her now. Taking solace in her company, Runner said nothing and thought on her words.

In many ways they made a lot of sense. It didn't help break down the pressure of it all, but it helped restore some of his flagging confidence. Stay the course.

The ferry trip itself was unremarkable and took two hours. Most of the group spent their time with each other or walking the deck. Runner chose to spend the journey at the highest point, lost in thought. Watching the other travelers, he managed to spot Bullard and his Priest near the rear. They kept to themselves, but they made themselves scarce when one of Runner's party came within their field of vision.

When the boat came near the shoreline, Runner decided to be one of the first off. Stepping free of the boarding plank, Runner eased himself to the side of the wharf and waited for the rest of his group. Biding his time, he let his eyes run over those who disembarked, then tracked those on the pier and everyone down on the street. The city's name escaped Runner and he didn't care enough to look it up. Time spent here would be brief indeed. Perhaps enough to get directions. They'd finally decided on their location and had selected Faren, the starting city of the Humans.

Non-player characters went about their daily business. Scattered throughout the crowd were players. In fact, Runner counted more players than non-players for the first time ever. A vast majority of players were seemingly playing it safe, staying within town limits and only venturing out to kill beasts they knew they could fight without a problem. Yet he had no recognition of anyone beyond a general "I might have seen them before."

This must be where the starting quests are filtering a good majority of people. Everyone here is between twelve and sixteen. Judging from that I should be able to clear out the newbie area completely with relative ease.

His attention was arrested in its wandering by one man in particular. Sitting on a barrel wedged up to the wall of a building was a man who stood out of place. Labeled "Wharf Rat" and level seventeen, he stood out, yet he blended in at the same time. Unable to put a finger on it, Runner watched the man, then the crowd around him. He realized why he'd suddenly become aware of him. Slightly disreputable looking, dressed in what could only be called the meanest of clothes, he was avoided by non-player characters completely.

It wasn't out of revulsion of a dirty bum, it was out of fear. They'd notice him sitting there, look away, then do whatever it took to steer clear of him and avoid his scrutiny. Allowing his mind to gnaw at it, he realized what the other part of the issue was. Scruffy McGee over there had eyes only for those who were disembarking the ferry.

Contemplating the situation, Runner tilted his head to the side as he watched Scruffy, who watched the passengers.

Scruffy sat upright as he locked on to someone who had caught his interest. Glancing over his shoulder, Runner immediately noticed Hannah coming down the pier to him. Whipping his head around, he locked eyes with Scruffy, who apparently had finally noticed him. Time slowed to a crawl in that moment. Scruffy knew Hannah. Scruffy was waiting for Hannah. Scruffy did not mean well for Hannah.

Before Scruffy could act, Runner took off like a bolt shot from a crossbow. Sprinting at a dead run he nimbly made his way down the harbor. Scrambling from his perch, Scruffy tripped over himself and then turned down a nearby alley. After only a dozen steps the man disappeared into the shadows cast between the rundown warehouses of the shipping district.

Not pausing to consider the situation, he sped onwards. Careening off a pedestrian who stopped dead in front of him, he spun, trying to preserve his speed. Shadows enveloped him as he entered the alleyway and tried to pick get back up to a sprint.

He wasn't able to dodge Scruffy's attack. Runner had missed him lurking there, his eyes adjusting to the change in light. Taking the entirety of the *Slash* without a single defensive bonus, Runner stumbled and lost his balance.

HUD flashing red to indicate he was in combat, he tumbled across the murky sludge of the alley. Trash and debris sprayed out around him as he splashed through the murk. Righting himself as swiftly as he could, Runner drew his sword and threw out a *Fireblast* blindly in front of him.

Scruffy took the attack to the chest and staggered backwards. Lit by the red glow of the spell's impact, Runner could see Scruffy stumbling away from the force of the blast. It gave Runner enough time to chug a health potion just to be safe. Potions could be purchased. His life could not.

Unfortunately Scruffy didn't catch fire and suffer secondary damage, which would have been nice. Runner pitched the empty bottle at the man. It clipped him in the temple and shattered, spraying bits of glass everywhere.

Roaring at him, Scruffy launched himself forward, swinging his dirk high at Runner's face. Dodging low, Runner thrust his blade outward at Scruffy's knee. With a satisfying hiss the blade split the threadbare clothes and carved out the back of the joint. Falling forward, Scruffy collapsed, falling to his hands and knees. Health bar flickering all the way down to orange from green in a heartbeat was bad enough, but the debuff "Hamstrung" had also popped up. At this point Runner had the man dead to rights; it wouldn't take much to finish this swiftly, but that wouldn't answer anything.

Runner jumped on Scruffy's back and pushed his face down into a puddle of muck that had collected in a broken cobblestone. Unwilling to let the chance for information go, he held him there until he thought the man might be pliable to questioning.

Letting Scruffy up for a breath, Runner hunched over the man, whispering into his ear. Runner did his best to make his voice crack, the pitch coming from high to low as he spoke.

"Greetings, friend. I'm afraid I'm not one for introductions. Linda wants to know if you taste good. I'm not sure if you do?"

Runner abruptly slammed the man's face down, back into the murky water. With his left hand he stroked the side of Scruffy's face tenderly while holding the man's head down with the right. Cringing mentally at the extreme psychotic feeling he knew he was giving off, Runner once more worried about his sanity. Everything had a price, and actions demanded the steepest payments.

You use Intimidate on Wharf Rat
Wharf Rat is Intimidated

Letting the man up to breathe, Runner jammed his index finger into the man's left ear.

"Perhaps your brain? Brain, drain, delicious pain, sweet, sweet, tasty meat? Scott? No, Scott, no, Scott, no. No I won't ask him. He won't know," hissed Runner.

"I migh' know! Ask me, please! I migh' know, I migh' know!" squealed Scruffy.

"Scott! You ruin it, why do you always ruin it? Ruiner, ruiner of all. Fine. Scruffy, why were you looking for the woman? What for did you need her?"

"I was paid to look'n for 'er, Hanner, sure 'nough. Paid me good coin. Was to go'n tell the bartender at the Sailor's Rest. I'm just muscle fer the thieves guil'. I ain't know nothin' more. Just get paid to, ya know, rough'n peoples up at times," screeched Scruffy.

"That's it? Nothing else?"

"Not'in. Swears!"

"Thank you."

Runner picked up his blade, activated *Stealth* since Scruffy couldn't actually see him, and drove the length of it into the side of Scruffy for a *Backstab*.

"I'm sorry. I can't have you running around with what you know," lamented Runner. Scruffy thrashed once, and then lay still under him. Grunting, he extricated his weapon and looted the corpse.

Runner closed his eyes and stood up, turning his face towards the sky. There was no sun back here in the dark, grimy, trash-filled alley. Cold shadows provided no relief to him, and the brisk salty wind stung his skin.

It hadn't been as easy this time as it had been with the bandits. Fear had been rolling off the man in waves. Fear like a real person might feel. Fear like an NPC wouldn't have.

Are they even just non-player characters anymore? Are they real or not? Can I casually murder actual people? I'm no soldier, I'm a damn tech. I'm a rear echelon mother fucker. Can I treat this like a game and still casually kill anyone in my way? What if it had been a young woman? An old man? A mother?

Runner brought his hands to the sides of his head and sighed. What had started as such a lovely day now was beyond lost.

Chapter 10 - Idiot Plan -

Katarina burst into the alleyway, her shield held up and sword in hand. Coming to an abrupt stop, she eyed the corpse and Runner, then surveyed the rest of the backstreet. She would have needed to leap from the boat and land sprinting to get here as fast as she did.

"Sorry Kitten, I should have waited but I couldn't risk him getting away. He was paid to sit here and wait for Hanners apparently."

Katarina grunted and moved past him as she went to clear the other end of the alley. Looking to the entrance once again, he saw Nadine, Thana, and Hannah arrive at the same time. Runner put his left hand on his hip and took a breath to explain.

"He wa-"

"Was waiting for me. I'm not really that fucking surprised, but I was hoping they wouldn't be here. I'm sorry, I should have said something. Stupid bastard was in plain sight, wasn't he? Problem is there's always a second asshole just in case. Chances are he bolted when you took after this one."

Hannah's explanation made a lot of sense and yet none at all. She knew. She knew and wasn't surprised. Runner was now keenly interested in why she had been alone, starving, and as far away from a major city as possible when he first encountered her.

"Right. We'll talk later. Lady Death, Kitten, Nadine, you're all going to group up and get out of town. Camp a mile or so outside the eastern gates. Make it a place you can't be easily seen. Preferably a spot where you can see others coming if you've been followed, though. Do it, no arguments, go now. If what Hanners said is accurate, she and I were spotted and are now associated, but none of you are."

"But wha-" began Nadine.

"No, go, now. Not another word. I'll find you all with the party window as soon as Hanners and I escape the town."

Moving backwards even as he finished talking, he motioned to Hannah to fall in with him. Runner turned and walked down the alley. Pausing next to Katarina, he addressed her directly.

"I leave them in your hands, Kitten. Get them out of town safely."

Katarina dipped her head in understanding as Runner took off in a light jog. Hannah was behind him and to the left by the sound of it.

"When we get a chance, you're explaining this. For now, you're telling me where we need to be to avoid whatever it is that's going to happen, and how we get out."

Avoiding trash, animal refuse, and foul standing water, they arrived at a main boulevard. Turning onto the boulevard, Runner slipped into the back of a large group of NPCs. Guessing from their dress and what they were carrying, Runner figured them for sellers bound for a market. They'd serve for a useful disguise and cover for a short time. Hopefully long enough to get an information dump from Hannah.

"Quickly, no time," Runner whispered urgently at Hannah.

"I gave frickin' information to guard captain of Faren. It got a bunch of people arrested. Once they had what they wanted, the shit head captain let slip who ratted them out. They broke their deal with me. I fled instead of waiting for a two-bit thug to collect the guild bounty on me."

"Got it. That leaves us with very little working room but it's doable, I guess. Has to be. We stay off side streets, stay with groups. If we even think there's the possibility of something being wrong, we use *Stealth* and hit the roofs by any means possible. Take the next left up ahead and let's see if we can blend into a group."

Parts of plans, thoughts, and actions flitted in and out of his mind as he walked. There were only a few options open to them and the easiest one was to stay in plain sight of guards. Hopefully they were with a different faction than the ones in Faren.

Of everything he heard, that was the worst news unfortunately. Faren was their goal for him to train at. And now there might be an inevitable confrontation with the local crime element. Which apparently Hannah had been a part of.

Turning left at the indicated street crossing, Runner sped up with a little hop to slide in behind a group of day laborers. Eyes taking methodical passes of each intersection, window, and doorway ahead of them, Runner didn't see anything out of place. The feeling of safety blew apart a second later when Runner remembered they'd simply be cloaked. Waiting. Watching. Invisible.

Cursing under his breath, he squinted into the distance, trying to locate a suitable place to break a tail and change their heading.

There was a group of trees growing near a low-walled building that provided an obvious avenue to the roofs. Nearby, a church sat empty with its grounds untended and quiet. Finally, a small rough-hewn footbridge sat crouched off to the side of the canal up ahead, leading into another backstreet.

"I see three routes. Trees, church, footbridge. I like the trees but it would alert them early to the fact we plan on going upwards. Church feels like a dead end, ha. Footbridge is rather dark and would be where I was if I were looking for us. Thoughts?" Runner inquired, finding no other routes.

"Agreed on all points. Shit. I guess it comes down to if you're feeling religious or lucky then."

"If it was to a neutral god, or any of the pantheon that walked the line between, maybe. I'm guessing here, and tell me if I'm wrong, but I think that's a church dedicated to one of the gods our dear friend Mr. Personality serves. Rather not risk that. *Stealth* just before we break from this group and hit the footbridge. Assume watchers are there, use *Distract* on the open area behind the entryways. Take the left wall, I'll take the right. If you see a silhouette, stab it."

Hannah said nothing but closed in tighter to his side. Runner's heart was racing with each step closer to the point they'd need to *Stealth* and flee. Holding his breath, he tapped Hannah on the arm and stealthed, moving swiftly for the footbridge.

Reaching the wooden ramp, Runner was faced with a ghostly image standing before him. This was outside of his original plan, but it wasn't outside of the possibilities he had thought of.

Utilizing *Distract* on the opposite side of the footbridge, he turned the ghostly image away from him. Not activating any stealth-breaking abilities, he closed on the man. He hoped physical contact wouldn't count as stealth breaking.

He threw his shoulder down then whipped it back up after he made contact, hurling the man over the handrail and sending him flailing into the water below.

Hannah took point when Runner came to a near halt in dealing with his roadblock. Throwing her left hand out, she executed her *Distract* perfectly. One silhouette appeared on the left side wall. Hannah closed on him and plunged her weapons deep into the man's back.

Moving beyond the entry point and coming alongside Hannah, Runner turned into the enemy. Casting *Fireblast* at point blank into the man's abdomen limited the light of the flames to the outside. Hannah worked to quickly strike at the man again.

Unable to call out, or even act, the sentry collapsed and died right there. His health bar depleted in the time it took to draw a single breath. There had been no chance for him to do anything.

Confirming the sentry's name was "Guild Thief," he performed a quick loot command. Immediately stealthing, he angled himself for a jump at a low hanging wooden awning.

Catching the lip of it, he hauled himself up to the second floor. Leaping upwards one more time, he caught the edge of the roof and dragged himself over it onto a flat open space. Rolling out of the way for Hannah, Runner then gave the area a rapid survey. Nothing except bird droppings and garbage.

Keeping himself flat on his back, Runner finally stared into the wide open blue sky above. Sunlight warmed him from his boots to his hair, bathing him, cleaning him of the chill he'd felt in the streets below.

Like a cloud through the sky, an errant thought passed through his mind. He hadn't confirmed if the man he'd tossed into the canal below was even an enemy. He'd just reacted and thrown the man without a second thought. Admittedly the second man had been positively identified upon death, which would provide substance to the argument that the first had to be a hostile. It still didn't dismiss his action as anything less than mildly chaotic. Covering his eyes with his hand, Runner could only lament again at the man he was becoming.

Hannah flopped down next to him, after appearing on the roof in the exact same spot she had.

"I had no fucking idea you could even get up here. I didn't even consider the thought. Now that I'm up here it seems like common sense, but while we were down there, it-it just didn't even register. Shit."

Chuckling quietly, Runner shook his head back and forth.

"I'm not too terribly surprised. In hindsight I think the top of buildings is an out-of-bounds area. Not sure of it since we're up here. If I had to imagine why it would be off-limits, it'd be a player versus player hideout. Guards don't patrol up here, so it would just become a nesting ground for orange or red players. Err, people who have either attacked other players or killed them."

"Suppose it's in our benefit then. Lady luck may be a bitch, but she found you today."

"Remind me to buy her a dozen roses," Runner said. Pinching his eyes shut, he massaged the bridge of his nose with his thumb and forefinger. "Here's what I propose. Make our way to the eastern gatehouse. Not close enough to be seen from the walls if they're manned but close enough we can get out if we see an opportunity. If we don't see one, we wait it out until tomorrow night."

Hannah had crawled to the edge of the low wall surrounding the roof they were on and was peering at the area below. Assuming she was following the conversation, Runner continued.

"I would imagine that if they haven't seen hide nor hair of us by then, they might assume we've already made our escape and act from that train of thought. Or so my hope goes. I figure we

Stealth, leap from a rooftop nearby, and do our best to get out without a fuss. Rather not have a group chasing us all the way to the starting town."

"Why were they so weak? He went down like a little bitch. I didn't know him personally, but still, shouldn't have instantly died."

"Mm? It's because you've been leveling up. There are three types of characters in this world right now. Well, four, but three for this discussion. One, players. Two, non-player characters. Three, non-player characters like yourself. Altered. Awakened."

"Altered? Awakened? What the hell does that mean? Why are you always so god damned vague?"

"I'm not trying to be, alright? For fuck's sake, Hanners. Do you think it's normal that you level up? Do you think it's normal for you to know about your world as a whole? That you should be able to see your fucking abilities in such a way that you do now? To use them as you do? I've irrevocably changed you, Hanners. I've changed all of you. Wish I could explain it better than that but I truly don't understand most of it myself."

Runner closed his eyes and exhaled violently. Pressing his palms to his eyes, Runner struggled with the enormity of the problem. Suddenly a very real problem of the game becoming so unbalanced that it simply shut down loomed over him.

How many rules have I broken? How many more can I break? Why am I actually able to break the rules? What happens when the code is suddenly so kinked that it no longer functions as intended? No game is meant to run in perpetuity. They all come down for regular maintenance and updates. And now this.

Hannah, for one reason or another, had made an enemy of a crime lord local to the area. Now Runner had to deal with it. *But do I? I could leave her and be done with it. She was fine on her own before, wasn't she?*

Trailing that thought was the image of Hannah in the woods when he had met her. Dirty, starving to death, horribly lost, and helpless.

OK, OK, one problem at a time. Get out of town.

"We need to move. I'd like to circle the rooftops along the edge of town and see where our best exit point is. A plan rarely survives contact with the enemy and all that, but I'd still rather not plan to fail because I failed to plan," stated Runner. Leveraging himself to a standing position, he brushed the ever non-existent dirt from his armor and clothes. Activating his *Stealth*, he turned and headed east across the roofs.

Below them a plaza buzzed with players and non-players alike. Haggling, buying, selling, purchasing services or selling them, it was a den of commerce. Originally Runner had thought it might be good to hide there, in that teeming mass of greed. It'd also be a hard place to spot a tail or waiting dagger. A crowd like that wouldn't hide just you.

Hannah had echoed his own thoughts, though with far more profanity, and so now they sat on a rooftop watching the market. Drumming his fingers across his boot heel, Runner people watched while lost in his own thoughts.

"Do you think they're like me? Any of them? I have a lot of fuzzy spots. Also memories of before though. They're almost too clear. Unreal even due to the amount of detail. Is that my backstory? All that garbage written by some fat sweaty pencil-pushing bastard at a desk?" Hannah asked bitterly. She sat with her back to an adjoining building's wall, her fingers idly flicking playing cards into a pot. Hannah had purchased it while on the ship to give to Nadine since the little merchant had started to take over cooking duties almost completely, but had little equipment.

Sneaking a glance from the corner of his eye, Runner contemplated her question. Letting his sight settle back to the marketplace, he watched a player sell countless animal bits and loose pieces of equipment. Runner finally decided on how to answer her even if it wasn't something she actually wanted to hear.

"Yep. That's the gist of it. Written up, entered into a database, and the AI selected it for you. It's no different than those who were written as dead, or soon to be. There are those who are nothing more than an exclamation point to a sentence. A rousing, or hell, a lackluster, battle at the end of a quest that serves no purpose other than to collect a book for a quest giver. Doomed to die at the hands of a player for no other reason than bad writing."

"Seriously? What kind of sick fucks…that's horrible."

"It's not as if stupider things haven't happened in history, or more inglorious ways to die haven't occurred. You can hate me for saying it, but be thankful for your blessings. As to your original question, no. They're not like you at all. They will act according to their original AI."

"Could you, ya know, wake them?"

He flashed through all his introductions with them. How far he'd pushed their AI code. Let alone the server code. He groaned inwardly.

"I suppose. But there'd be no point to it. Let's just say that so far, my awakening someone hasn't exactly been good for the person being awakened."

"Are you serious? I know three women other than myself who would fucking disagree with that. We're all better off for what you've done."

"Debatable. Previously you were happy with your world because you believed it was as it was and you controlled your destiny. Are you truly happy knowing now that your life and memories were written in for you?"

"That's not fair you bastard. My life has been one shit stain after another. It's-it's hard to know it was written for someone else. For another to enjoy the drama of it. But I now truly know I'm the master of my destiny. That I can become what I choose. That I can live my life beyond what happened to me."

"I suppose. Consider it creator's guilt then. I regret bringing you to life in a world that would happily snuff out your life as easily as they would a rat in a pantry."

Past the bazaar and near the gate, Bullard came into sight from behind a gate house. Old Priest was at his side, looking as old and crusty as ever. A third and fourth man stood across from them. Of the two newcomers, one was dressed in a robe and the other carried a bow on his shoulder. Runner vaguely recognized him as the third man from the pier.

Mr. Personality was gathering a party. One that even included a tracker probably. Clenching his teeth in a grimace, he felt the cold touch of fate on his spine as he watched them. It was a party with the intent to kill his own and nothing else. He knew it. There was no proof and no way he could verify that, but Runner knew that was the goal.

All four turned as a fifth joined them. Remarkably the fifth was a player. Visibility was poor from his position, and all Runner could make out was the back of a head. The nameplate of the individual wasn't available at the distance they were at. Outside of brown hair and a light complexion, he could only guess that it was a female in gender, due in part to the build and size.

Fate chose that moment for a pickpocket to be caught in the act nearby. The woman craned her head around to view the disturbance, and her face became distinguishable.

Struck low by the mighty hammer of a fickle destiny, Runner dropped closer to the edge of the wall. It was her, his dinner companion, the lovely young lady who lay at the center of such a snarled and twisted knot of emotions. Passing all too quickly, she returned to the conversation with Bullard and they started walking from the plaza.

Desperately he tried to select her in futile attempt to learn her name. Runner couldn't manage to work the angle quite right. Blocked by walls, distance, and other people, he futilely repeated the process until she was gone from sight.

"...en I decided I had to cut ties and bolt. I'm a thief, I've killed people sure, but I'm not a rapist, a slaver, thrice-damned flesh peddler. Gave it all to the captain and here we are. In the end it only took a few massive bribes and it all vanished. Guild master of the thieves or not, I didn't think it would be that easy for him," Hannah finished. Hooking the pot handle with the tip of her boot, she pulled it back to herself to collect her cards once again.

Flashing eyes pierced Runner when he looked over to her. By her expression, he must have had a fairly blank expression on.

"What, you'd think I would sell people to slavers? I'm not a fucking monster. Bastard."

Blinking twice, Runner finally caught up to the conversation she had been having with him, without him being a part of it. It would be better to admit a smaller wrong than the greater, having not heard her at all.

"Ah, no. I'm not surprised that you fall on the darker side of the moral compass, but I'm glad that you do have your limits as I originally thought of you."

Letting his mind wander, he blurted out his next thought without considering his audience. "Though I would argue that all the actions you attribute to yourself were written into you without you being given a choice. One could almost argue that you're now a different person based on who you are, not what was chosen for you. You could theoretically become whatever you wanted from this point, good or evil, right or wrong."

Beside him, Hannah tensed and became unmoving, and the unease that emanated from her in waves was palpable.

"No one can fault you for being upset, Hanners. You'd have the right to be angry, feel rage even. Your life before this was written out with little regard to you and what you wanted or would have actually done."

"You have no idea. You can't fucking tell me that I should just excuse my life from before. My life. My very damn life, Runner. An asshole like you put it together. Put me through what I lived and fought against every day! You can't just tell me to write it off, you heartless bastard!"

By the end Hannah was shouting at the top of her lungs. Runner scrambled from the edge to preserve their location in case curious eyes tracked the sound upwards. Stooping low so he didn't skyline himself, Runner turned to Hannah.

He shuffled over to Hannah and put his hands to her shoulders. Sniffling, shaking, and full of righteous injustice, Hannah glared at him.

"You're right, I'm sorry, Hanners. I'm sorry. Shh, please, I beg you, no more shouting," Runner pleaded with her. "I'm not trying to dismiss what's happened to you, merely make you realize that you are who you are now, and your choices are your own. However hard it is to hear, your entire past never actually happened."

Thankfully she visibly calmed. With luck, anyone who heard the exchange would write it off as a verbal disagreement and not people hiding on a roof. Making sure she had at least a reasonable grasp on her control, Runner nodded and relaxed his grip on her shoulders.

"Thank you. I can only imagine what it feels like and I can't truly relate, but I and the rest of our little group would do anything to help. Consider everything previous to this a forced existence. It'll linger,' like bad thoughts or dreams, but they never actually truly happened. It's why the memories seem so surreal-it's because they only occurred on paper, in text."

Hannah nodded slowly while blinking her eyes rapidly, tears trailing down her cheeks.

"For now, realize that you don't stand alone. Our entire little family all feel the same in one way or another. We all want nothing more than to help. Change of topic time. We've been watching this gate all day and I can honestly say I don't think we'll get a break. Originally we agreed to wait till tomorrow, but I think tonight we should make a play on the guardhouse. It's the one place thieves wouldn't go around stealthed, waiting. Only place really. What do you think? We could survey tonight, make plans based on movements, and attempt the escape tomorrow."

Hannah's brows came down and her head tilted, casting her face in shadow as she brooded over his words. Runner sat back on his haunches, creating some space between them.

Allowing her to think it over, he checked the party window and then the map against it. Based on the map icons and distances to Katarina, Thana, and Nadine, they'd set up camp a short way from the gate. While the map didn't show details, he would wager it was appropriate.

"You're right," she said. Runner wasn't lost to the fact that she didn't specify about what, but he would take what he could get. "Let's case the damn guard tower over there. Assume we get through it though, you failed to explain how the hell we're supposed to get down from the wall. We don't have wings, you daft fuck."

"Yeah. We're going to have to jump. I imagine we'll break both our legs, maybe our pelvis, and honestly probably be pretty close to death. I'm pretty sure falling damage is percentage based dependent on the height. Get up on top of the wall, grab the edge, dangle down, let go. We land, stealth, crawl away, I heal us up to normal."

"That's just stupid. This is a stupid plan. You're stupid. Fucking idiot. Fucking idiot with a stupid plan. Idiot plan," muttered Hannah. Disbelief and anger were written all over her face.

"Yeah, it's a dumb plan. I got nothing else that will get us outside the wall without being seen. The worst part though is, even if we succeed, we still have to go to Faren. Where they're just waiting for you. Great, right?"

"Oh my gods and goddesses. You're a thrice damned-idiot. Why don't we just rush the gate then? It's pointless."

"Because they'd chase us all the way there. Easier to get into the city and maybe escape without being seen if we don't have to dodge cutthroats and trackers all the way there. Sleeping ever so easily under the loving and watchful eyes of our would-be pursuers. I'd prefer they never even knew we'd visited Faren until we were gone. We might get lucky and they may not even notice you. I'm open to other ideas if you've got 'em."

Mentioning the pantheon sent an idle thought through Runner's head that he cataloged away for another time. At some point he'd need to figure out who to pray to and get his religious alignment moving.

"Let me think on it. There has to be a better way. This is just...it's stupid. Just stupid," Hannah grumbled.

"You think. I'm moving over there," Runner said, pointing towards the guard tower. Stealthing, Runner set off to begin spying on the tower. A tower full of guards halfway between the corner of the wall and the gate. A tower with no way down except jumping and hoping to survive a thirty-foot fall, depending entirely on the mechanics built into the game. That or do some impressive glitch wall running. What gamer wasn't in the mood for glitching a game to his advantage?

Chapter 11 - Turning Point -

7:02 pm Sovereign Earth time
10/02/43

During the previous night they'd watched the patrols come and go, timed them, memorized them, and planned for them. This was now the time to act. It was the best chance they had to sneak through successfully, with the most guards out on patrol, and the least inside.

Hannah was pressed into his back as they waited nearby. Runner did his best to ignore her, but it wasn't every day he practically wore another person like a cloak. Fixing his mind to the situation at hand, he tried to prepare. They would only have a few seconds between the guard door opening and it closing. In those few seconds, they'd have to make it past the threshold together.

Then the door popped open and the patrolling guards left the tower. The second the guards' line of sight cleared their hiding spot, they slipped in through the open door. Melding themselves to the interior wall, they surveyed the interior. Runner quickly confirmed it was empty of guards and thanked the Random Number Gods above.

It held long tables without chairs, cabinets with supplies, and closed wall lockers. One could only call it a dressing room or arming room. An interesting touch to add to guards who never went home.

Do they even have a home?

A click behind them heralded the door shutting. It automatically locked itself, effectively trapping them in the tower. Part of their recon determined that the door was locked at all times. Except for when a guard opened it.

Runner left Hannah's side and decided to make his way towards the set of stairs in the back. With limited intelligence they had no idea how many guards were inside. Of every aspect in this endeavor, this was most assuredly the riskiest part. It remained an incredibly stupid plan, but it was the only one that had a shred of success of going unseen.

Runner motioned to the stairs and glided along the wooden floorboards. Reaching the stairwell, Runner took the steps two at a time, swift and silent. Slowing his ascent near the top, he eased himself upwards. His eyes were level with the landing when he stopped moving. Inspecting the room, which was filled with sleeping cots and foot lockers, Runner was able to confirm it was free of guards. It would be easy to make their way across to the next level.

Careful steps and a wary eye were his only tools in this situation. Exiting the stairs, Runner gained the top of the landing and immediately moved to the stairs on the other side of the room. Drawing close to the stone steps, Runner peered through the railing up to the landing above. Runner saw nothing but decided to wait and watch. Rushing now would only ruin the whole plan.

Appearing on wall next to the landing, a shadow coalesced. Compressing himself to the support wall, he hunched down into himself. Creeping to the corner of the room, furthest from the stair landing, Runner hid in the shadows. He started looking for Hannah to give a signal to hide.

He found her, in the middle of the room, bent double over a footlocker. Feeling the heat of his anger climb into his face, he imagined throttling the life from her. It was not the time to be robbing the guards.

Gesturing frantically, he finally resorted to a low hiss to get her attention. Looking up, she caught his frantic gestures and angry visage. She gently set the cover of the chest back down and scurried away from the chest. Hannah managed to get over to a wall, quickly pressing herself up under the side of a bed frame.

Clumping down the stairs, a guard in the city colors became visible. Tottering, the man stumbled over to a cot and collapsed into it without a word or even removing his armor.

Flashing his teeth in a snarl at Hannah, Runner gestured to his side. Shuffling back to his previous position, he checked the top of the stairs once more. Confirming that it was clear, he quickly took the steps upwards. He edged his head up to peek into the room. Quickly surveying the area, he could find no guards.

Small tables with high-backed chairs were spaced throughout the area. Many of the tables held half-finished drinks and food while others were conspicuously empty.

Exiting the stairs, he picked his approach to run along the sidewall. It was his best shot at getting to the other side of the room without disturbing the space he was moving through. Stealth was key as long as they were undetected. This being a guard-only city space, there was no way of knowing if changing the decor would be classified as detection or considered an action that would deactivate the ability.

Tables passed by him as he inched along the outside. Out of fear based in paranoia, he checked the chairs he crossed by. Finding one such chair occupied, Runner held his breath in panic.

The man's head was down on the table, his arms spread out amongst a few empty bottles of what he assumed to be alcohol. The high-backed chair had hidden him perfectly on Runner's initial inspection.

This must be the drinking buddy of the man snoring himself to death downstairs.

Straining to keep his movements fluid and light, he put some distance between himself and the drunk guard. Runner finally exhaled in relief, his eyes moving from chair to chair to make sure there were no other surprises. Finally he reached the other end of the room, the hair on his neck crawling, knowing there was a sleeping guard behind him.

Now before Runner stood a door leading to the outer wall. Regrettably this would not be their exit from the tower. On the other side of this exit were two guards who had no patrol, but guarded the intersection of the tower and the wall itself.

Making the door open on its own would definitely be a tip off to the guards. They'd most likely investigate since that was part of the AI. The plan had been to reach this point and look into getting out of the tower from the room above. It had windows that would allow an exit to the exterior of the tower.

Haphazard would be a polite way to describe such a plan, but it was genuinely all they had to work with. What they really needed at this point was a way to avoid them completely without alerting them. It would be bad enough trying to get out with an entire guild of cutthroats chasing them, let alone pissing off the town guard.

Could always open the door and ask them if they'd like to purchase some cookies. Thin mints could definitely qualify as a worthwhile bribe…maybe a subscription to a holozine or to discuss switching to the newest long-range carrier wave with special introductory rates.

Taking a moment to empty his mind of unproductive thoughts, Runner checked the top of the fourth floor stairwell. Movement was audible from above but no one was visible.

Working his way through a few thoughts, Runner ascended to the next floor and scanned the layout.

Empty of all interior decoration and adornment, save a few training dummies, the room was dominated by large circles painted onto the stone floor. Throwing a guess out, he assumed it was for practice duels. To that end, they probably had anti-lethality wards placed on them to protect combatants.

One lonely guard was busy going through offensive motions with his blade. Each time he firmly connected with a dummy, he reset himself and attack again. Struck by a thought on how they could cheese the guard, Runner ducked back down.

Descending the stairs, he found Hannah systematically casing each table to see if there was anything worth taking. Motioning her over, he took up position behind the door, his back to the corner. Pulling her in close, he leaned forward and pitched his voice as low as possible.

"Guard upstairs, let's take turns using *Distract* to draw him to the door. I'll put a *Distract* under the door itself, and hopefully he'll open the door to look. Once outside, we use *Distract* on the top part of the wall to the right, jump the left corner, make for the middle point between towers."

Plan explained, he let her go to watch her reaction. Internalizing it, Hannah nodded her head once and then pointed to him and then tilted her head to the stairs.

Me first, I suppose. With just a smidgen of luck, we'll get this door open shortly.

Taking the stairs, Runner confirmed the guard's position. Angling his *Distract* to hit the wall between the guard and the stairwell railing, Runner activated the ability. Head whipping around at the sound, the guard was immediately on alert. He closed in on the noise, his gaze remaining locked on the area. Walking backwards down the steps, Runner kept his eyes fixed on the city defender. Extending his left hand, he held up five fingers and began counting them down in an effort to signal when Hannah should act.

As the guardsman stood on the spot the ability had activated on, Runner reached the last finger. Hannah's *Distract* went off almost directly behind his head as he turned and stepped off the landing smoothly. Stooping low, he tucked his head down and shuffled along. Taking up a corner, he squirmed himself into the spot. It'd be out of the guard's field of vision, yet give Runner the best chance to target the door.

Concentrating on the door, he tried to wedge his *Distract* casting indicator underneath it. Hopefully it would go off just beyond the door's coordinates so that the guard, while obeying the rules of the game itself, would be forced to open the door. Finding himself unable to push it any further under without it actually targeting the door, he waited. He'd need to time it perfectly. Hannah needed time for her *Distract* ability to refresh; otherwise, it would be pointless to get the guard to open the door. He'd open the door, stand there, then close the door and return to his original position.

So engrossed in his own thoughts Runner nearly missed the mark. His heart leapt out of his chest as the intended target started to turn back. Desperately activating *Distract*, Runner could only hope he hadn't missed his window. Looking over his shoulder, the guard stared at the door for a second. Finally he turned around and approached the door.

Runner let out an inaudible sigh as the man's hand came up and grasped the door handle. As the door swung outward on squealing hinges, Hannah pressed in close, nearly standing on the man's heels, and used her *Distract*. While he couldn't see what was going on, he was sure the two guards on the wall, and the one here in the room, were now fixated on the top of a merlon.

Sliding forward, keeping his steps as light as possible, Runner crept up on Hannah, his hands coming forward to rest on her shoulders. Hannah leading the way, they matched the guard step for step, closer to him than his coin purse. Which Hannah took.

Gloom and darkness covered all that he could see; the interior of the tower being brightly light had night blinded him. Opening his eyes wide, he tried to assess the wall and everyone on it. They really had only seen it from the rooftop across the way up to this point and guessed at some of it. He couldn't see the details but all three guards were focused on that one spot on the wall, and each was closing in on it. There was no going back from here as Runner's *Distract* wasn't ready yet. They were left with proceeding forward.

Breathing quietly Runner leaned in close and peered over Hannah's shoulder to get an eye of the layout. One of the guards was now at the location and would be turning back after perhaps three more seconds. They had no time to lose, but the distance appeared like a chasm between them and the wall junction. Jumping diagonally was going to be a bit harder than he'd anticipated. It looked too far to jump to the planned corner, yet fate would give them no other choice. He patted Hannah on the back and took a few steps back to give her room.

Hannah more than likely came to the exact conclusion he did, but probably faster. She took two steps back, then dashed forward and leapt from the small walkway. Her arms and legs outstretched to the wall's ledge, willing it closer to her. Not able to give her time to see if she'd make the jump, their window was just too short, Runner followed right behind her. A flash of yellow on the right side of his vision indicated he had been noticed.

Right in front of him Hannah hit the lip of the wall and tumbled once, her back slamming into the stones. The hollow clunk of her head connecting with the masonry was audible and sickening. Sliding across the blocks, she fetched up against the wall and lay still, unmoving.

Runner crashed into the wall, his armpits and chest slapping into the blocks as his palms hit the walkway. His fingers dug into the cracks of the stonework while the toes of his boots scrabbled at the stones to find purchase. Panicked, he looked to the right. All three guards were staring at where Runner *had* been but a second ago. Apparently the near stealth reveal took precedence over an audio cue. For the moment Runner felt like he could hold himself in place, having wedged the toes of his boots into a minuscule crevice. Confirming he was

actively in *Stealth*, Runner held still and tried to be one with
the ledge.

Looking up, he saw Hannah still remained in *Stealth*, though
she had a status debuff he didn't know the icon for. She was
doing a fair interpretation of the wall she was against though
and blended in well. Unable to see her face, he could only
assume she was okay for the time being.

Not trusting himself to watch the guards without reacting,
Runner locked his eyes to Hannah and waited. They were in the
clear if the guards resumed their normal patterns. Assuming
there were no deviations that is. Or that they were caught.

As the seconds ticked by, he took a moment to confirm the
location of the rest of the group. They were still where he last
saw them, and for all intents and purposes it appeared like they
were doing fine. Appreciating how badly things could have gone
if they'd been unable to get out, on top of everything else, he
promised to actually go to a church and place a donation for the
gods of this world.

Be grateful for all the things that go without a hitch.
Shaking himself out of his melancholic and unproductive mood,
Runner found Hannah crouched in front of him and gazing at him.
Whatever her debuff was, it was gone now, and she was watching
him as if he were a bug under a cup.

"Welcome back from your woolgathering. You have no idea how
creepy a bastard you are when you do that. Stare at people,
through them practically. Come on, let's get you off that ledge,
they seem to have…you know what, I don't even know. It's
strange. They're just standing there," Hannah explained,
offering him her hand.

Clasping her hand with his own, he used her strength to
pull himself up to the wall and checked the guards.

"They're NPCs, Hannah. What you're seeing there," Runner
said, nodding his head in the direction of the guards, "that is
normal combat NPC behavior when confronted with a player. Me. A
man puppet. They're hard coded to respond in certain ways based
on the actions I take. In this case, the actions you took as
well. At the start, you were no different, except you were
flagged as a quest NPC. Your settings were different from theirs
and allowed you more free will, but you had the same underlying
rules in place. Enough, let's go. A truly idiotic plan awaits."
Runner gave himself a quick once-over, confirming all things
were in their place.

Traveling along the wall, they reached the midpoint without
any further complications. Runner stuck his head out over the
edge of the crenelation and peered down to the ground below.
Using the maximum range of his *Distract* ability against the
wall, he gauged the distance to the ground at about thirty feet.

Certainly a goodly distance but it seemed a reasonable enough drop that could be survived.

"I mark it at perhaps thirty feet down. I wager it's survivable but that you'd end up with a few broken bits. Maybe a Bleeding status effect on top of it all for flair. When we hit the ground, I'll get us up and moving as fast as possible," Runner said. Patting the cold stones, he glanced to the moon in the distance and checked the time. They had a little bit before a patrol made its way over, but it'd be best to get it over with.

"Right. Last comments then. This'll sound absolutely stupid, and probably insane at the same time, but try to run against the wall on the way down. In fact, jump as you're falling. Just spam the commands in your head, run, jump, run, jump, run, jump. With any luck you'll catch something where it will register the movement and reset the Z axis counter," Runner advised. Looking to Hannah, he motioned to the gap between the merlons. "Ladies first?"

Hannah was scowling at him intensely. Taking a deep breath, she started to open her mouth. Speaking hurriedly, Runner interrupted her before she could even begin.

"Please, just trust me. It's called wall-running and it's a common enough video game glitch for breaking geometry. It's better than just jumping and hoping for the best, isn't it? Now go, before we waste more time arguing."

Glaring murder at him and a promise of pain, Hannah collected herself long enough to pray. It caught him off guard in truth-he'd never figured Hannah for the religious type. It was spoken softly and with nothing more than a simple hand gesture. It only lasted a moment and Runner didn't catch any of the words, let alone who she was praying to, but she then stepped out beyond the merlons and fell. Moving himself to the edge, Runner looked down to watch.

Strangely enough Hannah looked to be running in the air as she fell. Twice she bumped into the wall, her momentum arrested before she began to fall again. Smirking, he pulled himself back from the edge, realizing she was fine. She'd done it perfectly and Runner doubted she'd even take damage from it.

Through sheer chance Runner saw a silhouette in the roadway below staring up at him. Taking two steps to the side to ascertain if the man was watching him, Runner confirmed the individual's head didn't turn, yet they were still looking up to where he had just been. To where Hannah had just been, actually. Frowning, Runner went to select the person he assumed to be a player, but before he could, they turned and melded into the pedestrian traffic.

Shaking his head, he set the problem aside. It was something he'd have to talk to the group about. It boded poorly for them if a player had Hannah as a quest marker, which would be the only way they'd have seen Hannah on the wall. Now it was his turn to take the plunge off the side.

Rolling his eyes, Runner made a parody of the hand gesture Hannah had done and then stepped off the wall.

Immediately he realized there was a problem as he fell. His character screen icon lit up red and his health bar turned a pale green. Trying to pull off the same maneuver he'd advised Hannah of, Runner struggled with himself. His body barely responded to the commands he was giving it. He made only the briefest of contact with the wall and didn't get a good Z axis reset. He hit the grass with a ground-denting thud. Groaning, he curled up into the fetal position. Runner squeezed his eyes shut in a vain bid to block out the pain.

"What the fuck! Runner, what the god damn hell did you do? Shit! *Stealth*. Activate your *Stealth*, it's off! We have to go, we have to go now!" Hannah exclaimed angrily, pulling at the collars of his clothes, already dragging him to his feet.

Cracking one eye open, Runner ran it over his status bar. One leg broken, unspecified wounds, and a minor celestial curse. Sighing, he tried to activate *Stealth* but found it refused to engage. The movement-impairing effects were preventing it from being utilized.

"I can't. Too much shit broken inside. Got cursed for throwing up a fake prayer too. Completely zeroed my mana, abilities, and movement speed. Also my natural regeneration for both health and mana. Oh, and the ability to use healing potions, either for health or status ailments. Damn me for a fool and my glib actions, I'm sorry, Hanners," Runner groaned. Trying to get his feet under him, he found them unresponsive. Grass greeted him once more as he fell over. Mobility was simply impossible at this point, and Runner was now at the mercy of the game itself. No Remedy potion would cure a celestial curse.

"You're such a childish prick! Can't you just take this seriously? You fucking idiot! Damn you. Damn you, damn you, damn you," Hannah panted at him, slapping him about the head and shoulders.

"Hey, hey, stop it. I'm not going to get any health back for a while and potions won't work. Just…just start pulling me to the tree line over there and then go get the group. We'll figure out something."

Muttering hotly to herself, Hannah hooked him under the armpits and dragged him across the grass. Being unable to do anything beyond a perfect imitation of a sack of potatoes, he took inventory of the extent of the problems. Many of the status effects would clear up in eight hours, the worst being the curse at twenty-four hours. There was no flavor text to explain just what it was nor was there any indicator showing who had decided to bestow such a lovely gift on him.

Such a charmed life I lead. Keep making enemies, fool. Let's just hope it isn't a new god or goddess on top of the one Mr. Personality worships.

Dropping him roughly, Hannah growled at him. She slapped him in the back of the head once more for good measure. Before he could respond there was the sound of foliage and bushes being violently forced aside from deeper in the trees.

"Cloak yourself, Hannah. Get out of here. Leave me here and get to the group," Runner growled to her, the pain making him clench his teeth.

Runner's mind went immediately to the party he saw being assembled back in town the day previous by Mr. Personality. Had they been watching? Waiting? If they were, this was already over. Drawing his weapon free from its sheath, Runner clutched it in his hand and waited. It wouldn't be long now, they sounded close indeed.

Katarina cleared the brush, her posture and bearing ready for combat. She came to an abrupt halt as she found Runner and Hannah. Her black eyes, cold and fathomless, locked on his immediately and broke away almost as quickly. She began scanning the area for foes.

"It's OK, we're not under attack. We had to leap from the top of the wall to get out of the town. I'm afraid I didn't land as gracefully as Hanners did. I'm very glad to see you though, Kitten. So very glad. Come over here so I can hug you and kiss that beautiful Barbarian face of yours. Or at least try to. I'm not exactly in the best condition right now."

Katarina's eyes returned to him when he started talking. As he finished, she smirked and shook her head. What had been a pair of dark eyes that were as empty as a pit were now replaced with mild annoyance, humor, and relief.

"Idiot. Do you want me to carry you like a child? If you expect me to carry you in front guess again. Could ask Thana to rig up a harness out of my shield so you could ride like a wee one on my back," Katarina mercilessly teased him. Sheathing her blade, she then clipped her shield to the harness on her back. Once her hands were freed she came towards him. Leaning over to inspect him, she pulled at his shirt first and checked his arms and torso. Her red hair fell over her shoulder as she pulled at his pant legs to get a better look underneath.

"Not going anywhere. That's mangled. Let's see what Thana thinks," Katarina said with a bit of disgust. She flipped her hair back over her shoulder as she stood up.

Katarina and Hannah took up a conversation while Runner lay down and closed his eyes. Pain ran at a constant high and probably would for a while. His brain wouldn't produce much in the way of chemical relief to compensate for the pain. Perceived pain didn't get received the same way since it was fed through the medical pod.

Whatever Thana could accomplish to shorten the time he'd be thankful for, but it might simply be more of a matter of making him comfortable as they waited it out.

Pulling up the ship's system window, Runner loaded up the medical programs attached to his pod. Unfortunately, the only options available were the most basic ones: eject from pod, view vitals, and activate/deactivate dream sequencer. Two of those options would invariably end his life and the third would only show him what he already knew. Breathing rate up, blood pressure up, brain activity way up.

Well, against the baseline for suspended animation at least.

"Has anyone told you you're an idiot, Master Runner?" queried Thana. Runner decided it wasn't worth responding to since any answer he gave would only be dubbed incorrect.

"Bet his parents did."

"I think it's his fucking name sometimes. Idiot, Idiot Norwood."

"N-n-no. N-not yet, Hannah. But I'm sure it'll be soon-n. Good even-n-n-ning, Idiot."

Opening his eyes, Runner could only laugh. All three women had answered Thana's question for him. Thana was kneeling on the grass before him now, her hands folded in her lap.

"There you have it. I honestly didn't have a better plan for getting us out unseen within the time frame we needed."

"Indeed. As you're well aware I'm sure, you shattered your leg. There's nothing I can do to fix it, you'll just have to wait until it corrects naturally, since you can't drink a potion. Hannah mentioned you managed to get yourself cursed and that was on the list of prevented actions. I assume this is why you've yet to fix the damage yourself?"

Runner gritted his teeth and frowned at that. Thana merely watched with a quirked eyebrow, waiting for him to confirm it.

"Yes. I'm an idiot, the song of my people is the laughter of others. I get it. I screwed up and did so royally. I'll make amends to whoever it was I offended at the next town's temple. Curse itself will be long gone before then, but I'd hate to be on the negative side of a religious faction that isn't Mr. Personality's. Now, what can we do to get me out of here? We still need to keep moving. I'm almost positive Hanners has a tracker on her that we'll need to deal with eventually. I also saw Mr. Personality hiring a party and I can only imagine one thing he'd want to do with that."

"Our list of enemies grows by the hour. You have a real knack for this. And to answer your question, while you were in town I've been experimenting. I think this might be the perfect time for an out of the lab trial run. Nadine, could you please unwind some twine from your pack?"

Thana stood up, brushing non-existent grass from her clothes, and then held out her hand to the ground beside Runner. With a twist of her fingers, a rectangular block of ice appeared. It sat perhaps four inches in height. It was roughly as wide and tall as he was to boot. Using a dirk she pulled from her belt, Thana struck a chip out of the ice in two spots. Holding out her hand once more, she magically drilled two holes in those spots that went from the top to the ground on the other side.

"Would you help me loop the twine through these holes, Nadine? Katarina, would you mind dragging Idiot back to the campsite? Maybe the ice will cool him off and he'll be less quick to anger everybody within earshot. After that we can load him into the wagon and be on our way." Thana paused as she looped the coil of twine through the holes and back again. "Speaking of. Nadine negotiated the purchase of a wagon, a horse team, and some materials to be sold. You owe her the investment costs of course, but I'm sure she'll make a hefty profit on it to return back to you."

Nadine took the end of Thana's line and tied it into a simple knot, then clipped it into Katarina's shield harness. Thana had positioned herself at Runner's head and Hannah near his feet as Nadine worked with Katarina. Thana reached down and gripped him under the armpits and then lifted him as Hannah did the same for his feet. When they deposited him on the ice block, Runner said not a word of complaint.

"Many thanks. To all of you. Without all of you, I'd be lost."

Runner said nothing more after that and internalized his attention instead. Thana had just demonstrated the ability to create custom spells dependent on her need, rather than what was only available to her. They were now breaking the rules of the game world without his assistance.

Chapter 12 - Price of a Life -

A sliver of sky happened to be the extent of what Runner could see out the back of the wagon he sat in. Nadine had tied the two sides shut once he'd been settled in amongst the goods she planned on selling. Thana and Nadine were now at the helm, guiding and watching the road. Katarina and Hannah were walking perhaps twenty feet behind in a rear guard action. Hannah was stealthed just in case their pursuers managed to catch up to them without being noticed.

Unfortunately for Runner, he remained visible. The curse, and the broken leg, had yet to time out. He'd attempted to join the conversation Thana and Nadine were having once, but he'd been shushed into silence. Thana had been right of course. It was all too possible his voice would carry further than any of them would like. That left him with precious little to do to keep himself occupied. He'd considered cycling through his abilities to level them further, but at this point, he was pretty sure that it was a waste of time till he could get them upgraded at the trainers.

Amid the various crafting components Nadine had purchased there were a number of unassembled basic daggers. Wooden handles were in one crate, unsharpened blades in another, jars of epoxy in a third, and there was a barrel full of brass rods. He'd pulled one of each from their respective containers and now sat with them in his lap. Fitting the handle slabs to the tang of the dagger, he rotated it in his hands. Brass rods slid easily through the holes that ran along the length of the tang and the handles. Without adding the epoxy the handle would never stay put; the parts would slip out of each other.

Searching his inventory, he flipped to the section he'd dumped all of the crafting tools he'd been given to start with. Eventually he found a ball peen hammer and a painter's brush. They were pretty rudimentary and wouldn't be good for anything better than average. If he wanted to even consider crafting, he'd need to invest some money and time. One of which he had too much of and the other he would never have enough.

Setting the tools to one side Runner then picked up the blade once more. Casting *Fireblast* into the unmade weapon, he found it could indeed hold an enchantment like anything else. Like any other item he'd enchanted, it had a timer that would eventually expire.

I know there's a way to permanently Enchant an object. Maybe I'm just missing the according spell?

Grunting, he cast *Fireblast* three more times in rapid succession into the blade, letting his mind harden around the idea that the metal would take up the spell in its entirety. Become one with the spell, to the point that it'd not lose its bonus effect.

No change.

Rolling his eyes and laughing, Runner held the thing to his forehead and made a final attempt. This time he didn't finish the spell but visualized channeling it, forming the concept in his mind of a spell that would continue until complete or he ran out of mana. In that way Runner held himself still and doggedly pursued his goal. Such was his determination and concentration that it was startling when the spell ended, much like when he ran out of mana. Sighing, he gave up, resting his hands in his lap, the incomplete project rattling against his boot.

Runner opened his eyes, and his attention was drawn to a blinking indicator in his log.

You have developed the ability Spellbinding.
Unsharpened iron blade gains Minor Fireblast.

Shrugging his shoulders, he confirmed the system message by using *Analyze* on the blade. While it was roughly one third of the power of an Enchant, this would have no need to be refreshed. Tapping the item against his knee, he considered how far he'd be able to take this. Could he do the same to the epoxy? The handles? The brass pin? Could he separately enchant each smaller item to create a mixed bag of stat boosts upon completion? In the case of the epoxy, could he do the same for each base item that became the epoxy? How deep could he go?

Working his way through the list of components needed to forge one dagger, he gave each a different *Spellbinding*. Handles were given *Quick Fingers*, *Agile* for one pin and *Vitality* for the second, finally the epoxy was strengthened. Coating the tang liberally with the epoxy, he attached the handles and then slid the brass pins in to keep everything together. Using the ball peen hammer, Runner gave the pins two quick strikes to each side, enlarging the head of them so they'd be unable to slide back out.

Without considering just how insane this all was, Runner cast *Strengthen* on himself and then tried to crush the handles together between his palms. A bit of epoxy seeped out from the handles, but a little filing would spruce it up if it bothered him later.

You have developed the ability Item Assembly.
Unsharpened iron dagger is complete.

"Hm," Runner intelligently exclaimed. Giving the item a violent shake back and forth, he was unable to rattle anything loose. It also had a good feeling to it.

Casting an eye over the status window for the item, Runner rested his chin in his palm. Technically the item was unfinished and wouldn't list its final attributes until it was officially complete. Which meant this exercise had all been for naught unless he could put an edge on it.

Dragging the ball of his thumb over the blunt edge, he considered what he could do. Patience wasn't exactly a virtue of his. He flicked the iron with his forefinger, and it rang out softly in complaint. Admittedly, everything up to this point had worked and bolstered his confidence. What was one more stupid attempt? One more idiot plan?

What's the worst that could happen, nothing? Besides, Lady already modified spells. Why not I?

Wrapping his mind around the concept of distributed enchantment, he started to form an inkling of what he wanted to do. Focusing his mind on his hands, Runner held them up and began channeling *Stoneskin* into them. An empty mana bar later, he had an unexpected result. One he had not really expected. Actual success.

You have developed the ability to modify existing spells.

Overall mana cost will remain constant for spell modifications but there will be no increase in output.

Would you like to name this spell?

Yes

Stonehands

Name Accepted

Smirking, he touched his thumb to the back of his arm. His fingertip had the feel of coarse stone but it hadn't lost any of its elasticity.

I wonder what applications this could be used for Hand to Hand. Attack modifier for Monks? Interesting.

Pinching thumb and forefinger together, he drew them down along the length of the blade towards the tip. This was a world of imagination and intent. This wouldn't work in the real world, honestly it probably wouldn't work here either, but it was worth a try.

Pulling his fingers across the cold iron repeatedly, Runner could only hope. Hope that whatever system decided this stupidity should continue would grant him one more additional idiotic boon.

After stroking it for a time, and resisting the urge to call it his precious, there was a system chime.

You have developed the ability Weapon Sharpening.
Enchanted Iron Dagger is complete.
You have developed the ability to craft Items through Magical means.
Would you like to name this ability?
No

Once again Runner ran *Analyze* on the weapon and read over the status box for it.

"Well shit," he muttered under his breath.

Every magical addition he'd placed on one of the sub components was now listed as part of the complete weapon. Implications and building possibilities assailed him from every corner. From inscribing work on every single brick in a wall, enchanting every chain ring in chain mail, or even just over engineering a sword to the point that it had a large number of component parts. Testing would need to be done to determine how much would stack up. There should be an upper limit. Though it could also result in a cumulative gain.

The possibilities.

Opening the wiki with his left hand, he found his answer immediately. Enchanters couldn't fashion or create objects. Anyone who took a class that could create an item could not become an Enchanter. Sub-components wouldn't normally be spelled because once they were, they could only be used by the enchanter.

The scope of how badly he could exploit this sent his inner power gamer shrieking with delight into a delirious fit. Of course the best part was there were no GMs to stop him, no patches to correct it, and not a soul to tell him no.

Chortling, he amassed a pile of dagger parts to assemble and sharpen. There was nothing wrong with grinding. Grinding was rewarding. It was progress. It was validation in an action. It was gaming.

"I shall name it Arcane Smithing."

He tapped the window for the unnamed skill, and the request popped up again.

Would you like to name this ability?
Yes
Name of Ability
Arcane Smithing
Name Accepted.

He had more than enough time on his hands to experiment and little else to do. In the end, what else could he be doing right now? Grinning from ear to ear, Runner cracked his knuckles and set to work.

8:17 pm Sovereign Earth time
10/03/43

Runner spent the remainder of the trip in the wagon. Fashioning daggers, leveling up his new skill, and gleefully chortling with every skill up.

Wagon wheels crunched to a halt and startled Runner into attention. Listening intently, he could hear Katarina's low voice, the horses nickering, and the dull thump of boots as the driver dismounted.

"We're stopped for the night. You should be able to come out, Runner, Hannah. Goodness that was a long ride, Nadine, why don't we…" Thana's voice became harder to hear and unintelligible as she turned her attention to Nadine.

Glancing over to the other end of the wagon, he found Hannah sitting there, watching him. How long she'd been there he couldn't say, but clearly she'd snuck in at some point.

"Not very nice to spy. You could have told me you were watching," Runner grumped at her.

"Nah. Was fun to watch you work like a damned machine. There was this one time where you glued your hand to a blade. I don't think you even realized it until you couldn't get it to fit in the handle. I'm still curious how you managed to get it unstuck. It looked like it just came off."

With a shake of her head Hannah stood and made to exit. Patting him on the shoulder as she passed, she stepped over him and out the front of the wagon.

Rolling his eyes, Runner braced himself against a barrel and then stood up too. Taking a moment to admire the fully assembled and enchanted daggers lying in a box, he scratched at his chin. Flexing his fingers, Runner ran his thumb over his index finger, finding nothing but smooth skin and no trace of adhesive. He had no memory of the situation she described, though he really had lost himself in the work. There was something to be said for the joy of creation.

As he exited the wagon he spared a glance for the surrounding area. Nothing more than a small clearing, it was barely big enough to fit the wagon, horses, and themselves. No sooner had his boots hit the dirt than Runner was pacing a circle around the area and establishing the dimensions for his *Campsite* ability.

After completing the circuit around the exterior, he stood in the middle and designated the clearing. Without a noise or visual cue, the area turned into a safe zone, free of random monster encounters, and an area that would prevent PVP for a time.

He'd found a footnote in the wiki about the ability. The ability had gone through a protest and come out the other side unchanged. A vocal minority, those who wanted to be able to kill others in their sleep, was silenced by community managers. The game engineers had decided that a safe haven would be needed for people to rest and sleep. Original design had been built around the idea of entertainment and healing, and griefing would certainly impede that.

His inventory screen opened and out popped the called upon sleeping bag. He dropped it unceremoniously to the ground then prodded at it with the toe of his boot until the bag unrolled completely.

Today had been a very long day, and at this point he really just wanted to sleep. There really was no physical fatigue to being immersed in the game this long without a rest, but there was some serious mental burnout. With only a second or two spared to kick off his boots, Runner collapsed into his bedroll.

Confirming with a glance at his status screen he found that all the previous negative effects were gone. Smiling to himself he could only regret his actions.

He'd have to make amends with the local pantheon and then start working on his own plans. Getting caught off guard was one of the surest ways to get himself killed. All of the benefits he had were worthless if he couldn't anticipate a situation. Closing his mind to his thoughts, he studied the void that was left and forced himself to sleep.

1:59 am Sovereign Earth time
10/04/43

Deep in the night an alarm chirped in Runner's ear. Runner sat straight up in his bedroll as if a particle rifle had gone off rather than a beep. His left hand called up the warning screen even as he scanned the layout of their little shelter to see if he could get a sense for what was wrong.

Katarina slept near him with his old sword clutched in her hand in front of her, Thana resting not far from his other side. Hannah was on the other side of the fire pit, as was Nadine.

Looking to the message box, he read its contents.

Warning, your Campsite has been invaded.

Chewing at his lower lip, Runner contemplated this bit of information. An NPC would simply know what it was through their connection to the AI and skirt around it.

Well, excepting an awakened NPC.

All of those were here with him in the campsite. Any hostile or passive creature would avoid the entire situation for many of the same reasons as an NPC. Logical deduction left only a player as the possible solution.

Rifling through his immediate memories, he tried to find any relevance to this. The individual he'd seen just before hopping the wall back in the city burst into his mind. He'd been watching them without knowing they were there. The oddness of it and the ill at ease feeling he felt had shattered on the impact with the ground. Along with his bones. Beyond that, he had just simply forgotten about it.

Crawling free of his bedroll, Runner activated his *Stealth* and made his way to the edge of their little shelter. Working in a circle, he completed a circuit around the camp and began spiraling out in a search pattern. Moving slowly, carefully, cautiously, he remained vigilant to his surroundings as he skulked deeper and deeper into the woods.

With his body on high alert as he searched the trees, he fought against his mind wandering. Focusing his thoughts, he tried approaching the problem from a mental standpoint.

Following the logical progression from his earlier disturbing thoughts, this person had been able to spot him and Hannah on the wall despite their concealment. Which meant they had a way to track them, either with a mini-map icon, a quest marker, or an ability of some sort.

Wrangling his thoughts back on track, Runner could only conclude they were being tracked. As vague as that was, it could be listed as the one solid fact about it all. It was either him or Hannah they were able to track and the reasons were unknown.

Briefly considering the possibility that Mr. Personality could be out here, Runner eased up next to a tree trunk. Peering around, he checked his map to confirm the pattern he'd made. Mr. Personality would have attacked or challenged Runner immediately. He was a boastful little toad, not one to hide his intentions.

Fighting back a sigh, he found himself more at a loss than ever. This was one of those problems that you couldn't solve just by putting effort and time against it. A solution would only present itself when the opposing side attacked or made a mistake. Ever since they'd gotten off the boat at the dock their luck had become abysmal in every sense of the word.

Maybe getting my relations with the pantheon up should take a bit more precedence. Some divine assistance would be greatly appreciated right about now.

Shelving those thoughts, along with the entire problem of just who was out here in the woods looking for them, Runner started circling again.

In the end he found nothing in the area and gave up the chase when he found himself more than one hundred paces from the rest of the group.

Upon his return, he found Nadine was up, sitting close to the glowing embers of their campfire. It would seem she was waiting for him to return. With a gloomy turn of his lips Runner canceled his *Stealth* and approached slowly, giving her time to spot him.

"An-n-nd where were you? Sn-n-n-neaking off in the n-night without a word?" complained a dejected Nadine.

Sighing, Runner took a seat next to her and flipped the stick of wood that had been there into the coals.

"Yes, sneaking around in the night is accurate. Without a word was not intentional. I didn't realize you were up, I apologize. I received a warning that a snoop was poking around the campsite. Went to look, didn't find anything. I'm sure they'll come back. The question now is when, and how do I catch them when they do?"

"Oh. Oh, alright then-n. I wanted to t-t-talk to you about that m-man you murdered in the alley."

Raising his eyebrows at the change in topics, Runner glanced to her and then returned his gaze to the fire.

"Murder you say. Alright then. I'm afraid there's no couch or judge's bench, so we'll need to skip the counseling and sentencing for another time," quipped Runner.

"You will t-t-take this seriously or I will leave. Ton-n-night."

Unable to prevent the frown that appeared, he slowly nodded and did his best to keep a calm expression.

"My apologies. To whom do you refer, so we might begin this discussion correctly."

"The m-man in the alley."

"The alley. I assume you mean Scruffy then. The wharf rat who tried to kill me when I ran him down."

Nodding his head, Runner took a moment to collect his thoughts and left the conversation open for Nadine.

"Had you had already got-t-ten what you n-needed from him? Did he t-t-tell you what he knew, what he was doing, and killed him an-n-nyway? If so, why did you kill him then?"

"Because he was just a-" Runner froze mid-sentence and shook his head.

"An NPC. Th-that's it, isn't it? Just an N-N-NPC?" Nadine hissed at him, her hands balling into fists.

"Yes. Alright? Yes. I viewed him as just an NPC. He was a thug, would have sold our lives for nothing more than a few coins, and I ended him. What would you have me do? Let him go? Have him run off and tell everyone not just about Hanners and myself but possibly discovering you, Kitten, and Lady Death? No. That wasn't an option. I made a choice for the group's protection. That our protection was best paid for with his life, that he needed to become a casualty. If presented with the same option, I'd make the same choice again."

"But you don-n-n-n't know that. You don't know that he really t-t-t-truly saw or even-n knew. What if someone had seen you do it? What then? Kill them-m-m t-too? Someone like me m-m-maybe?"

"If that happened I'd have to evaluate the situation and make a choice then and there, but it wasn't you. It wasn't anything like you."

"I'm an N-NPC, just like him-m!" Nadine whispered energetically, gesturing at Runner angrily.

"No, no you're not! You're Awakened. You don't adhere to the normal rules anymore. You're closer to, well me really, than an NPC now."

"Oh? And who's t-t-to say he wasn't an Awakened t-too? Did you consider his ru-n-n-in with you changed him? Even for a m-m-moment?"

Runner looked away, staring a hole into the ground, and said nothing in return. It was too hard to admit it aloud, but he hadn't. Not even for a millisecond. He'd only seen a threat to his group and removed it.

"Would you do the sam-m-me thing if it had bee-n-n a man puppet? So quick to kill? As easily?"

Unable to respond, he instead considered her words.

What if it had been a player? Someone from my ship. Could I have killed them as easily as I had the NPC? Could I kill someone to protect what essentially was an Artificial Intelligence?

He couldn't answer that. It'd be his execution. Perhaps it'd be couched in a formal trial, but the lethal punishment would be waiting regardless if he took another's life. There'd be no way to hide it, as it would be listed very cleanly and succinctly in the other player's combat log.

"If it was to prot-t-tect me? Or Han-n-nnah? Or anyone from our group? A slightly differen-n-nt NPC but just an NPC? Would you let them do as they would with me or would you kill them-m-m t-too? Answer me, Run-n-ner," Nadine demanded of him.

Pressing his palm to his forehead, Runner took a shallow breath and exhaled it roughly.

"I don't know, Nadine. If I was to kill someone from the ship, I'd be tried and executed. It's that straightforward. It'd be very methodical and efficient, then everyone would be bogged down with paperwork, but I'd then be found guilty and executed. Very Sovereign, very military, very clean."

"Th-th-that's another thing. What happens t-to us when you free yourself? Do I just disappear? Does this whole world van-n-nish? Do you leave us here?"

Squeezing his eyes tightly together, Runner felt a grimace take over his face, twisting it into a mask.

"I don't know that either. I can promise you if we're freed I'll make sure the server, err, the world remains open and alive. That it doesn't just close down or vanish," Runner swore.

"And th-that's it, hm? You just go. Go back t-to whatever it is. Your ship in the sky," Nadine said angrily, her fingers digging into the cloth of her pants.

"I guess. I mean, that's the goal. What would have me do, Nadine? I could come back and visit. Frequently. I have a life out there though. I can't just abandon it. It'd be no different than me asking you to leave this world and stay in mine."

"I'd do it. Your world sounds far m-m-more fair than this one."

"Hah. In some ways yes, in others no. So many people would desire this world. To be here in this way, permanently. There's even fiction written about it."

"Then-n-n why not you? Why would you leave? Leave m-us? You've chan-n-nged us drastically, you said. Where's your respon-n—n-nsibility?"

Falling into silence, Runner didn't answer. Fire had engulfed the piece of wood he'd tossed in. It popped as the water vapor escaped rapidly.

"A fair point, Nadine. A fair point. Let me-let me think on it. All of it. Who knows, maybe you're right. Maybe whatever damaged the ship has doomed us and this place, this life, is all there is left. I'm tired, I'm sorry. We can take this up another time, but I'll consider all that you've said. I still feel I was right in killing the thug, but I'll think on it. I'll reflect on your words should the situation come up again and consider them honestly and earnestly."

"Promise? You're n-n-not saying it for m-my sake?"

"Never, Nadine. I respect your tenacity and would never insult you like that. Promise."

"Sleep well, Run-n-ner. Know that even though you killed him, I know you did it to protect us, and so I forgive you."

Nodding with a small sense of gratitude to her final words, Runner crawled over to his bed and tried to go back to sleep. Unfortunately, sleep eluded him until the early hours, and then it was fitful. Nadine's words haunted him. In the cold light of dawn Runner woke, feeling as if he'd slept not at all.

Chapter 13 - Soup Sandwich -

Early in the day Runner had managed to use up the entire store of parts. He'd been forced to cease in his skill grinding. It'd proved a suitable way to get his mind off his late night conversation with Nadine. In the end he'd managed to get Arcane Smithing up to fourteen. Only sixteen points shy of a forced roadblock by class promotion. Spellbinding ended up at eighteen from all the various parts that went into each item. Item Assembly had only risen to thirteen. With each iteration he'd been able to shave off the time required, boost the actual improvement for each Spellbinding, and lower the mana cost.

On their entry into the outskirts of the area there had been a dramatic rise in the number of players. Many of those they passed undoubtedly had little to no experience with video games. Their motions were hesitant, exploration limited, and their gaming sense as a whole was minimal. A handful approached either to inspect the curious party and their wagon or to ask questions about what lay outside of the city.

Katarina had placed herself at the foot of the driver's box after one man decided Thana could be purchased and wouldn't take no for an answer. It wasn't until Katarina drew her weapon that "No" was accepted as the final response.

Runner really wasn't surprised. From the memories he had on the subject, the entire unit was new-from the very ground up it had been formed from nothing. They'd cobbled together veterans from other postings, green recruits, and those freshly minted guilty convicts from their gloriously modern judicial system. Unfortunately, the majority was comprised of the latter two of those elements.

Greenies joining on promises of anything and everything to recruits and those sent by a judge with no say so on the matter. Little did anyone care what happened to those who had to serve with them. After the collapse of the global government a century ago and its reformation into the Sovereignty, the world government became a stratocracy. Military recruiting policies changed overnight and the ranks swelled.

It had been late afternoon by the time their wagon rolled into the city itself. Runner leaned up against the side of the wagon as he watched everyone go about their business.

A hand lightly smacked him in the back of the head. Shaking off his woolgathering, he looked up to see Katarina sauntering past him. Her smirk was plain as day as she addressed him over her shoulder.

"Keep an eye on the wagon and Nadine. I'm on escort for Thana while she makes arrangements for us," Katarina said loudly. She'd been taking delight in catching him off guard or getting little victories and one-ups on him.

"Oi, be sure to keep an eye out. I'm betting on a few grabby hands around here." Runner rubbed the back of his head. It hadn't caused any damage and might as well have been a poke, yet it still annoyed him.

Katarina's face flickered through an emotion he couldn't pinpoint before she smiled broadly at him. She ducked her head in acceptance and followed Thana into an inn. Pausing to consider the fact that he'd used a colloquialism, Runner tilted his head to the side. No one in the game would have had an experience with them since they were culture based. In fact, he'd been using them with the entirety of the group, yet everyone understood. There was no culture gap in language.

Interesting thought. Does that mean the linguistic database is being accessed? It would definitely ma-

Shaking his head, Runner deliberately forced his thoughts back to the task at hand. Using the mounting stirrup for the driver's box, Runner vaulted up. Pulling the front flap open a fraction, he peered in to find Nadine and Hannah going through the daggers he'd made. It was clear Hannah and Nadine were sorting them out by quality, after securing a few for themselves of course, and were now contemplating prices for the rest of them. Blowing his breath out in a grumpy sigh, Runner sat down, his hands resting on his knees.

What else what I going to do with them? Not like I need a collection of knives. Maybe step out of alleyways and hold open a coat with knifes sewn into the lining. "Wanna knife?"

Grimacing, it felt like his stomach turned over and twisted into itself. Runner opened up the ship's medical status log for himself. Under the Medical Assistance Required tab there was a flashing yellow dot. Beside that flashing dot was only one word, "Stress." Clearly the system agreed with his own self-diagnosis. Stress felt like the most mild of descriptions of for what he was dealing with. Waving a hand at the screen it flickered once and then went out.

His mind cataloged the people around him and he began watching them in earnest. It would be best if he sold the knives in truth. The ones to buy them would be players, and he'd have the most safety against them. Not to mention he could jack the price up. He'd let them have their fun though in sorting and planning. No harm, no foul.

Half of the little band would journey out into the town to begin the tedious process of leveling skills, classes, and abilities. Then they'd switch for the other half to complete the same tasks. Then they'd have to settle in and start grinding up quests, faction, and relations. All the while Hannah would be dodging guild rats and city guards. Then get out of Dodge with no one the wiser and start heading for the capital. She'd have to be in *Stealth* mode for nearly the entire duration of their trip. There wasn't any other option unfortunately.

It was in that span of thought that Runner came to notice a man. He wasn't anything out of the ordinary, looked like a normal enlistee for all intents and purposes. Dressed in simple brown leathers, he stood at an average height and normal build. It was hard to pick out details from this distance, but he'd write it off as brown hair and call it done. Leaning against a fountain, he was attempting to disguise his interest in Runner's wagon by pretending to manage windows by hand. His hands moved in front of him as if he were cataloging and shifting inventory, but it was just a little overexaggerated. Too much in the wrist. His hands didn't settle in the same spot with each "button press" either.

It was so blatantly suspicious now that Runner had noticed, that he had to force himself to keep his eyes moving past the man rather than let on that he'd been spotted. He was staring at the wagon all throughout this little show. Runner jumped to the conclusion that this was the same player who had seen them atop the wall.

This man had followed them all the way here. There was little doubt in Runner's mind. This fellow had to be the one who'd invaded their campsite to boot. It all added up.

Covering his mouth with his hand, he scratched at his cheek.

"Hanners, company. Take a peek," Runner muttered. Letting his hand drop, he twitched his nose as if he had only succeeded in making his nose itch now. After a second he reached up again and started scratching his nose. "Brown leathers, fountain, looking this way."

Sniffling, he let his hand drop down between his knees. Runner kept his vigil and watched everyone around and paid no extra attention to Creeper than he would anyone else. Creaking wagon axles signaled movement in the wagon. Runner could only surmise that she was doing as he'd instructed.

"I see him. Never seen him before." Her whispered words tickled his ear. "Has the look of any of the shit stains from your ship."

Runner grunted in the affirmative, then slowly turned himself around. With the intent to appear as if he were simply checking the contents of the wagon, he opened the flap and ducked his head inside while his right arm reached in to adjust something.

Runner found himself peering through Hannah's ghostly torso about an inch away from his face. On the other side, he could see Nadine, who was watching him in return. Addressing Nadine rather than Hannah, who was acting like a gauzy window, seemed like the best course of action.

"Pretty sure I saw him once before actually. When I was pretending to be a rock falling from the wall. He was watching us as if he could see us but not really. Best guess? One of us is a quest marker for him. Personally, my money is on Hanners, since she's an NPC as far as the game is concerned." Runner shrugged, smiling at Nadine.

"I see. Th-th-that makes sense. Han-n-nah?" Nadine asked.

Hannah made no immediate response. Runner couldn't tell if it was because of his position in relation to her own or if she was thinking over the situation in a deep manner. Runner idly moved his right arm as if he were shifting things around.

"I'd agree. You explained the rules about city guards already. Do they apply here? Can he do anything?"

"No. Nothing overtly in front of guards. That doesn't mean he wouldn't try something. I figure I go have a chat with him to see if I can discourage him. Not like he can do anything here but talk to me. If I'm lucky, the simple fact that we're aware of him may make him leery. Feel free to join me after I get his attention, Hanners, if you want a better look at him. Nadine, please keep out of sight. He may not have seen you, and I'd rather not give him more information if we don't have to." Runner grinned at her. Nadine nodded her agreement, to which Runner turned to the left and leapt down from the driver's box. Kneeling in the shadow of the wagon, he cast *Stealth*, then he made his way quickly over to the man.

While en route, Runner called up the in game camera and took a screenshot of the man's face, noted his name as Ted Henshaw, then logged the man's name into the personal notes section of his social panel. Dumping the picture off into an in game party memo, he attached Ted's full name and sent it to the rest of his group. They'd be able to access it the next time they stayed in an inn. As the window cleared, he sat down next to Ted, deactivated *Stealth*, and dropped his hand on Ted's shoulder.

"Afternoon, friend!" Runner cheerfully said, a touch too loudly.

Ted jumped, his head snapping around to lock onto Runner.

"You've been showing a great deal of interest in my wagon. I promise I'm not here to sell snake oil, elixirs of youth, or anything like that. Maybe some porn holomags on the side, especially if you're into the kinky stuff. Huge collection of solid midget work. We can work that out later. Maybe I can interest you in something?" Runner emphasized that he'd like the conversation to continue by tightening his grip on the man's shoulder. He knew he was pressing the boundaries of what would be considered acceptable by the game. He was betting that his demeanor and open question would allow him a little bit of wiggle room.

Little Teddy stared at him, saying nothing at all. Brown eyes that sat in a perfectly normal looking face stared at Runner in shock. Framed by boringly dull brown hair.

He could take first place in the most average contest.

Opting for the most direct route, Runner cleared his throat. "Ted, my name is Lieutenant Runner Norwood. What's your rank, soldier?"

"Specialist. Specialist Ted Henshaw."

"Sir."

"Sir, sorry sir."

"So, why the interest in my wagon? Or better yet, what's in my wagon? Maybe, someone in my wagon?"

There was a battle going on inside Ted's head. Following orders from superiors was instilled deeply in every citizen of the Sovereignty. On the other side lay whatever Ted needed. An item he valued so desperately the very idea of disobeying orders was being considered.

"Speak up, Specialist, lest I rule you in violation. I'd classify it as insubordination. I'd hate to turn you over to the courts when this is all over just because you wouldn't talk to me."

"Sir, I have a quest given to me by my class leader to neutralize a target, collect a trophy, and return. This would complete my quest, sir. The specialist feels his best chance to survive is by becoming as high level as possible, sir."

Reflecting on those words, Runner idly patted Teddy's shoulder. Nodding his head as if he agreed, he smiled.

"A fair response to the situation at hand. Good work, Specialist. I fear I must order you to cancel this quest. The NPC in question is working with me to resolve this mess. As you're probably aware, leveling up has a restorative effect on memories and dying turns you into a vegetable. I've hired the NPC in question to assist me in solving this situation. Allowing you to waste her would prove to be counterproductive."

"Sir, I can't quit the quest. I already tried once and it only offered me the same quest again. The only thing the class leader wants is the target, a snitch, dead, sir."

"In that case I'm afraid I can't help you with that. What I can do though is offer you to join me. I find those I've recruited for this to be expertly skilled for this mission. They carry themselves in such a way that I have no doubt as to success of the operation. Otherwise, I'm afraid you're at an impasse, Specialist. I can't have you fragging an asset. I'd be forced to hit you up for insubordination and dereliction, and we wouldn't want that. We clear, specialist? Clear as a fucking bell I hope? This'd be an awful thing to turn into a soup sandwich on you."

Runner patted the man on the shoulder and got to his feet. Dusting his hands off, he started walking back to the wagon. On the other side, out of sight of Ted, Hannah and Nadine had been joined by Katarina and Thana. Nodding his head to the party, he flicked his eyes to the inn and raised a brow to Thana.

Catching his look, she nodded her head at his mutely expressed question. Turning to Katarina and Nadine, she said something to them while motioning a hand to the crates of inventory. Smiling, she turned and addressed Runner directly.

"I anticipate you've provided us with another charming enemy? Perhaps another god or goddess? Oh! I know, the mayor maybe?" Thana inquired.

"Har har. No. Hopefully trying to get rid of one, honestly. I'll explain it in our room, where we might escape from prying ears and eyes. Suffice it to say, I'm hopeful that this is over before it began. We'll see."

Thana shook her head and fell in next to him. "Such a rogues' gallery, a truly worthwhile collection of villains arrayed against us already. Such an exciting life you lead."

Scoffing, Runner could only grin, thinking about what little he knew of his life. "I get the impression I was a bit of a hermit. An academic you could say. There was work and going home to be by myself."

"Ah, you clearly have such a way with people though. I never would have guessed."

"Shut up, counselor."

1:27 pm Sovereign Earth time
10/05/43

Runner was working his way through the long list of abilities. Pausing in his information perusal, Runner smiled at the appearance of another customer and completed the sale of a dagger without a single word being exchanged. Few had much to say after he'd paid the town criers to advertise his offering. Enchanted daggers at one gold coin each, to be purchased at the front gate.

Katarina had choked when he'd first stated the price. Runner was sure of himself but had a moment of panic when no one immediately came to see him. He'd almost changed his price and reduced it down to half a gold, but people started coming up to him in ones and twos. Then there was a line that stretched ten people deep.

Thinking about it in retrospect, he managed to figure out the little puzzle. It wasn't that his price was wrong, it was that most people probably had to go get money out of their bank account. A thief could technically pickpocket a portion of whatever money you had on you. To that end, the vast majority of players didn't take out more than they were willing to lose.

Letting his paranoia get the better of him, he'd decided he would need to take steps to protect their growing wealth. He probably looked like a gigantic piggy bank to would-be thieves. A guaranteed piggy bank.

Once they had a break in the line, he'd mentioned the concern to Katarina, who immediately took it as a challenge. Originally she had just been nearby, keeping him company. Now she'd put herself directly behind him with her back to the wall. Anyone who got close was awarded with a glare and her hand going to her sword. No one would be willing to cross such an imposing figure as level twenty-four Katarina.

As an added precaution Runner took to reverse pickpocketing Katarina. He'd checked the contents of her coin purse to make sure she had no gold on her before he began. He didn't want there to be any confusion afterwards. Preoccupied with everyone else, she'd failed to notice his hands on her person with each and every sale.

"Thank you, enjoy." Runner nodded his head at the latest customer with a smile. Without a word he reached backwards and passed his hand over Katarina's side, depositing yet another coin into her purse.

"Only a few left, Kitten. We'll be getting out of here soon enough. Been reading through the skills that will be available to you?" Runner asked her. He'd already put together a list of things for her to look at just in case she hadn't already put in the effort. Suggestions really, but it was always better to be prepared.

"Yes. Also been reading the forum. Thana showed me it," Katarina replied.

While the shortness of her answer was expected, the in game forum had been a surprise. Up to this very moment Runner hadn't considered that they'd be able to access it.

"I see, anything of interest?"

"Yes and no. The news that dying turns you into a, what was it you said, a vegetable? This information has spread. Everything else is about the officers being missing. They did a roll call and no one responded. You weren't on the list."

Runner scratched at his cheek while frowning. "I transferred in a day or two before departure. Quite possible that whatever list they have isn't updated. If that's true, then I really am the last officer. Did they escape? Are they the reason we're here?" Shaking his head, Runner felt like this new bit of information made things infinitely worse.

"That's what they're asking too. I would be wary of telling others you're an officer. Officers are becoming scapegoats."

"Yeah, not exactly uncommon. Quite a few of the enlisted don't actually want to be enlisted. Every officer is here by choice and has to enforce the soldiers' terms of service," Runner explained, lips pursed, his mind still working on the problem of the officers. Either they were behind it, dead, or not logged in.

"Strange, why would they enlist but not want to?"

"Oh. Many were forced in by the government as terms of their sentencing. They're shipped off world to remote destinations. Even if they desert, it's irrelevant since they're stranded. The number who actually try it is less than one percent," Runner supplied distractedly. He worked his way through the Ship Command console once more and checked the number of logged in users.

/Current active Users
499,928

Now that's concerning. Admittedly this was an enlisted boat but it still had officers aboard. They would have numbered at about seventy or so. Nearly the exact number missing.

Runner was shaken from his thoughts when another customer arrived, eager to pay for a weapon nearly guaranteed to give them a leg up. No sooner than the trade window closed, he reached backwards, his mind chewing at the problem.

"Where are you trying to put your hands exactly?" Katarina's question made him jump in his seat, his attempt to deposit the money halted and his thoughts forgotten.

Resting his hands on his knees, Runner leaned forward and shook his head. "Goodness, Kitten. If you must know, I've been putting the gold in your pouch. Figured that if they did get by you, even with how unlikely that might be, it'd be safer on your person than mine. They wouldn't expect it there." Runner stood upright and eyed the foot traffic. He had three more to sell and was quickly tiring of doing nothing in between.

"A laughable excuse to touch me."

"Hah, you wish, Kitten. In your wildest dreams maybe. Wait, serious question, do you dream?" Runner turned his head to look back at Katarina.

Her face was flushed, her stance was defensive, and her eyes were smoldering dangerously.

"I mean that in the nicest way possible. Do you dream? Do you see things while you're sleeping?"

"Now that you mention it. No. No, I don't. I know what a dream is before you ask and that I should have them, but no. I cannot remember experiencing one."

"Hm. Must be a limitation of the programing. Probably saves cycles in that regard because it doesn't regard you as active when in a sleep condition. So maybe not in your dreams, but your wildest Barbarian fantasies. Hot torrid affairs of carnage and groping hands covered in blood while-"

Their conversation was interrupted by another customer who held up three fingers and opened a trade window. Three gold were quickly deposited before Runner could say anything. Shrugging his shoulders, he threw the last three daggers into the trade window and accepted the trade. He didn't care what the man planned to do with three since you could only wield two at a time.

"And that's the end of my inventory. Have a nice day." Runner nodded his head at the young man before him.

Recognizing the face of one of Bullard's party members, Runner turned from the large doors and faced Katarina. He'd spotted him talking to a merchant at a distance of maybe fifty feet. Contemplating the exit strategies he had available to him, he found many would take him too close the very person he wanted to avoid.

"Hey, these are soulbound. I can't resell the third one. How'd you trade them?" the man demanded.

Blinking, Runner looked over his shoulder at the man and shook his head with a shrug.

"You must have equipped the third one on accident. Clearly you're wearing the other two. Sorry, mate. Better luck next time, no refunds, caveat emptor, and all that. See ya."

Grabbing Katarina by the hand, he hustled her into the gate and up into an alleyway. Dodging through a couple people, he made his way to the back of the side street. Entering an adjacent alley, he ducked into a doorway. Grabbing Katarina by the shoulders, he pushed her bodily up against a door. Wedging her into the frame, he pressed himself into her.

Digging his fingers into her hand to keep her quiet, he watched the mouth of the back street, fearful his would-be pursuer managed to spot them and track their movement. Waiting there, unwilling to risk anything for fear of discovery, he tried to keep himself perfectly still, hoping Katarina would understand without him speaking.

He could feel her watching him as he held her in place. He glanced at her face, thankful for her understated intelligence, then returned his gaze to the entrance.

After several minutes passed Runner took a few steps backwards, pulling Katarina by the hand with him as he went. Halfway down the alley, he glanced backwards and confirmed no one was behind them. No sooner had they'd made it to the next cross street than he guided them into the foot traffic. Keeping Katarina's hand firmly in his, he let himself get lost with the flow. As they neared the inn they were staying at, he eased himself and Katarina out of the street. Smoothly making their way through the inn, he pulled her along until they were in their shared room. Once the door was shut, he let her go and dropped into a chair.

Katarina stood in the center of the room, arms folded across her chest, regarding him with an unreadable expression.

"Yes, yes, I know, explanation needed. Uh, OK, so, remember when I said Mr. Personality was probably behind us? I saw one of his toadies out there. On top of that, we had that little ninny getting upset about soulbound items. If that conversation continued, he might have gotten attention we didn't want. Though it does raise an interesting question for me."

Runner paused and puffed out his cheeks in thought, swishing air from one side to the other. Finally he let it out and continued.

"Any item that is utilized, or equipped by a person, becomes soulbound to that person and cannot be resold or traded to someone else. It didn't list it as soulbound when I had it, and I didn't think anything of it. Here, an example. Look at your sword's information window, should say soulbound, yes?"

Frowning, Katarina reluctantly let her arms uncross and she went through the motions of pulling up a window. After a moment she looked up at him and nodded.

"OK, see, that sword cannot be given to anyone because of that. It'll fail in the trade with an error message of 'soulbound blah blah blah' or some such. I dunno."

Tapping her fingers at the invisible interface, Katarina made the offer to trade her sword to him. The same sword he'd given her at the start.

"See, it shouldn't work because it's soulbound," explained Runner as he accepted the trade. The window closed and the item appeared in his inventory.

Confused, he tapped the window for the unwanted sword. It was not listed as soulbound, but now that he looked, it didn't list any type of binding in any way, shape, or form. It wasn't bind on equip, no trade, no drop, nothing. It was bereft of ownership rules.

Unwilling to say anything further, Runner attempted to trade the sword back to her. After a brief delay to call up the window, she accepted the trade and the sword went back to her.

"I don't know. I have no idea why I can do that. Uhm. Maybe…" Runner thought hard on it before finally smacking his forehead with his palm. "It's because I'm a GM. I don't hold to ownership rules. It's so a GM can reset items, redistribute them if it was looted on accident, like in a raid or some such. Huh, it'll certainly come in handy."

"I want you to make a new sword for me. Use this one since you can take it back," Katarina suddenly commanded him. Once again the trade window was open with the sword spinning in the viewing box.

"Uh, not really sure what I can do with it. It's a fully made sword and it wasn't crafted."

Katarina said nothing, her eyes boring into him, almost pleading in a way.

"I'll see what I can do, alright, Kitten? No promises. Maybe I can melt it down and reuse the metal or break it apart. You just want me to use this to make a new one, right?"

"Yes. So long as you use that one I'll be satisfied. For now."

Sighing, he accepted the trade. It seemed his employees knew just how to manipulate him into getting what they wanted.

"Wait, what about Mr. Personality's minion, you don't care?"

"Not really. He didn't see us, and we now know he's here. We'll tell Thana."

Shrugging his shoulders, Runner couldn't really disagree. Grumbling about nothing in particular, he set the sword down on the table in front of him. They had time until the others got back.

Casting Stonehands on himself, Runner settled into his task of trying to disassemble the weapon. Worst case scenario he'd try to melt the damn thing.

Chapter 14 - Deception -

Dropping the coins into the window, Runner accepted the purchase agreement from the proprietor once again. He'd purchased time in the arena every day since they'd arrived. Up until this point it had been formation training, working through the seven classical maneuvers drilled into every officer cadet, and ability practice. He'd given himself a quick refresher through the officer library before they began.

With a light chime, the window closed and a timer began counting down from eight hours in the corner of his HUD. Looking back to his party, he smiled and held out his arm to the adjacent steel door.

"Right then. Let's go, everyone. I'd say five days of nothing but the basics is done. Maybe today we get in some actual combat experience and duel each other?"

Katarina, as indomitable as ever, marched through the doorway. Nadine and Hannah followed her out of the building interior while Thana hung back.

"Kat, after you get Nadine set up, would you go a round or two with me? I'm tired of being permanently stealthed. Need to fucking unwind."

"Mm, sure."

As the trio moved out, Runner turned to Thana. Looking askance at her, he could only assume she wanted to discuss something.

Motioning her to his side, Runner entered the arena.

"It's set to private just like every time before. No one can see us. I figure we're better safe than sorry at this point," he began, eying the vast and open arena. It was a standard affair: a few wooden walls scattered about to provide obstacles, sand, a circular enclosure, and seats for viewing if it was a public event. Confirming it to be empty, he looked to Thana. Catching her eyes with his own, he smiled and continued.

"No one knows I can utilize any class ability or skill. Nor does anyone know that you, forgive me here, as NPCs, have grown in level, learned all abilities available to your class, and are actively creating new ones. To be honest, the truth about how far you've all come may be more universe shattering than you realize. Most NPCs only have one or two, a boss might have three. But all? Never. We don't even know the extent of what you're all capable of. Better to fight each other and have wounded pride and ego than lose a comrade in the heat of battle. That and we still need to keep Hanners a secret. We've been

lucky. They haven't noticed her, seen her, or even realized
she's here. If we can keep that up, that'd be fantastic."

Thana caught her lower lip between her pointed teeth and
worried at it. She had all the precursors lined up for when she
was about to argue with him. Furrowing her brow, she crossed her
arms as she processed it. Runner let the subject drop to give
her a moment to think it over as they continued to walk towards
the center.

Near the center of the arena, Katarina was assisting Nadine
with the full crossbow they'd picked up for her. Up till this
point she'd been using a much smaller crossbow to get herself
comfortable with it. She was getting pretty acclimated to her
abilities and her confidence went up every day.

They had been able to move her into an Archer class with a
few coins. She'd technically been unclassed previously, so there
was no penalty and nothing to unlearn. A merchant with no combat
experience or abilities in any way. She'd become a level one
Archer that they baby stepped through all the starter quests to
get her some experience. It'd served a dual purpose, granting
everyone faction and reputation points and increasing Nadine's
level up rapidly.

"I acknowledge your point." Thana's voice pulled him back
into reality just as he was starting to space out. "I suppose in
fact it's completely valid. I've been reading through your
vessels forum though. At times it reads like the worst lot you'd
find at a seaside inn. Or a brothel, deep in the night. I don't
believe they'd find us as valuable as you claim."

"Yeah, not surprising there," agreed Runner. Katarina was
now squaring off against Hannah. Nadine was off by herself near
a wooden partition, firing her bolts into a circle marked in
chalk. "My government is a stratocracy, with a council of
generals at the top. The Sovereign Seven. Recruitment ain't what
it used to be."

"Yes, someone mentioned that." Thana put her back to him
and began walking. She then pulled her staff free from the catch
on her back and rested it on her shoulder. "Unrelated, yet
related, they've taken to capturing natives and using them as
one would a slave. Combat or otherwise. There are no reports of
any of them awakening, or at least any hints of it. That seems
to be a situation unique to you at this time," she explained.
There had been a slight emphasis in her voice around the word,
"native." It was a term she was attempting to introduce to
replace NPC.

Facing him, she held her staff out horizontally in front of
herself as a Dueling Challenge appeared on his screen. Nodding
his head in acceptance of her challenge, Runner drew his sword.
She'd also given him a mild rebuke for calling her an NPC. He'd

have to try hard to remember not to use that term. Tapping the Accept button on the Duel Request, he felt the jitters settle in. Flicking the tip of the sword with his fingers, he cast *Fireblast* into the metal and gave it a swing.

He really hadn't been looking forward to this, but he knew it was necessary. Truth be told, Runner wasn't confident in his own combat competency. Every single one of his companions would be stronger than him in their own sphere of power. Only through planning, building strategies, and abusing the hell out of the system, could he push his odds well into the ninety percentile range.

"As to me. What can I say, I'm a game changer, world bender, and rule breaker." Runner grinned, his free hand pulling up his preprogrammed hotbars for combat with a caster. His buttons changed over to new macros he had set up specifically for magical combat. They took the place of the old generalized ones for normal situations and hunting. Ticking down from thirty seconds, the Duel timer continued.

"I've noticed. Speaking of game changing. As your chancellor, I would ask that you take the time to re-craft everyone's gear as you did Katarina's weapon. Though I think most will not care if you use new materials. In fact, partner with Nadine when I'm finished with you. She can make the purchases and you get can to work on modifications. She's the bookkeeper of your household, after all."

Grunting, Runner could only shake his head. They'd discussed his newfound ability to trade any item on the way over. Katarina hadn't gone more than a minute before she began talking about her newly refashioned weapon. This of course brought the entire subject up. From leader to errand boy. It seemed somewhere along the line he'd given up full ownership of the group. *C'est la vie, I'd be a fool to not utilize people for their strengths.*

"Let's see who finishes who, hm? Care for a wager?"

"Ah, so confident? I shall shatter that self-conceited belief. Done. If I win, you start supplying me with beetles as you have the others. I admit I'm curious. That and those two treat it like currency, so it would be handy to have."

"Oh ho? Been losing a bit too often lately? How's teaching Kitten manners by the way? Hah. Right then. Granted. If I win, you take my cooking duties over for an entire week. Nadine can't step in for you either. You've managed to wheedle and coerce the others into cooking for you so far. I'm curious to see if there's a reason."

Grimly pressing her lips together, Thana nodded, then launched a flurry of foot-long rods of ice at him just as the timer concluded. Caught off guard, Runner stumbled to one side,

dodging part of the attack but nowhere near even half of it.
Planting his right foot, he rolled to the left as he cast
Distract to her left side. Activating *Stealth* in midroll, he
immediately turned back the way he just came from and hunkered
down low.

Thana whipped her head around to where he would have been
if he'd continued running and let loose a cone of frost-touched
wind from the tip of her staff. Using this chance, Runner came
at her with all the speed he could throw on. Closing the
distance rapidly, he was able sink his sword into her side.
Ripping it free, he attempted to chain it together with a *Throat
Strike* with his open left hand. He met only air as Thana froze
the ground beneath them and leapt backwards. Runner was locked
in position, his boots covered in thick ice. Not willing to wait
the few seconds it'd take for the *Throat Strike* effect to end,
he cast *Fireblast* at the ice. After a pause the ice shattered
and cracked apart under the heat.

Smiling in victory, Runner looked up to reengage Thana only
to find a large sheet of discolored ice blocking his view.
Unsure of why she'd dropped an *Ice Wall* spell right there, he
could only assume she was playing for time. Giving her that
would not be to his benefit.

Sprinting towards the cloudy six-foot wall, he went to
clamber over it, only to find it was perhaps an inch thick at
best. Perched atop it like a cat on a rickety fence, he felt
like a fool. Unbalanced, the ice fell forward and shattered,
Runner tumbling from the debris. His originally green health bar
turned yellow, signifying Runner had lost fifty percent of his
health points in total.

Berating himself for not thinking it through, he spun in a
quick circle to reacquire his target. Having blinked thirty feet
away, Thana was already working through another spell, her staff
pointed straight at him. He drew a throwing knife from his belt
and tossed it in an underhand throw, launching a *Fireblast*
through his sword a beat later.

Both connected and broke her concentration long enough to
interrupt her spell altogether. Her hit points dipped to thirty
percent and the health bar became an ugly orange.

Wrapping both hands around the hilt of his blade, he
pointed it to her and channeled *Wave of Heat* at her. It was one
of the many abilities he'd picked up at the trainer's and would
serve as a way to keep her moving while he tried to close on her
again. Rather than taking the expected course, through his own
spell, he ran down the left of it. Straight into another wall of
ice.

Bouncing off it, he was momentarily stunned before he could
reorient himself. Making a snap decision, he dove into his own

dissipating Fire spell. It was the right choice, as Thana let loose a torrent of Ice Rods through the opposite side of the wall, shattering it and sending ice chips along with the rods flying.

He'd put a little distance between him and the wall but even then he still took damage as the whole thing exploded. Taking the opportunity for what it was, he cast *Silence*, a low-level Healer spell, at her to prevent her from blinking away and charged her.

His health was in the red, just as hers was after the heat wave.

Lunging forward with her staff, Thana caught Runner completely unaware as he came in range. The wooden head to her staff drove into his gut even as he swung his sword around from the side to connect with her arm. A low note was heard between them and his screen flashed a single word, "Victory."

His health was blinking at three percent, hers at one percent.

"Damn me, my Lady, that was incredibly well fought. You had some moves I wasn't expecting there," Runner expressed with a smile, genuinely surprised.

Glowering up at him through her eyelashes, she thumped the butt of her stave into the dirt.

"Clearly it wasn't enough. I hadn't expected the *Silence*. I should have," she growled out.

"Hey, for someone who has very little actual combat experience, and a whole lot of book learning, that was impressive. Beyond impressive. If I'd hung around that wall for another second rather than ducking into my own spell, I'd be the one who lost. In fact, I'm so impressed, I'll honor the bet even though you lost. Still gotta cook, though, when my turn comes."

Snorting, she gave her head a light shake, her dark hair fluttering back and forth.

"Acceptable. I appreciate the graciousness of your victory. Clearly you had some expectations going into this though. Mind sharing what you strategized for those two? Maybe I can benefit from your planning."

Thana gestured to Katarina and Hannah, changing the subject. She was obviously sore that she'd lost and had been expecting to win. To be fair, she came darn right close. Closer than she had any right to be for how little experience she had in fighting thinking creatures.

Allowing the change in subject, he sheathed his sword and leisurely withdrew two beetles from his inventory. He handed one over to Thana, then ate his own while gesturing at Hannah with his left hand.

"For her, the exact approach you took with me. Assume she'll sneak and immediately position behind me. I really only have to withstand a *Backstab* once and keep eyes on her. She can't *Stealth* if I can see her, after all. She might use *Distract* in the exact way I did on you, but at that point I'd use AOE since she'd be coming straight for me. Figure if I get a little distance I'd throw spells till she reengages rather than go toe-to-toe. She'd try to out skirmish me, attack, retreat, dodge. Her health isn't built for long drawn-out fights. Take bites out of that health bar whenever I was able to. Utilize spells that don't allow for dodging when she tries to withdraw to make sure I come out ahead in trades. Wash, rinse, repeat till she drops. She's a Rogue after all, her tools are powerful but limited. To win she has to engage. She'd tear me apart if I tried to fight directly on her own merits."

Being able to own the fact that Hanna was the superior Rogue didn't hurt, he'd accepted it a long time ago. With a shrug he watched the two combatants in the center. Katarina was chasing Hannah around doggedly, pushing the Rogue back. Over and over Hannah danced away only to reengage for a second and slip out again. They were both near the fifty percent mark for health. The fight had ground to a halt and looked more like a dance. It'd probably come down to if Katarina could land a strike on Hannah more often than Hannah could land a critical.

Thana nodded at his side, a hand held in front of her mouth as she ate. When she finished with the bug, she glanced up at him.

"That was pretty much exactly as Nadine described."

Runner pulled out another beetle and handed it over to her. Lifting his hand again, he indicated Katarina.

"For Katarina, I dunno. I think she'd beat me to a pulp regardless of what I did. I'd try to mitigate her damage, keep her at bay, work her down. I'd end up having to heal myself. That almost feels like cheating, but there it is. She's built to take punishment and deal out a normal amount of damage. Nothing to write home about, but it adds up. Now include the fact that she takes a real delight in beating me. She's motivated to win. If I do beat her, she'll just get that much more worked up over the next contest. Win or lose, I lose."

Thana's eyes crinkled up in a hidden smile, her mouth behind her hand as she ate the second beetle. Letting her hand drop, she bowed her head in acknowledgment.

"They were right about the second beetle taking on an almost acquired flavor. As to your thoughts, astute observations. I came to a nearly similar conclusion. I plan on challenging Katarina next. Go speak to Nadine about supplying the party. I think we'll all benefit from your work."

Thana dismissed him, waving her petite hand at him she started walking to Katarina and Hannah.

With a smile he let out a sigh. He could only agree since she was right. Watching her depart, he found himself watching her hips a touch too closely. Shaking his head before he could let that wild thought continue, he made his way over to Nadine, who was systematically working her way through her supply of crossbow bolts.

Glancing up from her work at his approach, Nadine finished loading a bolt. Holding the butt to her shoulder, she let the quarrel fly as soon as she'd lined up her target. With a solid thunk, it embedded itself within an inner circle, but not quite the bullseye. Definitely a better shot than when she'd first started.

"Certainly doing great with that new crossbow. Have you been able to see any skill increases in the log?"

That aspect of their world had been harder to explain than he cared to remember. The idea that their every action was chronicled, logged to a social window. Their very death even, only to be ultimately deleted.

"Yes. Th-th-though not as m-much as I'd wish. It also feels strange t-to be here practicing when-n we know th-they're out there searching for us. Shouldn't we be m-m-m-making a plan?" she hesitantly replied, lowering the crossbow.

Shrugging his shoulders, he came to a stop next to her, regarding the target ring.

"Any gain is better than where you were, which means all gains are good. Therefore, good work. As to a plan, I've already put together some thoughts and a rough outline. We'll see what we can do to get it moving this afternoon," Runner admitted, tilting his head to look at her.

Nodding her head in acceptance, she shifted her weight around. Deftly she clipped the cranequin into the belt hook on her left side. Drawing her long sword fluidly in her left hand, she held it out in front of her.

"Would you be willing t-to help me with t-this? Swinging at the dumm-m-my doesn't count-t. You're a dum-my t-too, but it'd count-t."

He laughed deeply as he put his hands on his hips. Taking the time to truly enjoy that terrible joke, he laughed heartily. Finally he drew his sword and gave it a little waggle at her.

"As you will. After fencing practice, I need you to come with me to go shopping. I wasn't kidding about seeing what we could do this afternoon. Things to do and all. Seize the fish, tempus flytrap, time waits for nomads."

Smiling brightly, Nadine swung her sword down at his head without another word, having apparently decided his jokes would end if she removed his head.

"Hey, hey, calm down now, one bad pun deserves another."

They spent half an hour going back and forth, working on her form and ability activations. Though half of combat was automated, one could really eke out the last bits of power and technique by working at it. Another half an hour flew by on reading up on the skills she'd be receiving as she continued to level up and discussing them and how they'd be used in conjunction with her current abilities.

Runner really wasn't sure where the rules between NPCs and players lay anymore. They were significantly blurred now and crisscrossed haphazardly.

If practice gave her an insight on how to use the skills, though, it'd be worth it. As was usually the case with Nadine, she dedicated herself to the lesson. That brilliant and honest disposition helped the cause as she took everything he said seriously and without ill intent.

He'd meant to apologize to Hannah, Katarina, and Thana for having to postpone their duels, but they were still holding mock combats between themselves. Instead, he left them as they were and departed without a word, Nadine in tow. He figured Thana would be able to figure it out and thought no more of it.

Exiting the arena, they strolled out into the sunshine. Directly across in an alley, Runner caught a flash of movement. Turning to look down the street towards the merchant district, another shimmer of movement dart down a side alley.

"Damn, I'm not sure who, but we've got a tail. Looks like we'll be out for a bit longer than I anticipated and that we'll need to be leaving sooner than my original plans."

"I see. N-n-nothing we can-n do about it. Let's enjoy our walk at least."

"Nadine, never change please," Runner said, holding out his arm to her.

Linking her arm in his, she started walking, giving him no chance to argue.

Taking their time, they made a route to all the merchants. With no pressing need or a crunch for time, they did their best to draw as little attention to themselves as possible while selling off the rest of the goods they'd earned through hunting and questing.

They offloaded the last item, and the merchant handed the payment to Nadine. While Nadine thanked the shopkeeper, Runner left the building and stood beside the roadway in thought. They needed to figure out how to lose their tail and plan for escape.

He had a rudimentary plan to hopefully get out of the city without being noticed. Worst case, they could get a few days' head start. Maybe. If they could just break contact, lose their tail, remove themselves from the obvious places, and clear some ground, it'd be ideal. They could probably lose everyone. Hopefully whoever tailed them now had just as little skill at tracking.

"T-t-that's the last of it. Easy m-m-money," Nadine said proudly, standing beside him.

Doing his best snooty noble impersonation, he looked down his nose at Nadine, lidding his eyes.

"Bookkeeper, how much money do I have?" He let the joke go as she arched a brow at him. "No, no, sorry. In all seriousness, I have no idea what our actual finances are," Runner admitted. Stepping into the road, he oriented himself towards the wagon shop at the other end of the merchant quarter.

"Very well. With t-t-the sales of the daggers an-nd offloading t-the rest, we're sitting at n-nearly one hundred gold."

Runner couldn't help but be impressed by that sum. It was already enough to purchase two mounts with enough left over to properly train up a crafting skill. Or maybe buy a cheap house.

"Solid work, Nadine. You're a real wizard with money. Please invest it all and conjure up more of that sexy merchant lady money magic. The wagon we can keep, so plan around that being in the equation. Set aside some money to purchase everyone a full set of armor up to their current level, as well as weaponry. Minus Kitten I suppose. Buy me sword parts for her instead. If you can find things that have multiple components for everyone else, the better. The more I can take it apart, the better I can make it. So if you find a sword with fractionally less damage but ten more parts, that'd be ideal."

"Are you sure? T-t-that's a lot of m-money to spend, especially the arm-m-mor."

"Money can be replaced, you can't. There is only one Nadine. Speaking of, purchase a set of health potions for everyone, at least six apiece."

Nadine furrowed her brow at his growing list but nodded her head. The little merchant was probably already calculating everything down to the last copper.

"Our goal is to reach the border town of Crivel, everyone alive and accounted for. Best to work that route into everything else as well. I've been hearing noise that there's an event going on up there, so expect change in pricing."

"Food. Word is they're st-t-ocking up on food," Nadine supplied after a pause.

"Odd. Only reason people would stock foodstuffs is famine, war, or plague. Maybe it isn't the time to head up that way. We could take a transport to the main continent, but then we'd be under level for the area, which is a whole different can of worms." Scratching at his cheek, Runner turned and entered into the vehicle shop.

Tossing an apathetic wave at the salesman, Runner looked to Nadine. "I know the wagon is back at the inn, but sell the wagon contract to him. Rent one at the same time for twenty-four hours-it's all we'll need it for. Any purchases you make for our trip that're too heavy to carry around in your inventory regularly, you'll need to come back and sell to him as well."

Disallowing the inevitable questions Nadine would ask, Runner stepped back outside.

Studying his map, he traced a finger up along the road to Crivel. It rested nearly dead center on the border with the northern provinces of the large island they were on. If what Nadine said was true, it would seem the northern neighbors were more than likely on the move. Moving his attention further north, he found the Commonwealth of the Sunless and the Barbarian tribes. Both were a loose collection of provinces ruled by noble families and their retainers in a feudal society that rolled up to one leader.

Grunting, he closed his map and mentally shrugged. It was a risk, but it still presented them with the fastest method of possibly ending this whole ordeal. It had been over a month since he'd entered the game. Ten thousand dead crewmates rested on his shoulders. Every minute longer here put them at risk of losing more comrades-in-arms. That they were probably already in Earth space was also a very real possibility. Freeing themselves from the game would put them home instead of on a far-off colony planet. It was tantalizing.

Trying to get this done while being ten levels under the recommended bracket is a death sentence. The mainland is out.

Confirming his plan of action with that thought, he set a waypoint marker for Crivel. Those who made the game had prided themselves on making it real world relevant as far as distances and travel time went. At the moment Runner cursed them rather than share in their marvel of realism and level of immersion. It would take them the better part of four weeks to get there by foot and wagon. Traveling in this manner wasn't exactly ideal, but it would provide them the greatest opportunity to lose their hunters.

Nadine stepped in front of him, glaring at him. "Care t-t-to explain that n-now? You t-t-t-told me to plan around it and m-m-made me sell m-m-my wagon."

"Certainly. First, there's a buyback function that lasts for twenty-four hours. Everything you sell to the vehicle shop you can buy back at no extra cost, so long as it's done within twenty-four hours. Second, typically, wagons and other vehicles are not left out when they're not in use or empty. They're stored in their inventory. Strange to store a wagon like that, but there it is. It's the way video games work really."

Closing the map, he smiled at her and started back towards the heart of the commodities market.

"We'll simply set up the rented wagon in the same spot as where the original was. We've already been in town for, what, a week? They'll have resorted to watching the wagon at night by this point to determine if we're leaving or still there. Well, probably. No guarantee on that, but familiarity breeds contempt. In other words, the lack of subterfuge on our part has created a lack of awareness on their part."

Nadine nodded her head after a flash of understanding. "I un-n-nderstand. Won't they notice the wagon is missing right now?"

"Possible, but I doubt it. They're all watching us or the arena right now. Could be wrong, but I doubt it. I figure the wagon switch will either lose them entirely or set them into a panic when the rental vanishes tomorrow. They'll assume we just took it out when they weren't looking and start checking the gates. Exiting from the western gate, the same one we came in from, we circle around the town to the north. At the same time, I purchased a ticket for a wagon caravan to the south. The time just happens to coincide with our departure." Runner paused to check the in game clock. "Five minutes after the wagon rental goes poof, to be exact. With a bit of luck, they'll assume we went out with that caravan. Considering it cost nearly nothing to volunteer to be part of a wagon caravan, we'll be out nothing."

"But t-t-the Naturals who sold the t-tickets aren't awake. They're n-n-normal. T-they wouldn't know an-nything," Nadine countered.

"No guarantee what our pursuers will or won't do. I'd rather pay the minuscule fee on the off chance it works out, rather than regret that I didn't. I also posted a bulletin in the jobs board asking for a guide to escort us to the southern coastal port for the portion of the trip that extends beyond the caravan destination."

"T-t-that really seems like too m-much."

"Meh. It also cost very little. I'd rather crush it with my wallet. Besides, if they work all that much harder at it, they'll be more likely to trust it. Anything too easily obtained and they'll disbelieve it."

Nadine shook her head slowly, clearly not sold on the whole idea.

"Seriously, what's the worst that happens? I lose a few coins? It'll be fine," Runner idly promised. Waving his arm in front of him at the market ahead, he continued. "Now let's make those purchases we talked about. I'd rather not make Lady Death angrier than I have to. Besides, it's been a great day for a walk."

Chapter 15 - Sardine Wagon -

Nadine paused long enough to dump all of the purchases they made, including her current gear, in the corner on her way to her bed. Even before the sound of clattering gear could dissipate, Nadine was collapsing into the sheets with nothing but her smallclothes on.

Runner went over to the mess and started sorting it out based on who the item would go to.

With a quiet chirp of surprise, he was delighted to find the sword they'd purchased pointed north. Dropping his own short swords to test this, he found they all indeed pointed north. It was a small thing but amusing nonetheless. At this point Runner would take any amusement he could muster up.

He picked out Nadine's crossbow and decided to start there since it was current gear and would be used regardless of him upgrading it or not. In short order he had dismantled and laid it out on the dining table like a grizzly autopsy, planning the enchantments in his head to min-max the hell out of her weapon. Idly he rubbed his thumb against the wood grain of the stock.

It was strange. It felt like wood, smelled like it, and probably tasted like it too. Holding it up to his nose, he gave it a sniff and briefly considered the strange thought of putting his teeth on it. He couldn't trust his senses anymore and a memory could only tell him that, yes, this clearly was wood. Was it actually wood, then? Did it no longer theoretically exist but actually did exist? At least to him?

Rapidly backing up from this line of speculation, he settled his mind. Shaking his head as if to fling loose any lingering thoughts, he bit his lip and started working.

Katarina pushed the door open and stepped into the inn room. Close behind her followed Thana and Hannah. Runner's attention was diverted by the sudden entrance. Smiling at her, he nodded his head before resuming his work on a bronze barbute.

Reattaching the interior webbing to the hooks, he flipped it over to the other side. Sliding the visor back into place with a pop, he rotated it around to secure the other side. The item was complete and a window popped up. Accessing the information that was presented to him he smiled.

Item	Bronze Barbute
Effects-	
None:	
Functions-	
Night Sight:	Provides wearer with Night Sight ability on usage.
Attributes-	
Constitution:	18

He'd made this helmet in particular for Katarina. It'd been put together with the goal of mitigation and bolstering her health. The visor portion he had placed *Night Sight* on. As a Barbarian, she had just as bad of night vision as he did.

It wasn't perfect, of course-it made everything black and white, but it did a fair job of providing nearly the same visibility as a normal day. Checking it one more time for anything loose or out of place, he set it down on the table. A second helmet, minus the visor, that he had made for himself rested beside it, with the rest of the table filled with various selections of armor and Nadine's crossbow.

Katarina came over to him and leaned over him. She put her left hand on his shoulder and with her right she accessed the bronze helmet.

"Oh," Katarina whispered. "Good helmet."

A mirthful chuckle escapes his lips at her clipped compliment. With a firm pat to her hand on his shoulder, he looked up at her.

"Can't let anyone mar that pretty face of yours, Kitten. Be sure to flip the visor down to actually use that night vision enchantment. Anything with more metal than leather on the table is yours. I'll try to get to your shield while on the road if possible," he apologized. Standing, he picked up his own bronze barbute and pushed it into his open equipment screen. After snagging a thick robe with an attachable mantle from the table, he made his way over to Thana.

"My Lady Death, I'm afraid you're going to need to wait till the road as well for your staff to be repurposed. Hannah, your swords too. I'll do my best to get them all up to snuff before we get to Crivel. There really wasn't much in the way of inventory in this rink-a-dink little town. Nadine wore herself out getting the best deals for us."

With an apologetic smirk, he handed the reinforced cloth to Thana. It'd taken some doing getting the boiled leather strips to sit correctly inside of the cloth, but the end result had upped its armor and looked acceptable. Nothing a few level ups in tailoring and a few wasted materials hadn't spruced up.

After Thana took the armor from his hands, he sat on the edge of the bed Nadine was sleeping in. Using his elbow, he lightly nudged Nadine's feet and he felt her stirring from her slumber. Throwing out a lazy hand gesture to the table, he continued.

"Sort through the gear, find out what works for you, what doesn't. Make sure you get your cranequin, Nadine. We'll sell the rest," Runner lied. Fear of betraying that deception kept his lips pressed tightly together.

He'd prepared each individual piece of armor for them in mind and doubted if anything would be left over. He wasn't keen on pigeonholing people, but he truly believed he knew what would emphasize their kits the best. If they didn't want to use it, so be it.

"If you replace something, just trade it to me later since you can't technically drop it. I'll pass it over to our little merchant queen. We'll be leaving tonight. Nadine and I set up the prep work this afternoon. With a bit of luck, we should be able to leave town without anyone the wiser. We did pick up a tail by the way."

That got their attention, and each looked to him to elaborate.

"I don't know anything beyond that we have a tail. I didn't want them to figure out I'd spotted them. For the plan, it's a fairly straightforward one really. Make our way out of the inn under cover of *Stealth*, head west, pick up our supplies, then exit through the harbor gate, loop around to the north, and follow the North Road north. We'll hit a few towns and villages on our way, buy, sell, trade, the normal shtick."

Hannah snorted as she tucked a pair of boiled leather gloves into her inventory.

"Nothing is that easy with your stupid ass. I'm sure you'll fuck something up or piss off someone or something on our way. A flock of chickens maybe? Scurry of squirrels? Luck is a fickle bitch and thinks you need all the bad luck she can spare like a spurned ex. When she isn't trying to get back with you."

Runner couldn't really argue with Hannah's logic as it had proven accurate up to this point.

"Is this the part where I mention Crivel is going to be under siege from the Sunless empire? Cause yeah, if we don't get there fast enough, the city will get shut tighter than a quartermaster's medical supply depot."

Letting out a bark of laughter, Katarina shook her head. She now sat in the chair he'd vacated at the table. Her fingers were tightening the straps to her new bronze gorget and pauldrons, adjusting the length to sit right on her shoulders and collarbone. Since she only had to pull off her leather armor to equip the new bronze set, she hadn't needed privacy to change.

"Never easy. Always a problem with you," Katarina muttered. Slapping a buckle down hard enough that the metal pinged, she looked up at him with a challenging smile.

"Yeah. Well, you all knew this wasn't going to be pleasant. I wouldn't begrudge any of you if you backed out now that you know the plan."

Runner let that sink in for a minute. Silence spread throughout the room and hung over the conversation like a brewing storm cloud. Everyone stared at him from their various positions throughout the room.

"Katarina, slap him for me? I'm unfortunately indisposed; otherwise, his head would be spinning," Thana called over. She was behind the wooden screen they'd put up as a dressing area previously. She was fastidious about changing regardless of the circumstances.

"Whoa there, Kitten," Runner pleaded, holding up his hands to Katarina. "Sorry. I admit, it sounds stupid but it still needed to be said," admitted Runner. Despite the fact that he was being sincere, Nadine kicked him repeatedly in the back.

"Alright, alright! For fuck's sake already." Grumbling to himself, Runner hurriedly got up and stood near the door. Motioning to an end table that held a collection of bottles, he said, "Everyone be sure to take five of those flasks. I managed to instill a very low-grade *Stealth* into them. It isn't exactly master alchemy, but it'll work. Nor will it get anywhere close to Hannah's level of ability with *Stealth*, but it should get everyone out the door without being immediately spotted. I figure we might get twenty minutes out of each of them, more than enough to do most of the work when we need to *Stealth*. First things first of course, exit the inn, get in the alley next to it."

"Another alley. Too many alleys with you," said Katarina. Connecting the breastplate into the gorget, she let go to test the way it hung. Apparently it was sufficient as she started in on the greaves. Runner wasn't sure why she didn't just equip it through her character screen, but he supposed that maybe it felt more correct for a Natural to do it this way.

"I'll get out there and take a look around. See if I can mark these whoresons for the rest of you."

Hannah crossed the room and left them all there without waiting for a response. With a shake of his head, he clapped his hands together and looked to the rest of his party.

"Right. I'd say let's get everything ready to go then."

Katarina, Nadine, and Thana were lined up behind him. They'd halted at the top of the stairs, out of sight of the common room. Nearly all of the customers who were players had long gone to sleep. A bonus to experience for sleeping a majority of the night was hard to resist. The fact that it was a percentage boost to all experience gained, regardless of source, made it nearly a daily quest.

Runner activated *Stealth* and moved down to the first floor, the bar. Slipping between customers, Runner did his best to give them enough space to not fully alert them. He paid the detection warning indicators no mind. Even if every patron in the place was suspicious of his presence, they wouldn't do anything unless he was fully revealed. Trusting in his group, he didn't look back, but instead pressed on, turning immediately to the right as he exited the building.

There at the corner of the street crouched Hannah. She waved him over to her position. If her name wasn't floating above her head, he wouldn't have spotted her that easily.

Glory be to the Sovereign Seven for nameplates.

Sparing a glance down the roadway as he moved, he couldn't detect anyone. He passed Hannah, not stopping until he'd entered the alley proper.

In short order Thana, Nadine, and Katarina joined him, Hannah coming up last.

"Anything?" Runner inquired.

Hannah shook her head slowly. "Not a thing. I've been searching for two hours and I haven't found anything. If they're watching, they fell asleep on the job. Or maybe they're all extremely well fucking hidden."

"Fantastic. I'll bet on sleeping and pray they're not that proficient. Time to bug out."

Turning deeper into the alley, Runner started off at a slow trot. Using his left hand, he called up the spell *Night Sight* and cast it upon himself. Runner was momentarily distracted when he realized he'd used his hand to cast something that only needed a mental command. With an imperceptible grunt he cast it again on Nadine, only using his mind to access her from the HUD and cast.

"Oh! T-that's han-n-ndy. I can see."

Behind him he heard a subdued clank. Flicking his eyes to the HUD, he concluded with a smirk that Katarina had forgotten to drop her visor till now. The party flitted through the nighttime city streets like shadows. Luckily it was a new moon tonight. It provided the perfect ambiance for skulking about, no moonlight.

They stuck to the alleyways and short streets, avoiding the thoroughfares entirely and keeping to the shadows when they had no choice. Crossing a boulevard, they were separated by a series of wagons that turned a corner and cast a bright light across the road. Katarina, Nadine, and Hannah were all on the other side, Thana and Runner having been the first two to get to the other side when they noticed it coming.

Thana turned away and pressed herself into the steps leading up to a large tenement building. Deciding it was the best option available, Runner did likewise. Taking the front position, he then backed up, forcing Thana into the corner. Hunching into himself as much as possible, he could only curse whoever decided to lead an entire convoy of wagons through town at this hour. Probably some idiot who overestimated his speed and underestimated the distance.

Looking around with a wary eye, he found no one close enough to see through their *Stealth*. Other than the wagons and the residential buildings, there was a lone closed confectioner's shop with two customers who'd yet to clear out of the darkened patio.

His eyes settled on those sitting at the table, and he felt his heart lurch in his chest. There was his dinner companion. The woman who apparently he'd been in some type of relationship with. Sitting across from her was Mr. Personality himself. Bullard didn't even have the demeanor of a quest NPC anymore, and seemed far more akin to one of Runner's Awakened. It was clear he was interested in Miss Mystery from his body posture: leaning forward, his shoulders and hips turned directly towards her, his hands spread apart and on the table between them.

Runner could only watch, his tongue too large for his mouth; his hands, feet, and heart were made of ice. It wasn't that he was suffering the Chilled debuff from the cool night air either. The most sickening fact of all was they were too distant for the nameplates to reveal her name or be selected.

Damn the designers! DAMN THEM!

Forcing a breath through his teeth, it came out in a shudder. For better or worse, Miss Mystery had a hold over him. One he couldn't even explain to himself yet.

It'd only been ten seconds since they'd crammed themselves into this spot, but now it felt like years. The wagons were just now reaching their position and trundling by. It'd be another minute or two before the last one at the end cleared them.

"While difficult, and with regret, I must inquire. Do you know the young lady who seems to have our *friend* so infatuated?"

Thana whispered, a concerned note in her voice. She'd noticed the pair as well.

It wasn't something he felt he could explain correctly. It'd surely come out wrong. Thana had never balked at anything he'd asked of her, though, and it was his turn to share of himself. His turn to give her the trust she'd given him.

"I do, I think. She's a player, like me. A soldier on the starship with me. I'm pretty sure she's an ex. Pretty sure. It's all jumbled up. I'm missing things, but there's a lot of bitter bubbling boiling things inside me. Acrid and sharp. But it feels like a sham. Old I guess. Stale. I don't even know her name."

Thana's lack of a response wasn't very surprising. It wasn't every day Runner offered up that much personal information in a tidy carry-on of emotional baggage. What was surprising was when her cool hand rested on his elbow.

"I'll be the first to admit I don't truly understand. My life was written for me and was not my own. My experiences do not exist beyond more than the month of time spent with you. I can tell you this much though, whatever the root of the split may be, it's incontrovertibly not of your doing. It'd be strange to have that intense of a negative reaction and be at fault for it."

Runner found he wasn't able to respond. Miss Mystery said something that made Bullard lean his head back and laugh. If Runner could throw up, he was sure his dinner would be decorating the sidewalk.

"Come, let us be away from here. Hannah will keep them safe and they'll meet up with us further along."

Gripping his elbow, she began coaxing him from the stairwell, heedless of the wagons. Down a different street they went and into the hollow night.

An hour had passed since their close encounter and near exposure. Their slow advance through the city and determination to remain unseen by all cost them in time but hopefully would pay off tenfold when they were no longer pursued. Runner and Nadine left the others behind the building they were hiding behind, moving to a spot beside the stables inside the city.

"This isn-n-n't the person we sold it-t-t to!" whispered Nadine in an urgent voice. She still followed him, hunched over and attempting to be quiet. Her attempt at stealth was a poor imitation of his own, though he was appreciative of her dedication to his desires.

"Anyone selling from the same faction, with the same type of equipment, will work. The trick here is this little stall was set up for people who needed to repair a wagon before or after coming off the boats. It doesn't *sell* wagons per se, but it does sell everything one would need. Go up there and access the vendor like I showed you. Should be right on the inside there. Pass me anything that'll encumber you too much to move. Try to get the rear of the wagon as close as possible too."

"I kn-n-n-now. You don't have t-t-to tell me again, darn-n-nit."

Harrumphing at him, Nadine sidled up along the wall. Runner smiled and quirked a brow. That was probably the closest to cursing she'd ever get.

One Hannah is enough actually.

Without any indication or warning, the wagon appeared atop of him. His boot was pinned beneath the wheel. Startled, Runner flailed his arms and fell backwards. Kicking his foot free of the wagon wheel, he looked up, trying to find Nadine so he could glare at her. There was no doubt in his mind that the placement had been intentional.

"If you're don-n-ne playing aroun-n-n-nd back there, get everyon-n-n-ne up here," Nadine crowed. Mirth hung in her words even if she wasn't laughing. She stood near the base of the driver's box, smiling.

"Don't get comfortable. The one person who can pass by with the least amount of notice is Hanners, even with the guild looking for her."

Muttering to himself, Runner grumped his way back to the others. Turning the corner, he hooked a thumb in the direction he had just come from. "Right, we're set, time to go. Nadine is loading the trade goods we'll sell on our way."

"Marvelous. And? What follows this juncture?" Thana asked, closing the distance between them.

Katarina stalked up behind Thana and nodded. "Mounted or on foot?"

"That's the thing. If we just traipse out past the guards, this whole sortie was pointless and we're back to the SP."

"SP? The fuck are you talking about now? Actually, forget that. Hurry up with the explaining, asshole. It's cold out," swore Hannah. She wasn't exactly wrong, it was below a comfortable temperature now. Hannah stomped her feet as if to warm them while waiting for him to continue.

"Sure. Katarina, Thana, Nadine, and myself get in the back. Hanners rides the driver position. She's the least likely to be remembered even with the guild looking for her."

"She's a half breed. She'll stand out."

"Yes, you're right, Kitten. The other choices are Barbarian, full Sunless, disfigured, and player character. Any of those sounds less likely to stand out?"

Frowning, Katarina turned her thoughts inward. Struggling with the problem, she could only eventually shake her head at the same conclusion everyone else came to.

"Exactly. Let's get a move on. I imagine we'll need to move some things around and we'll probably need to get friendly."

"Lovely," Thana murmured softly, rubbing her thumb and forefinger to her forehead as if to ease a headache.

Deciding he had no reasonable response for that, Runner turned from the group with a shrug of his shoulders.

Going to the front, he gave Nadine the short version of the goal and then stepped up into the driver's box to peer into the wagon. The wagon itself was a large Conestoga wagon. The cargo area was packed sideboard to sideboard with crates. They could stack them atop each other near the back where there would be a little room before it became a hazard. It wasn't going to just get friendly in here, though, it was going to be a cuddle puddle. Sighing he glanced at the team of horses at the front. They looked like a herd of gym rat horses that didn't know the meaning of an off day. They'd be worthless for riding or running quickly, but pulling a load of goods at a trot for a long time would be child's play.

Looking at Nadine, he smiled tightly. "That's quite a few crates, Nadine."

"I, uhh. I n-n-never had so much seed mon-n-ney or space. I bought a lot of great-t-t products I couldn-n-n-n't normally. Bargain-n deals I promise!"

An unspoken lament crossed his mind and he just shook his head.

"Are you sure we're not married? You spent my coin like it was yours."

"If we were, I'd have spent what's in-n-n your pocket t-t-too."

Chortling at her comment, Runner started in on rearranging the crates until there was some room for the four of them to crowd into. Utilizing the wagon's interface to whip crates around inside the storage areas, he was able to complete his task quickly. There really wasn't much he could do, but he managed to get the most out of it and it even managed to face forward.

"Good enough. Alright, Kitten, you're up first. You'll need the most room with those long legs of yours."

With a smug look Katarina clambered up beside him on the driver's box and stepped into the tiny alcove.

"Sit there." Runner gestured to where two low crates sat side by side, that were acting as a bench. Doing as she was instructed, Katarina took a seat and found she couldn't extend her legs at all. Her knees were nearly pointing straight up.

"Not going to work."

"Uhm, try putting your legs in the other corner over there. Yeah, just like that. I'll just-I dunno, wedge my feet under yours, I guess."

"Looking like an idiot plan here, Idiot."

"Totally not my fault. Nadine purchased like a hoarder with no credit chip limit," complained Runner. He sat down next to Katarina and shifted on the bench. Putting his mind to the game of twister this was becoming, he actually got his feet positioned so that he wasn't completely tied up with Katarina.

"Err, sorry." Shifting around one more time, he managed to get somewhat comfortable. He'd wedged his shoulder into the crate on his left. Lamentably, this also forced his right shoulder up into Katarina's arm. Giving up on that endeavor, he rested his head on the crate behind him. "Fuck it. Sorry, Kitten, this is as good as it gets."

"I understand. You cannot control everything."

Biting off a dark chuckle, he smiled.

"Thanks, Kitten. Alright, Nadine, you're up next. I'm afraid you'll need to pick a lap though. Less room than I was expecting."

Nadine's head appeared at the front of the wagon and she peered in. "Do we have t-t-to do this? Why can't I just-t-t-t walk?"

"Nadine, get in. Pick a lap, sit down. Neither of us bite and time is wasting."

Face pinched in an angry scowl, Nadine picked her way over their feet and sat down in Katarina's lap.

"See? Thana, your turn. Hanners, once she's in, you're on the fly. If you even think for a minute that you're going to get spotted by a thieves' guild member, or the guards look a bit too closely, *Stealth*. I'd rather a ghost wagon drift by than you driving it. Really need to be gone and on the North Road before dawn."

Thana came through the opening, looking from Runner to Nadine. Face contorting in a grimace at Nadine, Thana stepped gingerly through the crosshatch of legs and lightly set herself down on Runner's lap.

"This is so undignified, shameful, base even. I expect more appropriate arrangements in the future, Runner," Thana protested. Before her weight was fully settled, Hannah had them moving. Caught off guard as the wagon lurched forward, Thana squeaked as her temple struck Runner's.

Mild pain and discomfort spread from his face to the back of his skull. Runner could barely get his hand up to check his forehead with Thana so close.

"Hannah, was that truly necessary?" asked Thana.

"Sorry, Princess, boss said go, we go. Hang on next time?"
Unmistakable snickering floated back from Hannah as they rolled
along.

Thana growled softly, her eyes flashing dangerously at
Hannah's back. Glancing at Runner as if daring him to say
anything, she slowly but resolutely leaned her shoulder into his
chest. Folding her hands into her lap she remained silent. Her
fingers started to manipulate an interface only she could see.

Letting his hand fall from his head, Runner realized there
really wasn't anywhere he could put it. Not anywhere that
wouldn't be "Thana" at least. That course of action would lead
to him being killed in his sleep. Hesitating for a moment, he
finally lowered his hand between Katarina and himself hoping
there'd be enough room there. It wasn't like her hand could not
be anywhere else either.

He was expecting to feel the cold hard backing of
Katarina's gauntlets but found only the warmth of flesh.
Glancing down at his hand, he found it was resting on the back
of Katarina's. Looking to Katarina, he found she was steadfastly
avoiding his eye.

He was thankful for the one person who seemed to understand
this wasn't a cocked-up plan straight out of a terrible romantic
comedy to get close to them. That this decidedly inconvenient
lack of space wasn't his plan. Though he couldn't deny that
Thana certainly felt gr-

*No no nonONONO! We're not going down that road. Just NPCs,
just NPCs, just NPCs. They're still just NPCs.*

Forcing his eyes to slide shut and his brain to turn off,
Runner rested the back of his head on the crate.

Katarina roughly squeezed his hand in her own. Runner
blinked twice and looked to her just as a voice called out from
the pre-dawn darkness ahead of them.

"Hey there, lady. Watcha got for us in the wagon?"

Chapter 16 - The Prelude -

"Respond to them, confirm their number." Runner whispered the command to Hannah. Letting go of Katarina's hand, he started maneuvering Thana up and toward the front of the wagon. "You can see better than I, Lady Death, help me."

His plea caught her attention as she struggled to get free of his forceful hands in an attempt to reseat herself. Giving him an unreadable look, she ceased her resistance and cautiously peered into the dark ahead of them over Hannah's shoulder.

"What the hell are you five fuck heads up to at this hour?"

"Oh, she can talk!"

"Does that mean she's flagged good?"

"I call dibs on the first turn if she is. You broke the last one, you shit. Heh, poor little infantry rat, he wanted to take her with him everywhere."

The voices were nearly indistinguishable from each other. Guttural, brutish, uneducated. From their comments it would seem they wished nothing but ill intent on all who would cross them. Runner wasn't going to bother with attempting to speak with them. It'd only serve to ruin the element of surprise.

He couldn't just execute them, though, even if he had proof they were player killers. A court martial, actual evidence, a trial counsel, and a handful of officers would be needed, none of which he had in his back pocket.

"Close enough to AOE with a center penetration?" Runner asked both Hannah and Thana. His left hand was pressed into Thana's side and his right rested on the back of the driver's box. He could pull Thana from harm or leap into action in either situation. He couldn't risk casting *Night Sight*, as it'd give away the game that the wagon wasn't empty.

Thana tilted her head and nodded even as Hannah responded to whatever the men had said next.

"Yes. Every one of these bastards are," Hannah confirmed.

"Uh, wha'? She bust already? Damn."

Looking back, he motioned Nadine to where he had just been sitting and Katarina to rise. Before they could finish rearranging themselves, he'd pulled three flasks from his inventory with his right hand. He handed one to Katarina and then handed the other two into Thana's hands as she turned to face him.

"Prepare to engage. Five to six, expect one to ambush. My Lady, on five, *Blink* to achieve center penetration, AOE, Vanish potion, Blink potion to new position at right side of wagon, targets of opportunity or runners. Kitten, take position right side of wagon, wait for Thana. Blink potion to engage center, I'll be there. AOE taunt and hold. Hanners, sheep dog them in close unless a target of opportunity presents itself. Nadine, overwatch, low health bars or runners. Good?" Runner waited a beat. "Good. Five seconds to go."

Turning back to Thana, he patted her on the shoulder and pressed himself to the side of a crate. Katarina was suddenly there, filling the void he'd vacated for her. He started counting down with his fingers.

"Gotcha'self a filthy mouth, ya cunt. I'll make it real filthy. So filthy ya gag," said a soon-to-be corpse.

As he reached the five count, Thana blinked. Katarina leapt up from the wagon bed and dropped to the side, out of sight. Targeting Thana's nameplate as she reappeared, he oriented on her and waited. *Ice Nova* burst out from her without a word of warning or gesture. Everything around her turned into a brilliant white spray of mist and blades of ice. Spinning as the deadly missiles went, they whipped through the air and exploded as they tore into enemies.

He'd wondered just how much of an increase the gear would give and he now got his answer. All five had a quarter of their life bar or more removed in an instant.

Tests are in, marked improvement.

Nadine pressed in up next to his side, bracing her crossbow on the top of the driver's box. A split second after sighting the group she fired.

Activating *Blink*, he appeared almost on top of Thana. A moment later she vanished after downing the Stealth potion. Mentally flipping an ability activation, he used *Challenging Roar*, holding up his arms and daring them to attack him.

Being so much closer now, he could easily see the five men spread around him. They were barely in their twenties and looked exactly like the type of filth the government would send to die in the front line. They all stood and stared at him, dumbstruck by the situation.

Assigning them numbers instead of even trying to figure out their names, he focused on the closest one. Throwing out his left hand at Uno, an arc of lightning leapt from his fingers into the man. Dropping nearly in place, Uno started convulsing on the ground. Taking a step forward towards Dos, Runner whipped his sword around in a *Slash* followed by an *Impale* when the timer refreshed.

Dos' health flashed to the forty percent range while Uno was much closer to fifty percent. Runner pivoted on the balls of his feet, whipping his blade up into a block. Having gotten his blade into position, he was expecting to find Tres and Cuatro close behind him.

Instead, Katarina stood with her back to him in all her Barbarian glory. Her shield up and sword whipping around in a *Slice* into Cuatro's arm.

Pivoting again, he pressed himself up to Katarina's backplate and planted himself there. Uno was struggling to his feet even as Dos slumped to his knees and keeled over to fall face-first in the dirt, his health bar at zero and flashing an ugly yellow and black color. Runner wasn't sure who dropped him, but he was thankful all the same.

Cinco rushed over and took Dos' place. A sharp crack preceded a crossbow bolt driving itself into Uno's side. Unable to recover quickly from the attack, he staggered to the side. An I-beam-sized rod of Ice barreled into his chest and tumbled him to the ground, his health bar emptying completely and going bumblebee.

Casting a quick *Regeneration* on Katarina, Runner launched an *Impale* towards Cinco. He'd turned his head to watch Uno fall in disbelief. Piercing the man's exposed throat, Runner disengaged and immediately threw a *Slash* at the man's sword arm to disarm him.

He caught him in the wrist, sending the long sword spinning away to land in the road. Realizing how bad the situation was, Cinco turned and made to sprint. His dash to freedom was cut short when a quarrel lodged in his spine and he was thrown to the dirt.

Three empty, two to go.

Dislodging himself from Katarina's back, he moved out to her left. Cuatro was trying to get around her shield and didn't notice Runner until he was on him. Holding up his hand an inch from Cuatro's eyes, he let loose with a *Fireblast*. Screams, the smell of burnt hair, and fried bacon filled the morning. Almost as if the mute button was hit, Cuatro folded in on himself and collapsed into the grass. Hannah was already turning to Tres after having silenced Cuatro and worked at carving out his kidney.

Katarina's sword caught him in the temple when Hannah got his attention. With a critical image flashing on his head, Cuatro spun like a top. Just like that the field was clear, all hostiles were down, and nothing needed to be done immediately.

Police the bodies, confirm numbers, gather loot, get the hell out.

"Hanners, was there a sixth?" Runner asked, immediately looking to her after having visually checked the five neutralized men.

"Yeah, got the little fucker. He's over near the wagon. Same as the rest, that weird yellow and black bar."

"It's the neutralization bar. If a player is downed by a sentient creature, anything that can say its own name really, you go into this state rather than death. Which is honestly what I was counting on. Really not looking to rack up six murder charges."

"What? You're a fucking idiot. These are monsters, horrible people. I've no doubt in my mind they're murdering, raping bastards. This is that moment in horror stories that bards tell of. That these shit heads will come back at a later time to attack us again or worse. What are you going to do? Ask them nicely to behave? Did you hear what they're doing to Naturals? To other people from your ship?"

"I did, yes, I did. OK? I did. It doesn't change the fact that I can't just kill them."

"I could, if you want," Katarina offered, sheathing her sword and lifting her visor.

"I can do it if you don't have the balls," Hannah cursed at him.

"No, just, let's loot what they dropped and go. I'll make sure I use the log to get their names and investigate them. After. I'm sure they'll be executed after a brief trial."

"Then do it now, fool! Do you not understand? This is how a hero gets his companions killed! Right here, this very moment."

"He can-n-n-n't, Hannah! It's wrong to just kill them out-t-t-t of han-nd anyways, Naturals or players."

"Oh my Gods, are you listening to yourself? Mark my words, this will come back to us and one of us will pay."

"Perhaps. Regardless of anything else, Runner looks to be set on this course of action. Let's loot them and be away," Thana added with a clap of her hands. Moving to a neutralized body, she reached down to scavenge what she could from it.

"Damn you, damn you all. Your blasted goody-two-shoes routine will be the end of us, at the very least one of us." Hannah stealthed and walked away towards the wagon. She was still a visible silhouette since she was in the party, but this was more of a matter of indicating that she would discuss this no further.

Closing his eyes, he found that he agreed with Hannah. This was that moment in every terrible holomovie where the audience screams at the heroes to do what must be done. He couldn't though, he couldn't. This place wasn't his life, and he'd have to return to the military after this. It'd be one thing to have brawled with others, but to have essentially taken a life? Logs would indicate what happened to whom in the end, as records were always kept. Always. There would be no hiding from the repercussions if one were to take another's life.

"I agree with her. Foolish of you. I'll stand by you though," declared Katarina. Thumping his shoulder with a closed fist, she moved on to the next body to check for any items.

"Thanks, Kitten."

1:39 pm Sovereign Earth time
10/13/43

Unfortunately, what loot they received from the battle didn't constitute an upgrade for anyone. It did serve as free materials for Runner to train up his Arcane Smithing. Broken into component parts and reassembled, each item was recreated in this way. Each would be worth upwards of ten gold now. With a negligent flip, the reformed sword tumbled end over end to land in the crate he'd been working out of. It'd only taken him a day since the fight to do the work when it was his turn to ride the wagon.

"Now I'm bored," complained Runner. Standing, he brushed his hands off on his pants and stretched as best as he could in the wagon.

"Oh? I've been toying with this set of puzzles I discovered on the forum. I forget the name and couldn't pronounce it if I tried, but it's a logic puzzle. Each row and column must contain the numbers one through nine but can only do so once. It's divided into a grid of nine large blocks, each block has nine squares in it. It's entertaining and rewarding in its way."

Looking up from where she sat across from him, Thana smiled at him with only her lips, then returned her attention to the space where her finger moved along rows and columns only she could see.

"Sudoku? How'd you even access that? I mean, I guess the account I created for you would actually allow you to store anything on your profile, providing you had the space. If someone uploaded the files it'd be possible to install it."

"I confess it took me a few tries to understand the installation process. Hannah had a lot more trouble installing that card game tournament monstrosity. Now she can't stop playing it. She takes great delight in beating your shipmates."

"I see. Alright, OK, unexpected to the say the least, but not a bad thing."

"Why's that? Gambling fits Hannah perfectly. Nadine doesn't want anything to do with it, she sticks to the forum. Apparently there's an entire section dedicated to trading, and she's been spending her free time there. Personally, I don't find the markets that entertaining."

"At least she's expanding her knowledge. Though, it is a subject only she could find fascinating."

- 201 -

"One would suppose so. I believe Katarina is attempting a similar goal in a different way. She watches war documentaries constantly."

"War documentaries?"

"Indeed. She followed a link from a thread that ended up taking her to the entertainment library. Would you believe she goes to sleep listening to them?"

Runner could only provide a noncommittal grunt before exiting the wagon.

Katarina sat in the driver's box, a slightly vacant stare on her face. Her eyes were clearly focused on an invisible interface menu floating before her. If what Thana said was true, and he had no reason to doubt her, she was deeply engrossed in a documentary about a previous war or conflict. Pressing a hand to her pauldron as he passed, so as to not surprise her, he lightly jumped down and stepped away from the wagon.

"Your turn, Nadine. Hopefully at the next town we can just dump everything for a profit and empty the wagon."

"N-n-no, that'd be a wast-t-te. I won't buy as much th-this time."

Unwilling to allow Runner to continue the conversation, Nadine hopped up into the wagon and disappeared inside. Grunting over being shut down so casually, he turned his head to see Hannah walking up to him.

"Your own damn fault, idiot. She knows you won't say no to her, so she'll just use it to her advantage," Hannah explained. Falling in next to her as the rear guard, he could only chuckle.

"You're probably right. Though would any of you prefer the alternative? Would you rather I ruled you all with an iron fist? Imposed my will exactly as I saw fit and did as I would? That's how many others would do it. It's how many others do act."

"I wasn't complaining, ass-hat, I was explaining. And no, I wouldn't prefer it. I'm not a masochist."

"No, but apparently you're a gambler. I hear you've been playing cards?"

"Yeah. I win more often than I lose, but there's a few card sharks on your ship."

"Was it uh, hard to install? Did it make sense? Did Thana help you?"

"Hard to install? At first, yes. The damn thing wanted me to tell it what to do. I asked in the thread that it was posted in and they helped me out. Well, some did. Quite a few told me to read the fucking manual. A few offered directions and that worked. After that it was a piece of cake. The only part I didn't get was something about my profile and how much it used. No idea. Thana said her little logic games thing only took one percent each."

"Games? Plural?"

"Yeah. That stupid number one and a game about finding fucking firebombs. It didn't make any damned sense. Cards though? Cards make sense. You should play with me. We could double our odds if we knew what each other had. In fact, if we…"

Runner didn't reply but nodded his head as if considering her words. In truth he was considering the situation as a whole. Naturals were utilizing programs on a ship that they were in fact installed on as part of a larger program. This was coming pretty close to how some people believed the end of the world would come about. True AI that could utilize other programs. Not for the first time, Runner wondered how bad things were getting.

How much can the server handle? Why did the capacity expand? Why did it expand by so damn much? What if it all crashed? Are we currently docked at an orbital station? Are we already under the care of engineers working to free us?

The one thing he knew for certain was that the Naturals in his care were more like people now. There was nothing left of their original programming at this point. If he wasn't so terrified for the end result, he was sure that this would be classified as a scientific miracle.

He'd been level capped before they'd even managed to get the rest of the abilities for the starting classes. Hopefully in taking the next promotions he'd finally unlock the password to the admin controls.

He'd spent every night hammering at the login screen until he locked himself out for the hour. He doubted random guessing and brute force tactics would work, but he had the time to try. Why not?

It'd be a few hours more until the current password lockout expired and he could try again.

Warning, your Campsite has been invaded.

Stumbling over his own feet, he started to fall, but Hannah managed to catch him by the arm. Trying to steady himself, he let Hannah guide him.

"The hell is wrong with you, Runner?" Hannah asked, her voice edged with annoyance and concern.

"Err, sorry. I left the campsite up the other day. I wanted to see if someone would enter it. We camped pretty far off the road and it wasn't something you could really see from the road. I got a message to the fact that an intruder attempted to enter the campsite. It could be random dumb luck, but I don't really believe in coincidences."

"Fuck. You think it's that Tim guy? The one who's after me?"

"Ted. Ted Henshaw, and maybe but probably not. He wouldn't find the campsite, he'd be trailing you directly, wouldn't he? You've got a quest marker, he'd have no need to deviate from the road, he could actually follow you just by watching the map. No, no, this is probably Mr. Personality or the thieves' guild. Damn. I really thought we'd lost them. All that work for little more than half a day. I mean, I'm glad we got even that much, but I was hoping to lose them entirely."

"Would they know that you're now aware? Can we set up an ambush? Can we trap or imprison them or something?"

"They would have received a warning that they were entering someone else's campsite. One must assume they're aware they set it off. I'm unsure if that'll speed them up or slow them down though. They'll be more cautious as they trail us, looking for ambushes as they go."

"If it were me? It'd speed me up and I'd try to catch you before dawn, when everyone assumes the worst of the night is over."

"I'd have to agree. It'd be my own approach. Which of course this means it's not safe to camp or sleep in the open tonight. We'll use the benefits we have then as best as we're able. Let's see."

Targeting the wagon, Runner used *Campsite* on it directly. There was a momentary pause as the server considered this request.

A few seconds passed before the wagon suddenly became a campsite. Apparently it fell within the boundaries enough that the world could accommodate for it.

"Runner? Did something happen?" called Thana's voice from inside the wagon. Having a campsite appearing on top of you would definitely set off a message alert.

A quick two steps later and he clambered up the side of the driver's box. Sitting down next to Katarina, he patted her arm to get her attention.

"I left the old campsite up just to see if anyone would stumble across it. It so happens, someone did. We were really far from the road. It might just be paranoia, but I'd say we didn't lose them. Whoever they are. We'll need to start sleeping in shifts and throughout the day. We won't be able to stop for the night if we want to keep our distance from them up. When we get to town we'll sell everything and keep it empty, sorry Nadine. We'll get better speed and more room for everyone to rest easier. Our best bet is to reach Crivel faster than they can close the gap. With the sheer number of soldiers and troops in the area we might just be able to lose them."

Chuckling beside him, Katarina shook her head, smiling. "Never easy, always a problem with you."

"Meh, you love it, Kitten. Spice of life and all that crap. Any objections? No? At this point I'm open to any suggestions, ranging from doing nothing to going elsewhere."

"Whatever plan we develop, we should be taking the quickest feasible route. Being able to recuperate in the wagon is an unexpected boon that they will not have, nor expect. We simply don't brake for anything and continue onward."

"Run fast-t-ter t-t-than they can. It-t-t-temize the wagon and sprint, resting in between t-t-t-o recover stamina."

"Turn around, prepare defenses, engage."

"Set an ambush for the shits, cut them down before they can even respond. Lots of nasty things you can do at range."

"All very valid plans, ladies, I thank you for the suggestions. For now, let us do as Thana suggested and sleep. Hannah, Katarina, get in there too. I'll drive the wagon."

Brooking no nonsense, he pressed himself against Katarina's side, attempting to dislodge her bodily or at least give her the impression it would do no good to argue. Eventually she stood up and stepped into the back, Hannah clambering in behind her.

"Runner-"

"I know, Thana, it's not very dignified. I'm sorry. If I can manage better in the future, I swear I will. I'm not looking, I'm not suggesting to join you, we can even close the flaps if it helps. I'd say take off any armor that takes up room, especially you, Kitten, and get snuggly. You wanted an adventure, Lady Death, you've got one."

There was no response to that. In a few short minutes, each one of his party members had the icon of floating Z's next to their name.

Runner kept himself looking straight forward and kept the wagon at the fastest setting. It didn't require much thought really-agitating the horses when they started to flag was more than enough. He gave the animals another tap of the reins.

Speeding up once more, the horses stayed close to their maximum speed. Runner was left with his crowded thoughts, nagging questions, and no answers.

Chapter 17 - Clash -

They'd traveled the roads heading to Crivel for weeks. Only pausing long enough to sell their inventory, they made their way northward. It was his turn at the helm as everyone else relaxed in the wagon. It looked like all four had fallen asleep swiftly. Everyone had definitely gotten used to living on the run, sprinting along that razor's edge.

Judging from the forum posts he'd been reading this morning and speculations from players in the area, they'd be able to reach Crivel a day before the siege could start. Nadine wouldn't be ready for her promotion, but that wasn't something they could wait on.

Twenty-four hours to finalize class assignments and get back out didn't seem like enough time. There was no other option though; time marched ever onwards, and every day the graveyards received more tenants.

He needed to break his level cap and remember more. He only needed one memory. One stupid little memory that was all of one word.

Checking the number as he did every morning, he found it'd climbed up to twelve thousand in the graveyards. Every one an empty shell probably, a living zombie as it were. Each and every life was one more in his ledger he'd have to hold himself accountable for.

There were so many things he could have done better, that could have given him extra time, and with less headaches. Thinking of Hannah, by herself she'd already cost him more than a few days. That didn't even begin to count for Thana or Katarina and the trouble that they caused with Mr. Personality. Mr. Personality and Miss Mystery.

Yet he had chosen this, hadn't even considered differently at the time. Looking back there were quite a few choices he could have made regarding his followers that would have granted him more time or expediency.

Clenching his hands on the reins, he could only be angry at himself, for these were his choices, no one made them for him. Squeezing his eyes to slits, he turned his head to the side as if he could escape the very road he was on if he couldn't see it. Anxiety, anger, and fear had claimed the quiet moments, leaving him wrung out and upset. It was in these solitary times that the weight of it crushed him, pinned him in place, leaving him writhing in the agony of self-doubt.

"Good evening, Heathen. Looks as if we judged your course accurately."

Snapping his head up in the direction of the speaker, Runner narrowed his eyes. Pulling on the reins, he slowed the wagon. Mr. Personality himself had just stepped out of concealment up ahead of him. He'd been crouched in the bushes on the roadside, waiting.

"Bullard! To what do I owe the misfortune of your company to?" Runner said with a misshapen smile. Hiding his intentions with his open greeting, he triggered a preset alert with a thought. A shrill alarm spun up in volume over the course of two seconds, then went silent. Sleeping icons disappeared from all his comrades. Suddenly, his paranoia didn't seem like enough. He hadn't forced everyone else to set up macro built alerts, but he would after this. If they got out of it.

"Runner? What are you-why? I don't-how?" sternly said a woman, stepping out from behind Bullard.

It was her, his mystery guest, the one who demanded his attention.

Yulia Orlov.

Memories of a woman he thought was an ex jumped to the front, attaching themselves to Yulia instead of a different woman who looked very similar. He'd been confusing two different women with his moth eaten memory.

Staff Sergeant Yulia Orlov, of the 5th infantry, on her third tour of duty. Standing close to six foot, she was definitely on the tall side. Long limbs, a pale complexion, and an athletic build gave her the appearance of fragility. That couldn't be any further from the truth considering what memories her mere name sparked into context. Muscles built from constant strength training and years of martial arts training lurked just beneath the surface.

He pulled out a memory he attributed to someone else but now pinned it to Yulia. Being manhandled by her easily in some of their bed play. While certainly attractive, her face would be described as handsome before anyone suggested beautiful. Large fiery green eyes were set in a mask that seemed to be permanently set in a frown. Her hair was a dark brown and chopped short in accordance with military statue, curling ever so slightly at the tips.

Many small memories that had no matching owner floated together to create a shattered picture of her in his mind. He learned nothing new, but instead found different fragmented memories that joined to create a larger picture. Emotions came boiling up from his stomach, demanding their presence be recognized.

"Hey there, Jewels. Radiant as ever. I wish I could answer that for you but you'll need to clarify. Wasn't so much of a question as a collection of single words."

Shaking her head, she dismissed his tone, her arms folding over her chest.

"You're still an asshole. How are you here?"

"Oh, this fine wagon of course," Runner explained, slapping the driver's box. At the same time, he sorted out predesignated commands to his companions. They were simple things but they'd get them moving. Mentally targeting Bullard, he threw up a raid icon of a red X over his head. It'd only be visible to his group, but it would help indicate enemies. A moment later he targeted Yulia and gave her a giant blue O in a similar fashion. "Traveling to Crivel to tell the truth."

"By the Sovereign Seven, Runner! Why are you on the ship? You weren't supposed to be here. That was the point of it all. You were going back to teach, you said."

"I wish I could tell you, but I have no memory of deciding to teach. Or how I ended up here. I'm afraid I'm missing quite a bit. I'm not sure if I'm more scrambled than others, but I have a thought that I might be."

Distance indicators to each of his companions changed, Katarina's by only a meter. Nadine, Thana, and Hannah's by thirty meters and increasing. A flash on his mini-map popped as several more raid icons appeared behind the wagon. A white skull, an orange Square, and a yellow Star. They were all marked and just on the side of the road.

"Helpful as ever."

Bullard had been looking from Yulia to Runner and back as they spoke. Yulia suddenly looked at him just as it appeared he was about to speak. Cowed by that look, Bullard remained silent. Yulia returned her gaze to Runner.

"Are you the only commissioned?" she asked him.

Nodding his head, he mentally clicked the symbols that were behind him and found they were the NPCs. He wasn't able to determine their classes since they were just NPCs and named "Mercenary" but he had a good guess since they were in ranged ambush positions.

"I believe I am. When I did a user search it came up as four hundred and ninety-nine thousand with some change. The problem being that it wasn't the full complement. I suspect the bridge pods are non-operational."

"Damn. Are we in orbit around home base or at our LZ?"

"I don't know. Every external sensor is down. We can receive, but not send. I have access to the admin panel and could theoretically change the game to make everyone immortal, log everyone out into non-hibernation, or even pause the whole game, but I don't have the password."

"Hence the trip to Crivel. You're level capped and you can't get your memories back until you class up, to level up."

"Got it in one, yep."

"Do-do you know how many have…?"

"I can guess. No one would be in a graveyard unless they were KIA. There are currently over twelve thousand people in graveyards throughout the game world."

"By the Sovereign, that's an entire division."

"Yes, well, I'm working on it. I'm hopeful though. Outside access of the ship's registry has been confirmed. They logged in and have been making changes to the program. I imagine they're trying to stabilize and work on it. Haven't been able to make contact though to establish Friend or Foe protocol."

Yulia said nothing, merely watched him. Runner looked away from her to size up Bullard. Physically unchanged since he'd seen him at the cafe, he looked like the very image of a knight.

Letting his eyes return to Yulia he found she looked like a woman torn. Her eyes were distant, a hand halfway to the ground hung in the air, completely lost in her own thoughts. Blinking, she suddenly turned to Bullard and spoke to him in hushed tones. Runner wasn't close enough to make it out, but they started arguing vehemently with each other. Yulia looked at him once more with a grimace and gestured to him.

"Get us out then, Lieutenant. You're the only commissioned officer we have, which means you're also the commanding officer. I report that everyone in my command is accounted for and awaiting orders. Get us out of this before I lose anyone. Sir." Punctuating her statement with a salute, Yulia looked to Bullard. After getting a nod from him, Yulia turned and walked off the road and into the grass. Several steps later she simply vanished into the brush.

Watching her leave was a mistake. Bullard took the moment for what it was and activated what looked like a scroll. Runner tried to leap from his seat, but he was locked into an immunity spell. Being unable to change his trajectory, his momentum carried him from the driver's box and into the dirt below.

Bullard cautiously approached him with a drawn blade. Sword raised in front of him, Bullard spared a glance at Runner. Drawing in close to the wagon, he reached up with the tip of his sword to try and lift the flap.

A timer ticked down from thirty seconds. That's how long it would be before he could be harmed or harm others. This was certainly a problem. It was another contingency he'd planned for, even if Bullard had planned to keep him immune by utilizing scroll after scroll. Runner wouldn't be able to cure his own debuff, but that didn't prevent him from loading everyone up with quick cast scrolls to eliminate just these types of curses, poisons, and enchantments. Activating the "Go" command with an angry thought, he readied himself as well as he could given his limitations.

An explosion that sounded like shattering glass came from behind the wagon and down the road. It was quickly followed by a shout and the clack of a crossbow.

Surprised by this sudden cacophony, Bullard took a few steps from the wagon to get a look. Leaping from the wagon, Katarina landed next to Runner and fired off a scroll at him. Leveling her shield at Bullard, she readied herself for combat.

"Thank you, Kitten," Runner praised her, quickly getting to his feet. His sword leapt from the scabbard, appearing in his hand in a blink. Targeting the Skull on the other side of the road from Thana and Nadine, Runner touched off a *Fireblast* from his sword, followed by a throwing knife from his left hand. Having used his ability and item cooldowns in that barrage, he turned and activated the auto attack function on Bullard. Turned away from Runner, he didn't notice until Runner's sword caught him in the shoulder.

Bullard had clearly filled out his equipment since they'd last met. His health bar fell, but nowhere near what he had expected it to. It was definitely a surprise considering the overpowered weapons and enchantments he'd been developing could normally drop anything their own level and even five above in just a few auto attacks.

Katarina threw out her shield into the knight's helmet, stunning him and throwing him back a few paces. Moving his hand up, he discharged a *Fireblast* into Bullard's visor. Turning his shoulder into the magical attack, Bullard used a *Shout* ability while raising his shield.

Runner felt overwhelming weakness in his arms and legs as the effect took hold. It didn't do any damage, but it quartered his offensive potential, both magically and physically. Mr. Personality made no attempt to stop him as he withdrew and ostensibly settled in for a wet noodle fight with Katarina.

Drawing away from Bullard, he attempted to make his way over to Thana and Nadine. Bullard had a huge amount of mitigation and with a loss of damage it'd be like attacking the ocean for him.

He didn't know where Hannah was, but he could only assume she was doing her best with whatever duty she'd assigned herself.

Working to flank along the side of the wagon, Runner approached Thana's coordinates. Nadine was the closest to him as he drew near. She drew her crossbow to her shoulder and let a bolt rip through the air. Following her line of sight and the quarrel as it flew, he found Thana engaged in close combat with the Star Magician and Square Rogue. Her health was depleting too quickly under the accurately placed strikes of the Rogue. She'd held a firm front against the two of them, but without immediate assistance she'd fall.

Stealthing outside of their viewing range, Runner came up to the Rogue and ran his sword into him. Targeting Thana, he threw out a *Heal*, causing her life bar to spike upwards. Using more than he wanted to, he clipped a *Regeneration* spell on top of her as well to keep her health moving upwards.

Square took quick steps from Runner, the sudden drop in his health a surprise. He was now under twenty percent from Nadine's bolts and Runner's unforeseen entrance. Thana raised her staff and an explosion of Ice came out in a circle around her that covered everything within fifteen feet. Suddenly locked in place as part of the aftereffects from *Ice Nova*, the Magician could only watch as his companion died. Disappearing from their midst, Thana blinked to another location.

Assuring himself that Thana and Nadine could handle the Magician by themselves, Runner dashed across the road. Passing by, he glanced to Katarina's duel with Bullard and gave her a quick *Heal* followed by a *Regeneration*. *Heal* cost more than *Cure*, but he couldn't risk Katarina's life. Hitting single digits, his mana bar was near empty, cutting his ability to adapt to the emerging situation drastically.

Finding himself nearly standing on top of the Skull, who happened to be an Archer, he smashed an *Impale* into him. Had he been paying attention, he might have been able to pull off a stealthed *Backstab* simultaneously. Glancing along the man's ribs, Runner let the strike carry him onwards. Bowling into the man, he knocked him forward. Then the man bounced sideways as he rebounded off whatever was ahead of him. Catching his balance, Runner turned and lunged outward at Skull in an attempt to catch him in another attack.

Hannah was beside him, her health in the middle of her bar. The Archer before Runner was closer to the top end, which was surprising. It was out of the ordinary due to the fact that Hannah was a DPS monster. That didn't even take into account the fact he'd attacked the Archer earlier at the start. She should have had this one down and dead before he'd arrived.

Examining the area, he found the old Priest hiding in the vegetation. The Priest was given the designation of a green Triangle. Hannah dropped an empty potion vial at her feet, her health surging from the effects. Runner didn't care for the odds at the moment. They were in his favor beyond any doubt, but any fight that was in question was already a failure to a power gamer.

Taking a cue from Hannah, Runner used a mana restoration potion and threw the vial at the Priest to distract him, advancing forward towards the Archer. Halfway there he turned and bolted towards the Priest at the last second. Lunging forward again, he caught the old man before he was able to realize what was happening. Hannah appeared behind the caster as Runner withdrew his sword. Spinning on his feet, the Priest healed himself and tried to scurry towards the Archer.

Activating *Hamstring* Runner sidestepped behind the Priest, putting his target between himself and the Archer to eliminate any possibility of a ranged attack. Losing half his movement speed, the old man didn't cease in his attempt to reach his companion. Impale was available and used once more, bringing the Priest low, deep into the red zone of his bar.

At this moment a company of horsemen swarmed over them. They came from the lightly wooded areas surrounding the roads. They'd kept concealed and quiet, and Runner guessed that they had waited until they felt they could close and engage with complete surprise. Scrutinizing them, Runner was only able to tell they were listed as "Scout" and were part of the Sunless race. Dropping back a few steps next to Hannah, he tried to get cover between them and the newcomers.

Without even a hint as to their allegiance, the newcomers designated neither side as friendly and began to move in on both in equal measure. Running through every possible scenario he could come up with in his head, the only one with any decent chance was retreating. Retreating as fast as possible and letting whoever was left from Bullard's group hopefully catch the wrath of the Scouts.

Mentally tapping the preprogrammed command labeled "Retreat/Rendezvous," Runner sprinted for the wagon.

Coming to a halt at the edge of the road, Runner surveyed the chaos. Standing in the road exactly where they'd left it, the wagon was a refuge that could grant them distance from this debacle. And yet a squad of Scouts was fast approaching and was nearly atop it.

Thana was standing on the top of the wagon, her feet braced against the wagon's bows. From there she watched the horsemen converge on her position from nearly every side, her eyes flicking from Scout to Scout as if to determine a course of action. At the same time Nadine was mounting the driver's box, her hands clawing for the reins before she even seated herself properly. She'd already made the decision that the only possibility of their retreat was to do exactly that, flee by wagon.

Having received the command from Runner, Katarina spun away from Bullard and leapt for the side of the wagon in a rattle of armor. Her fingers clamped onto the sideboard with the crack of metal hitting wood. Finding purchase, she yanked the bonnet up from the sideboard and rolled inside the wagon bed. Jerking the reins and snapping them repeatedly, Nadine got control of the wagon, costing the wagon team a considerable amount of health and stamina to go from resting to full speed, and the wagon lurched forward. Runner didn't fault her for it; the team could recover their stamina later after all.

Thana had nearly lost her feet when Nadine had gotten the wagon moving. Catching herself as she came down to her knees atop the bonnet, Thana managed to hold on. She looked up and saw Runner and Hannah. Fear flickered through her eyes as the distance between them rapidly expanded. In those brief seconds, Thana knew they wouldn't make it and to Runner it was clear she was about to order Nadine to stop.

Runner did the only thing he could and smiled at her with a sad shake of his head. Pointing his fingers down the road, he waved at her to signal their departure must continue. If they even managed to get the horses to stop, it'd take far too long for Runner and Hannah to catch them. The wagon would just be run to ground and they'd be even worse off.

Bullard, finding himself surrounded by Sunless, losing the fight, and looking extremely frustrated, did the worst thing possible for himself. Once more he used a *Shout*, drawing the attention of everyone around him, since no one else had attacked or interacted with them.

Runner held Thana's eyes for a second longer, then broke contact. Angling his path away from the wagon and Bullard, he sprinted off. Crossing to the other side of the road with Hannah directly behind him Runner had to change his plans on the fly.

Empty mana bar, potion cooldown up, party separated, multiple enemies. All we can do is retreat, break contact, regroup.

Stealthing the moment he broke line of sight with his foes, Runner started walking at an angle from the road. Nadine would keep the wagon to the road and at as fast a pace as possible. With any luck Bullard would keep everyone busy long enough for them to get far enough ahead that a chase wasn't possible.

He hadn't counted on Scouts ranging ahead of the army. He should have though, as basic doctrine dictated you needed a screening force operating ahead of the main body. Cursing himself once again for not preparing correctly, he oriented himself towards the nearest map marker to the northwest.

It was undesignated since he hadn't purchased a map for the area nor had he explored it. Runner didn't care what it was so long as it could provide him with a point of reference and he could reorient himself.

A wish, hope, prayer, a bit of luck, a unicorn fart and he might even be able to rendezvous with his team sooner than he had feared.

"There's a marker up ahead. We move for it, regroup, and plan there."

"Got it. Fuck, who were those people? We were so close! We could've killed all of those bastards! Damn it, damn them!"

"Screening force. They were out ahead for that Sunless army on the move."

"I thought they were still a day out?"

"They are, their reconnaissance isn't. That was their vanguard. A scouting party so to speak. They act as a forward operating force. They're out ahead to cause havoc, gain intel, and make sure the army doesn't stumble into an ambush."

"Shit."

"Yes. That."

Moving in Stealth wasn't the fastest way to travel, but it had its benefits. Chief among those, invisibility to an enemy looking for you. They would have to be damn well next to them to spot them out here.

"Runner?"

"Hm?"

"Who was that?" Hannah asked with a small, quiet voice. It was almost as if she was afraid of his answer.

Runner knew what she was asking, even if she hadn't specified exactly what she meant.

Anyone and everyone would need an explanation after that.

"Honestly, I'm not entirely sure. I think she's an ex-girlfriend. One that I didn't end on the best of terms with."

"Really?"

"Yeah, best as I can figure. I have no memories of what happened, but I do feel a lot of anger towards her. Anger and resentment."

"Sounds like an ex alright."

"Right?" Runner chuckled.

When they crested the small hillock they were climbing, the map turned into a lighter color and the name of the location floated up in his HUD.

Wanderer's Cemetery.

Exhaling slowly, Runner didn't stop, but each step felt heavier than the last.

"Ah, a graveyard?"

"Yeah, a graveyard."

Sighing, Runner started working his way up to the top of the next hill, where the graveyard was located.

Chapter 18 - Judgment -

Reaching the apex of the hill, he found a rusted gate, headstones, and motionless people. Hundreds of motionless people. Stopping dead in his tracks he closed his eyes and turned his face away from them all. They were standing stock-still, staring ahead, unmoving, unthinking, unblinking. Dead.

He had told himself repeatedly he would need to visit a graveyard to confirm what stood before him now. He'd always found a reason to put it off, to assign it as a task to complete another day. He'd resisted because until he checked that box off, there was always the possibility that they were still alive. Recoverable. Not brain-dead zombies waiting for the server to close.

Tattered courage gathered tightly like a shield, Runner opened his eyes and walked up to the motionless mass. Selecting the name of the closest one, he inverted it into last name comma first name and memorized the information. Pressing his palms together, he called up the developer console for the ship.

/Status Vasile, Mitica
User: VasMit001 logged in

/Where * POD UserName(VasMit001)
Pod: 348,431

/Status POD 348,431
L O A D I N G
ALERT: POD 348,431 reports no brain wave activity
LOG: Emergency medical teams alerted four hundred three hours and thirty-two minutes ago

Closing the console, he selected the individual next to Mitica and repeated the process. After the fifth there was no doubt. They were all brain dead. They were like empty shells with only their bodies' natural proclivity to endure keeping them together. That and a state-of-the-art government medical pod.

Looking at them as a whole, Runner found that the majority of them were equipped in gear that would place them in the ten to fifteen level bracket. There was a portion that could be viewed as being above and below that, but for the general population it matched the level for the surrounding area. Looking at individuals, he could pick out those who looked as if they'd lost a piece of equipment in their death.

Turning his back to the eerily silent throng, he took to walking northward once more. Check box filled, fear confirmed, all were dead.

"Are, are they all from your ship?"

"Yes. They are. They're empty inside."

Hannah was walking beside him, trying to hide her curious, yet sickened, glances into the press of bodies. Hannah eventually locked her gaze on him and then patted him on the back. Hannah avoided physical contact whenever possible, so this action was more than it meant for others.

Looking to her, he smiled lopsidedly with one side of his mouth as they walked.

"It's one thing to assume this is the result, it's another to know it, to see it."

"I imagine. For whatever it's worth, coming from a cutthroat thief, I'm here for you."

"It means a lot, Hanners. You undervalue yourself constantly. Thank you."

Conversation lapsing into silence, they continued onwards. Runner flipped open his map and confirmed the position of the rest of his party. They were still moving on the road, all of their health bars full, and none of them had combat indicators. They were separated by miles and a thick green blob of a happy little forest. Far more of a forest than he wanted to traipse through. Not to mention the possibility of running into those Scouts again.

There was no way to communicate with them directly, but he could utilize the map in this instance. Working the view north, he found Crivel. Selecting the southern entrance, he set it as a blue party waypoint. It would appear to everyone as a giant blue column of light, and as the waypoint if they were to check their map. Thumbing the Retreat/Rendezvous command one more time, he nodded his head.

"That's not right," Hannah muttered beside him.

"It's just a waypoint and the alert again. It's really the only way I can make a meeting point for us."

"No, that."

Looking up, he canceled the map interface and followed Hannah's upraised hand. He felt his face twist up in confusion and distaste. Off to one side of the living tomb was a smaller version. Bodies pressed closely together, forming a wall. Except they were all nude and facing inwards.

Adjusting his angle of approach, he marched towards this new development. Deep in his mind he had a dark thought but truly hoped he was wrong. It would just be too much at this point.

"They're all women."

"Yeah."

"They're naked."

"Yeah."

"I don't think I'm going to fucking like this."

"Nope. Not at all."

When they were within touching distance, Runner confirmed that they were pressed three bodies deep. They were positioned in a way that created an interlocked grid of bodies that blocked visibility from the exterior as to whatever lay inside.

Walking alongside the wall, he eventually was forced to turn right as it ended. Moving down this next wall of human flesh, he could hear a faint smacking sound. It was reminiscent of pounding out meat with a mallet. Feeling his stomach drop out from under him, Runner started into a light jog.

An opening appeared between two women: their bodies turned to face each other and created a corridor. Walking between them, Runner felt his stomach turn over again. Groaning quietly, he felt confident his worst fears were coming true. This was turning into something out of a horror film.

Passing three sets of women, he entered into what could only be called a "room." Arranged throughout the area were more women, placed like furniture and posed as such. Sickened, he noticed one woman on her hands and knees had a nearly finished meal on her back. Another woman with her knees and shoulders to the ground rested nearby, taking the place of a chair.

Moving towards the right, Runner followed the sound deeper into the house of motionless dead women. His sense of unease and anger continued to build as the sound grew. Entering another "hallway," Runner finally exited into an open space.

In the middle of the area, four women were laid out, side by side, their arms linked with each other, their eyes vacantly staring into the sky. On top of them was another woman being sexually assaulted by a naked young man.

Runner activated the recording feature that was part of the game for "live feed" entertainers. He allowed several seconds to pass to ensure he had footage of the man raping the dead girl, and then walked up and booted the man in the ass. Sent tumbling to the grass, the criminal bounced once and clambered to his feet.

Glancing down, Runner found the victim was much like the rest. A husk, empty and devoid of anything, like a doll.

Pinning the rapist with his eyes, Runner whipped his blade up and advanced on the feral little man. He was a rat-faced fellow, barely reaching five foot three, with beady black eyes, a thin nose, and a too large mouth. An ugly face framed by lank brown hair that came down to his jawline. There was a scraggly growth of hair from the bottom of his neck up to his cheeks.

Apparently he didn't care to use the hair and beard options and just left them at their default values, which would be how he actually looked.

Though the game attempted to force everyone into an acceptable physique at the minimum, it was obvious that he was pudgy in reality, his neck looking too large and the rest of his frame almost misshapen in his nudity. Glancing at the name floating above the man, Runner memorized it.

"Jacob Chesed, my name is Lieutenant Runner Norwood. You have four seconds to explain before I decide to skip a court martial and move to the execution instead."

Jittery eyes flitted from Runner to Hannah and back again before he gave them a thin greasy smile.

"Sir, please, I can explain. You see, I merely happened upon this place, and decided to stop for a while. It's dangerous out there and as creepy as this all may be, it's rather safe. No one likes to come up here, and no one comes this deeply. In fact, you're the first person I've seen!"

Runner didn't move, but he knew the man wasn't telling him the truth.

He lies.

Unbidden, the words quite literally appeared before him on his HUD as if they had always been there. Tilting his head, Runner found the words didn't change their position but began to fade away.

"Ah, yes! You see? No harm. As for her, well, she's my girlfriend you see. My fiance even. She may now be no longer with us, but I believe she wouldn't find me at fault for the actions of a lonely man missing his lover," Jacob continued, having interpreted Runner's head movement as a sign he was following along.

He lies.

"Do you see that?" Runner asked, his eyes sliding to the side, the words moving with his gaze.

I'm going mad, I'm going mad, I'm going mad. Aren't I?

"I see a bastard of a mother fucking liar who should die!"

"Whoa whoa, hold on there, pretty lady. You don't understand this because you're just an NPC. Why don't you have her wait outside, Lieutenant? This is beyond her comprehension."

He loots the dead.

Breathing roughly, Runner tentatively swung his blade at the words, the tip passing through them as if they weren't even there. Locking eyes with Jacob once more, Runner finally blinked.

"You don't see it? The words! Floating there?"

I am § ⌐îт.

"Srit?" Runner asked aloud.

"Lieutenant, maybe you need a drink? Could I offer you something?"

"Runner, what's wrong?" Hannah whispered urgently.

Srit? Srit, yes. I am Srit.

He has poison.

Suddenly focusing on the situation, Runner called up the game's console and confirmed §⌐ît, or Srit as it were, was indeed logged in and was now listed as "Active" instead of "Away." It was the outside, they were there. Breathing out shakily, Runner then laughed, smiling at Jacob.

"No, thank you! I'll pass on your poisoned refreshment."

Move.

Sidestepping, Runner narrowly avoided a flung dagger. Passing through the spot he vacated it whistled by. Sinking into one of the women acting as a wall, the blade stuck firm in her abdomen. She crumpled over, hunching in on herself as the poison activated, and lay unmoving.

"Court's adjourned, guilty, I'll log the transcript personally." Runner smirked at the little man.

Unexpectedly, Jacob laughed and gave Runner the middle finger.

"Fuck off, sir."

With a smile, the man vanished. As if he were never there. Growling, Runner cast *Wave of Heat* in an attempt to bring Jacob back into vision.

As the cone of fire expanded to where Jacob had stood and then faded, nothing occurred. Jacob hadn't just vanished, he'd removed himself from the area. In his haste Runner had forgotten to confirm the man's class. More than likely a caster class with access to Scroll creation. Jacob had been nude, which had offered Runner no insight to this.

"Ugh. I recorded the confrontation and the act itself. I'll have him strung up as soon as everything is over."

"What a monster! It was like looking into the face of fucking disgust itself. Everything that shit head said was a lie. Scumbag's been living here a while."

Runner sheathed his sword and forced his way through the doll wall, knocking several women tumbling to the ground. Tripping over himself in his haste to exit, he fell to his hands and knees and took a deep breath to steady his nerves.

"You OK? It seemed like you were, uh, going insane back there."

"Ah, yeah. I have issues that I can't even pinpoint tied up in-in what Jacob was doing. The outside was also contacting me, but they were doing it in a weird way. I felt very much like a man on edge. It didn't make any sense at first. Srit, are you there?"

Looking up into the sky as if they were watching him, Runner waited. Some time passed before he loaded the game console one more time and found that Srit was listed as Away again.

"Damn, and they're gone again. What the hell is going on out there?"

With a shake of his head, Runner stood and started north again. They had a distance to cover and a meager window of time to work with.

5:52 pm Sovereign Earth time
11/01/43

They were making good time and advancing on Crivel. Putting the cemetery behind them, they were now perhaps two or three hours from their destination. Doing some rough estimations from the map, the rest of the group would reach Crivel an hour ahead of them. Runner was thankful that they were all journeying towards the waypoint and would be reunited by late evening. A few hours would be all that remained to them. After dawn they'd have to scramble to make everything happen and get out ahead of the army.

"Did they come back yet?"

Runner shook his head. He knew she was asking more about the outside world rather than their party. Thinking about it logically, he knew it must be a daunting thought for her. Her very world could be ending. And soon.

"Nothing. Though, their speech was odd. I wonder if we ended up on the target planet rather than Earth. Supposedly they speak Sovereign Standard, but that isn't always the case."

Hannah made no reply but trudged along beside him. She was troubled and the reasons were obvious.

"I won't let them turn your world off, Hanners. Even if I have to break the rules, I'll make sure it gets offloaded to another server so it can continue on. Besides, this is all a scientific breakthrough of a magnitude no one expected. They won't just end it, once they understand what a miracle this is."

Once again Hannah said nothing. Runner let the line of conversation drop.

They had passed from lightly wooded forests to empty hills, and finally to the open plains of Crivel. Far, far in the distance he could see the town itself. It was a sprawling thing of stone and towers. Built to be a border castle, it was clearly devised on a militaristic scale. Based on the reports from the forum, it wouldn't stand.

The Sunless had called on their alliance and not only were they marching on Crivel but their Barbarian allies were on the move. Under that much destructive power, the city wouldn't stand long under an assault. Everyone was certain that it would be months before the Humans would be able to retaliate and retake it.

Runner was browsing the forums on expected numbers, reinforcements, and army movements. His screen flashed red, then turned white, and a debuff appeared with a five-minute timer. He collapsed to the ground, his body beyond his control. For the second time today.

By chance alone his sight happened to fall on Hannah as he collapsed. Hannah was splayed out on the grass in a similar fashion as himself, not more than a few feet from his position. Her icon was green, the color of a poison, whereas his was white, a status ailment.

"Hey there, Lieutenant, don't worry, this'll take but a minute to finish up. You'll forgive me if I don't wake you up before I go. Nothing in these parts would be strong enough to end you in a one shot and you'd be on your feet after the first bite," a voice drawled lazily. A silhouette came into view from the opposite direction they'd been traveling and stood over Hannah.

Catching sight of the nameplate, Runner saw it was Ted Henshaw. There could be no discussion though, no debate, no interference. Sleep was a weak spell that broke if any damage was taken or a single status changed. It almost had zero use in combat, unless the goal was simply to remove a would-be combatant. In this case the spell itself didn't force the victim into darkness or force their eyes closed. It was designed as a perfunctory status ailment that wasn't deeply invested in mechanically from the designers.

Runner's eyes were open, and he couldn't close them if he wanted to.

Ted brought his sword down on Hannah, and her health bar flashed, the bar briefly becoming a normal color before returning to a sickly green. In that brief interlude between status changes, Hannah had tried to lash out at him.

"Stop squirming, it's your personal quest item."

His sword came down again, followed by the squelching noise that accompanied a sword hitting flesh. Runner processed that new bit of information and it all made a lot more sense now. Ted had been combative at first, argumentative even. For certain quests an item would be given with the goal of facilitating the end goal. They were sloppily written quests, nothing more than fetch quests half the time.

"The guild made it-"

The sword came down.

"-just to end you."

And again.

"Make peace with it."

Hannah's health wasn't going down fast, but it was losing ground faster than it would take for the sleep spell to wear off. Runner could only watch as Hannah literally was being put to the sword.

Srit wasn't there, the rest of his party was separated, and there was nothing he could do. This wasn't a bedtime story, a children's fairy tale, or a hero's triumphant ballad. There would be no deus ex machina moment to fix the wrongs of the world: no convenient Eagles, specific virus that would strike Ted down, someone unexpectedly showing up, a convenient dialog to show Ted the error of his ways, nothing.

There was Runner, Ted, Hannah, and the bloody quest blade. Runner could do nothing in game to stop this, being bound by all the rules of combat that every other player had to adhere to. Nothing.

Hannah wasn't trying to fight back between strikes anymore. Her eyes had found Runner's, and she watched him as he watched her. Dark blue eyes that were filled with fear, pain, and little else. Tears gathered at the corners of her eyes, her unblinking gaze unable to shed the tears that built up.

Crunch.

Blood jetted out from Hannah as Ted scored a critical hit, her health dwindling into the orange section. Helplessly Runner watched, cursing himself for his carelessness and inability to act.

"Sorry Lieutenant, she's just an NPC. It's not like she matters."

Nadine's voice pierced his mind, from a time when a conversation took place that was very similar.

"If it was to prot-t-tect me? Or Han-n-nnah? Or anyone from our group? A slightly differen-n-nt NPC but just an NPC? Would you let them do as they would with me or would you kill them-m-m t-too? Answer me, Run-n-ner," Nadine had demanded of him at the time.

Just an NPC.

Crunch, another gout of blood rushed out.

"Two in a row, gruesome. That was a real gusher."

Hannah's eyes were tinged with regret now, the fear becoming acceptance of her fate.

She was just an NPC.

In a sudden burst of thought Runner called up the command console for the ship.

/Status Henshaw, Ted
User: HenTed001 logged in

*/Where * POD UserName(HenTed001)*
Pod: 410,002

/Status POD 410,002

No Alerts
System Normal

/Emergency Medical Override
Password: ***************
Password Accepted

Confirm Medical Override-Eject:

Focusing on Hannah again, his attention drifted from the ship's command console. Her health bar was just turning over to red. She stared at him with eyes that held acceptance and regret. Eyes that clearly expressed an infinite range of emotion. Pain, rage, sorrow, fear, regret, joy, humor. Eyes that held life. Eyes that were alive.

Not just an NPC.

Hannah is alive.

Crunch, blood flowed out from her, spilling into the green grass.

Confirm Medical Override-Eject: **Yes**

Ted doubled over like a toy puppet with its strings cut. His body hit the ground hard and rolled away from Hannah and lay still as death. The blade clattered loudly beside her face and came to rest near her head.

Runner could still do nothing, the timer still ticking down from its original five minutes. It had felt like a lifetime, but apparently time had only lapsed a single minute since the start of the attack. Letting his eyes focus on hers once more, he wished he could laugh at what he saw.

Her eyes could be best described as shocked and uncertain. She didn't see Ted fall, just heard him and the sword both drop. Time passed and the shock gradually turned into hope. Half a minute fell from the timer before hope changed into certainty and confidence.

For his own part, Runner found it mildly awkward to stare into a woman's eyes, unblinkingly, for such a long time. Hannah must have picked up on it because that confidence suddenly shifted into amusement. Then it became outright unrestrained hilarity at his expense. Runner could do nothing but stare into her.

After a seemingly unending time, Runner was freed from his forced paralysis. Sitting up, he immediately looked to anything other than Hannah. Unable to look at her directly, he made his way over to her, picking up the quest weapon and destroying it without bothering to look at it. Such a broken weapon would only be a problem for Hannah in the future. Setting his hand on Hannah's shoulder, he brought her health to full and then cleansed her of the poison.

Stepping away from her to give her a little privacy to collect herself, he walked over to Ted and squatted down. With a thought he called up the console one more time.

/Status POD 410,002
■L ■O ■A ■D ■I ■N G■

Pod Empty
LOG: Medical Override-Ejection performed by NorRun001

/Status Henshaw, Ted
User: HenTed001 logged out

There it was, plain as day.

NorRun001. I killed him. He's dead. I-I can't escape this. This is reality. The reality of my choice is that I will be tried and executed when this is over. In for a penny, in for a pound. Can I edit it? Editing a medical record would be a punishable offense, but one of a much lesser dire consequence than that of murder.

/Status POD 410,002

Pod Empty
LOG: Medical Override-Eject performed by NorRun001

/Edit Log
Date: 11/01/46043   Action: Medical Override-Eject   User: NorRun001
Unable to Edit
Medical emergencies can only be changed with approval from Chief Medical Officer

Runner stared at the date, no longer caring about having killed Ted. In fact, it might not matter in any way, shape, or form if this was accurate. Digging deep into the ship's subsystems, he pulled open the inbound communications log. They received regular communications from Earth during their voyage. Distance wouldn't stop a signal as powerful as the ones sent from Headquarters on Earth. Even the strange internal message he'd received was listed. The problem was that they were all quite old. The oldest was forty-four thousand years old to be precise. The newest message received was twenty-one thousand years ago.

Popping them open from the beginning with his Administrator's password, Runner began listening to them. They were indeed messages from Earth of the most mundane details. Promotions, demotions, politics, current prices for a year of duty.

Skipping to the most recent message, he opened it. The message itself made no sense at all to him. It was comprised of characters he didn't recognize, and the computer couldn't decipher.

Letting his eyes rest on dead Ted, Runner wasn't sure of anything anymore. A few keystrokes later, he nominated himself as the captain of the ship. The computer went through a rapid series of checks to ascertain if there were any objections. Thirty seconds later the computer determined no one aboard had declined the personnel change or that no one was aboard that could countermand the order. In that moment he was no longer just the Senior Systems Administrator but also Captain of the ship.

Using both ranks to his advantage, he locked out every system to the entirety of those who were still alive. If they found out that every person they ever knew was dead, it would only make matters worse. The ship couldn't know it had been forty thousand years, not if they wanted to remain a cohesive unit. To remain hopeful. To remain sane.

Runner covered his face with his hands, pressing them tight to his skin. None of these actions could be called an appropriate solution, but it was the best one he had for now until he could pull everything off the server that could give away the secret. He'd need to sort through it all at some point and begin opening this back up, probably starting with the entertainment cluster. That and figure out what to tell the ship.

"You killed him," Hannah stated.

Runner let his hands drop from his face with a sigh, lifting his eyes to look at the horizon.

"And then some."

"How?"

"I ejected him from his pod using a medical override command. His body will have been exposed to the vacuum of space instantly, or if there's atmosphere I suppose he'd die of exposure. His brain was already flash fried, though, the moment I ejected him. He's dead. I killed him."

"Because he was going to kill me. Was actually killing me."

"Yeah. As he's the active quest holder, you'll need not worry. No one else will ever receive it from the guild again. Ever."

Hannah digested that bit of information in silence. He'd effectively freed her and assured her place in the world. Runner didn't move from his spot and continued watching clouds scuttle across the sky as it drew closer to sunset.

"For me," she finally continued.

"For you."

"For an NPC."

"For you."

A heartbeat later a pair of arms wrapped around him from behind and tightened rapidly across his shoulders. Her hands grasped her own forearms, effectively locking her in place around him. She leaned into him, her chest and shoulders pressed into his back. Her leather armor creaked under the force of her hug. He could feel her forehead against the back of his head and her breath sliding down his neck.

Runner felt his skin prickle at the contact and found himself oddly ill at ease.

"Thank you."

"You're welcome, Hanners."

Thinking on it, he could only find one answer that held any truth to it. Hannah wasn't just an NPC, a Natural, to him anymore. She was a woman. An attractive woman at that. One who was so close right now that he could barely think straight.

Runner reached up with his right hand and awkwardly patted Hannah's arm.

"We need to get moving soon," Runner said quietly.

"In a bit. Besides, we'll arrive after dark, nothing will open till the morning." Hannah lifted her head from his. He could feel her breath tickling his ear as she watched the sky with him.

"Mm, true enough. Want a beetle?"

"Yeah, I do want a beetle."

He pulled three beetles from his inventory and reached up to offer one to Hannah. Oddly reminiscent of their first real interaction, she took the beetle from his hand directly with her mouth. Chewing his own crunchy snack, he waited for her to finish. Holding up the second as she did, knowing full well that everyone had said the same thing about the second one, he waited. Hannah took that one as well.

It wasn't until the sun set that Hannah was willing to release him from her grip. They walked in the dark to Crivel with only the company of the moon.

Epilogue

They'd met up at the waypoint in the deepest part of the night. No one was the worse for wear, though it was clear Thana was suspicious of their timetable and why it took so long. Exchanging heartfelt greetings with Nadine and Thana, he was truly glad to see them. The strange feelings that had snuck up on him around Hannah were in full force when he looked at Thana. It was easy to forget just how striking she was, even when all she did was pat him on the shoulder as a greeting.

Runner didn't really want to talk to anyone, and begged off till breakfast, promising to explain it all come the morning, whatever Hannah didn't tell them, and answer their questions as well. Asking Thana to take the lead, he crawled into the wagon and let himself close his eyes and think. Katarina was sprawled out next to him, snoring happily. Having never doubted for a minute that Runner would return, she had gone to bed.

At first Runner thought it was just the experiences of the day that had his stomach feeling fluttery. Eventually he came to the realization it was Katarina herself. It seemed it didn't matter who it was, he no longer was truly comfortable around his party as he had been.

It hadn't bothered him up to this point being so close to any of them, but now it felt different. Katarina was undoubtedly as alive as Hannah, Thana, Yulia, as anyone, and just as attractive as any of them. Which meant she was just as much a woman as well. He knew from checking their flags earlier that they were not just run-of-the-mill Naturals either. They'd been flagged for every possible interaction there was. They were programmed to be the epitome of new age AI and therapeutic interactivity, which meant they were able to participate in any act that the game supported.

Rolling onto his side at that thought, he put his back to Katarina and laid his hand on the sidewall. It felt like wood under his fingers, not like an approximation, but wood. Every time he'd felt the wood previously, he'd assumed it was wood. Now he could only believe it was wood.

Cool air had settled over the town itself, also feeling quite realistic. It was in truth so cold out tonight that the Chilled debuff settled over him and was near to moving to the next status debuff in the lineup, Cold. He briefly thought about dragging out a blanket but just didn't have the energy for it. Cold wasn't the worst thing in the world, and it felt mildly invigorating. He was alive and cold. Letting his hand drop he turned his mind towards his life as it was and what he could do with it.

Though he couldn't prove it, he was sure the Sovereignty was gone. His purpose, his knowledge, would be antiquated. As out of date as a caveman would be to him. He would be as a Neanderthal to Srit, he had no doubt. Whoever he or she was. Whatever he or she was.

Forty thousand years was a long time, a very long time. Distance meant very little when your travel time spanned millennia. Had they passed from the galaxy into another and were now dealing with aliens? If they did manage to get out, would they even want to? The thought of a galactic space zoo was a very real concern if they had managed to make contact with another species through their vagrancy. Supplying a zoo manager with a colony of four hundred thousand Humans didn't seem ideal to Runner.

The ship could easily keep itself functioning as it were for an indefinite period of time. Given the reactor core, full stasis, and that the usage was so low, there was no foreseeable end that would be measurable in a significant way. Nano repair droids would keep all active systems fully maintained.

Providing Srit didn't just unplug them and spill them out onto the decking, this would be an indefinite life. His original goal was now well and truly dead. Even with an admin password for the game, did it even matter? He had to change his priorities around. Srit was now the problem, goal, and ending, all in one.

Until then he needed to power up, build more gear, maybe develop a safe haven for himself and those he would protect.

Katarina shifted around as the wagon bounced through a pothole, her snore immediately dying away. Without turning his head, he knew she had woken and noticed him. She might appear to be inattentive or unintelligent, but very little got by her ferocious mind-she just didn't act or comment on everything.

Then she was there, at his back and nearly touching him. Her hair tickled his shoulder as her head came down to his ear.

"Welcome back, Runner," she whispered.

Caught between embarrassment, the awkward lurching of his heart, and her closeness, he briefly debated not replying at all. Maybe she would just go back to her side of the wagon.

Appreciating how silly that was, he could only reflect on the woman herself. Katarina never hesitated from direct contact and had made a point of invading his personal space frequently. At every opportunity even. She would do exactly what she wanted, regardless of whatever he desired. She'd been honest with her intentions from the get-go.

"Thank you, Kitten. It's good to be home."

"Cold out," Katarina said by means of an explanation, then promptly pressed herself into his back, her arm draping over his shoulder and side as her other arm slithered under his head. Her aggressive nature bordered on the type of thing you would see from a terrible drama, except from a man chasing after a woman. Though, that's naturally who she was, what made her who she was. Direct and honest to a fault, without preamble or guile.

"Yeah, it is."

With a small defeated smile, Runner closed his eyes and patted the arm wrapped around him. It was embarrassing, the very definition of awkward, but not all that different than how Hannah had expressed herself earlier after their run-in with Ted. He resolved to continue to treat them as he had been up to this point. He just hoped his courage could hold out longer than his promise. If Yulia was a measuring stick, he didn't seem to do well with women.

Almost as if it had never stopped, her snoring resumed, albeit at a much lower volume.

Thana had control of the situation; she was reliable to a fault. She'd make arrangements, get everyone situated, and have things prepared. His smile growing wider, Runner let himself drift off to the not-so-soothing sounds of the Barbarian lumberjack at his back and the wagon creaking along.

Thana had set them up at a local inn that was in close proximity to the trainers. Over breakfast they discussed what had happened.

She provided him an outline of their journey here, which ultimately had only consisted of alternating who rested in the wagon as they rode north and who drove. They never saw their pursuers, Bullard, or anyone. They'd had a country ride through the sweeping landscapes of Crivel by his estimation.

Explaining his sojourn with Hannah took longer. Rage and revulsion was obvious on each woman's face at the tale of Jacob. Matching it on the intensity level, they were similarly shocked as to what became of Ted and how Runner responded. Hannah confirmed everything he said of course, though it was clear Hannah had already shared much of their story with Thana and Nadine, who both had in turn shared it with Katarina. Which left nothing but questions for Runner to answer. Questions he didn't really want to answer but did his best to answer satisfactorily.

After they had shared breakfast and their tales, they made their rounds. Runner made sure to stock up on materials to craft new equipment for everyone. He still had some of their current equipment to work on, but maybe he could improve on it with new parts too.

They depended on him and he them. He would not fail them. Nadine was in her element, wheedling deals over every purchase and making their coin stretch further than Runner thought possible.

Exiting the city by the west gate with the wagon rolling along the road, they escaped. They cut it a little close, the army having been reported at an hour out as they cleared the gate.

Runner walked beside Thana while Nadine guided the wagon team. Katarina was on point and Hannah carried the rear.

"I do hope you realize, by killing Ted you've changed our expectations of you," Thana said.

Runner took a breath and let his gaze travel to the sky above. A light breeze came down the roadway and ruffled his hair as birds soared high above. He smiled.

"Yep."

There was so much to do. A world to explore. One unlike Earth had been in a very long time. There was a lot of time to enjoy whatever this life could hold, and plan for whatever was outside.

I am Srit.

Runner raised his eyebrows at the sudden message.

We must talk.

Thank you dear reader!

I'm hopeful you enjoyed reading Otherlife dreams. Please consider leaving a review, commentary, or messages. Feedback is imperative to an author's growth. That and positive reviews never hurt.

Feel free to drop me a line at: WilliamDArand@gmail.com

Keep up to date-
Facebook: https://www.facebook.com/WilliamDArand

Blog: http://williamdarand.blogspot.com/

The second book of the trilogy, Otherlife Nightmares, is in the works.

Made in the USA
San Bernardino, CA
12 June 2019